W9-CHV-620

TWIG CREATED BY SKOTTIE YOUNG & KYLE STRAHM

PRODUCTION ARTIST RICH FOWLKS WITH RYAN BREWER

IMAGE COMICS, INC. • Robert Kirkman: Chief Operating Officer • Erik Larsen: Chief Financial Officer • Todd McFarlane: President • Marc Silvestri: Chief Executive Officer • Jim Valentino: Vice President • Eric Stephenson: Publisher / Chief Creative Officer • Nicole Lapalme: Vice President of Finance • Leanna Caunter: Accounting Analyst • Sue Korpel: Accounting & HR Manager • Matt Parkinson: Vice President of Sales & Publishing Planning • Lorelei Bunjes: Vice President of Digital Strategy • Dirk Wood: Vice President of International Sales & Licensing • Ryan Brewer: International Sales & Licensing Manager • Alex Cox: Director of Direct Market Sales • Chloe Ramos: Book Market & Library Sales Manager • Emilio Bautista: Digital Sales Coordinator • Jon Schlaffman: Specialty Sales Coordinator • Kat Salazar: Vice President of PR & Marketing • Deanna Phelps: Marketing Design Manager • Drew Fitzgerald: Marketing Content Associate • Heather Doornink: Vice President of Production • Drew Gill: Art Director • Hilary DiLoreto: Print Manager • Tricia Ramos: Traffic Manager • Melissa Gifford: Content Manager • Erika Schnatz: Senior Production Artist • Wesley Griffith: Production Artist • Rich Fowlks: Production Artist IMAGECOMICS.COM

TWIG, VOL. 1. First Printing. November 2022. Published by Image Comics, Inc. Office of publication: PO BOX 14457, Portland, OR 97293. Copyright © 202 Skottie Young & Stupid Fresh Mess, LLC & Triple Entendre LLC. All rights reserved. Contains material originally published in single magazine form as TWIG # 5. "Twig," its logos, and the likenesses of all characters herein are trademarks of Skottie Young & Stupid Fresh Mess, LLC & Triple Entendre LLC, unles otherwise noted. "Image" and the Image Comics logos are registered trademarks of Image Comics, Inc. No part of this publication may be reproduced o transmitted, in any form or by any means (except for short excerpts for journalistic or review purposes), without the express written permission of Skottie Youn & Stupid Fresh Mess, LLC & Triple Entendre LLC, or Image Comics, Inc. All names, characters, events, and locales in this publication are entirely fiction Any resemblance to actual persons (living or dead), events, or places, without satirical intent, is coincidental. Printed in Canada. For international right contact: foreignlicensing@imagecomics.com. ISBN: 978-1-5343-2346-9 Creator Exclusive Variant: 978-1-5343-2579-1

WRITTEN BY
SKOTTIE YOUNG

ART AND DESIGNS BY
KYLE STRAHM

COLORING BY
JEAN-FRANCOIS BEAULIEU

LETTERING, LOGO & SERIES DESIGN BY
NATE PIEKOS OF BLAMBOT®

EDITED BY
JOEL ENOS

COVER BY
KYLE STRAHM

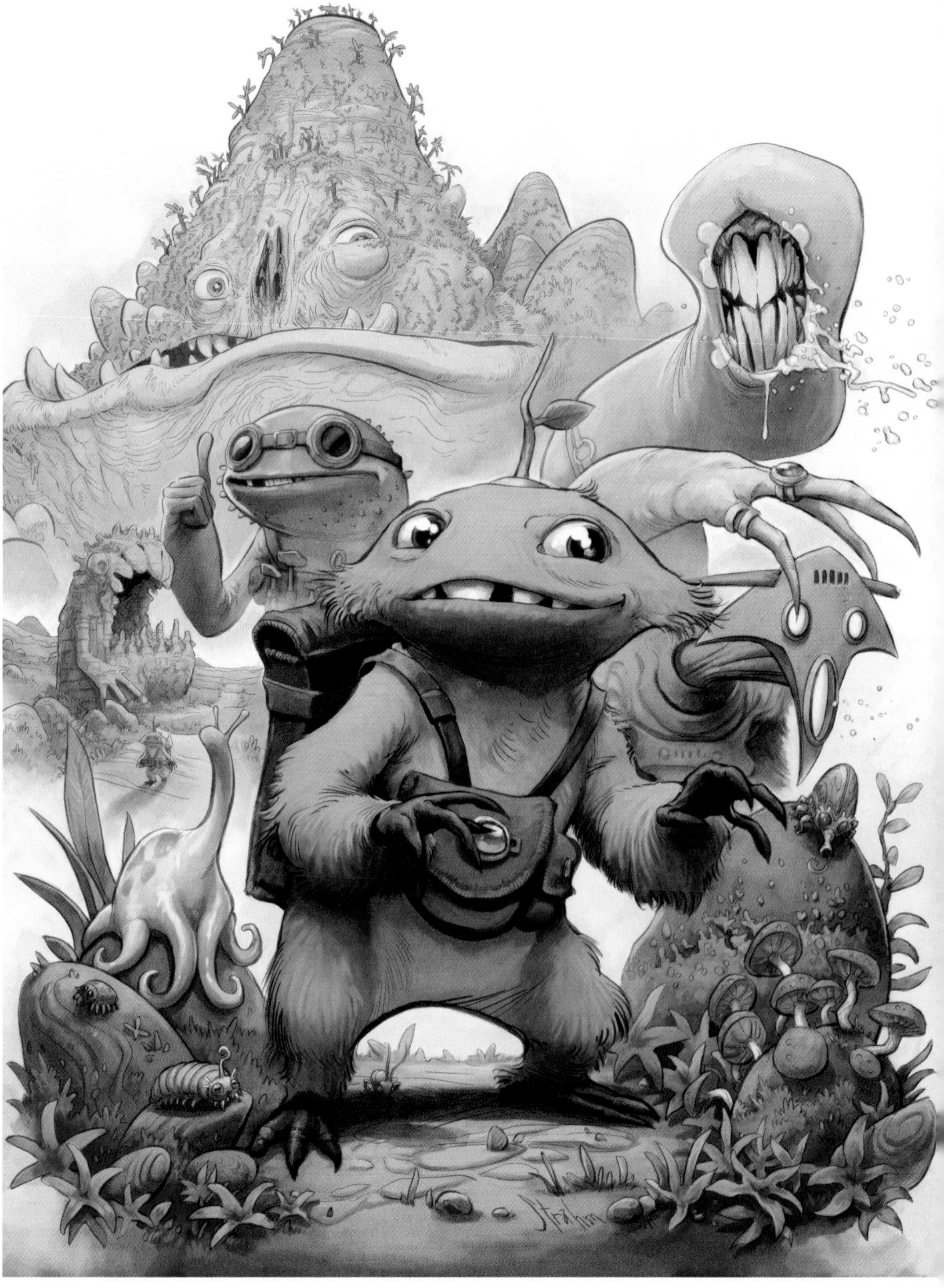

ONE

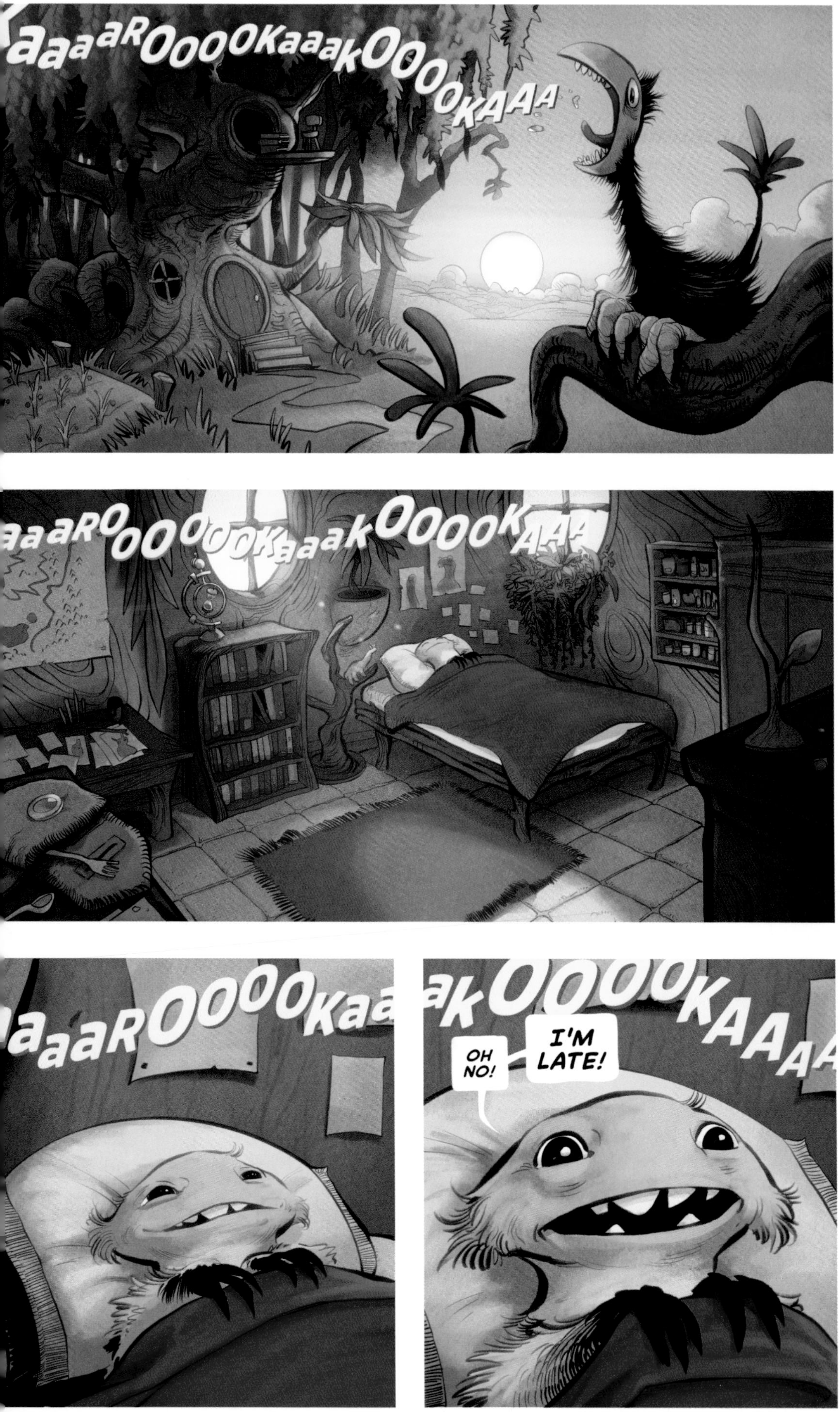
aaaaROOOOKaaakOOOOKAAA
aaaROOOOOKaaakOOOOKAAA
aaaROOOOKaa
akOOOOKAAAA
OH NO!
I'M LATE!

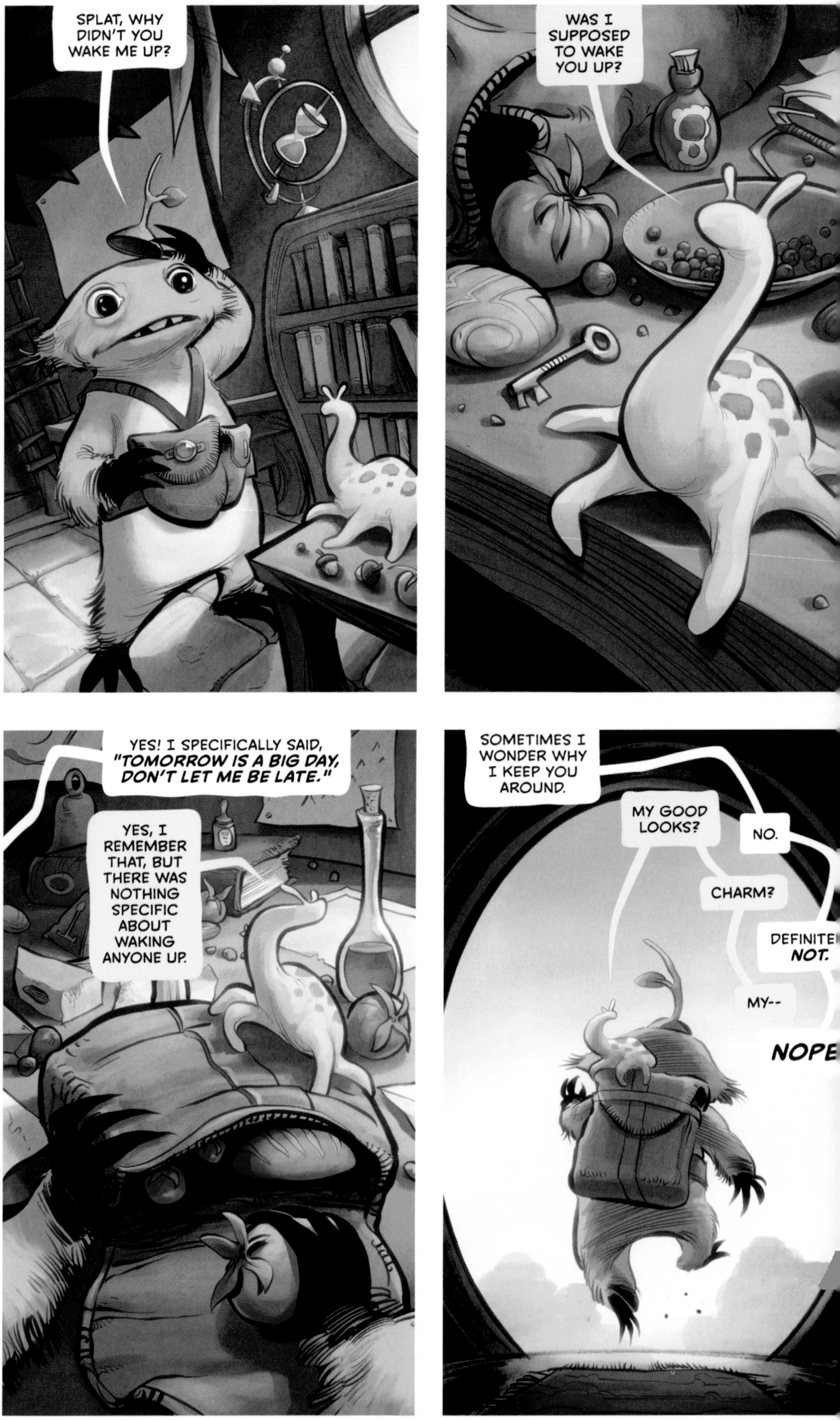
SPLAT, WHY DIDN'T YOU WAKE ME UP?
WAS I SUPPOSED TO WAKE YOU UP?
YES! I SPECIFICALLY SAID, *"TOMORROW IS A BIG DAY, DON'T LET ME BE LATE."*
YES, I REMEMBER THAT, BUT THERE WAS NOTHING SPECIFIC ABOUT WAKING ANYONE UP.
SOMETIMES I WONDER WHY I KEEP YOU AROUND.
MY GOOD LOOKS?
NO.
CHARM?
DEFINITE
NOT.
MY--
NOPE

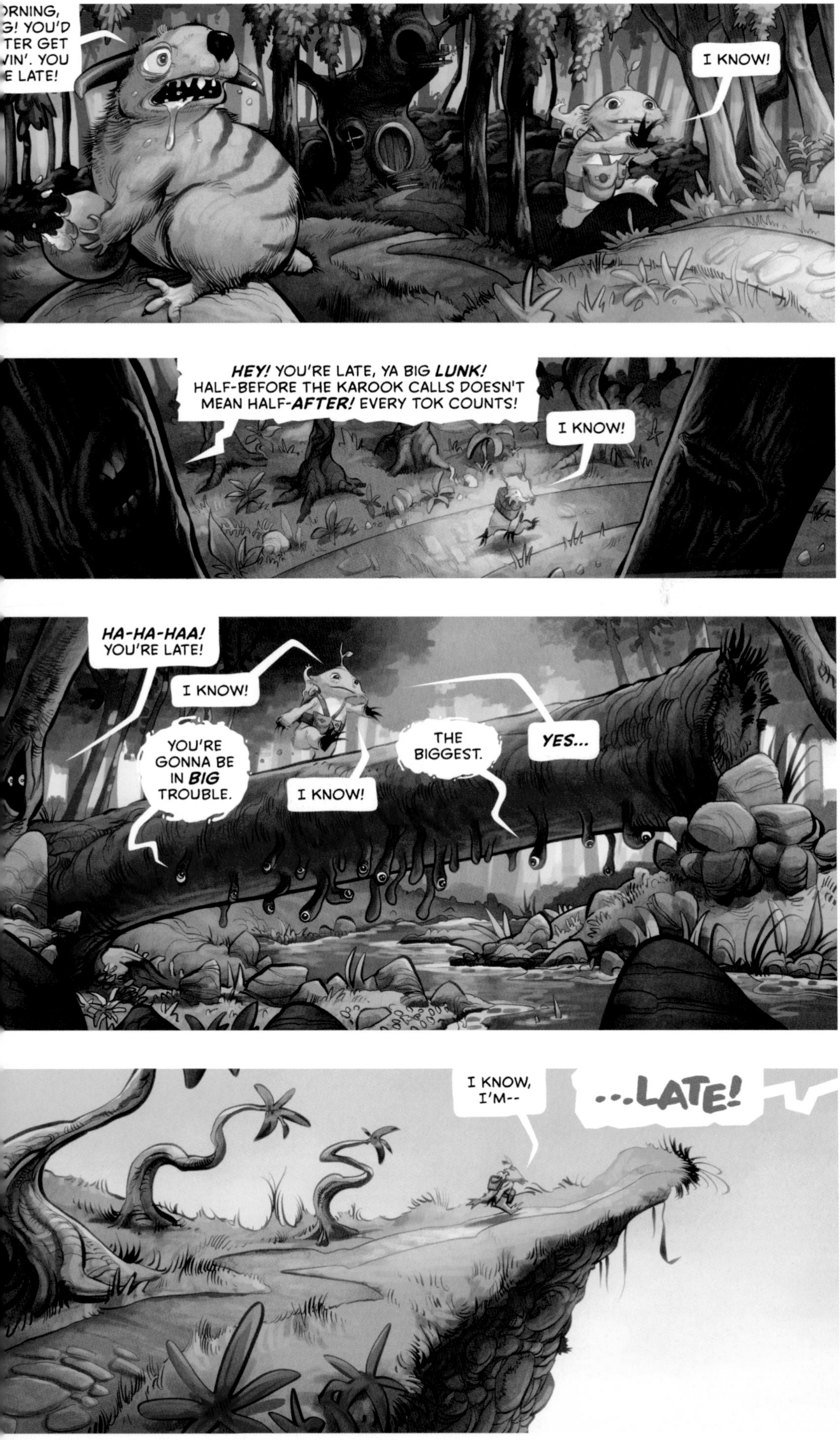

ORNING, G! YOU'D TER GET VIN'. YOU E LATE!
I KNOW!
HEY! YOU'RE LATE, YA BIG LUNK! HALF-BEFORE THE KAROOK CALLS DOESN'T MEAN HALF-AFTER! EVERY TOK COUNTS!
I KNOW!
HA-HA-HAA! YOU'RE LATE!
I KNOW!
YOU'RE GONNA BE IN BIG TROUBLE.
I KNOW!
THE BIGGEST.
YES...
I KNOW, I'M--
--LATE!

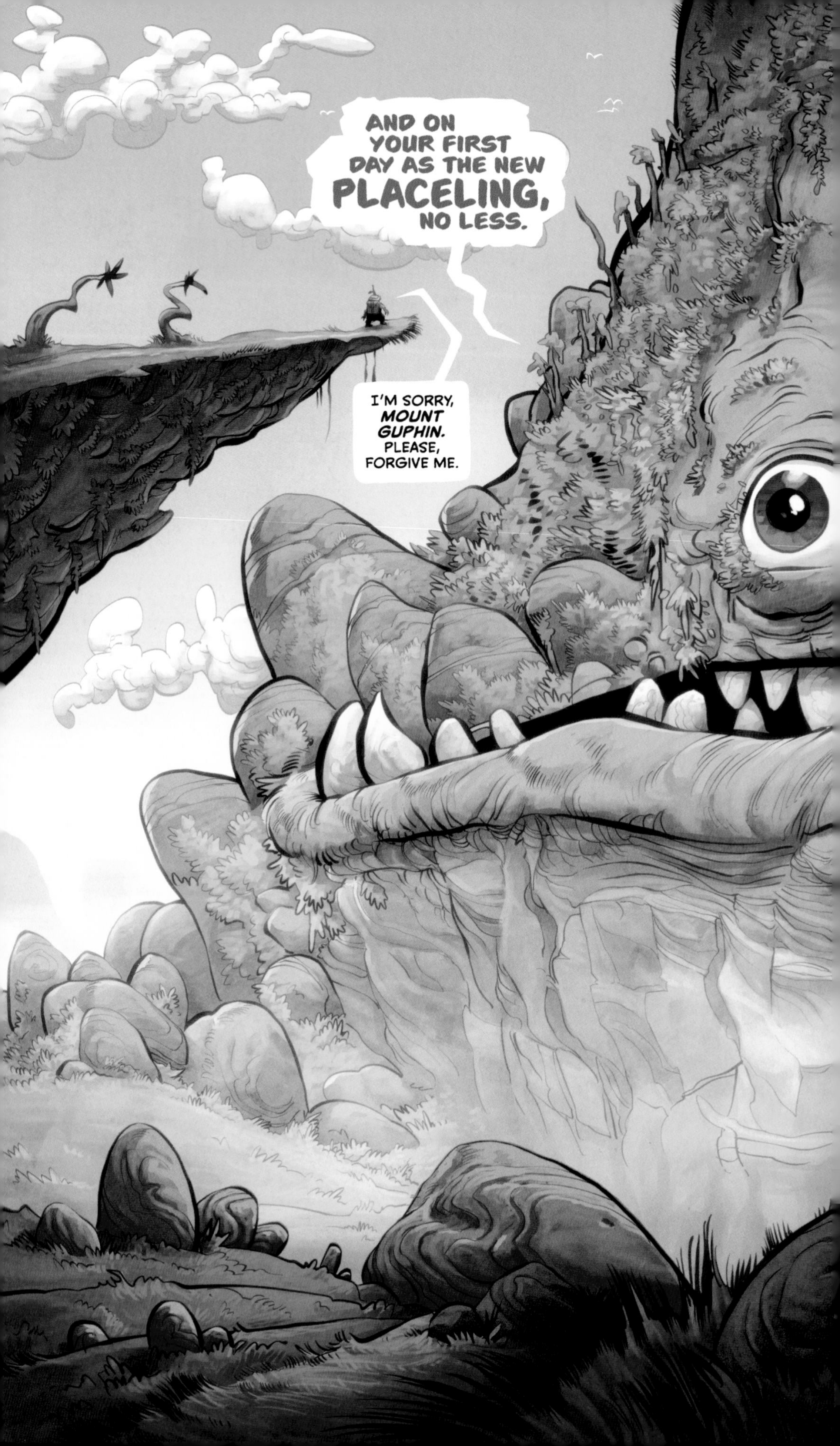
AND ON YOUR FIRST DAY AS THE NEW PLACELING, NO LESS.
I'M SORRY, MOUNT GUPHIN. PLEASE, FORGIVE ME.

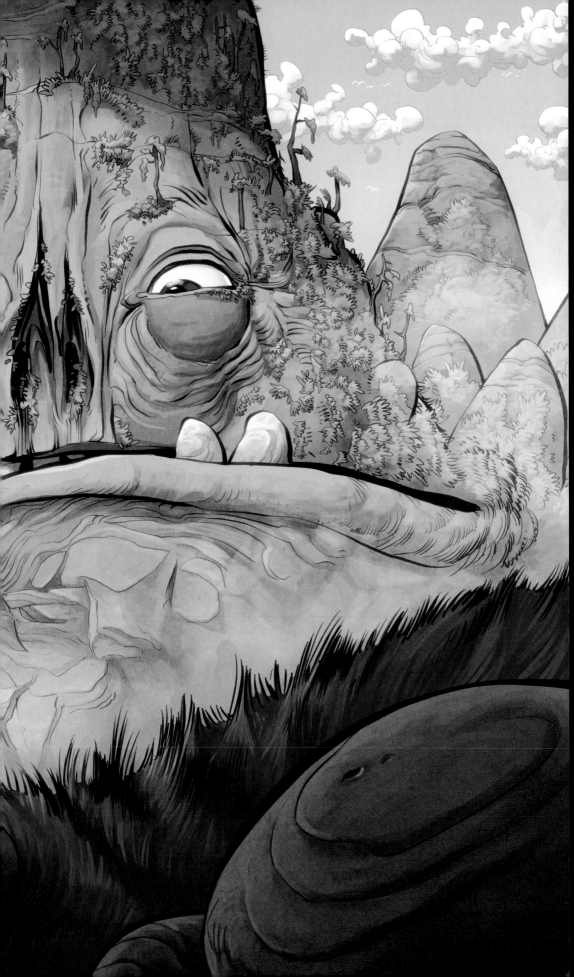

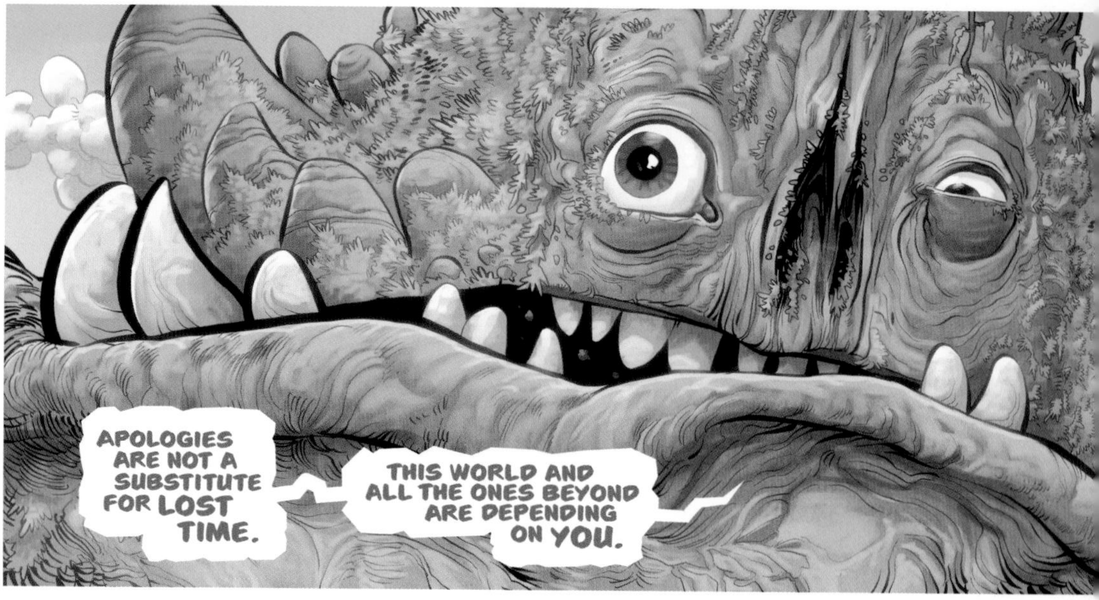
APOLOGIES ARE NOT A SUBSTITUTE FOR LOST TIME.
THIS WORLD AND ALL THE ONES BEYOND ARE DEPENDING ON YOU.

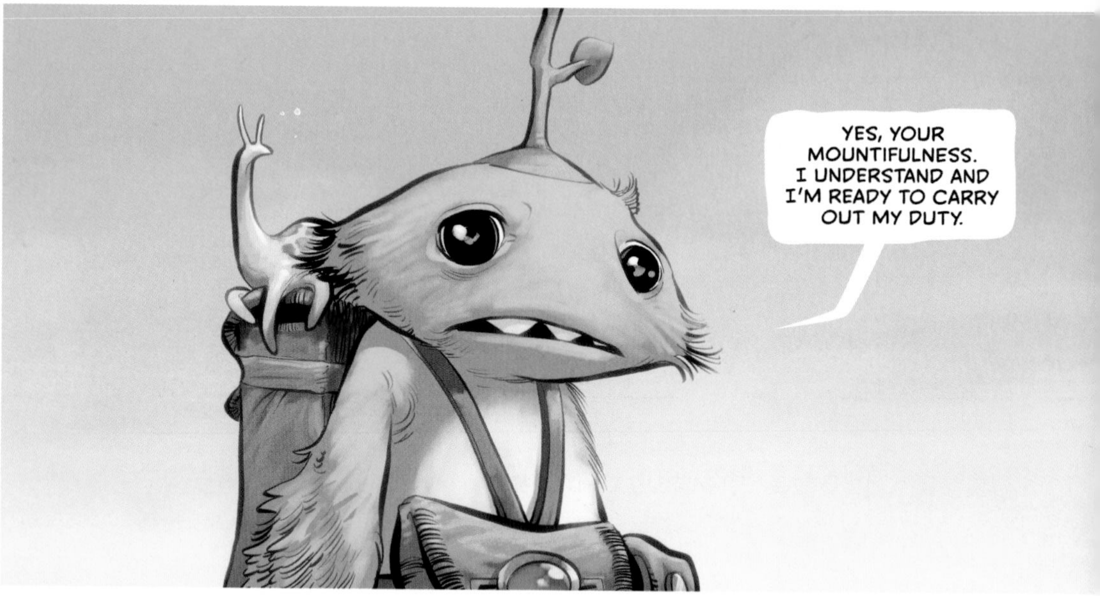
YES, YOUR MOUNTIFULNESS. I UNDERSTAND AND I'M READY TO CARRY OUT MY DUTY.

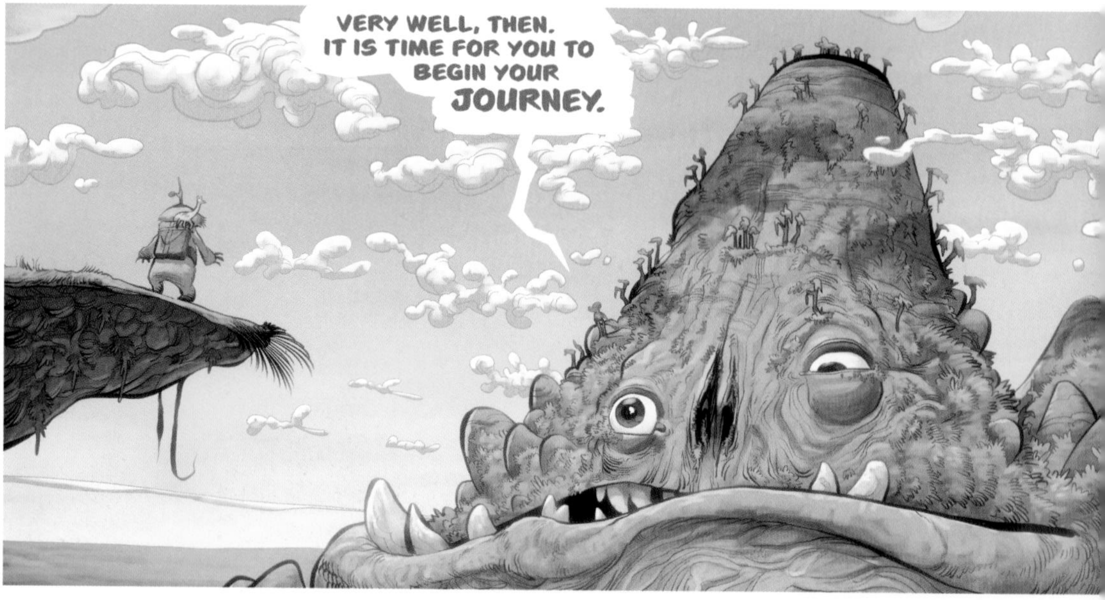
VERY WELL, THEN. IT IS TIME FOR YOU TO BEGIN YOUR JOURNEY.

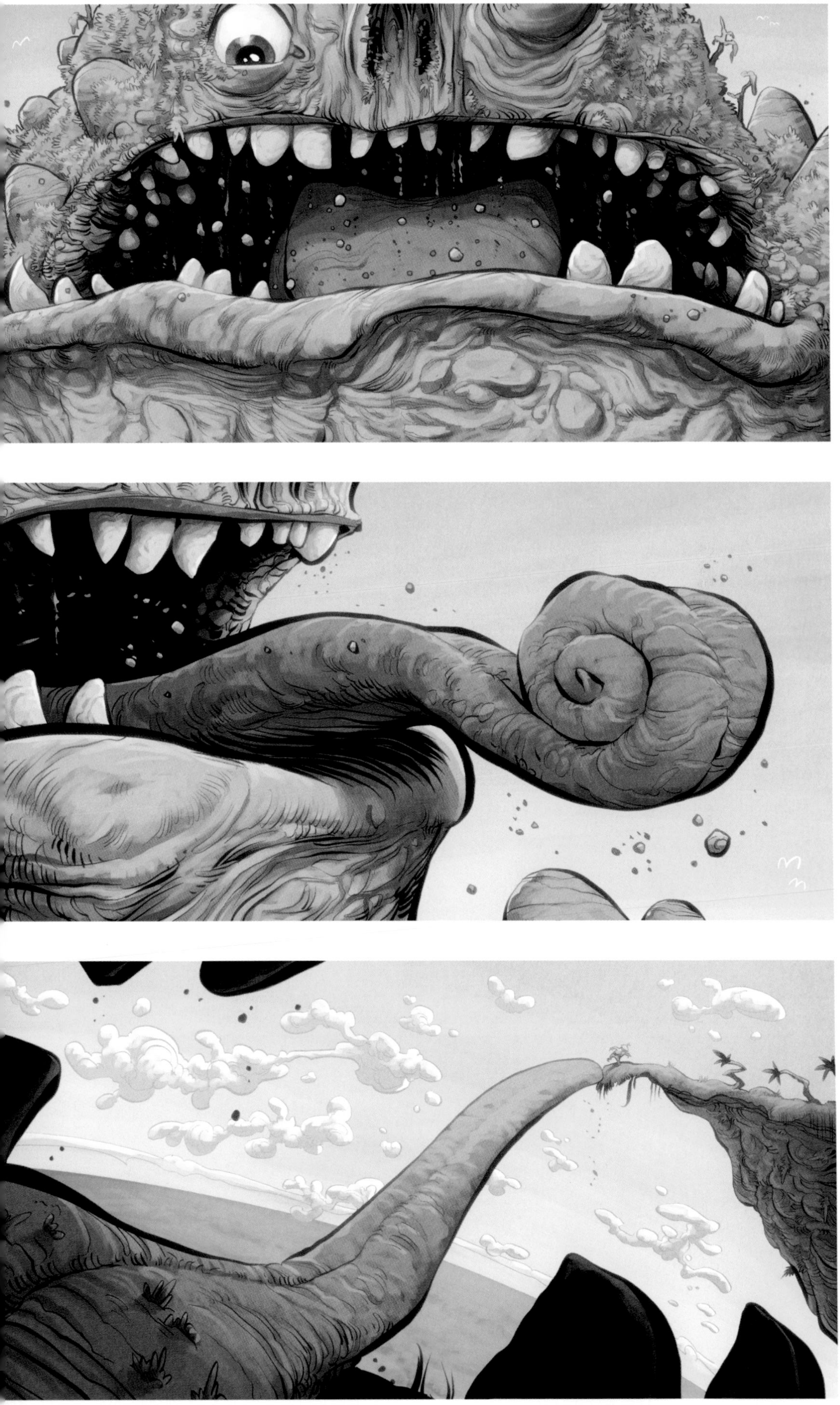

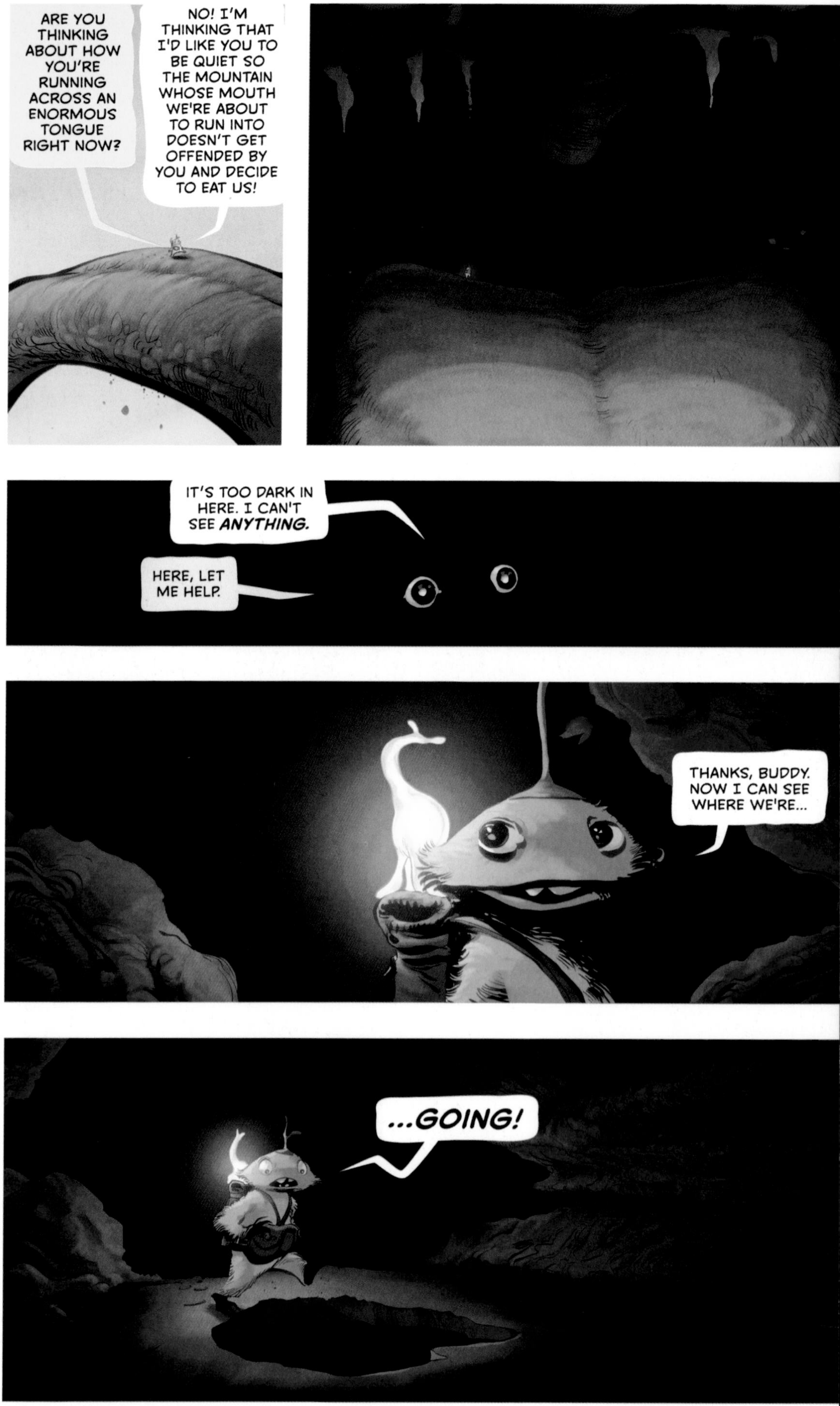
ARE YOU THINKING ABOUT HOW YOU'RE RUNNING ACROSS AN ENORMOUS TONGUE RIGHT NOW?
NO! I'M THINKING THAT I'D LIKE YOU TO BE QUIET SO THE MOUNTAIN WHOSE MOUTH WE'RE ABOUT TO RUN INTO DOESN'T GET OFFENDED BY YOU AND DECIDE TO EAT US!
IT'S TOO DARK IN HERE. I CAN'T SEE *ANYTHING.*
HERE, LET ME HELP.
THANKS, BUDDY. NOW I CAN SEE WHERE WE'RE...
...GOING!

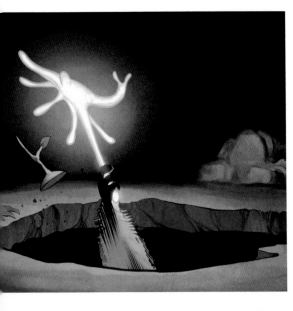

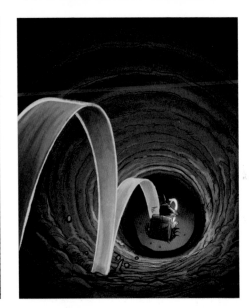

OOF!

THAT WAS QUITE THE TUMBLE THERE, FELLA.

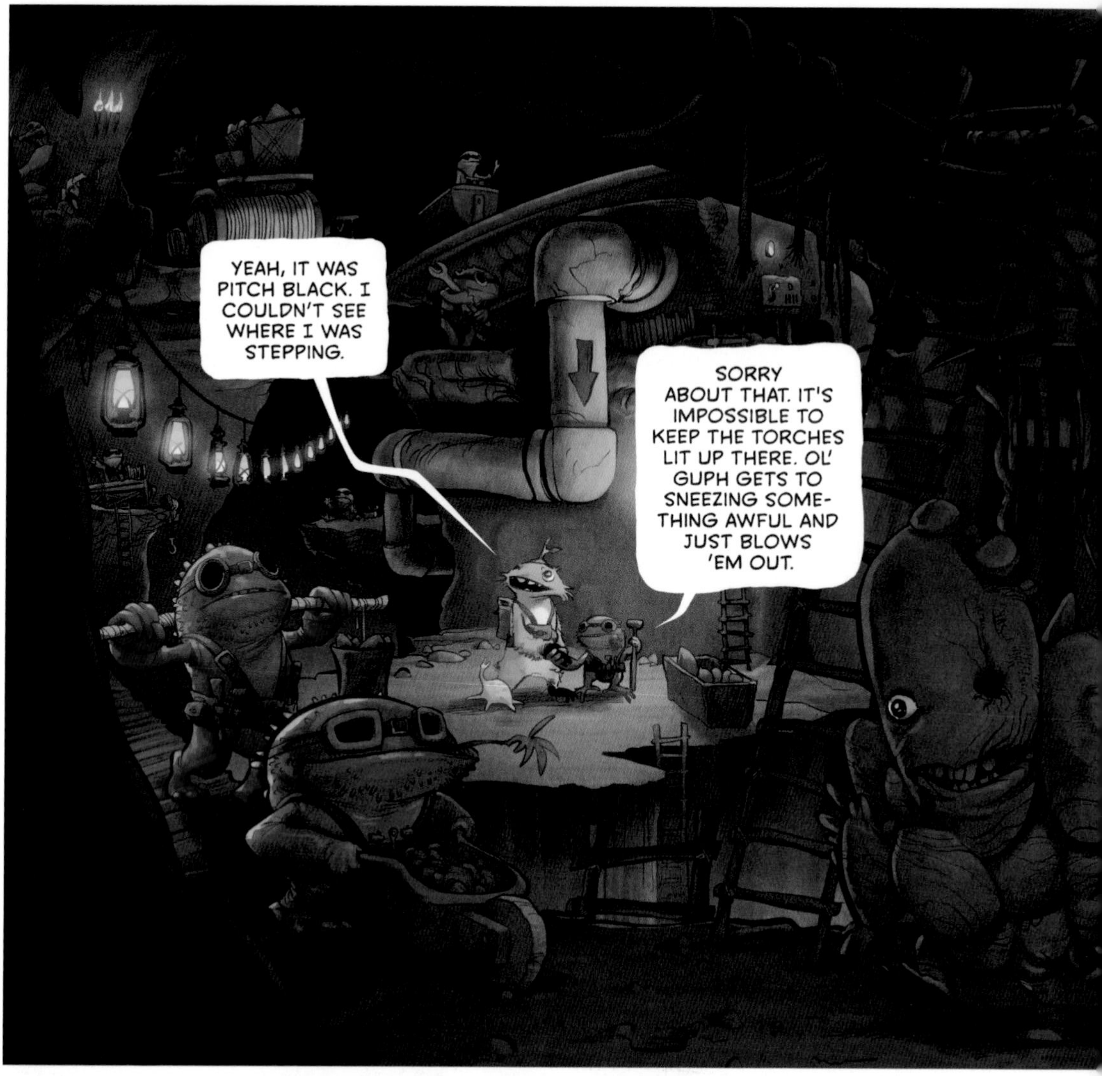
YEAH, IT WAS PITCH BLACK. I COULDN'T SEE WHERE I WAS STEPPING.
SORRY ABOUT THAT. IT'S IMPOSSIBLE TO KEEP THE TORCHES LIT UP THERE. OL' GUPH GETS TO SNEEZING SOME-THING AWFUL AND JUST BLOWS 'EM OUT.

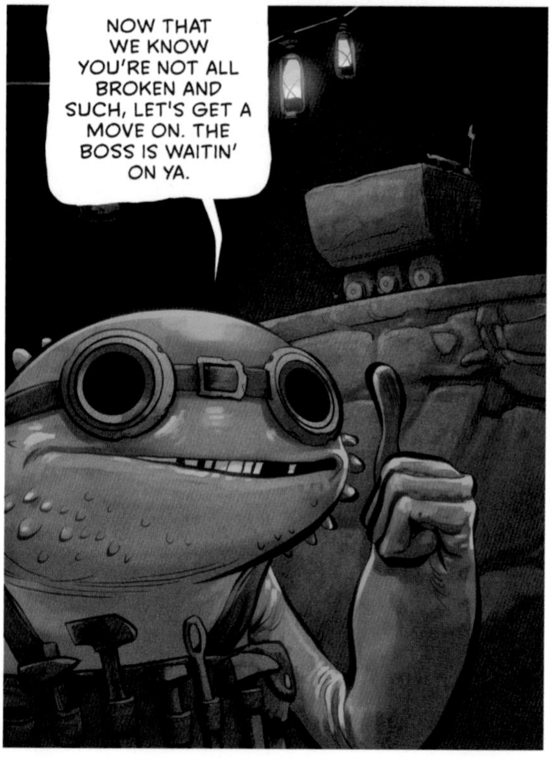
NOW THAT WE KNOW YOU'RE NOT ALL BROKEN AND SUCH, LET'S GET A MOVE ON. THE BOSS IS WAITIN' ON YA.

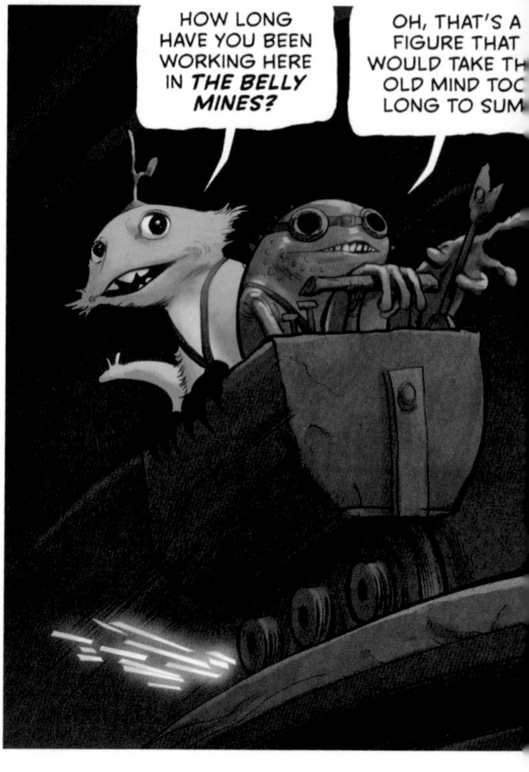
HOW LONG HAVE YOU BEEN WORKING HERE IN ***THE BELLY MINES?***
OH, THAT'S A FIGURE THAT WOULD TAKE TH OLD MIND TOO LONG TO SUM

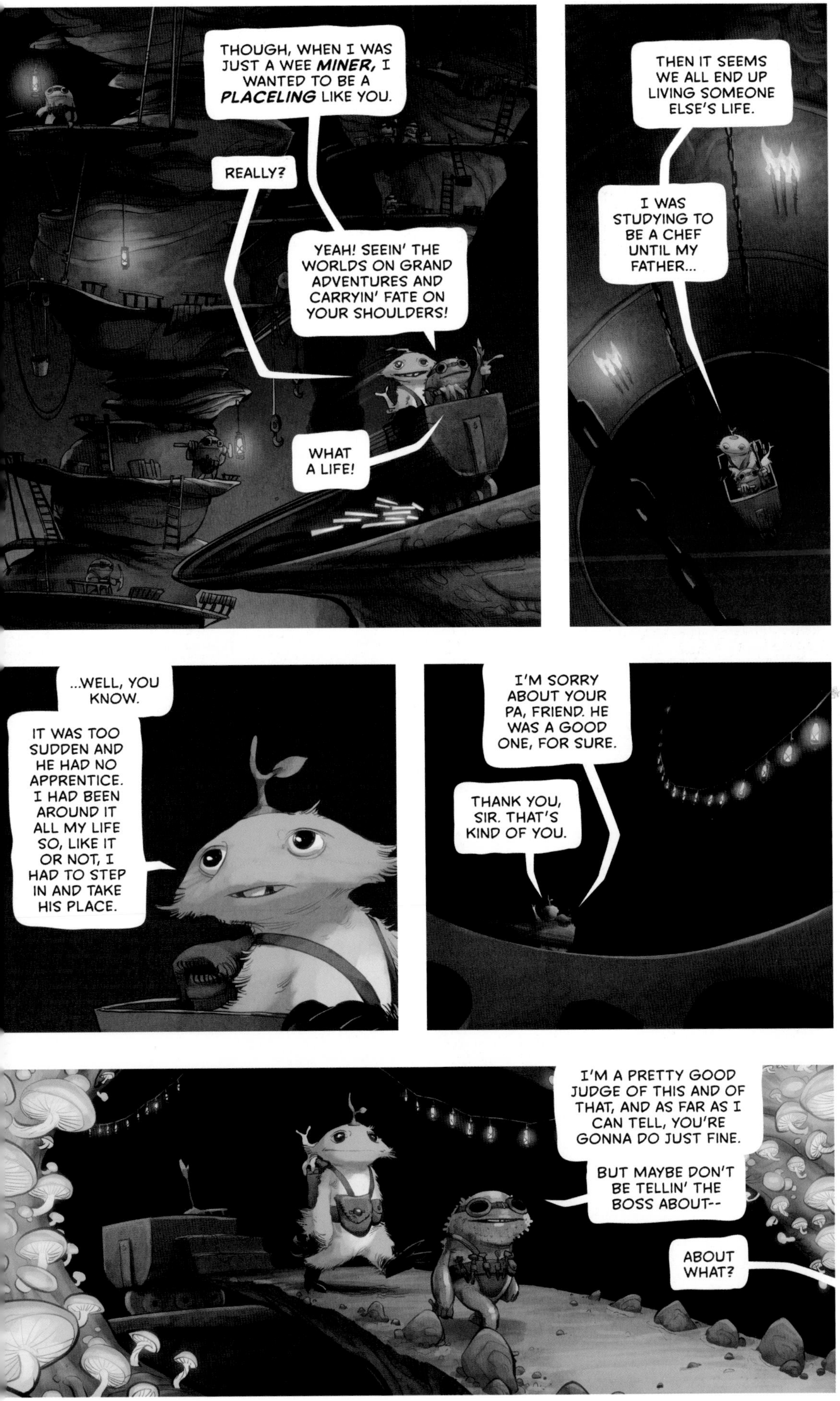
THOUGH, WHEN I WAS JUST A WEE *MINER,* I WANTED TO BE A *PLACELING* LIKE YOU.
REALLY?
YEAH! SEEIN' THE WORLDS ON GRAND ADVENTURES AND CARRYIN' FATE ON YOUR SHOULDERS!
WHAT A LIFE!
THEN IT SEEMS WE ALL END UP LIVING SOMEONE ELSE'S LIFE.
I WAS STUDYING TO BE A CHEF UNTIL MY FATHER...
...WELL, YOU KNOW.
IT WAS TOO SUDDEN AND HE HAD NO APPRENTICE. I HAD BEEN AROUND IT ALL MY LIFE SO, LIKE IT OR NOT, I HAD TO STEP IN AND TAKE HIS PLACE.
I'M SORRY ABOUT YOUR PA, FRIEND. HE WAS A GOOD ONE, FOR SURE.
THANK YOU, SIR. THAT'S KIND OF YOU.
I'M A PRETTY GOOD JUDGE OF THIS AND OF THAT, AND AS FAR AS I CAN TELL, YOU'RE GONNA DO JUST FINE.
BUT MAYBE DON'T BE TELLIN' THE BOSS ABOUT--
ABOUT WHAT?

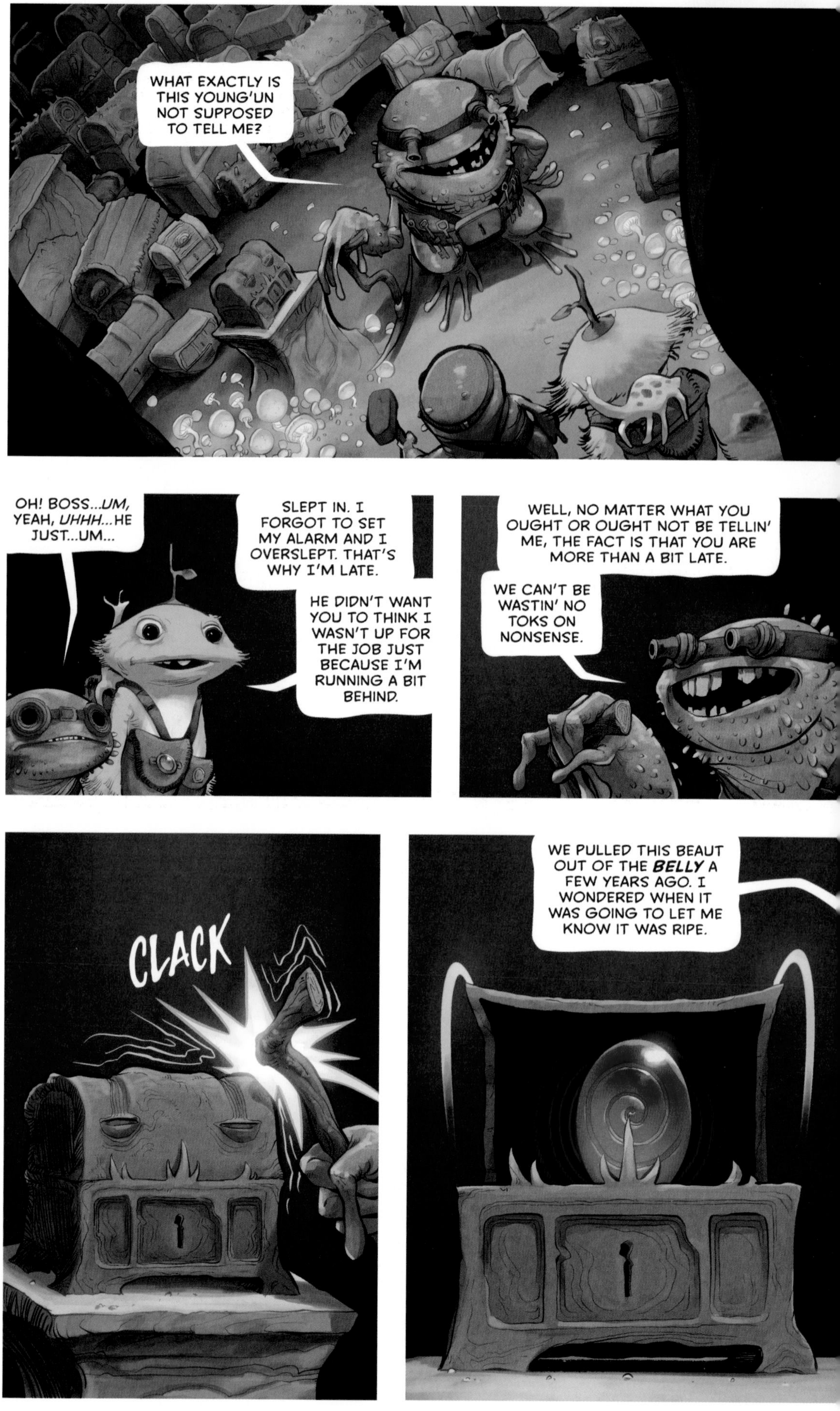

WHAT EXACTLY IS THIS YOUNG'UN NOT SUPPOSED TO TELL ME?
OH! BOSS...*UM*, YEAH, *UHHH*...HE JUST...UM...
SLEPT IN. I FORGOT TO SET MY ALARM AND I OVERSLEPT. THAT'S WHY I'M LATE.
HE DIDN'T WANT YOU TO THINK I WASN'T UP FOR THE JOB JUST BECAUSE I'M RUNNING A BIT BEHIND.
WELL, NO MATTER WHAT YOU OUGHT OR OUGHT NOT BE TELLIN' ME, THE FACT IS THAT YOU ARE MORE THAN A BIT LATE.
WE CAN'T BE WASTIN' NO TOKS ON NONSENSE.
CLACK
WE PULLED THIS BEAUT OUT OF THE ***BELLY*** A FEW YEARS AGO. I WONDERED WHEN IT WAS GOING TO LET ME KNOW IT WAS RIPE.

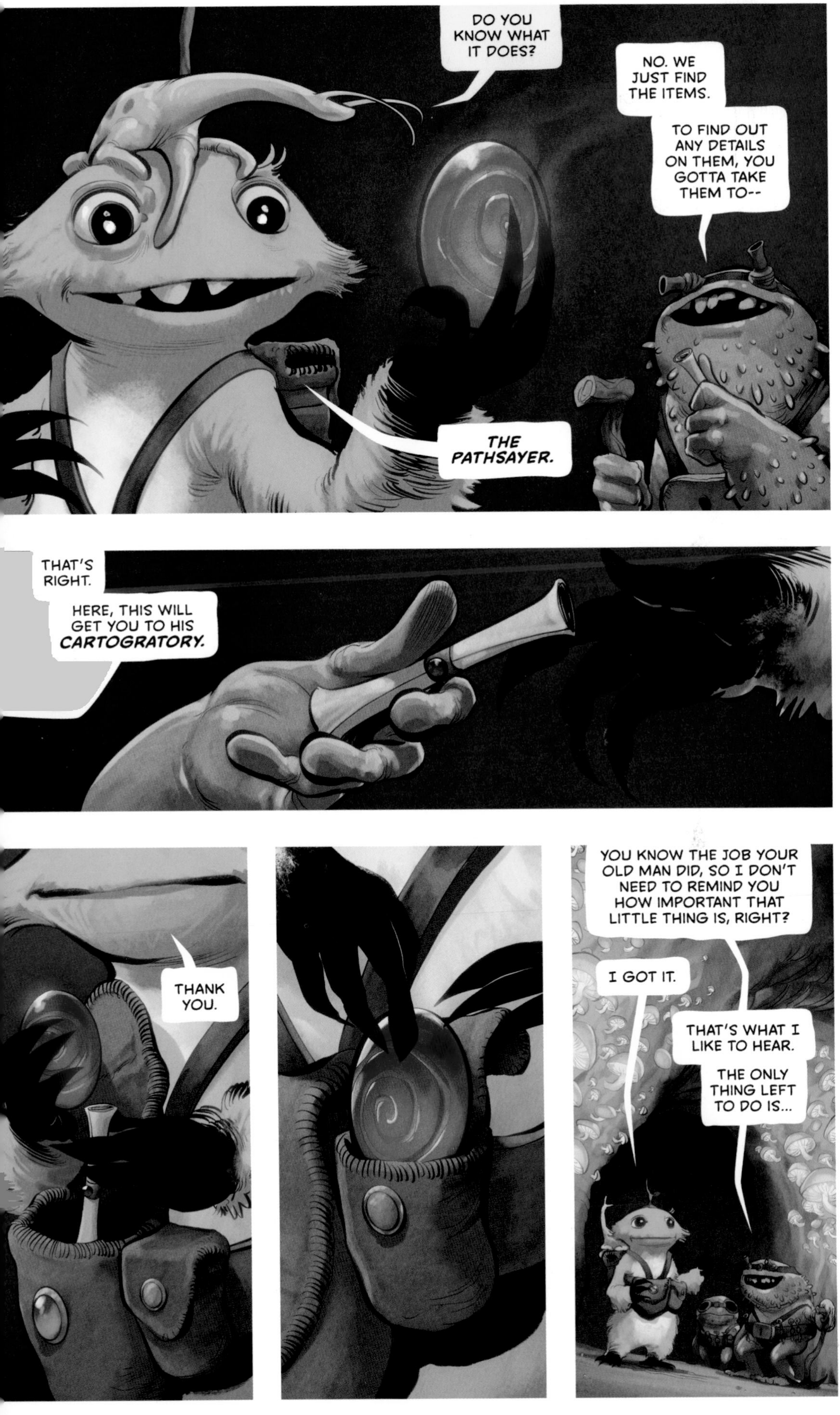
DO YOU KNOW WHAT IT DOES?
NO. WE JUST FIND THE ITEMS.
TO FIND OUT ANY DETAILS ON THEM, YOU GOTTA TAKE THEM TO--
THE PATHSAYER.
THAT'S RIGHT.
HERE, THIS WILL GET YOU TO HIS CARTOGRATORY.
THANK YOU.
YOU KNOW THE JOB YOUR OLD MAN DID, SO I DON'T NEED TO REMIND YOU HOW IMPORTANT THAT LITTLE THING IS, RIGHT?
I GOT IT.
THAT'S WHAT I LIKE TO HEAR.
THE ONLY THING LEFT TO DO IS...

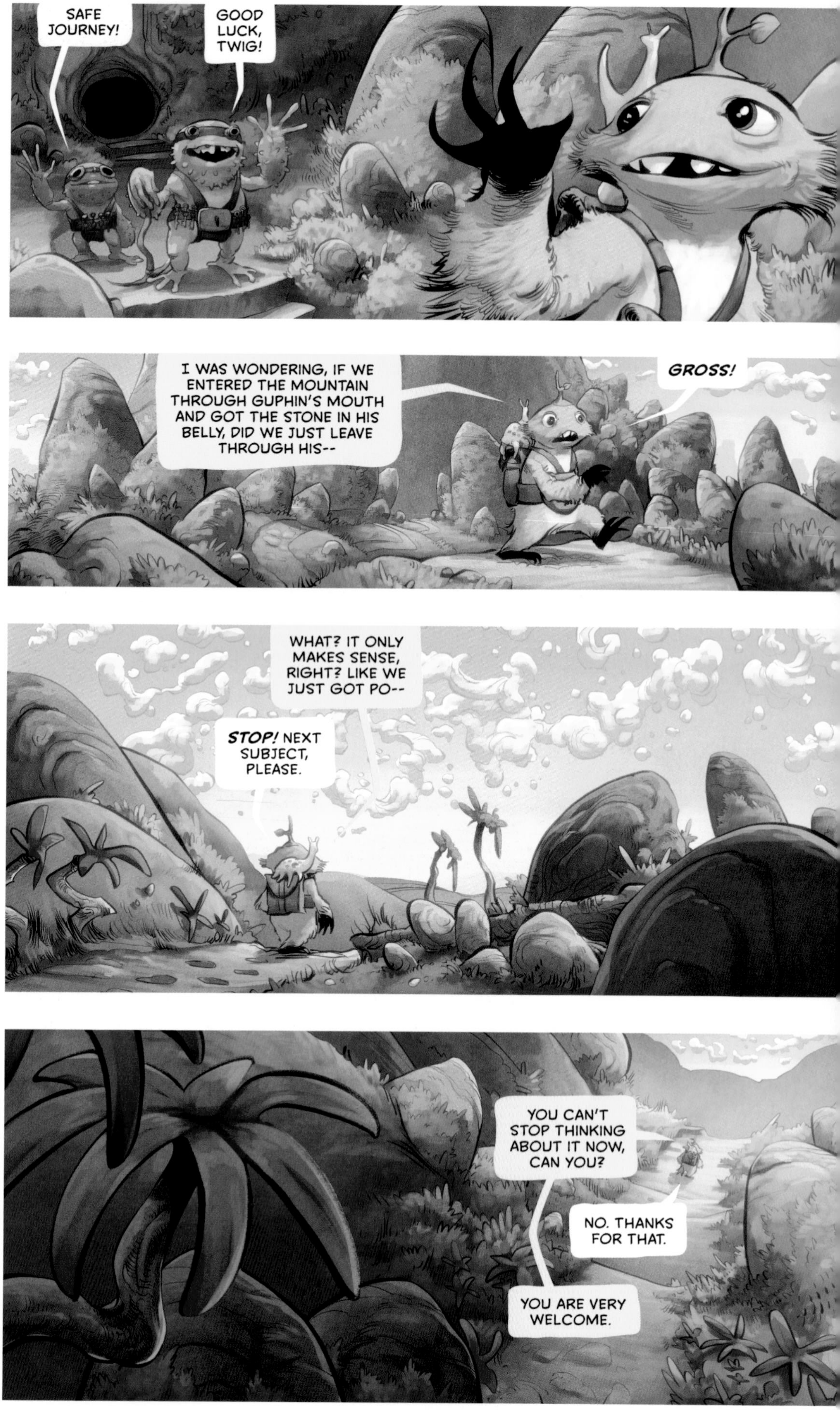
SAFE JOURNEY!
GOOD LUCK, TWIG!
I WAS WONDERING, IF WE ENTERED THE MOUNTAIN THROUGH GUPHIN'S MOUTH AND GOT THE STONE IN HIS BELLY, DID WE JUST LEAVE THROUGH HIS--
GROSS!
WHAT? IT ONLY MAKES SENSE, RIGHT? LIKE WE JUST GOT PO--
STOP! NEXT SUBJECT, PLEASE.
YOU CAN'T STOP THINKING ABOUT IT NOW, CAN YOU?
NO. THANKS FOR THAT.
YOU ARE VERY WELCOME.

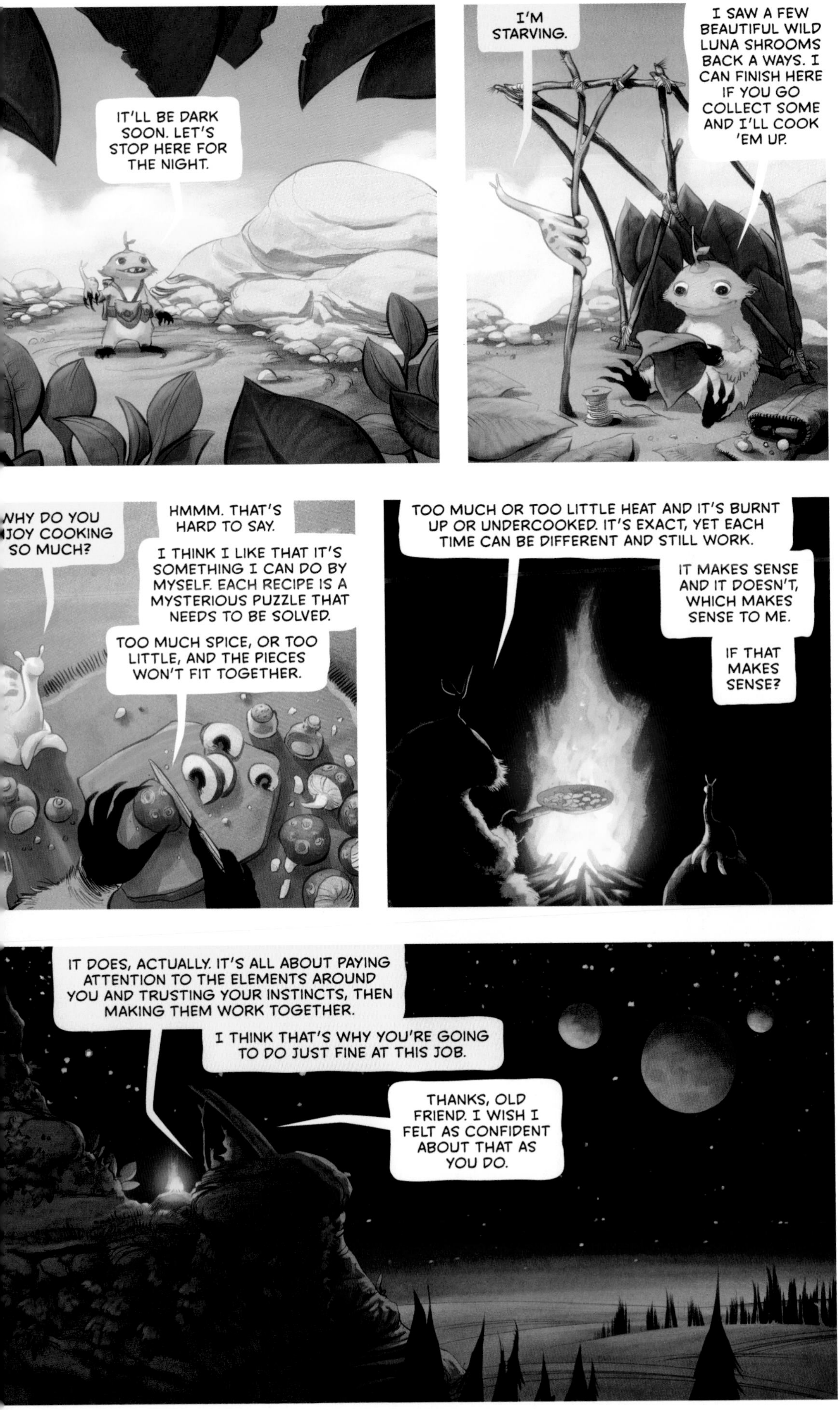
IT'LL BE DARK SOON. LET'S STOP HERE FOR THE NIGHT.
I'M STARVING.
I SAW A FEW BEAUTIFUL WILD LUNA SHROOMS BACK A WAYS. I CAN FINISH HERE IF YOU GO COLLECT SOME AND I'LL COOK 'EM UP.
WHY DO YOU JOY COOKING SO MUCH?
HMMM. THAT'S HARD TO SAY.
I THINK I LIKE THAT IT'S SOMETHING I CAN DO BY MYSELF. EACH RECIPE IS A MYSTERIOUS PUZZLE THAT NEEDS TO BE SOLVED.
TOO MUCH SPICE, OR TOO LITTLE, AND THE PIECES WON'T FIT TOGETHER.
TOO MUCH OR TOO LITTLE HEAT AND IT'S BURNT UP OR UNDERCOOKED. IT'S EXACT, YET EACH TIME CAN BE DIFFERENT AND STILL WORK.
IT MAKES SENSE AND IT DOESN'T, WHICH MAKES SENSE TO ME.
IF THAT MAKES SENSE?
IT DOES, ACTUALLY. IT'S ALL ABOUT PAYING ATTENTION TO THE ELEMENTS AROUND YOU AND TRUSTING YOUR INSTINCTS, THEN MAKING THEM WORK TOGETHER.
I THINK THAT'S WHY YOU'RE GOING TO DO JUST FINE AT THIS JOB.
THANKS, OLD FRIEND. I WISH I FELT AS CONFIDENT ABOUT THAT AS YOU DO.

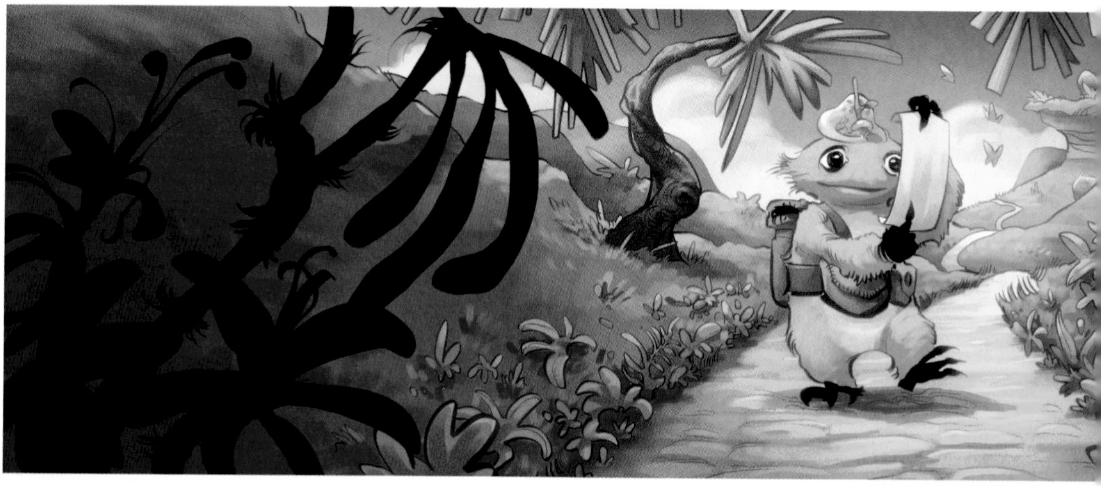
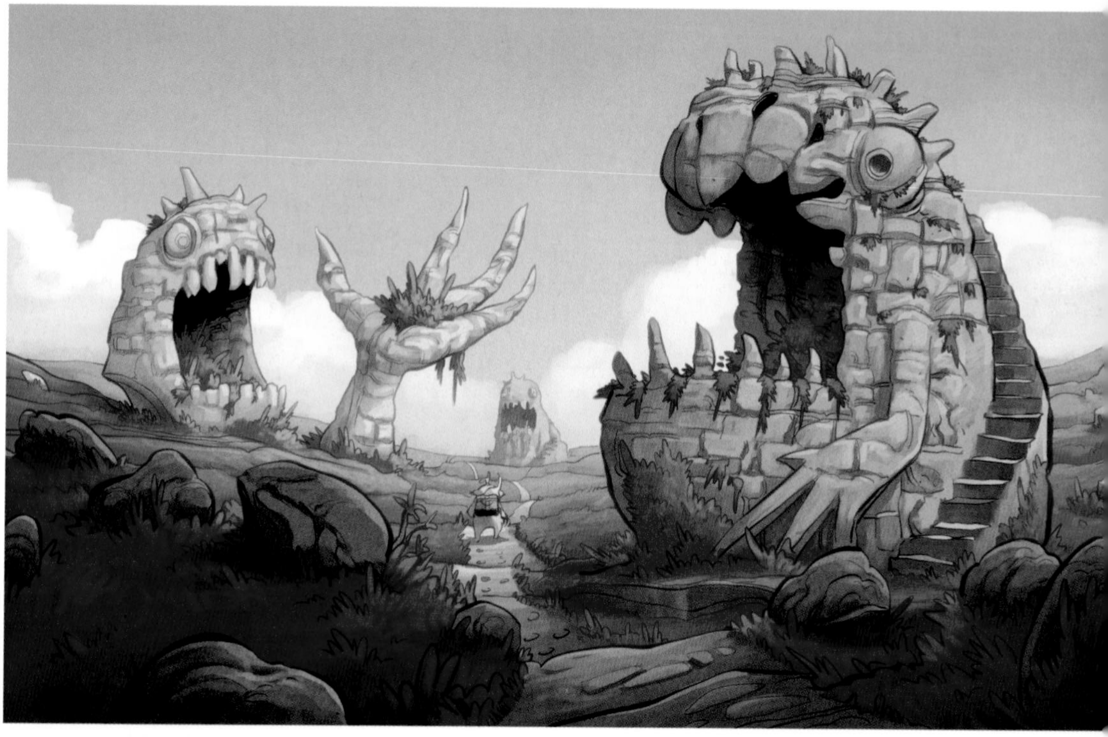
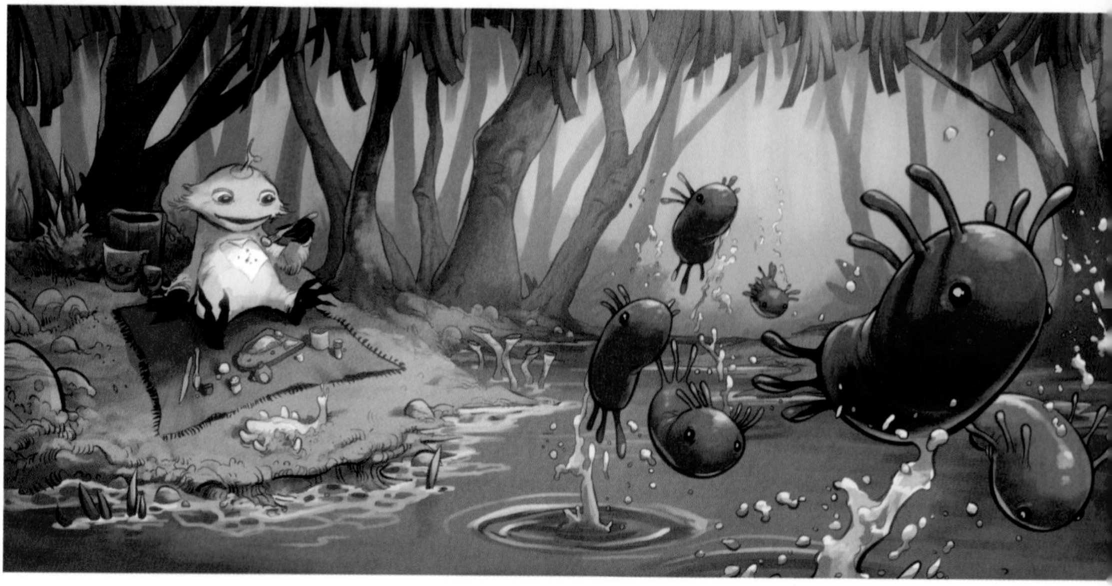

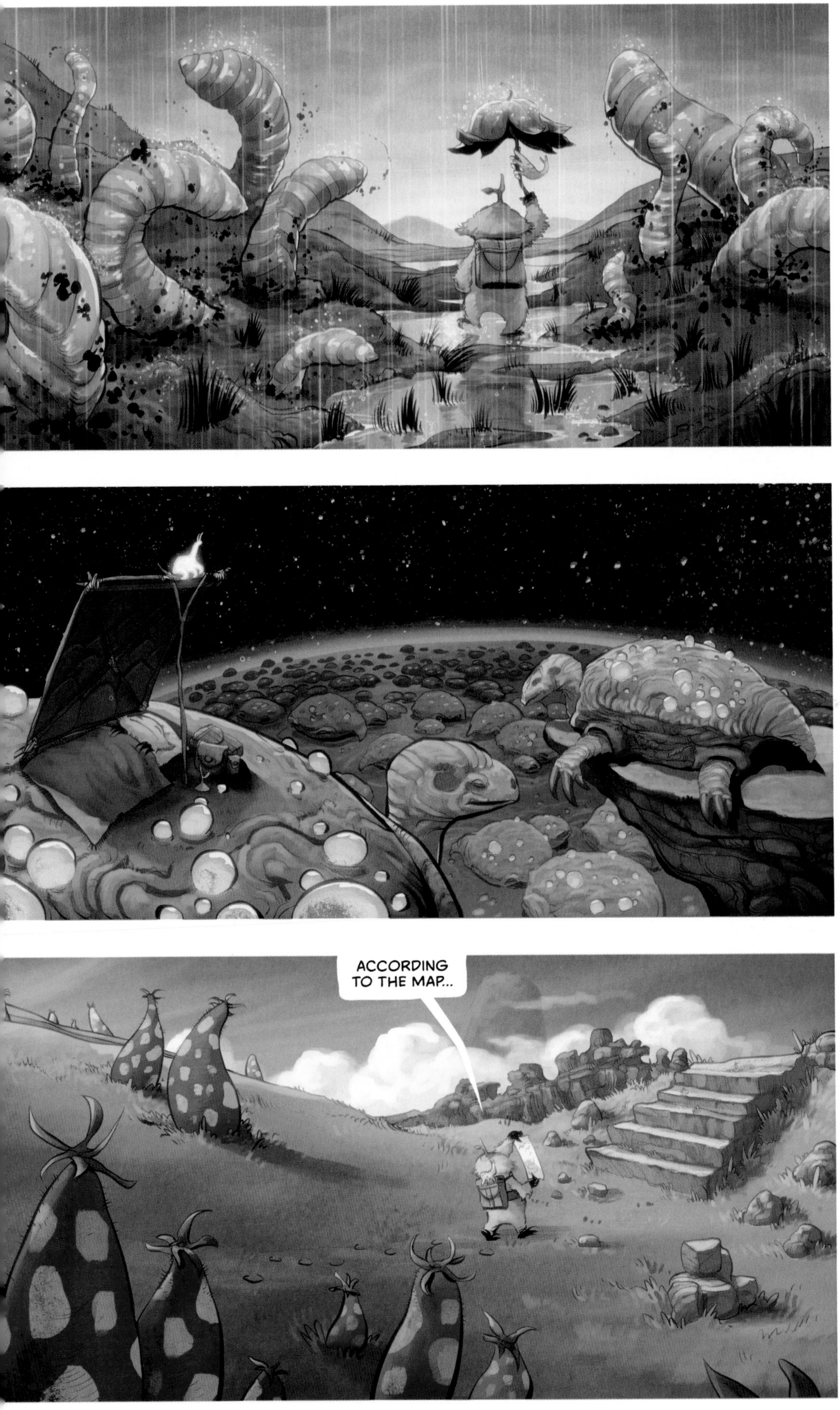
ACCORDING TO THE MAP...

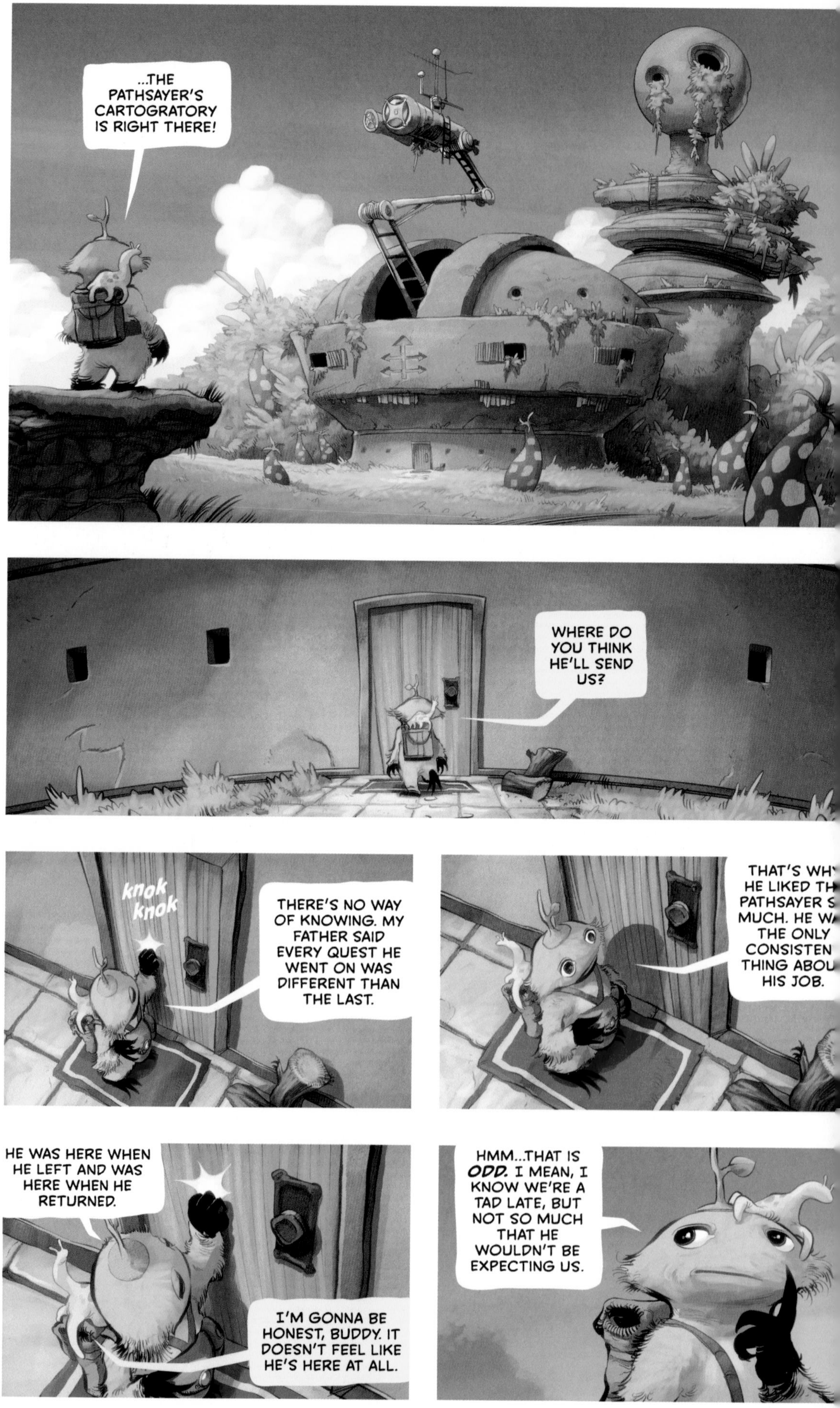

...THE PATHSAYER'S CARTOGRATORY IS RIGHT THERE!
WHERE DO YOU THINK HE'LL SEND US?
knok knok
THERE'S NO WAY OF KNOWING. MY FATHER SAID EVERY QUEST HE WENT ON WAS DIFFERENT THAN THE LAST.
THAT'S WH HE LIKED TH PATHSAYER S MUCH. HE W THE ONLY CONSISTEN THING ABOU HIS JOB.
HE WAS HERE WHEN HE LEFT AND WAS HERE WHEN HE RETURNED.
I'M GONNA BE HONEST, BUDDY. IT DOESN'T FEEL LIKE HE'S HERE AT ALL.
HMM...THAT IS ODD. I MEAN, I KNOW WE'RE A TAD LATE, BUT NOT SO MUCH THAT HE WOULDN'T BE EXPECTING US.

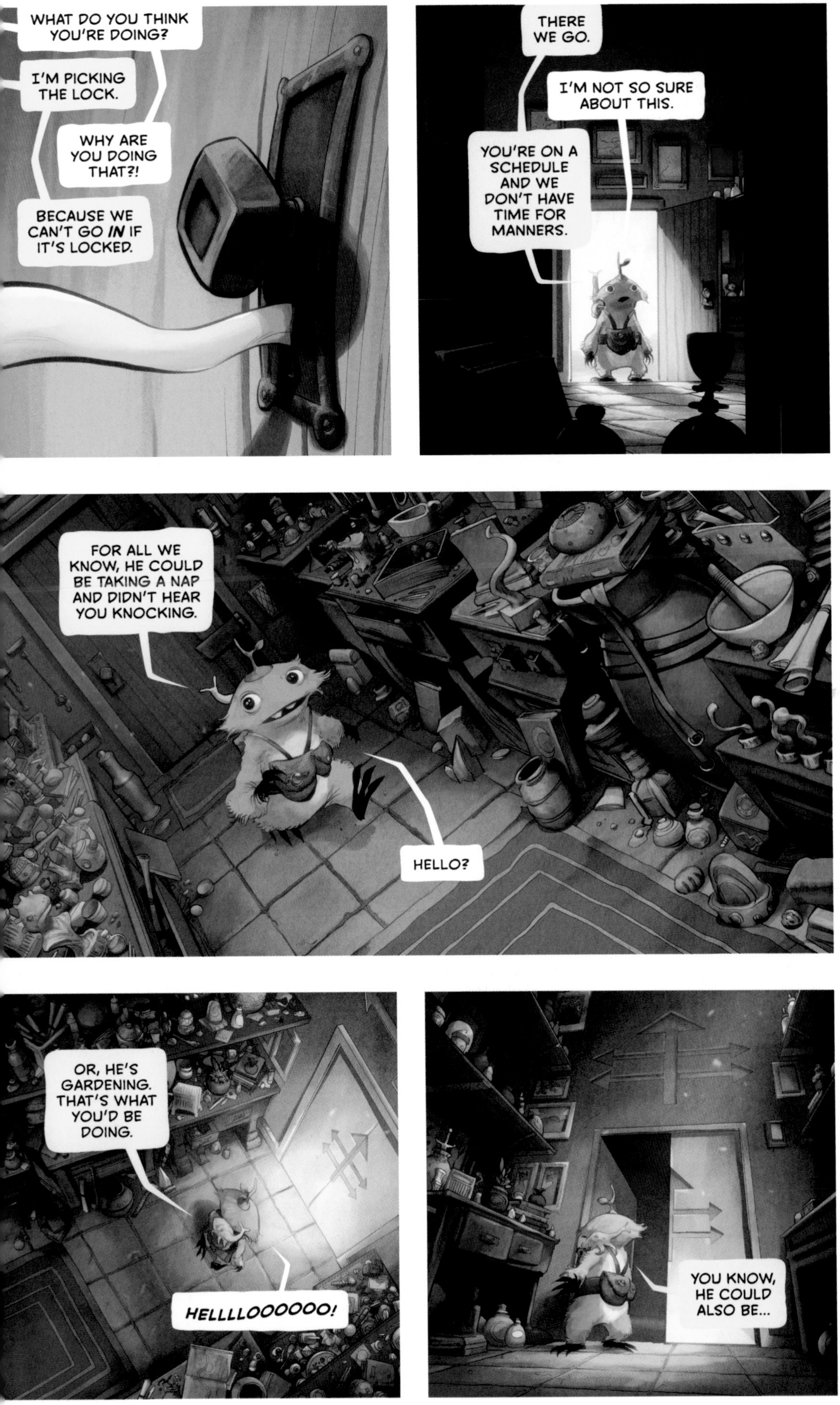
WHAT DO YOU THINK YOU'RE DOING?
I'M PICKING THE LOCK.
WHY ARE YOU DOING THAT?!
BECAUSE WE CAN'T GO *IN* IF IT'S LOCKED.
THERE WE GO.
I'M NOT SO SURE ABOUT THIS.
YOU'RE ON A SCHEDULE AND WE DON'T HAVE TIME FOR MANNERS.
FOR ALL WE KNOW, HE COULD BE TAKING A NAP AND DIDN'T HEAR YOU KNOCKING.
HELLO?
OR, HE'S GARDENING. THAT'S WHAT YOU'D BE DOING.
HELLLLOOOOOO!
YOU KNOW, HE COULD ALSO BE...

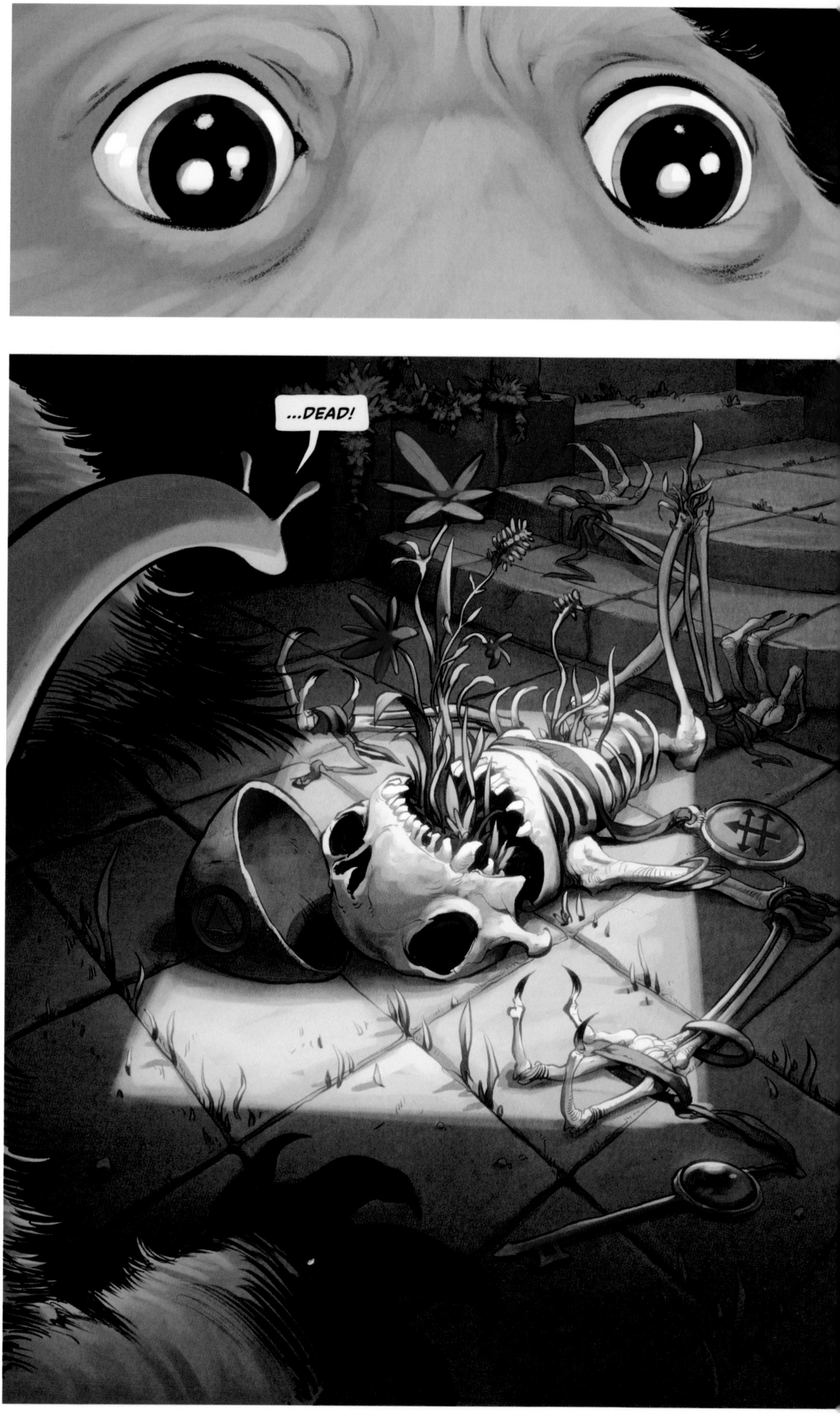
...DEAD!

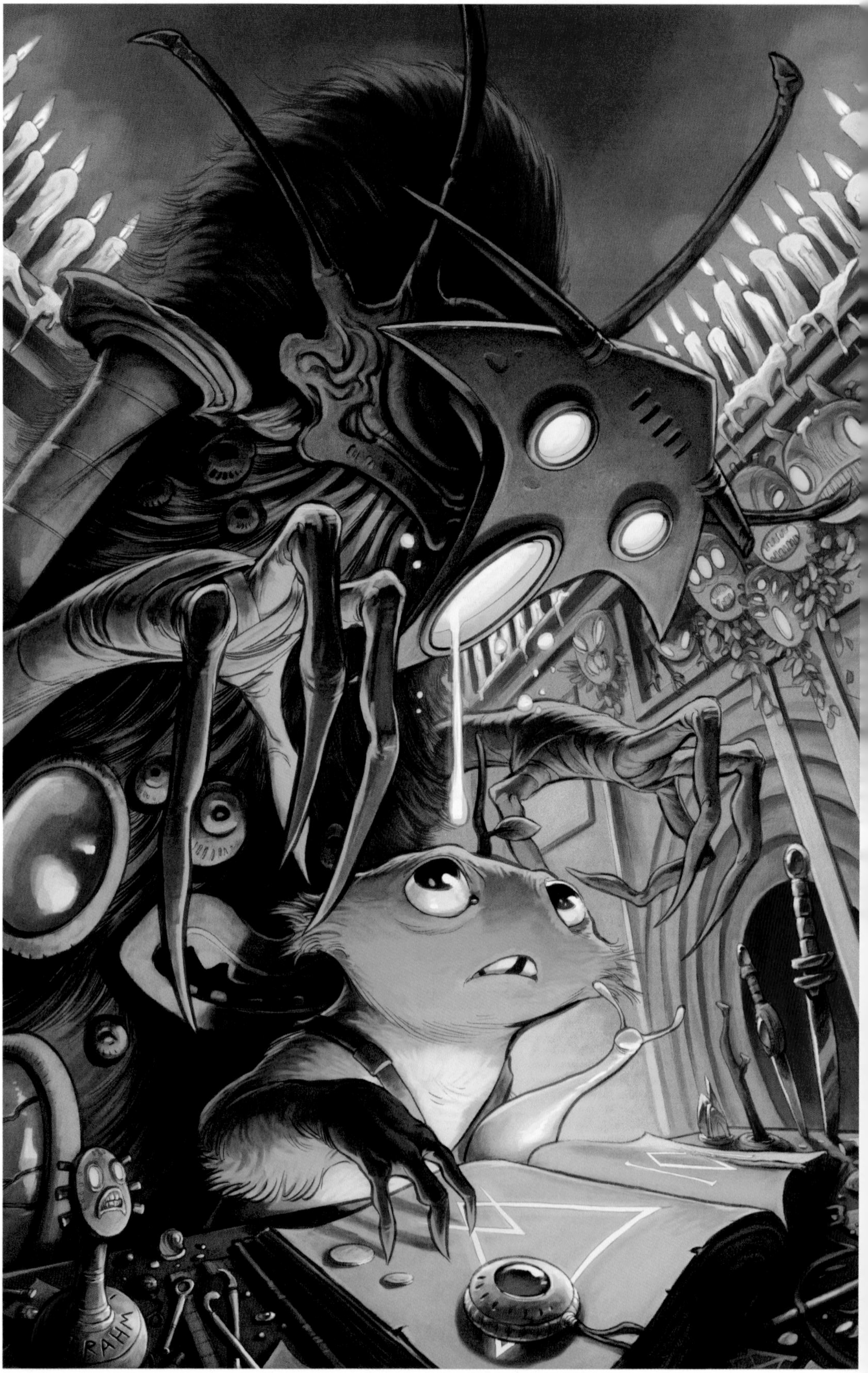

TWO

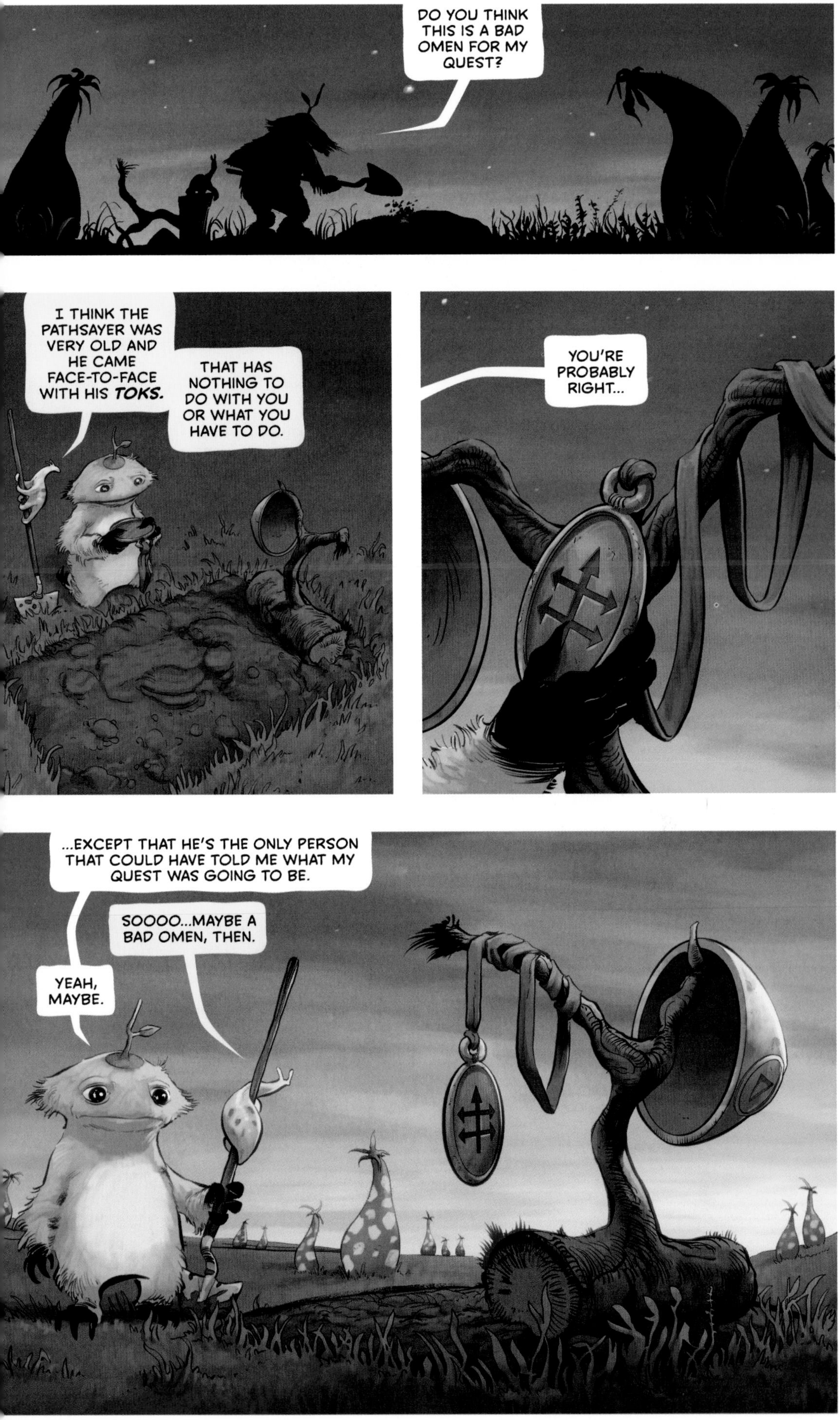
DO YOU THINK THIS IS A BAD OMEN FOR MY QUEST?
I THINK THE PATHSAYER WAS VERY OLD AND HE CAME FACE-TO-FACE WITH HIS *TOKS.*
THAT HAS NOTHING TO DO WITH YOU OR WHAT YOU HAVE TO DO.
YOU'RE PROBABLY RIGHT...
...EXCEPT THAT HE'S THE ONLY PERSON THAT COULD HAVE TOLD ME WHAT MY QUEST WAS GOING TO BE.
SOOOO...MAYBE A BAD OMEN, THEN.
YEAH, MAYBE.

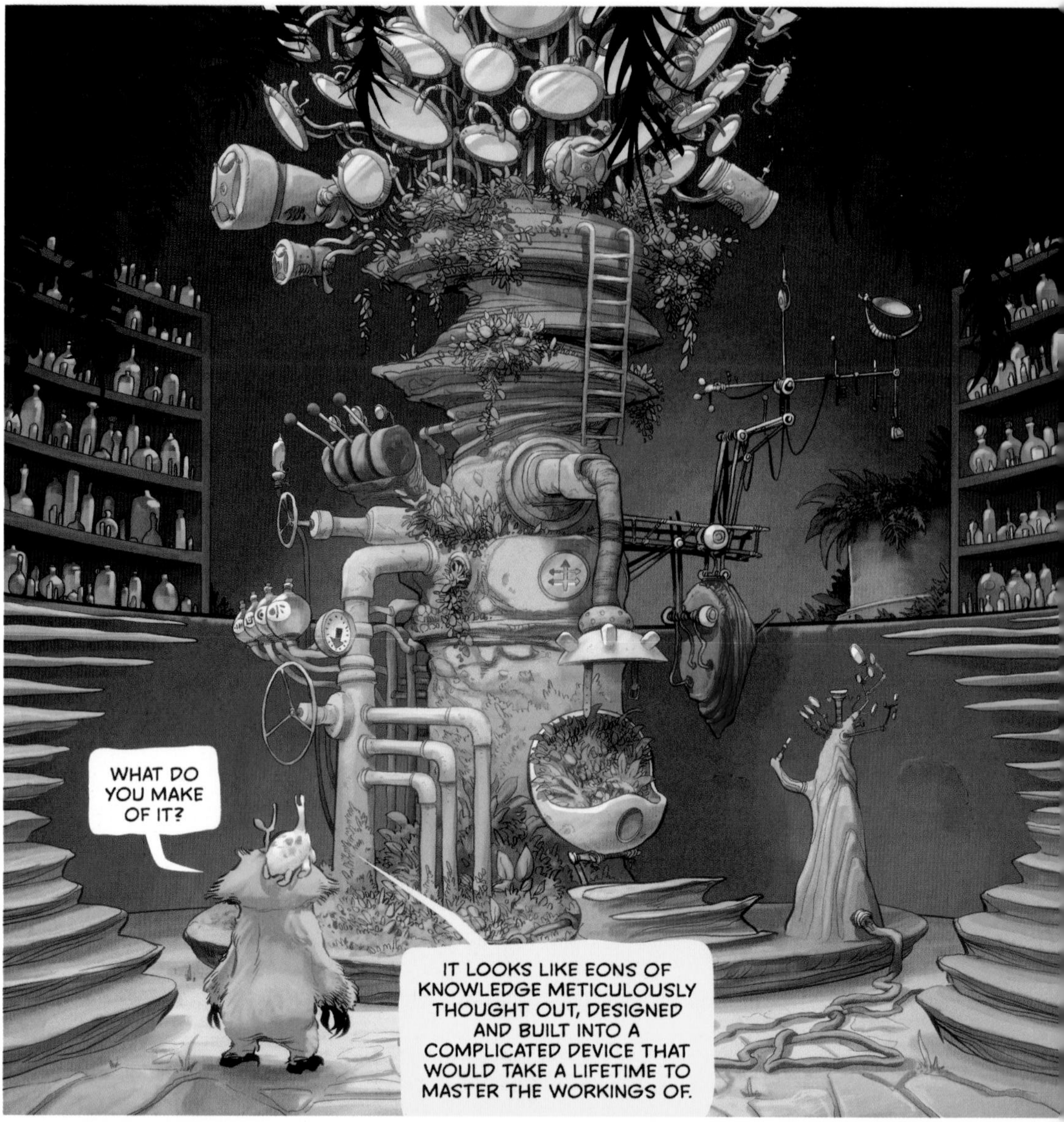
WHAT DO YOU MAKE OF IT?
IT LOOKS LIKE EONS OF KNOWLEDGE METICULOUSLY THOUGHT OUT, DESIGNED AND BUILT INTO A COMPLICATED DEVICE THAT WOULD TAKE A LIFETIME TO MASTER THE WORKINGS OF.

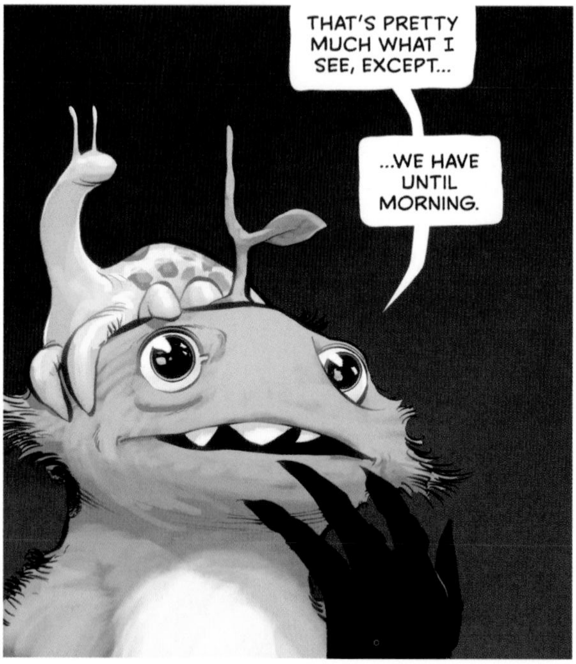
THAT'S PRETTY MUCH WHAT I SEE, EXCEPT...
...WE HAVE UNTIL MORNING.

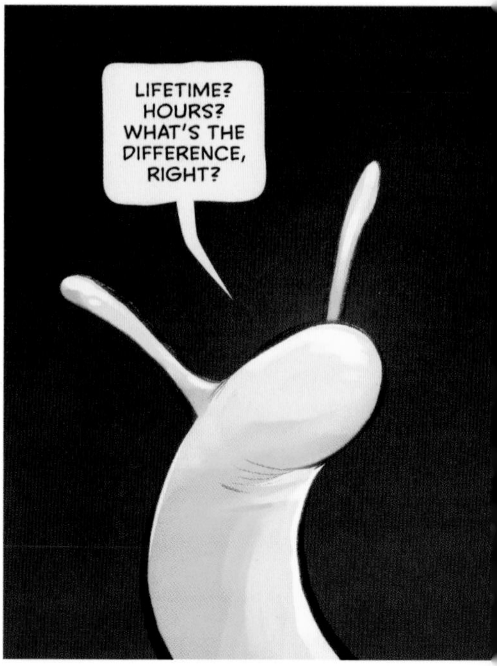
LIFETIME? HOURS? WHAT'S THE DIFFERENCE, RIGHT?

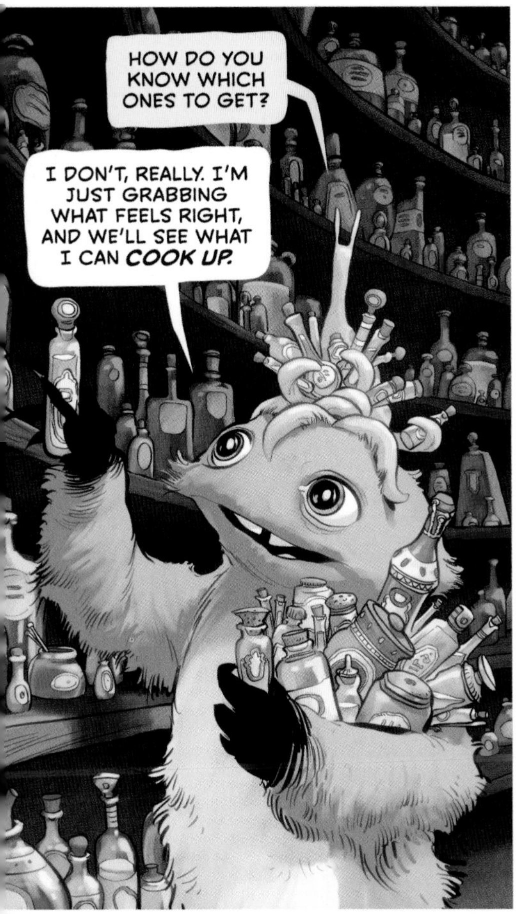
HOW DO YOU KNOW WHICH ONES TO GET?
I DON'T, REALLY. I'M JUST GRABBING WHAT FEELS RIGHT, AND WE'LL SEE WHAT I CAN ***COOK UP.***

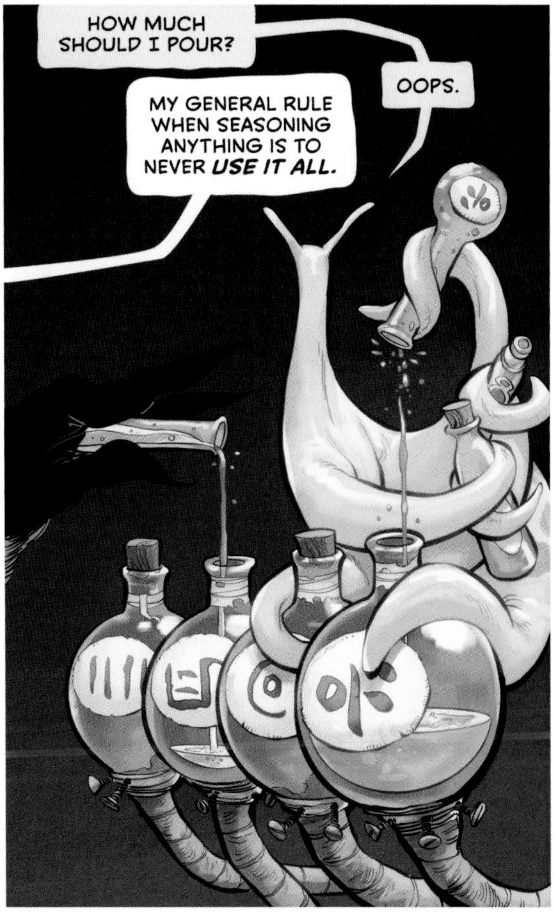
HOW MUCH SHOULD I POUR?
MY GENERAL RULE WHEN SEASONING ANYTHING IS TO NEVER ***USE IT ALL.***
OOPS.

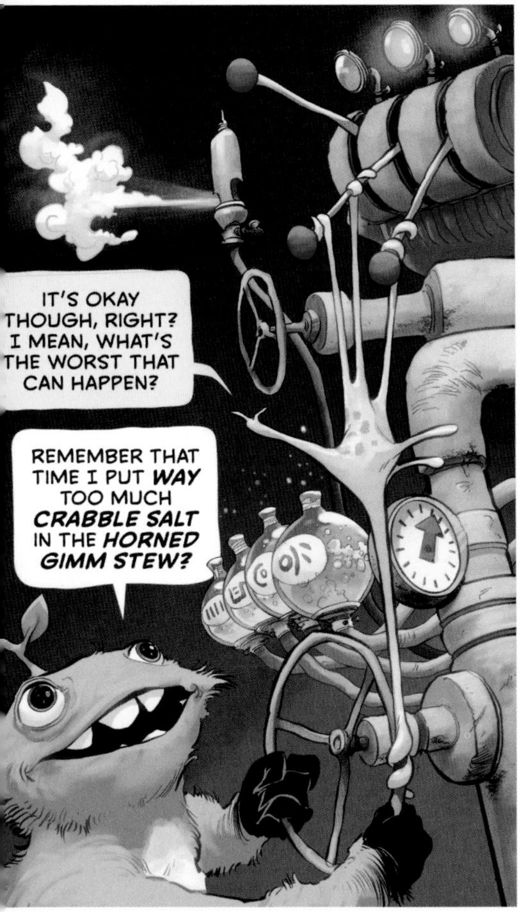
IT'S OKAY THOUGH, RIGHT? I MEAN, WHAT'S THE WORST THAT CAN HAPPEN?
REMEMBER THAT TIME I PUT ***WAY*** TOO MUCH ***CRABBLE SALT*** IN THE ***HORNED GIMM STEW?***

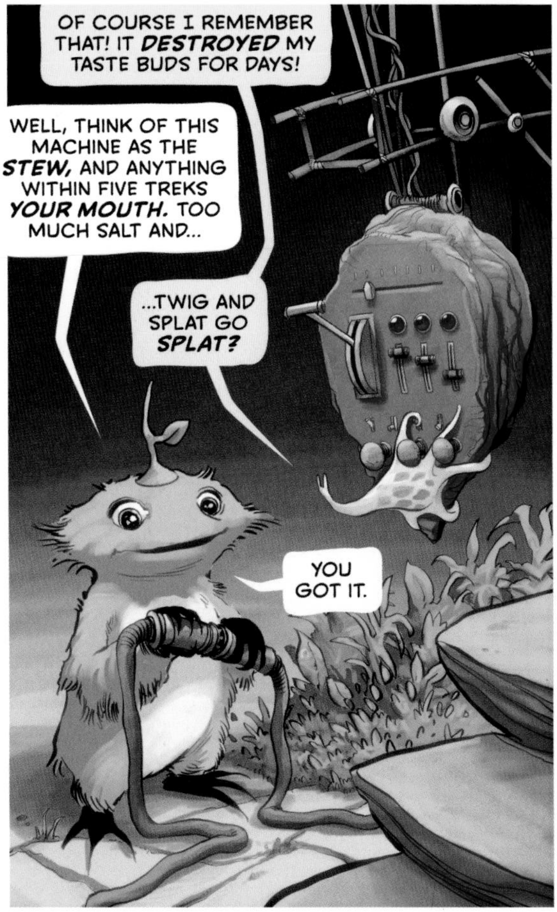
OF COURSE I REMEMBER THAT! IT ***DESTROYED*** MY TASTE BUDS FOR DAYS!
WELL, THINK OF THIS MACHINE AS THE ***STEW,*** AND ANYTHING WITHIN FIVE TREKS ***YOUR MOUTH.*** TOO MUCH SALT AND...
...TWIG AND SPLAT GO ***SPLAT?***
YOU GOT IT.

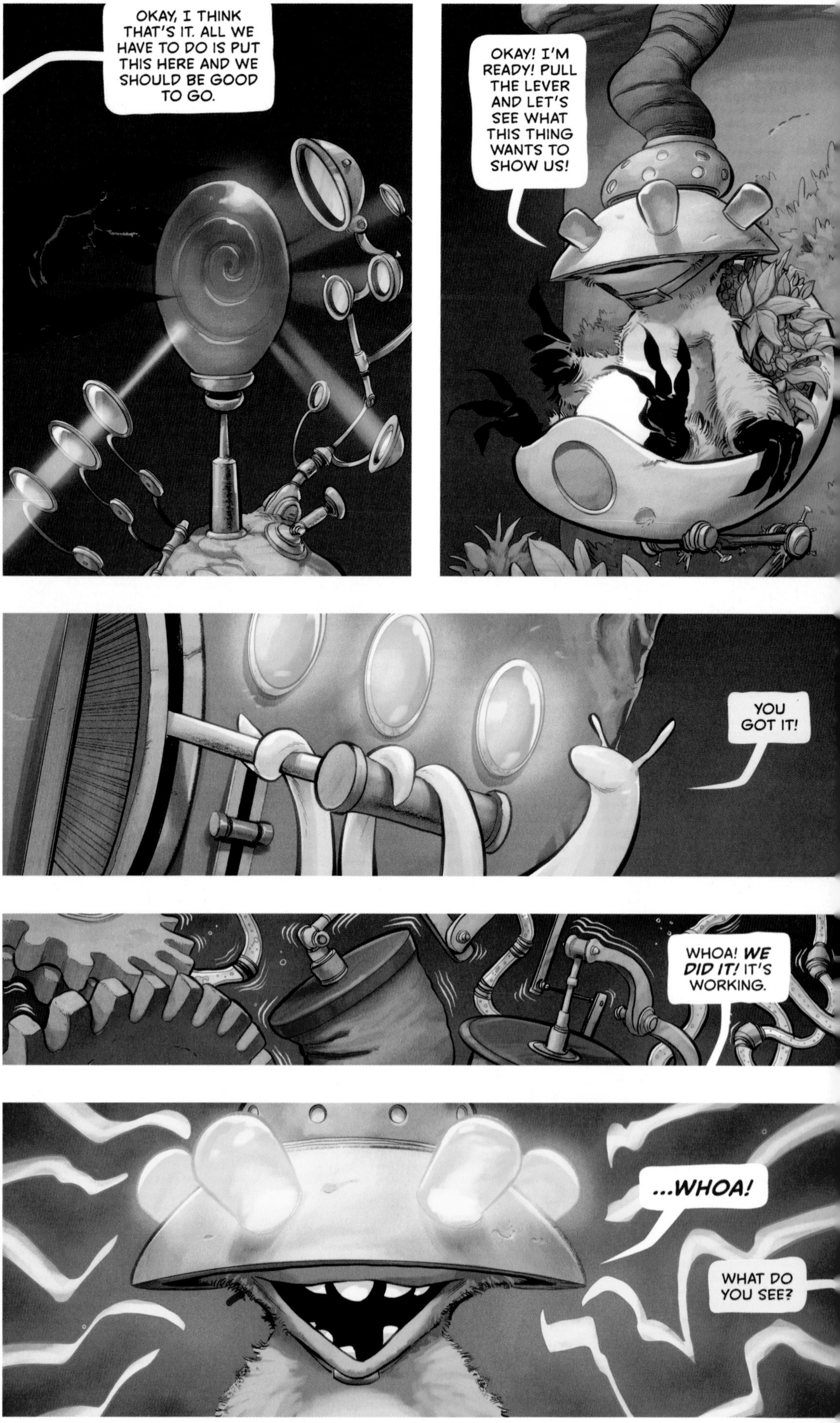
OKAY, I THINK THAT'S IT. ALL WE HAVE TO DO IS PUT THIS HERE AND WE SHOULD BE GOOD TO GO.
OKAY! I'M READY! PULL THE LEVER AND LET'S SEE WHAT THIS THING WANTS TO SHOW US!
YOU GOT IT!
WHOA! ***WE DID IT!*** IT'S WORKING.
...WHOA!
WHAT DO YOU SEE?

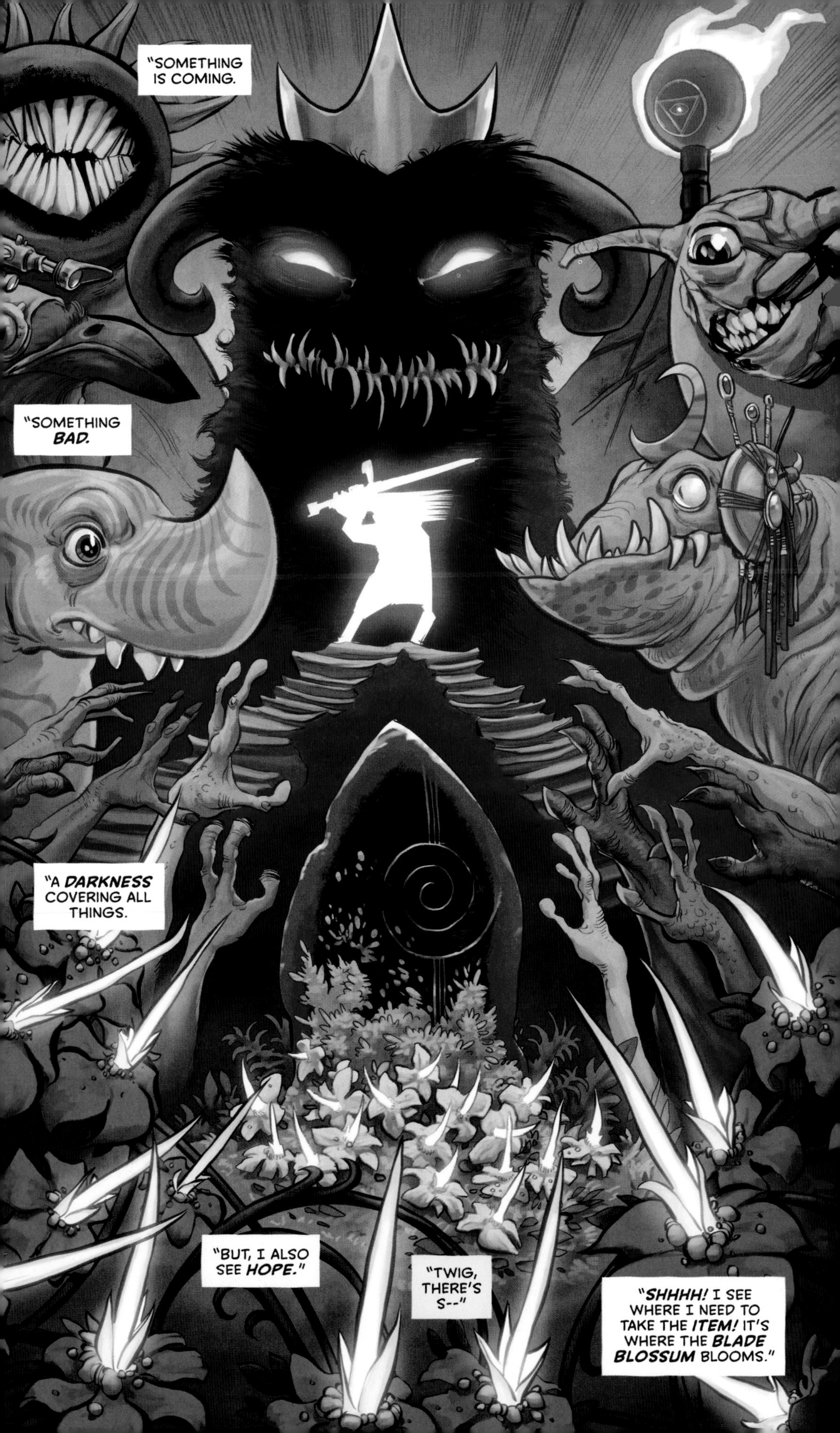
"SOMETHING IS COMING.
"SOMETHING *BAD.*
"A *DARKNESS* COVERING ALL THINGS.
"BUT, I ALSO SEE *HOPE.*"
"TWIG, THERE'S S--"
"*SHHHH!* I SEE WHERE I NEED TO TAKE THE *ITEM!* IT'S WHERE THE *BLADE BLOSSUM* BLOOMS."

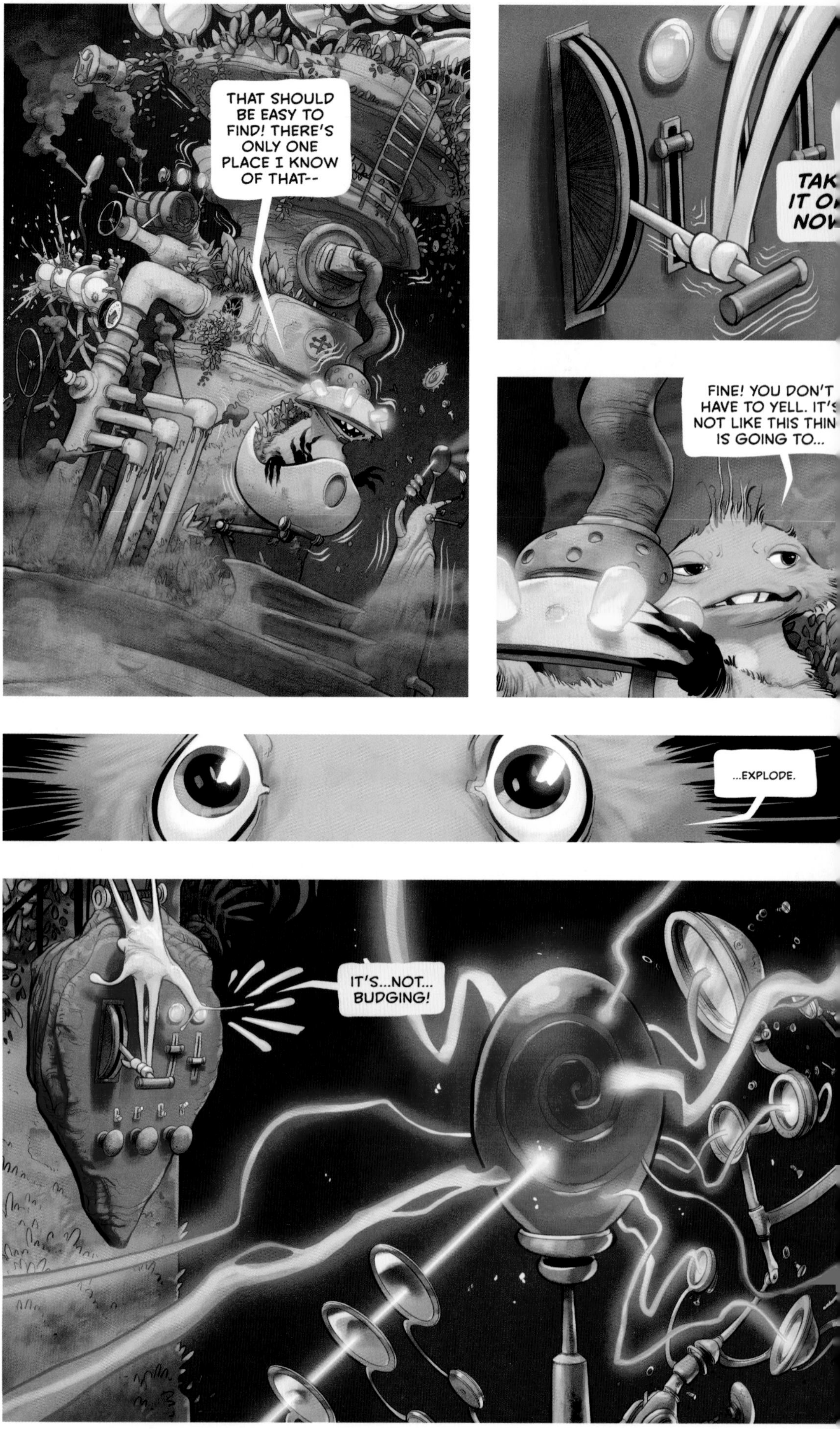
THAT SHOULD BE EASY TO FIND! THERE'S ONLY ONE PLACE I KNOW OF THAT--
FINE! YOU DON'T HAVE TO YELL. IT'S NOT LIKE THIS THIN IS GOING TO...
...EXPLODE.
IT'S...NOT... BUDGING!

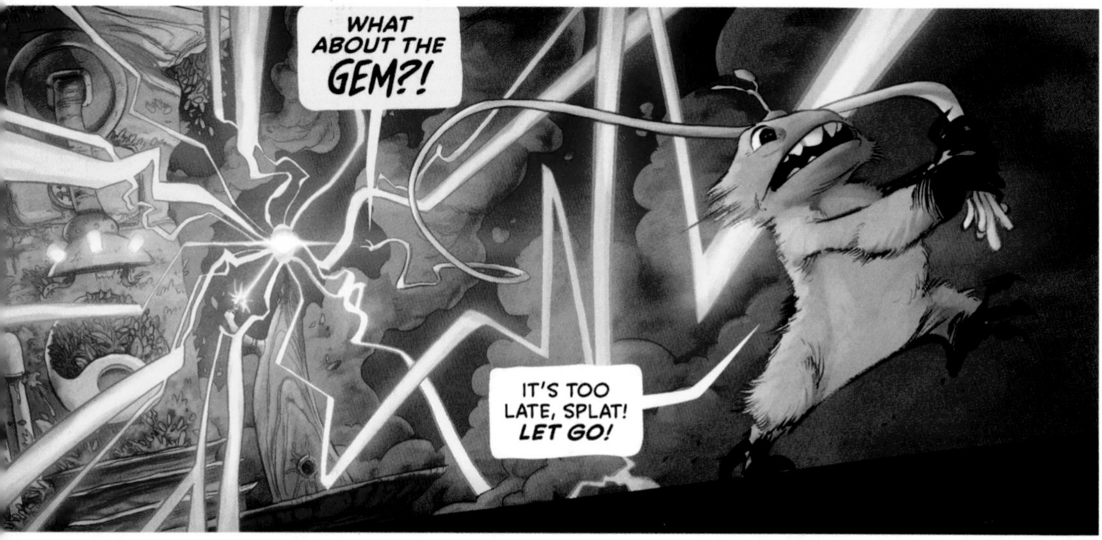
WHAT ABOUT THE GEM?!
IT'S TOO LATE, SPLAT! LET GO!

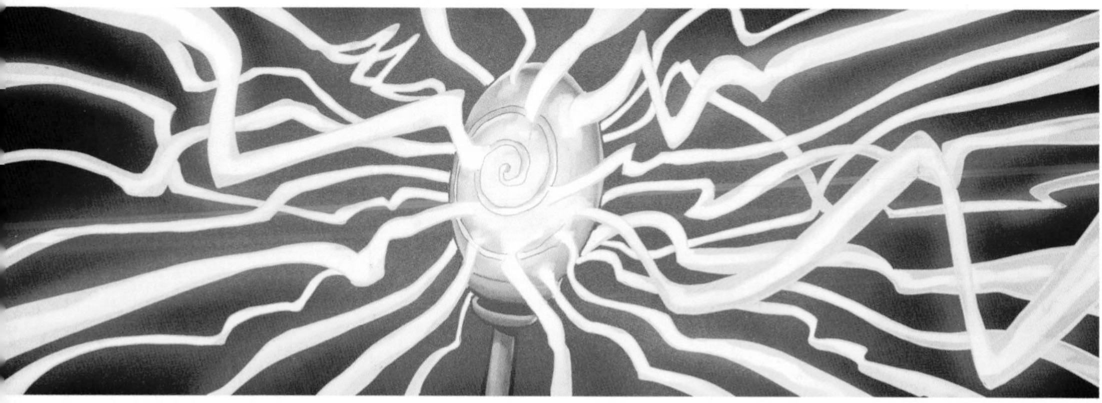

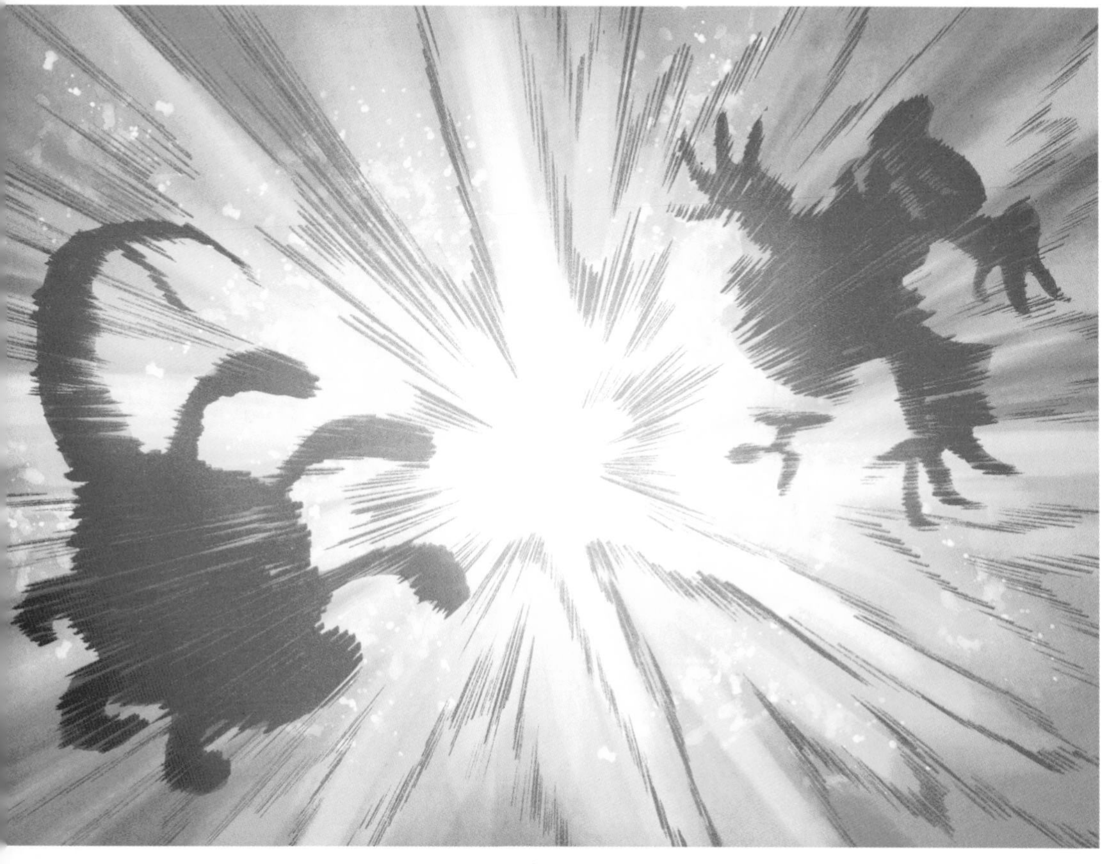

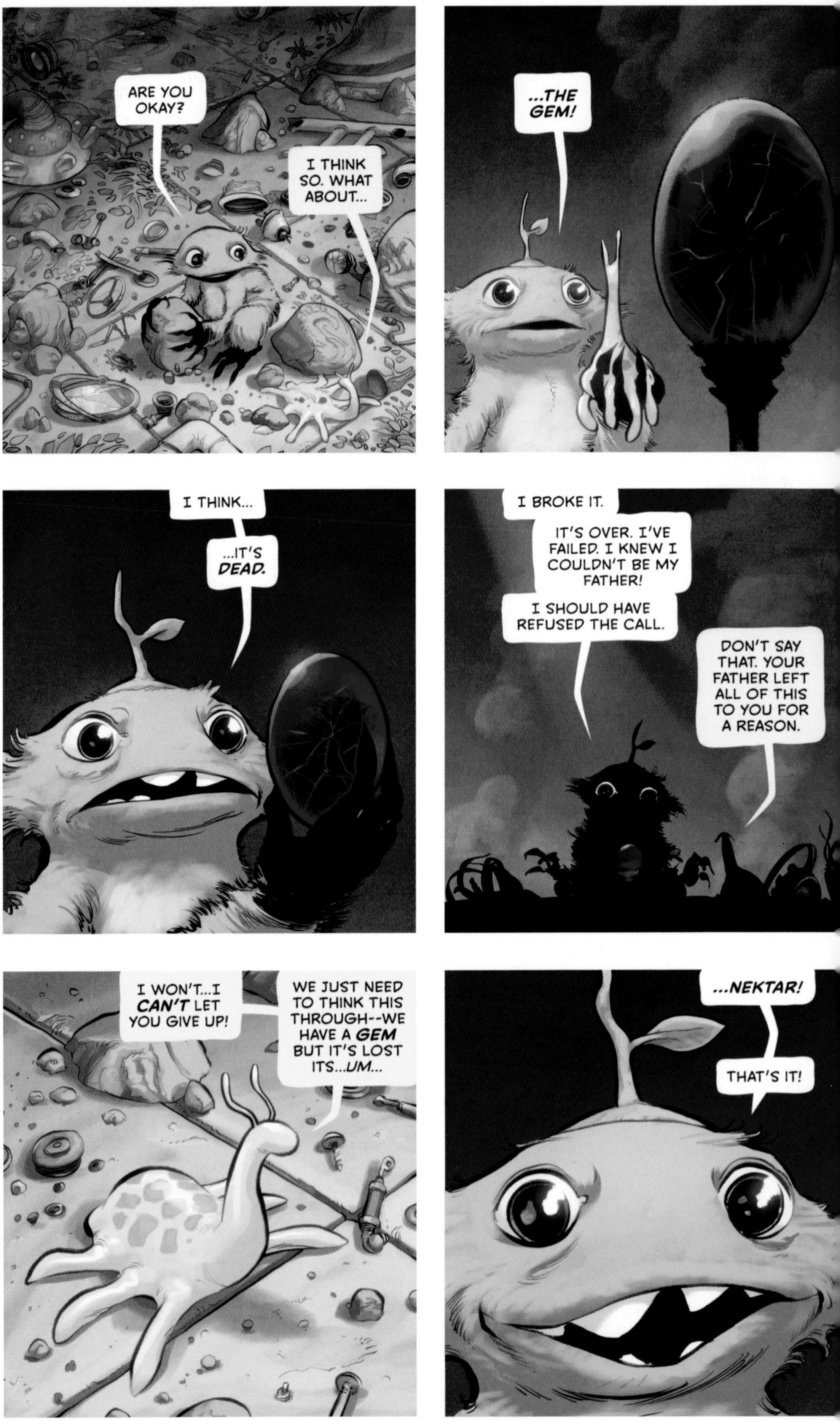
ARE YOU OKAY?
I THINK SO. WHAT ABOUT...
...THE GEM!
I THINK...
...IT'S DEAD.
I BROKE IT.
IT'S OVER. I'VE FAILED. I KNEW I COULDN'T BE MY FATHER!
I SHOULD HAVE REFUSED THE CALL.
DON'T SAY THAT. YOUR FATHER LEFT ALL OF THIS TO YOU FOR A REASON.
I WON'T...I CAN'T LET YOU GIVE UP!
WE JUST NEED TO THINK THIS THROUGH--WE HAVE A GEM BUT IT'S LOST ITS...UM...
...NEKTAR!
THAT'S IT!

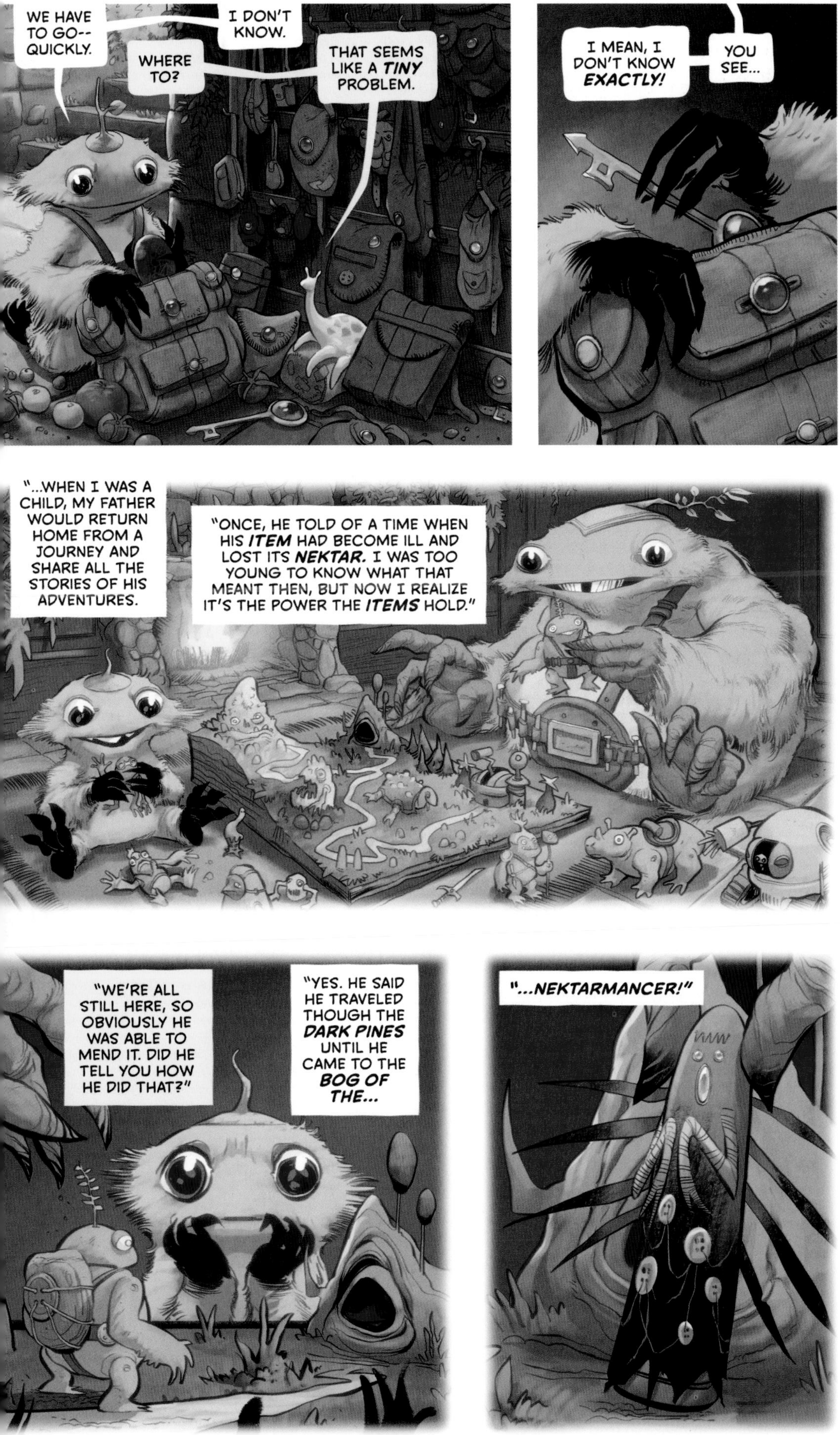
WE HAVE TO GO-- QUICKLY.
WHERE TO?
I DON'T KNOW.
THAT SEEMS LIKE A *TINY* PROBLEM.
I MEAN, I DON'T KNOW *EXACTLY!*
YOU SEE...
"...WHEN I WAS A CHILD, MY FATHER WOULD RETURN HOME FROM A JOURNEY AND SHARE ALL THE STORIES OF HIS ADVENTURES.
"ONCE, HE TOLD OF A TIME WHEN HIS *ITEM* HAD BECOME ILL AND LOST ITS *NEKTAR.* I WAS TOO YOUNG TO KNOW WHAT THAT MEANT THEN, BUT NOW I REALIZE IT'S THE POWER THE *ITEMS* HOLD."
"WE'RE ALL STILL HERE, SO OBVIOUSLY HE WAS ABLE TO MEND IT. DID HE TELL YOU HOW HE DID THAT?"
"YES. HE SAID HE TRAVELED THOUGH THE *DARK PINES* UNTIL HE CAME TO THE *BOG OF THE...*
"...NEKTARMANCER!"

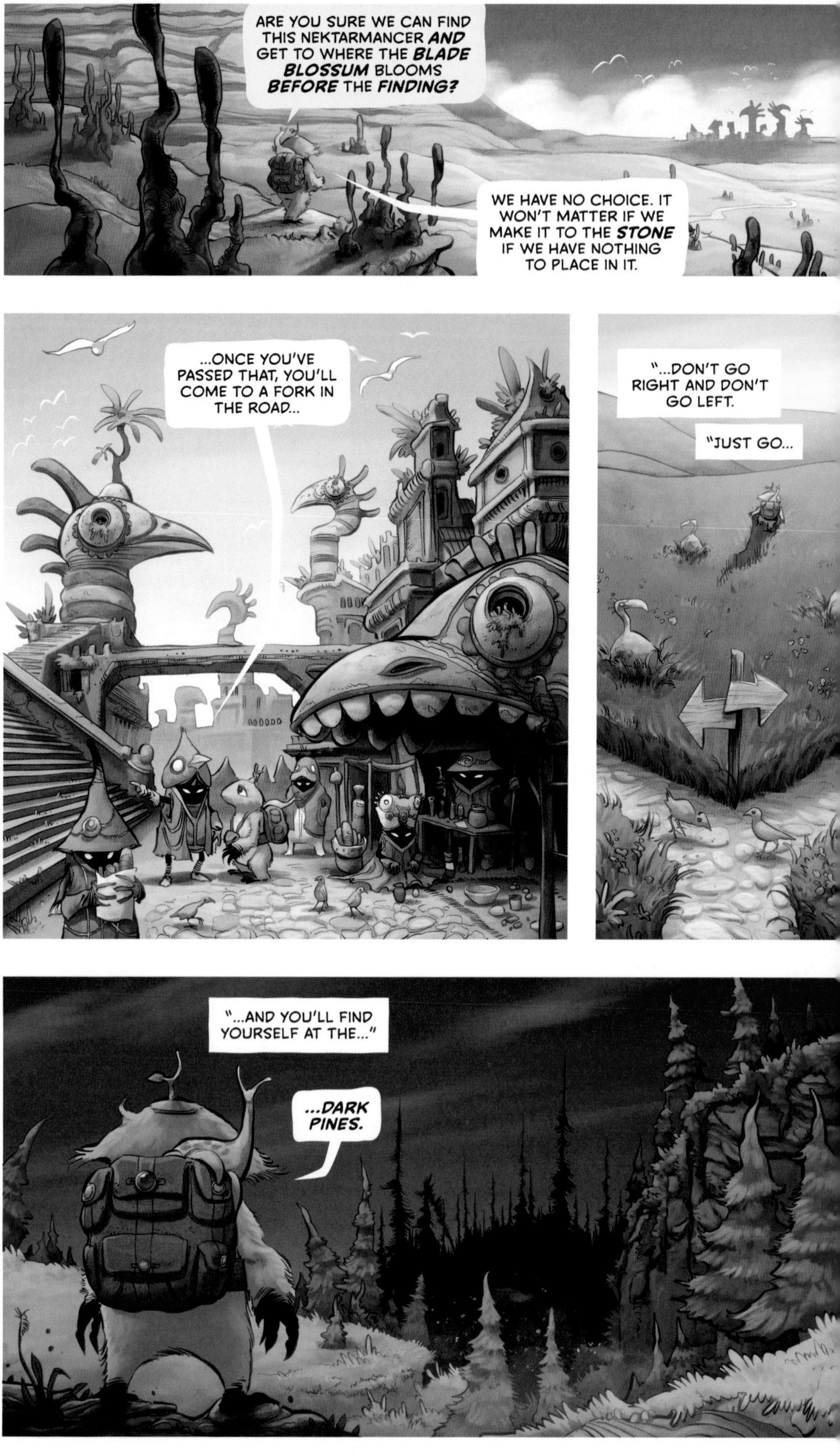
ARE YOU SURE WE CAN FIND THIS NEKTARMANCER AND GET TO WHERE THE BLADE BLOSSUM BLOOMS BEFORE THE FINDING?
WE HAVE NO CHOICE. IT WON'T MATTER IF WE MAKE IT TO THE STONE IF WE HAVE NOTHING TO PLACE IN IT.
...ONCE YOU'VE PASSED THAT, YOU'LL COME TO A FORK IN THE ROAD...
"...DON'T GO RIGHT AND DON'T GO LEFT.
"JUST GO...
"...AND YOU'LL FIND YOURSELF AT THE..."
...DARK PINES.

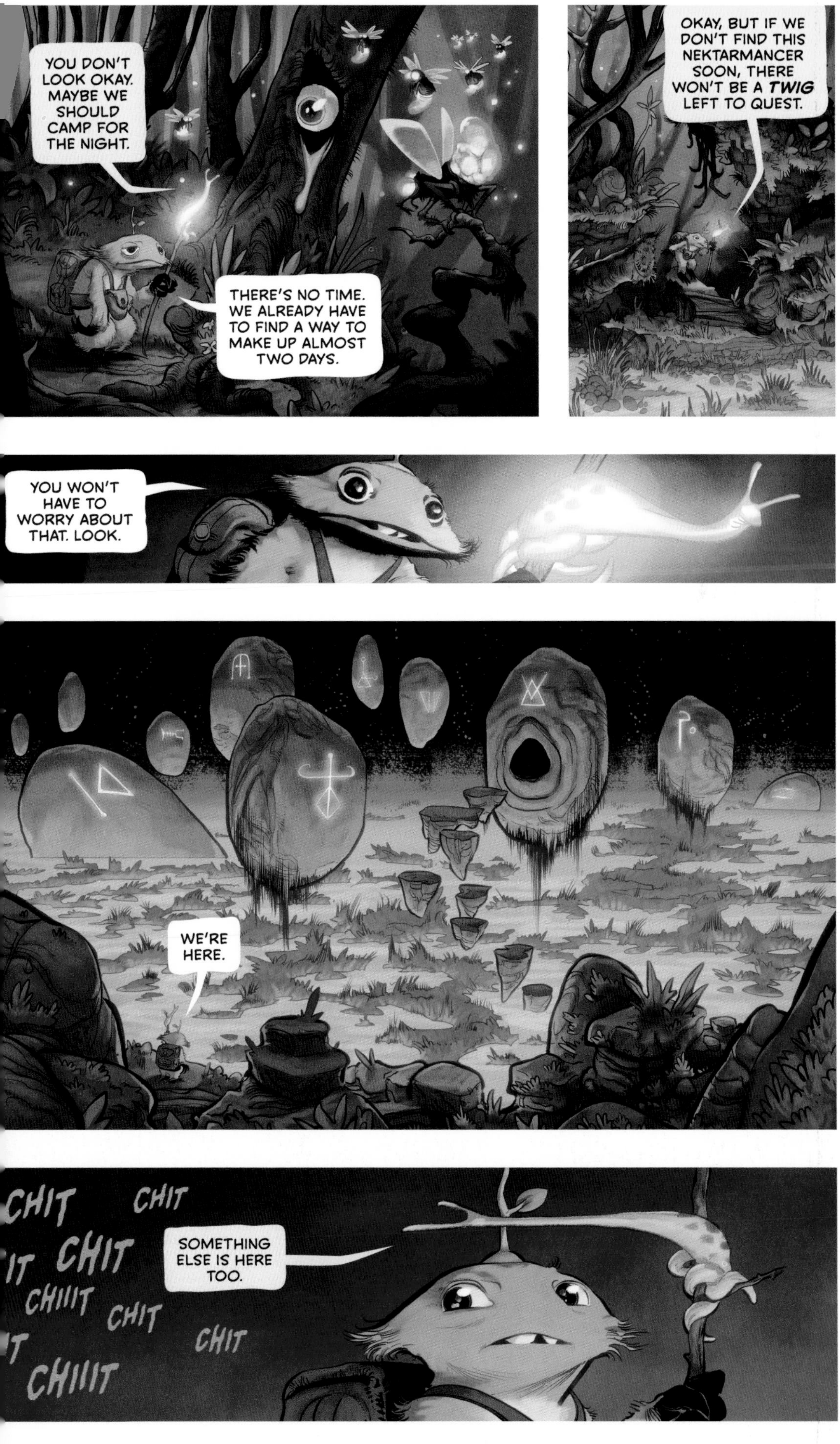
YOU DON'T LOOK OKAY. MAYBE WE SHOULD CAMP FOR THE NIGHT.
THERE'S NO TIME. WE ALREADY HAVE TO FIND A WAY TO MAKE UP ALMOST TWO DAYS.
OKAY, BUT IF WE DON'T FIND THIS NEKTARMANCER SOON, THERE WON'T BE A ***TWIG*** LEFT TO QUEST.
YOU WON'T HAVE TO WORRY ABOUT THAT. LOOK.
WE'RE HERE.
CHIT
CHIT
CHIT
CHIIIT
CHIT
CHIT
CHIIIT
SOMETHING ELSE IS HERE TOO.

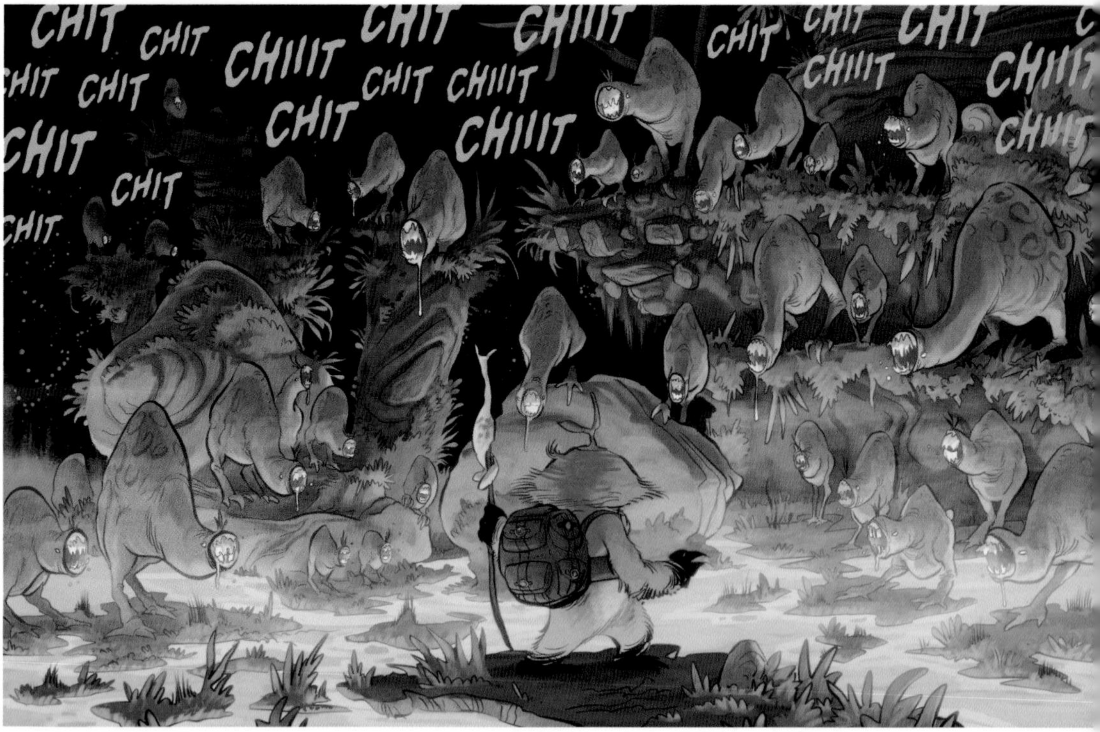
CHIT
CHIT
CHIIIT
CHIT
CHIIIT
CHIT
CHIT
CHIIIT
HIT
CHIT
CHIT
CHIIIT
CHIIIT
CHIT
CHIT
CHIIIT
CHIT
CHIT
HIT

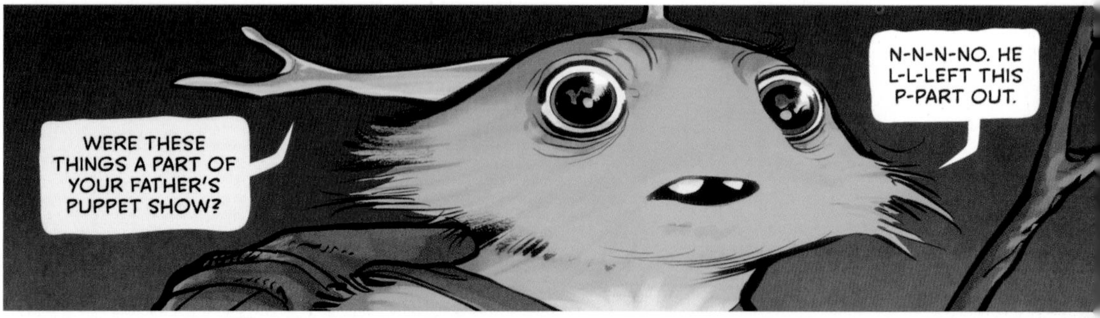
WERE THESE THINGS A PART OF YOUR FATHER'S PUPPET SHOW?
N-N-N-NO. HE L-L-LEFT THIS P-PART OUT.

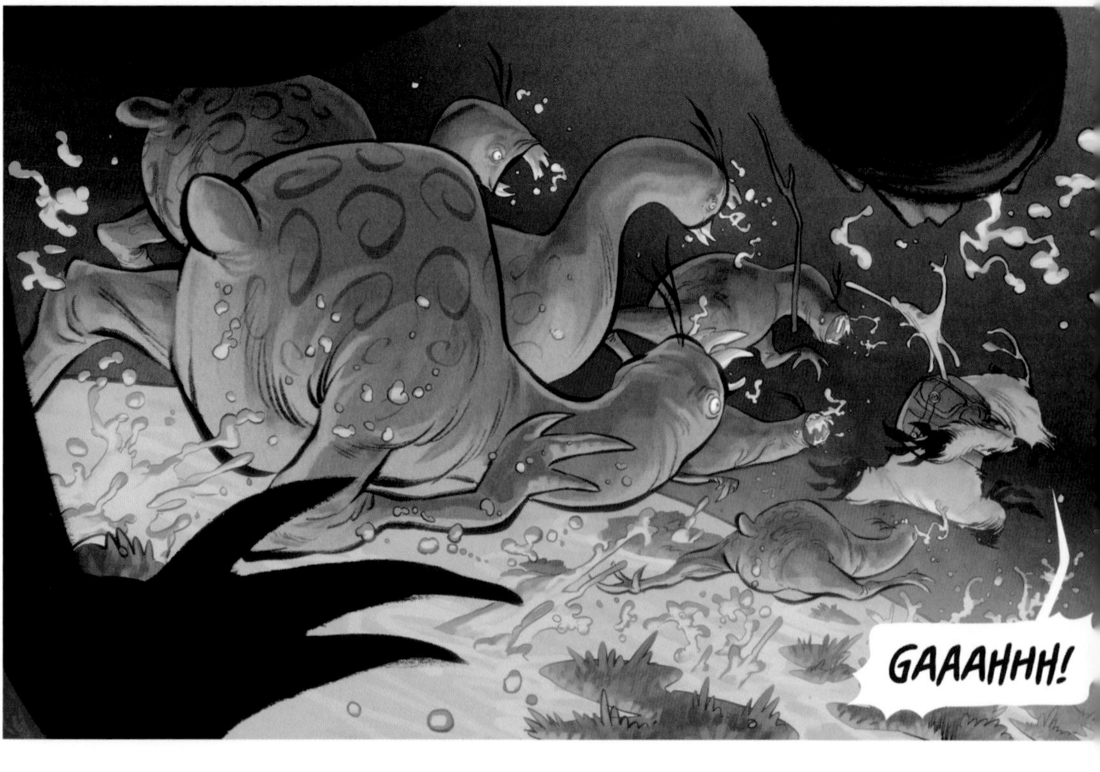
GAAAHHH!

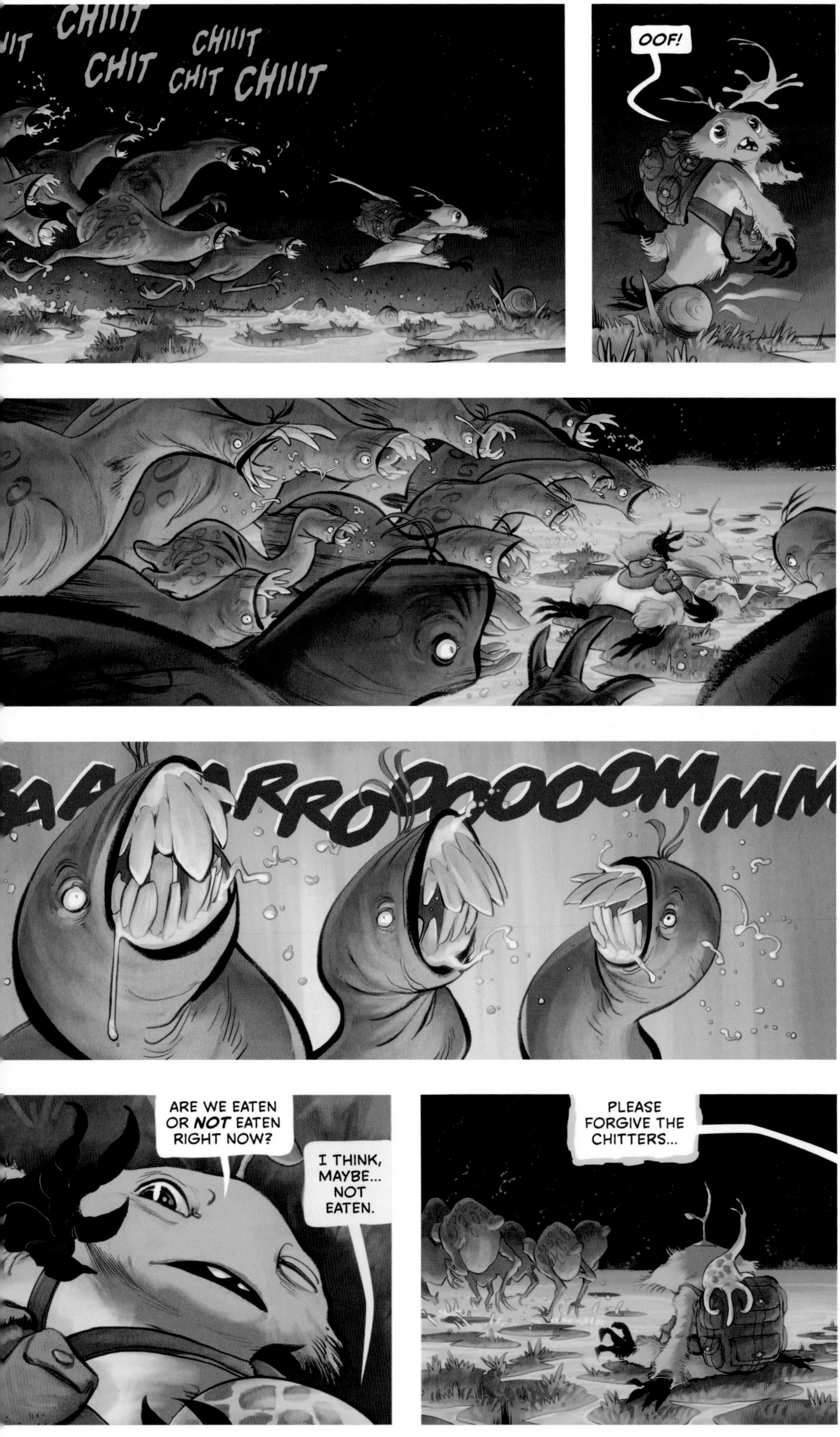

CHIIIT
CHIT
CHIIIT
CHIT CHIIIT
OOF!
OOOMMM
ARE WE EATEN OR NOT EATEN RIGHT NOW?
I THINK, MAYBE... NOT EATEN.
PLEASE FORGIVE THE CHITTERS...

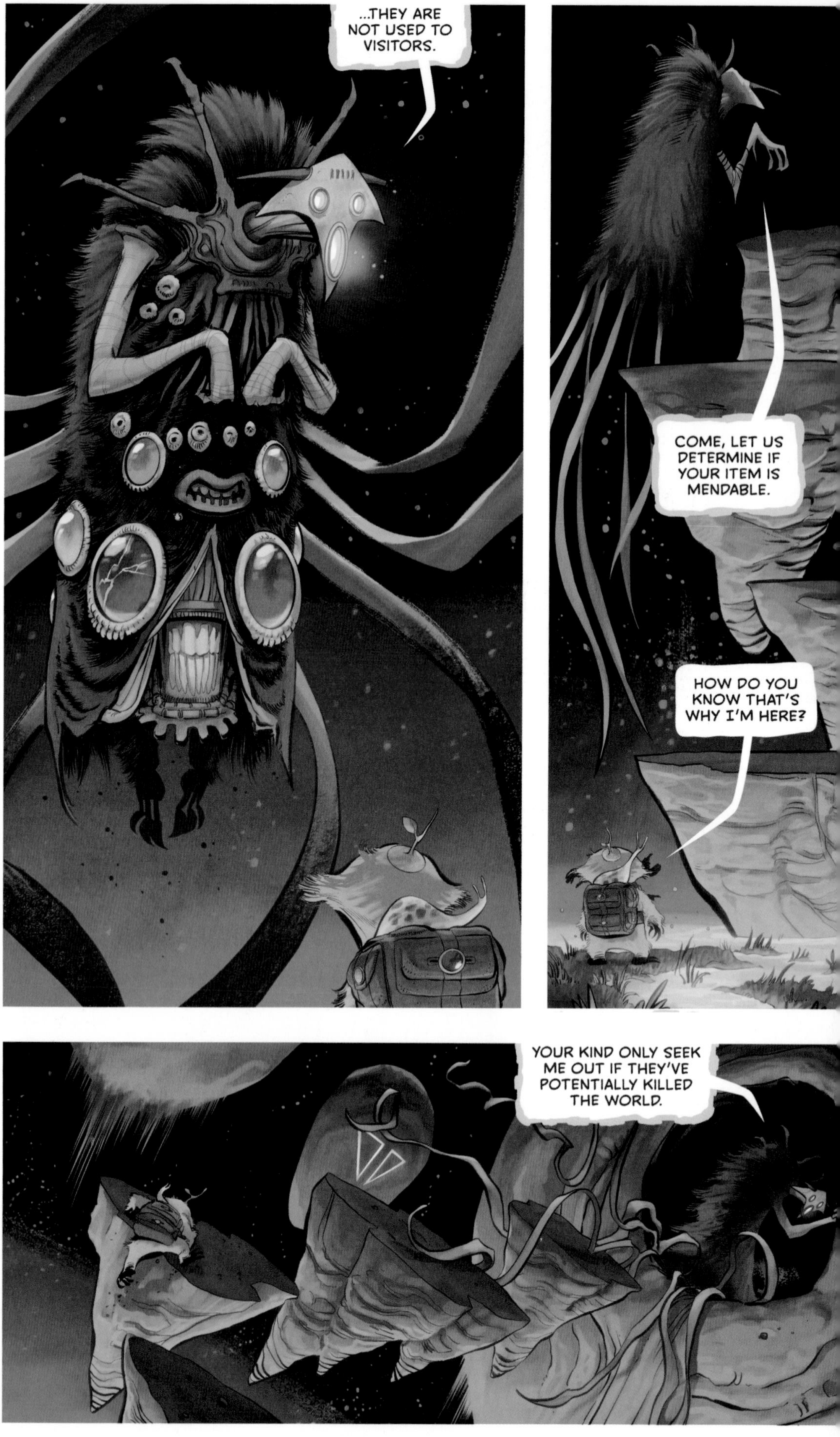
...THEY ARE NOT USED TO VISITORS.
COME, LET US DETERMINE IF YOUR ITEM IS MENDABLE.
HOW DO YOU KNOW THAT'S WHY I'M HERE?
YOUR KIND ONLY SEEK ME OUT IF THEY'VE POTENTIALLY KILLED THE WORLD.

THIS IS WORSE THAN I COULD HAVE IMAGINED.
OH, NO. ARE YOU SAYING IT CAN'T BE FIXED?
WAS SAYING AT, THEN I OULD HAVE ID *THAT.*
NOT A SINGLE DROP REMAINS IN ITS CORE. THIS WILL MAKE IT VERY DIFFICULT TO DETERMINE THE REMEDY.
I NEED MORE TIME WITH IT.
I'M AFRAID I DON'T HAVE *MORE* TIME TO GIVE.
YOU SEE, I WOKE UP LATE WHICH MEANS I STARTED THIS JOURNEY COMPLETELY BEHIND, WHICH MEANS--
THAT YOU OULD HAVE OT BEEN ATE, THEN U WOULD NOT BE HIND, AND THEN...
...YOU WOULD NOT BE TRYING TO HAND THE BURDEN OF *YOUR* FEAR OF TIME OVER TO ME.
GULP!
NOW, AWAY WITH YOU! I HAVE ANSWERS TO FIND AND YOU HAVE TO SLEEP.
THERE IS A SMALL DEN DOWN AND TO THE RIGHT.

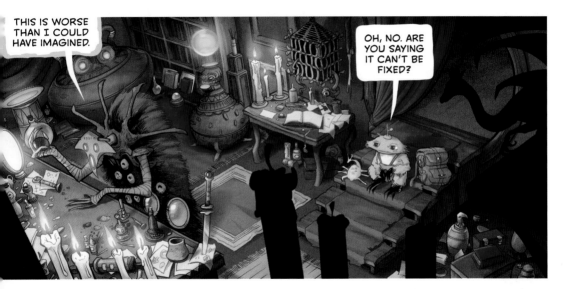

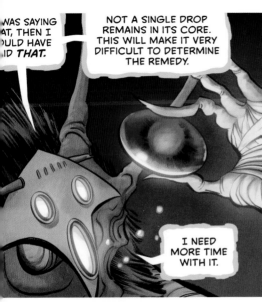

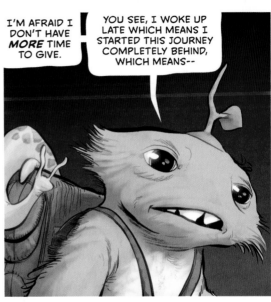

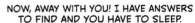

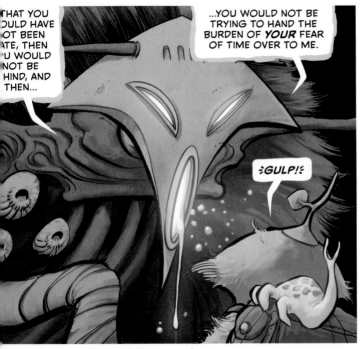

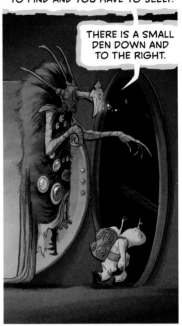

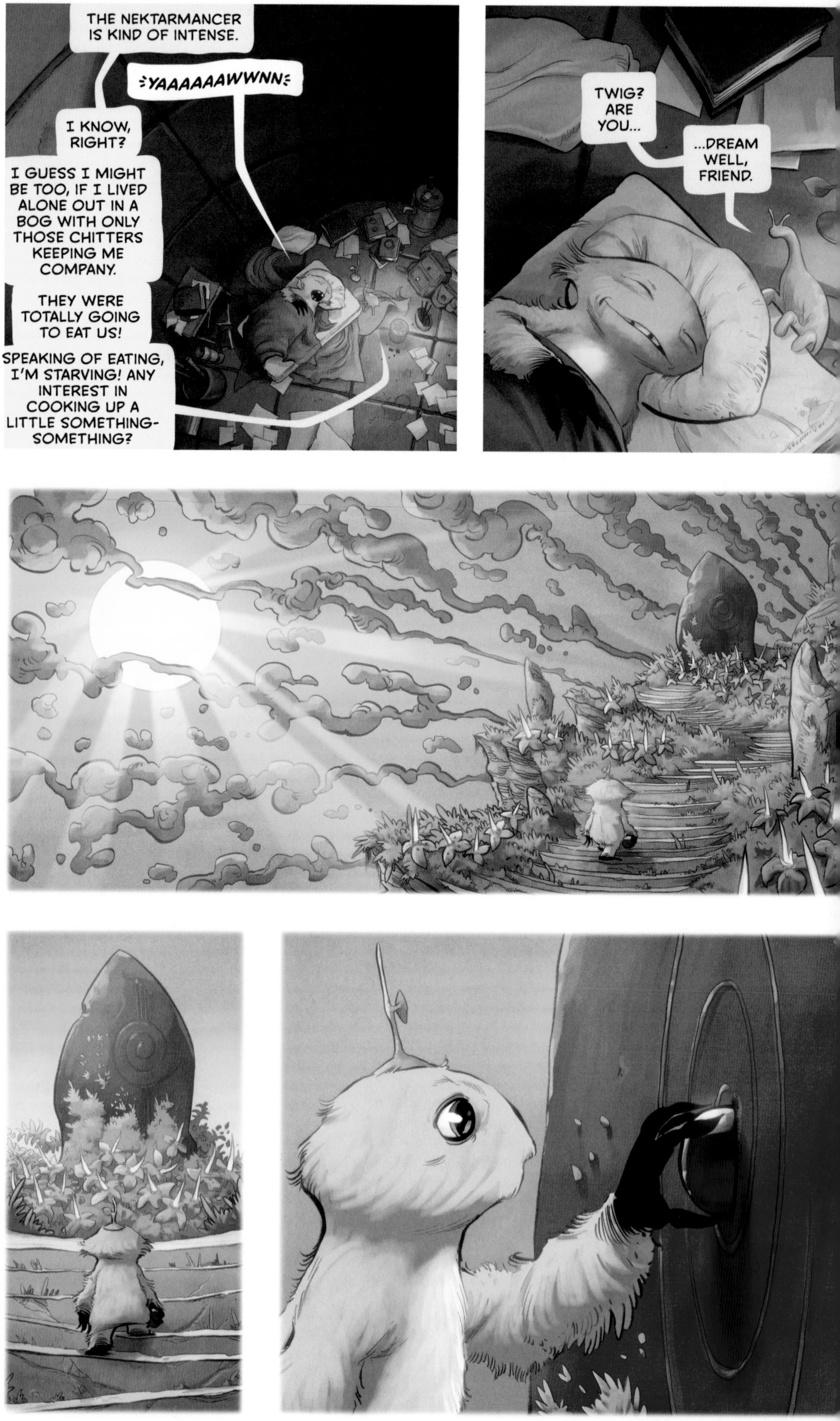
THE NEKTARMANCER IS KIND OF INTENSE.
YAAAAAAWWNN
I KNOW, RIGHT?
I GUESS I MIGHT BE TOO, IF I LIVED ALONE OUT IN A BOG WITH ONLY THOSE CHITTERS KEEPING ME COMPANY.
THEY WERE TOTALLY GOING TO EAT US!
SPEAKING OF EATING, I'M STARVING! ANY INTEREST IN COOKING UP A LITTLE SOMETHING-SOMETHING?
TWIG? ARE YOU...
...DREAM WELL, FRIEND.

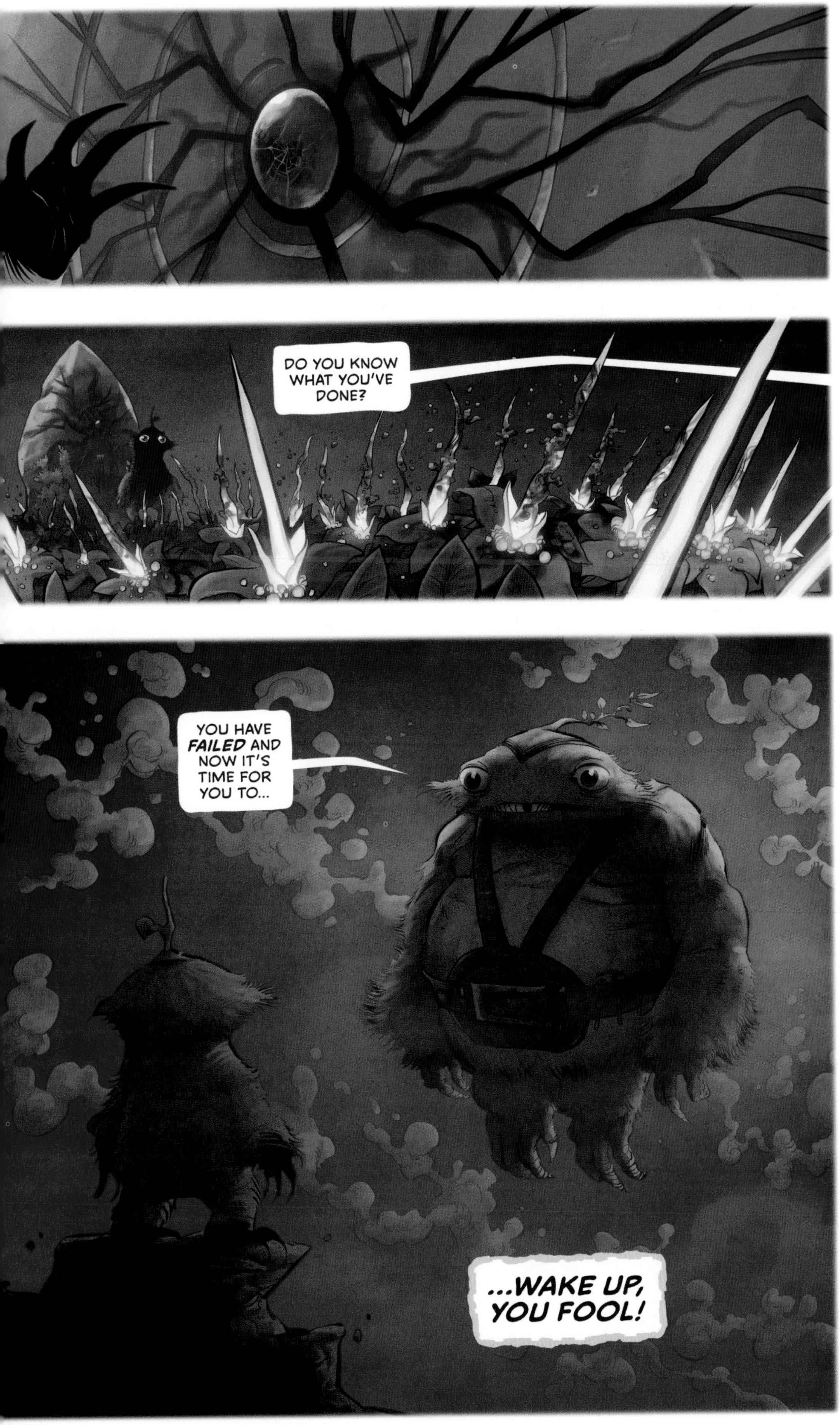
DO YOU KNOW WHAT YOU'VE DONE?
YOU HAVE *FAILED* AND NOW IT'S TIME FOR YOU TO...
...WAKE UP, YOU FOOL!

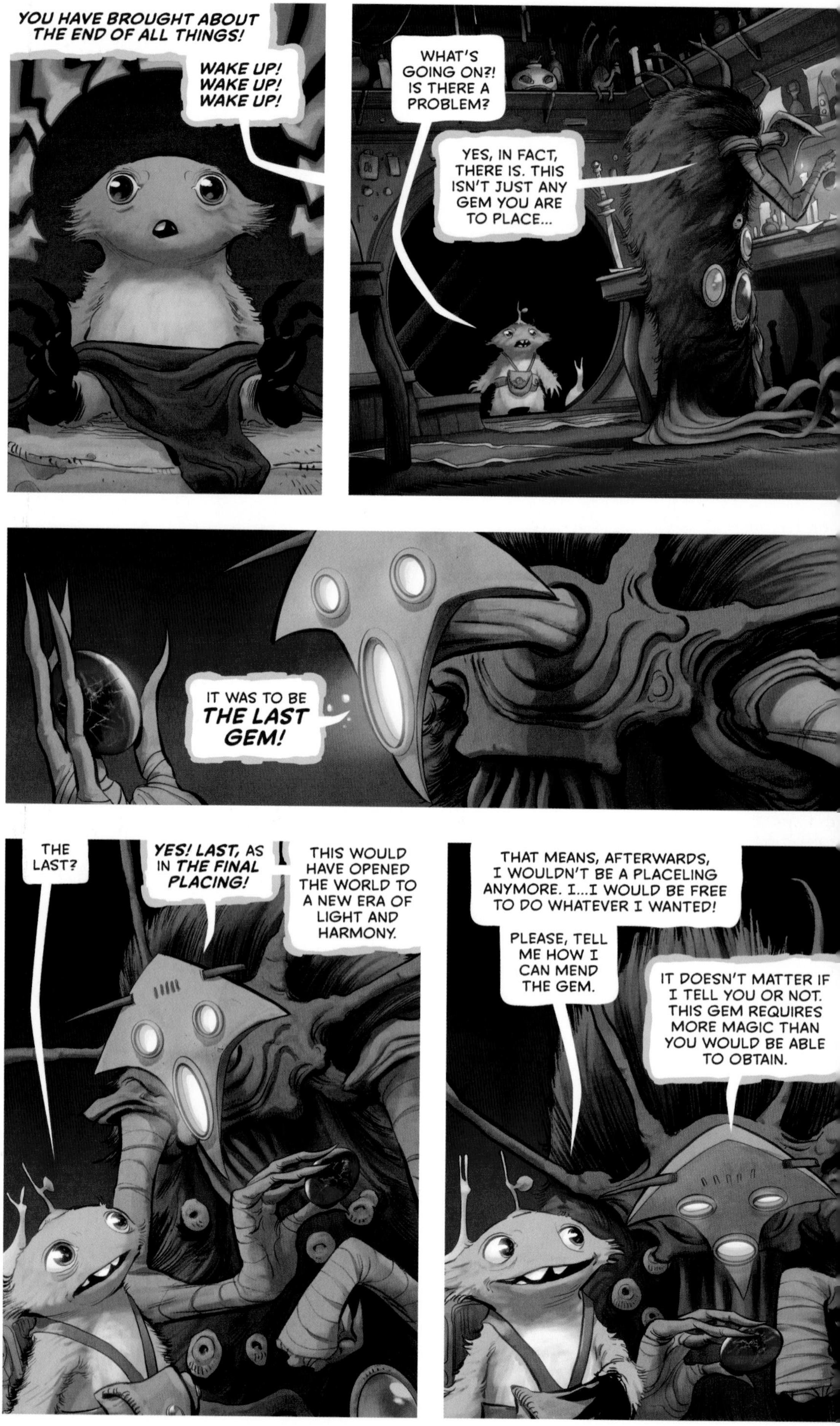
YOU HAVE BROUGHT ABOUT THE END OF ALL THINGS!
WAKE UP! WAKE UP! WAKE UP!
WHAT'S GOING ON?! IS THERE A PROBLEM?
YES, IN FACT, THERE IS. THIS ISN'T JUST ANY GEM YOU ARE TO PLACE...
IT WAS TO BE THE LAST GEM!
THE LAST?
YES! LAST, AS IN THE FINAL PLACING!
THIS WOULD HAVE OPENED THE WORLD TO A NEW ERA OF LIGHT AND HARMONY.
THAT MEANS, AFTERWARDS, I WOULDN'T BE A PLACELING ANYMORE. I...I WOULD BE FREE TO DO WHATEVER I WANTED!
PLEASE, TELL ME HOW I CAN MEND THE GEM.
IT DOESN'T MATTER IF I TELL YOU OR NOT. THIS GEM REQUIRES MORE MAGIC THAN YOU WOULD BE ABLE TO OBTAIN.

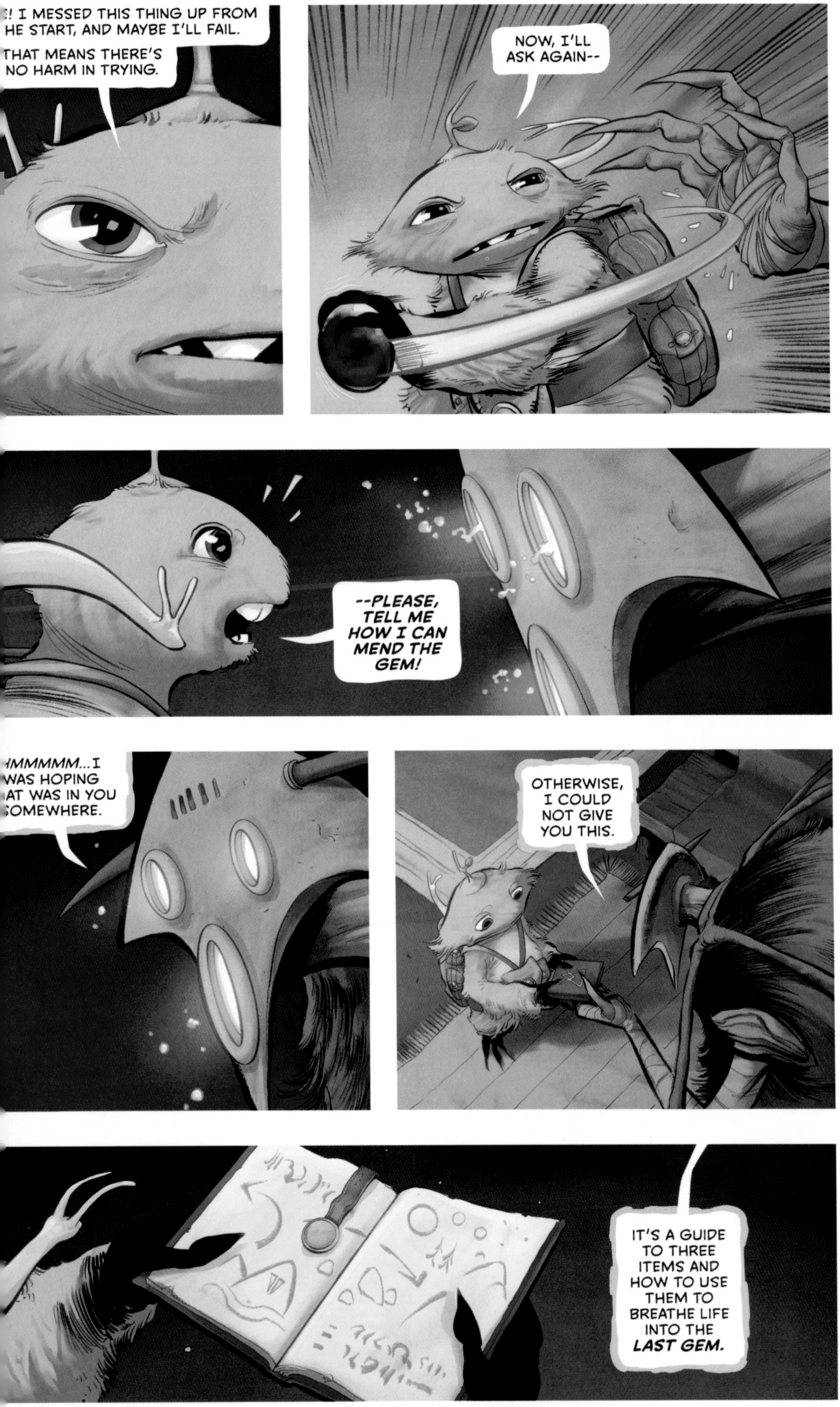

I MESSED THIS THING UP FROM HE START, AND MAYBE I'LL FAIL.
THAT MEANS THERE'S NO HARM IN TRYING.
NOW, I'LL ASK AGAIN--
--PLEASE, TELL ME HOW I CAN MEND THE GEM!
MMMMM...I WAS HOPING AT WAS IN YOU OMEWHERE.
OTHERWISE, I COULD NOT GIVE YOU THIS.
IT'S A GUIDE TO THREE ITEMS AND HOW TO USE THEM TO BREATHE LIFE INTO THE LAST GEM.

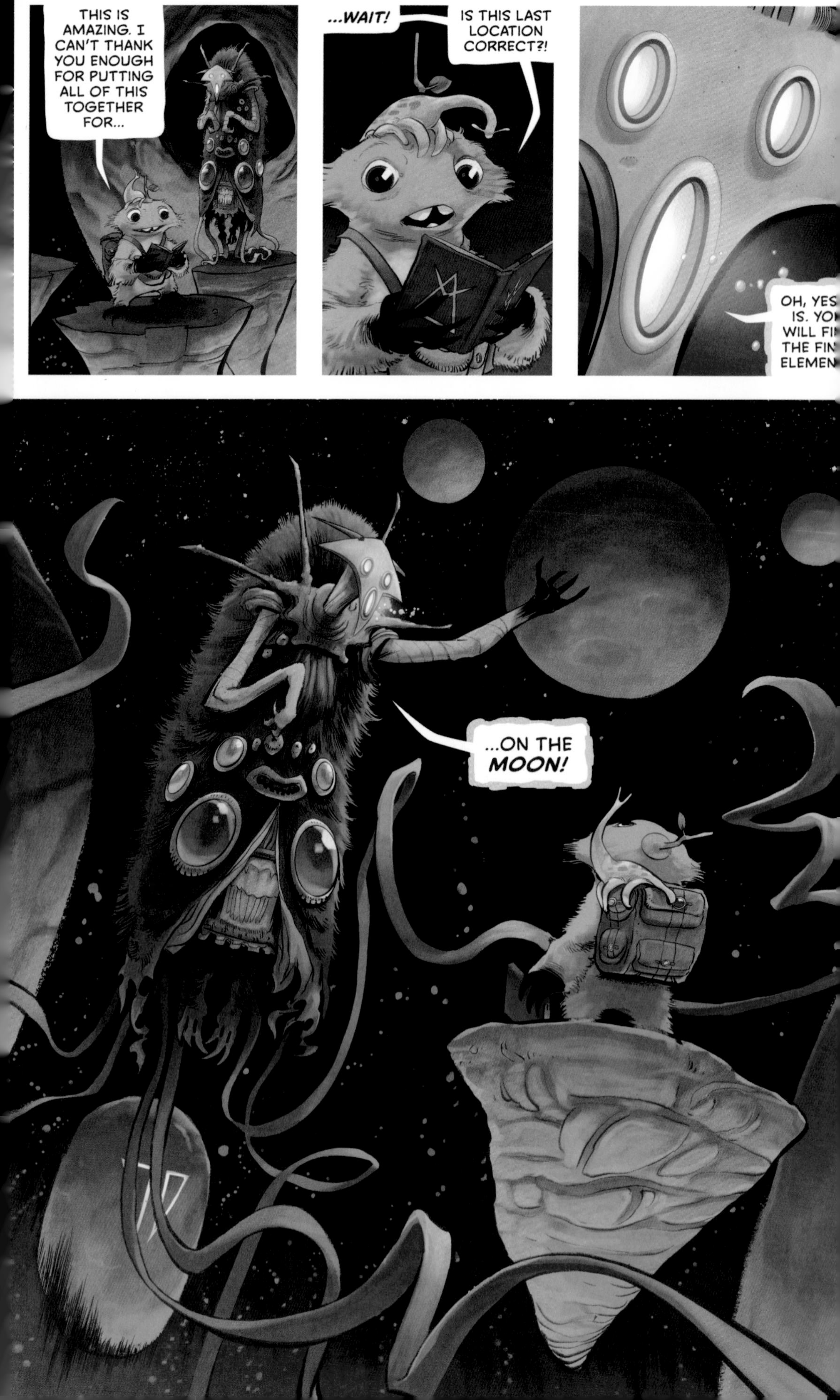
THIS IS AMAZING. I CAN'T THANK YOU ENOUGH FOR PUTTING ALL OF THIS TOGETHER FOR...
...WAIT!
IS THIS LAST LOCATION CORRECT?!
OH, YES IS. YO WILL FI THE FIN ELEMEN
...ON THE MOON!

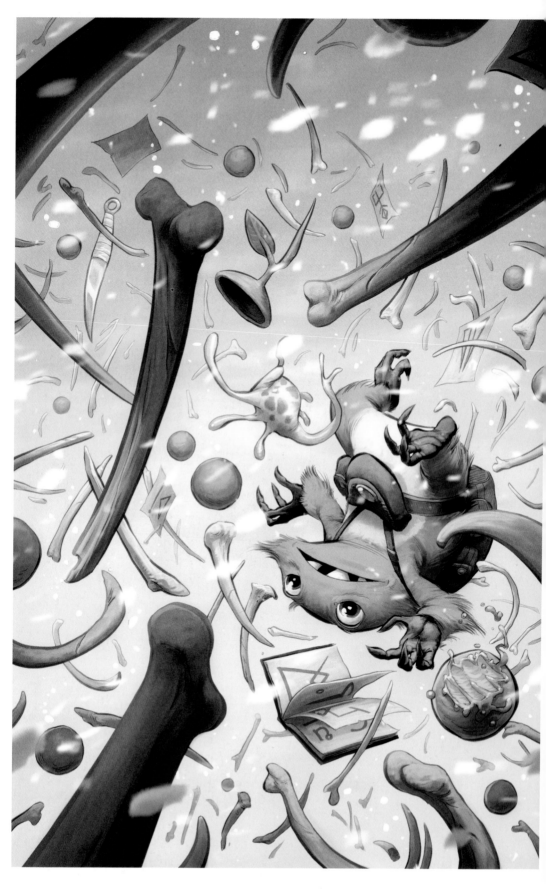

THREE

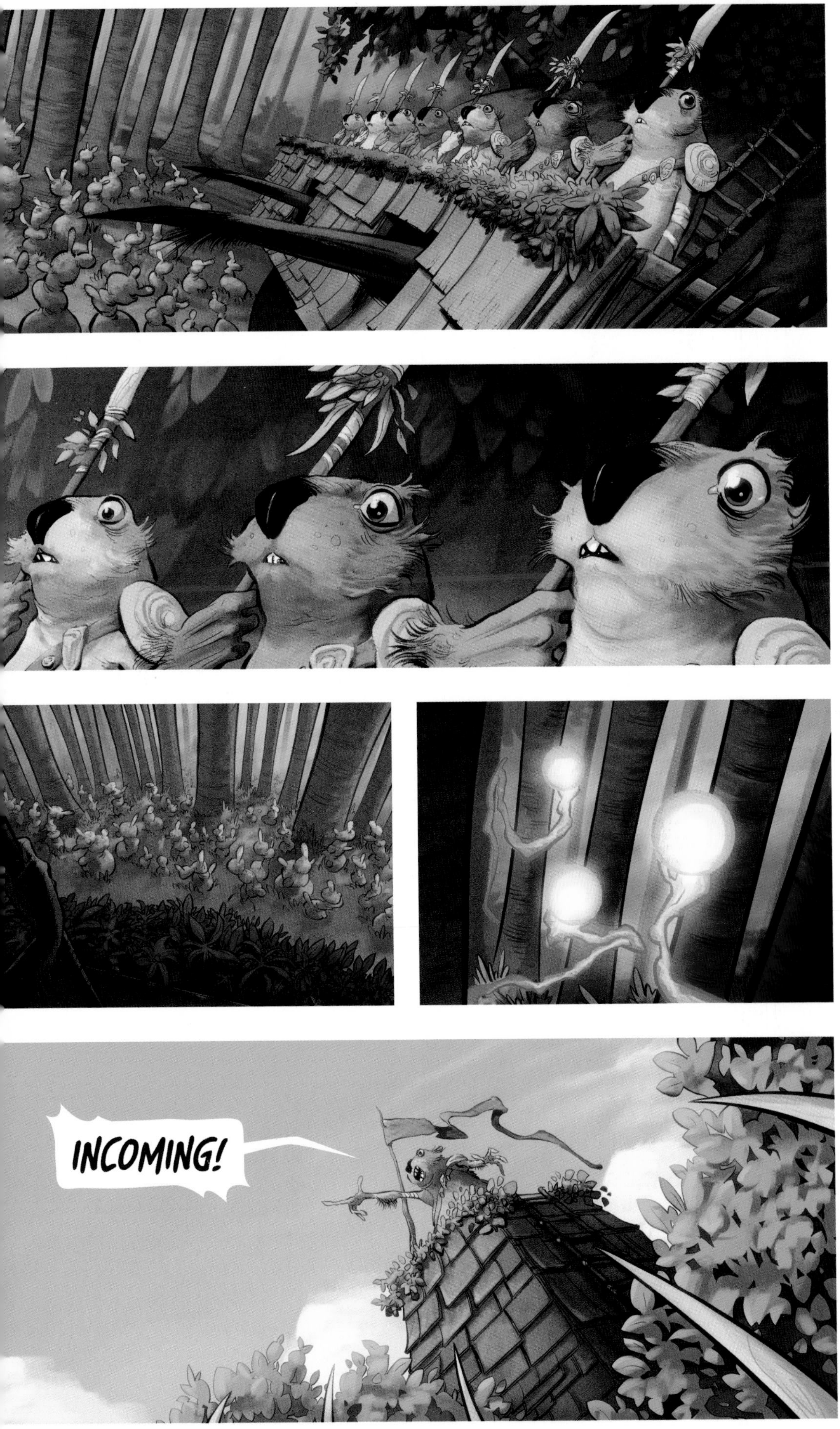
INCOMING!

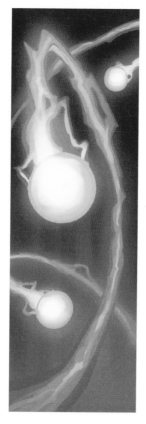

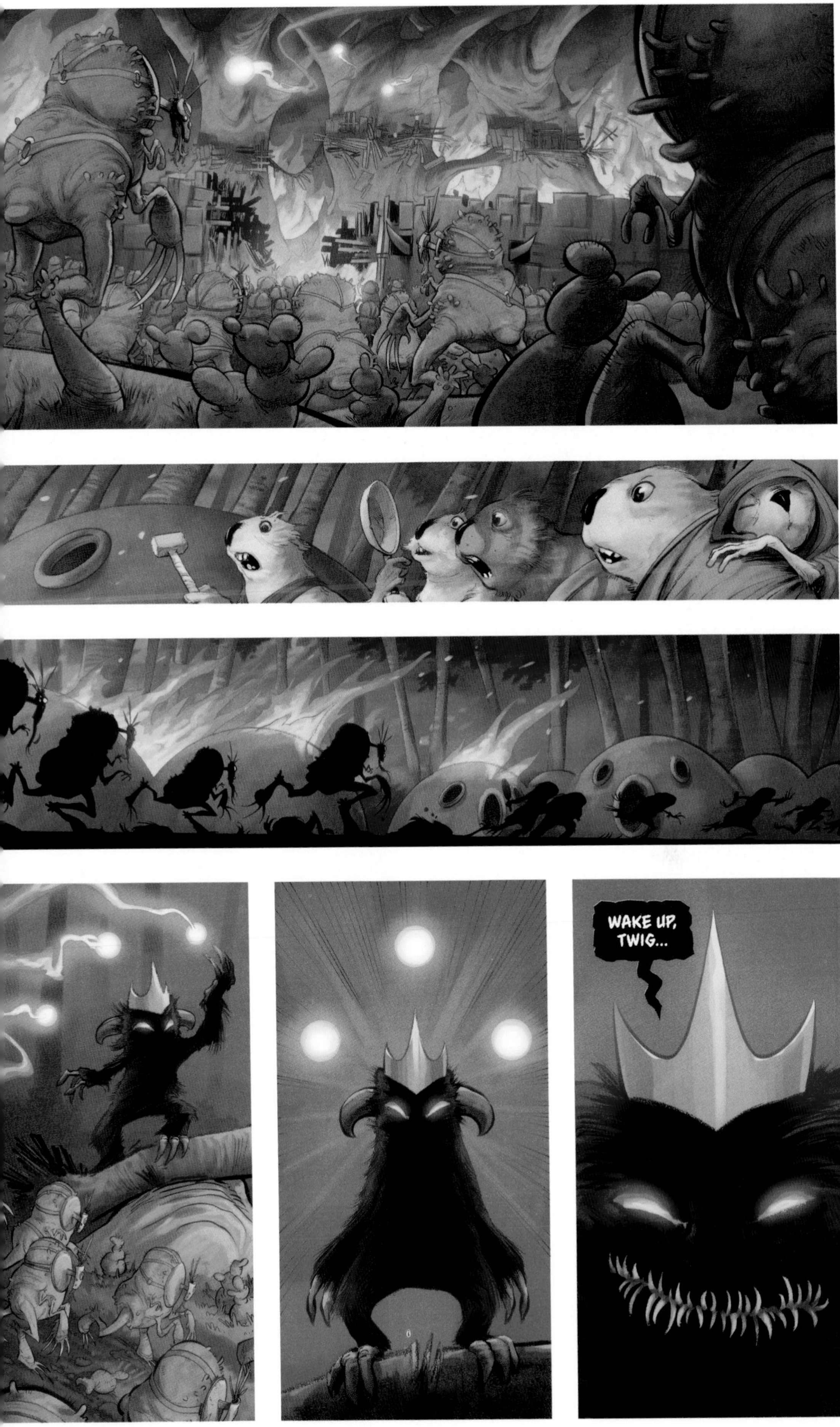
WAKE UP, TWIG...

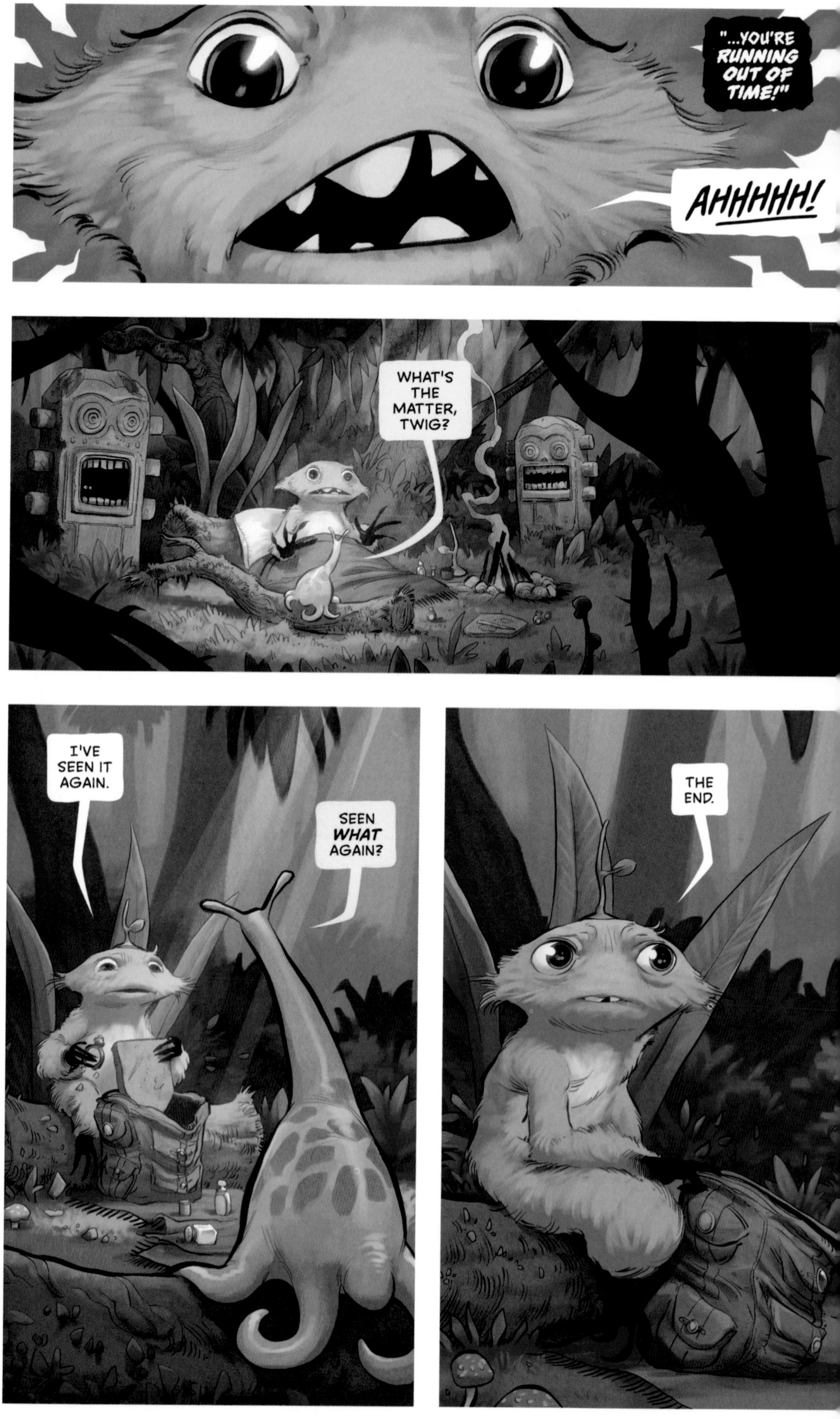
"...YOU'RE RUNNING OUT OF TIME!"
AHHHHH!
WHAT'S THE MATTER, TWIG?
I'VE SEEN IT AGAIN.
SEEN ***WHAT*** AGAIN?
THE END.

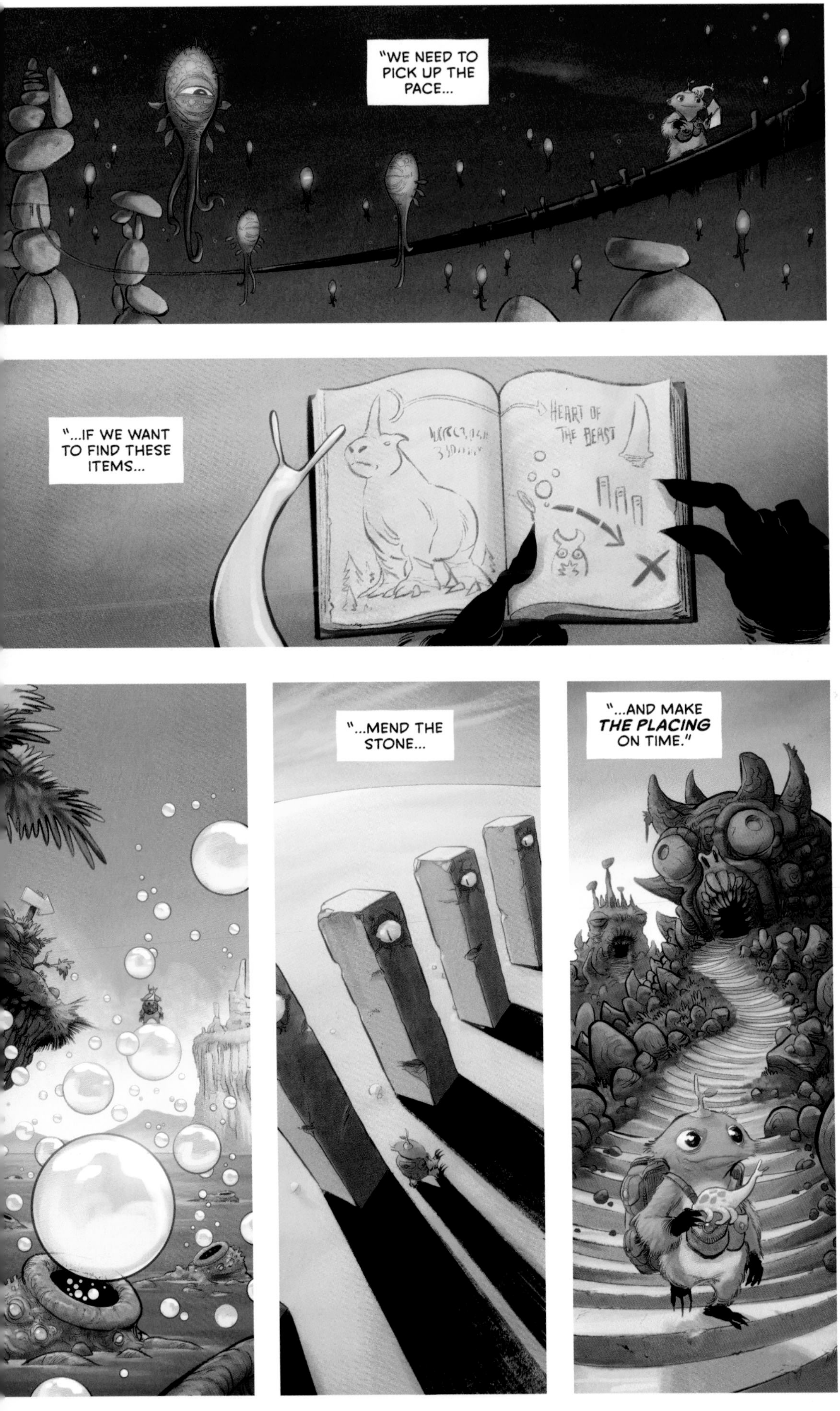
"WE NEED TO PICK UP THE PACE...
"...IF WE WANT TO FIND THESE ITEMS...
HEART OF THE BEAST
"...MEND THE STONE...
"...AND MAKE *THE PLACING* ON TIME."

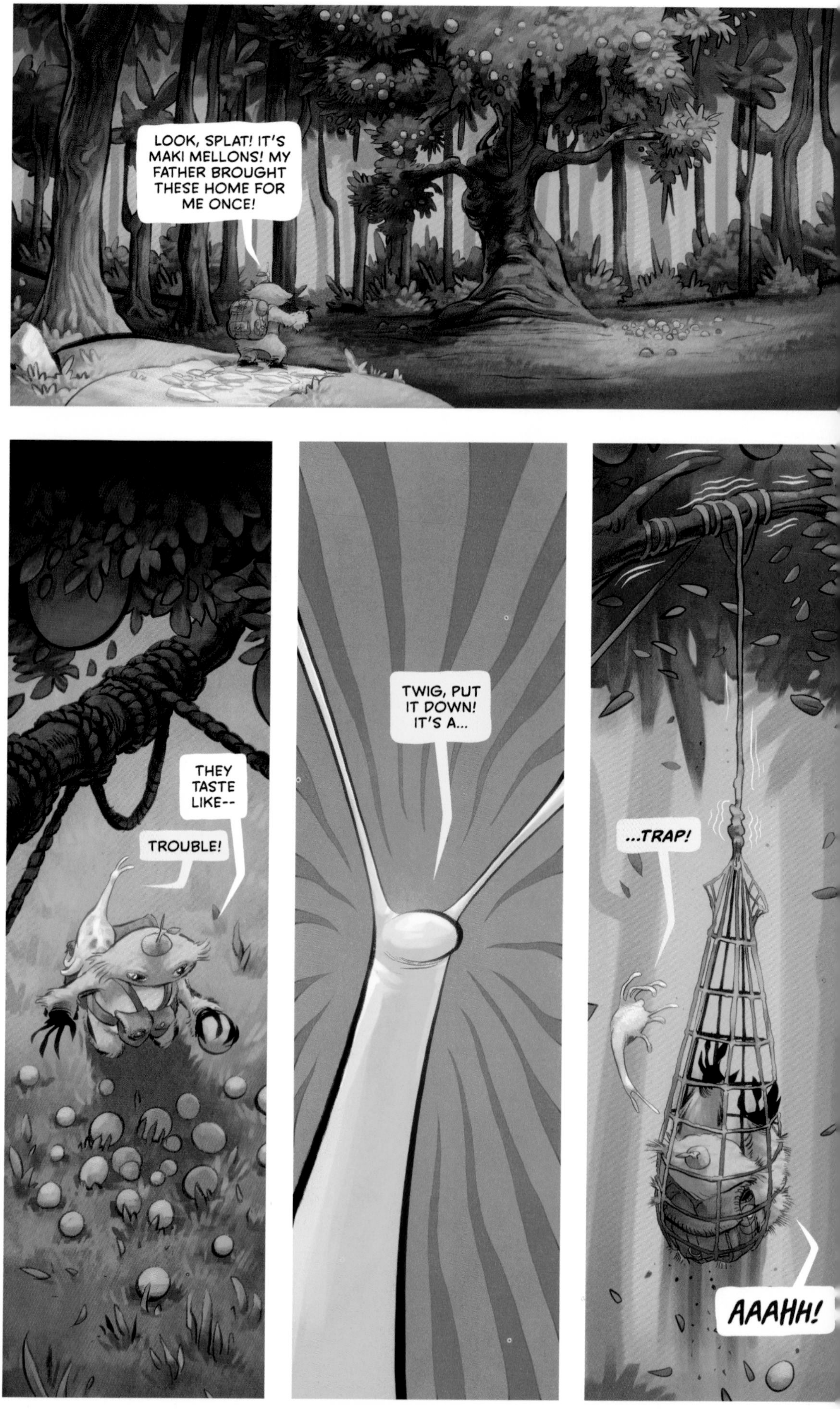
LOOK, SPLAT! IT'S MAKI MELLONS! MY FATHER BROUGHT THESE HOME FOR ME ONCE!
THEY TASTE LIKE--
TROUBLE!
TWIG, PUT IT DOWN! IT'S A...
...TRAP!
AAAHH!

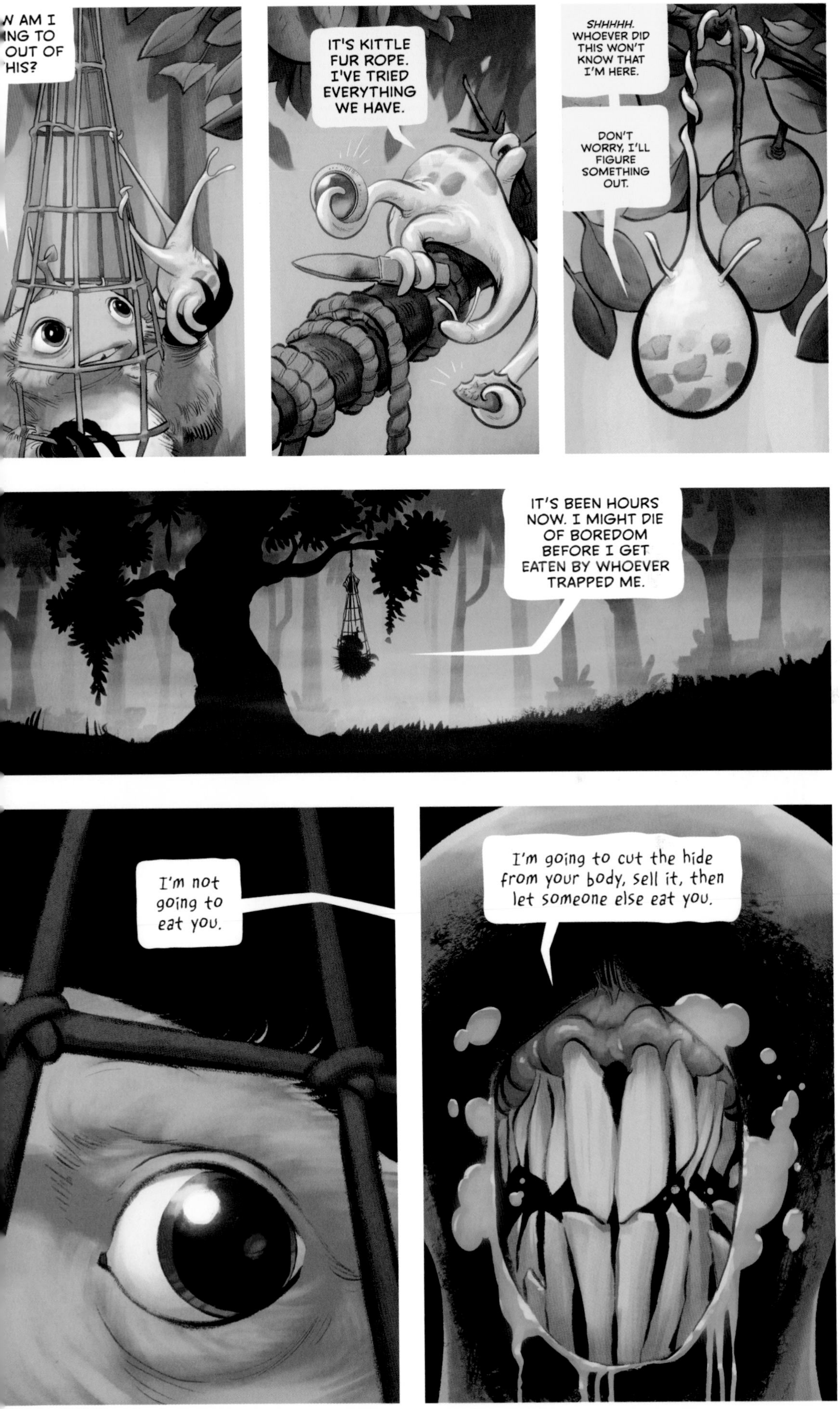

N AM I
NG TO
OUT OF
HIS?
IT'S KITTLE FUR ROPE. I'VE TRIED EVERYTHING WE HAVE.
SHHHHH. WHOEVER DID THIS WON'T KNOW THAT I'M HERE.
DON'T WORRY, I'LL FIGURE SOMETHING OUT.
IT'S BEEN HOURS NOW. I MIGHT DIE OF BOREDOM BEFORE I GET EATEN BY WHOEVER TRAPPED ME.
I'm not going to eat you.
I'm going to cut the hide from your body, sell it, then let someone else eat you.

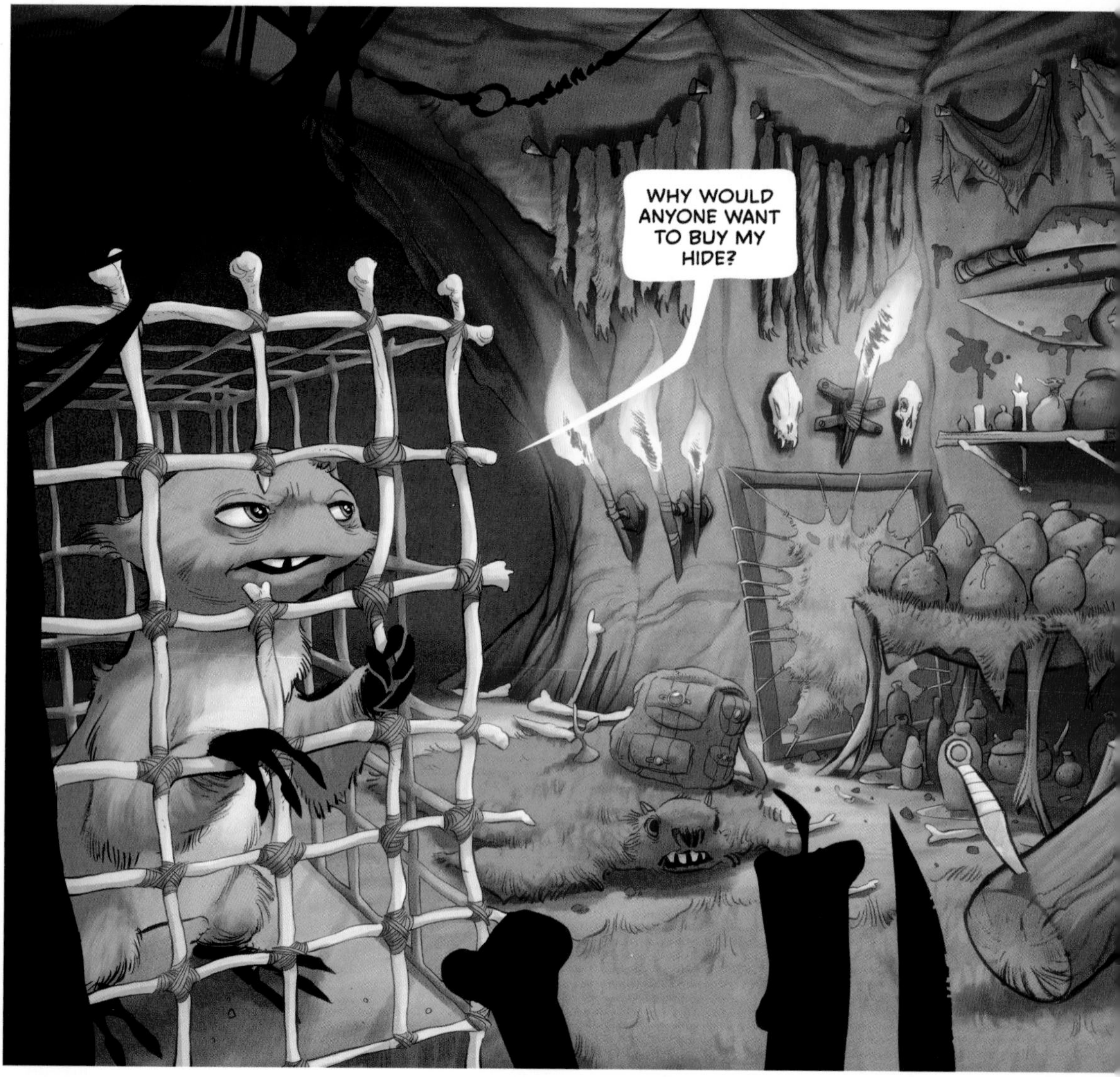
WHY WOULD ANYONE WANT TO BUY MY HIDE?

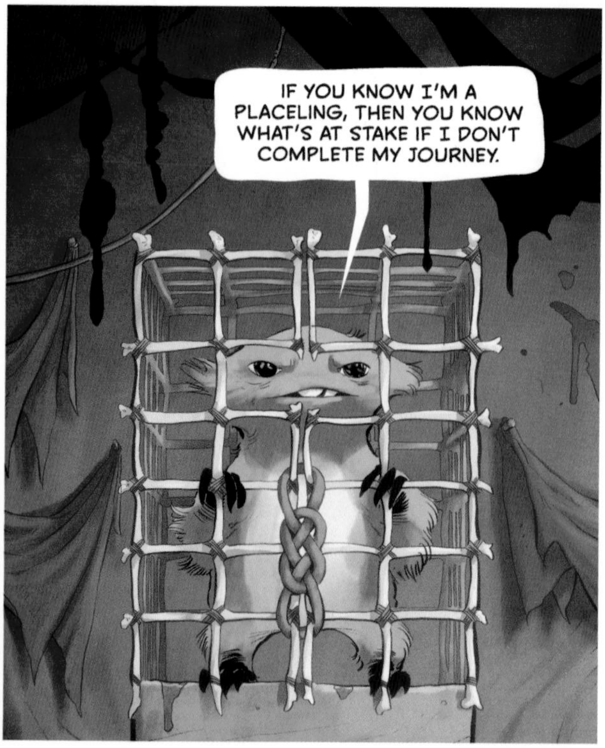
IF YOU KNOW I'M A PLACELING, THEN YOU KNOW WHAT'S AT STAKE IF I DON'T COMPLETE MY JOURNEY.

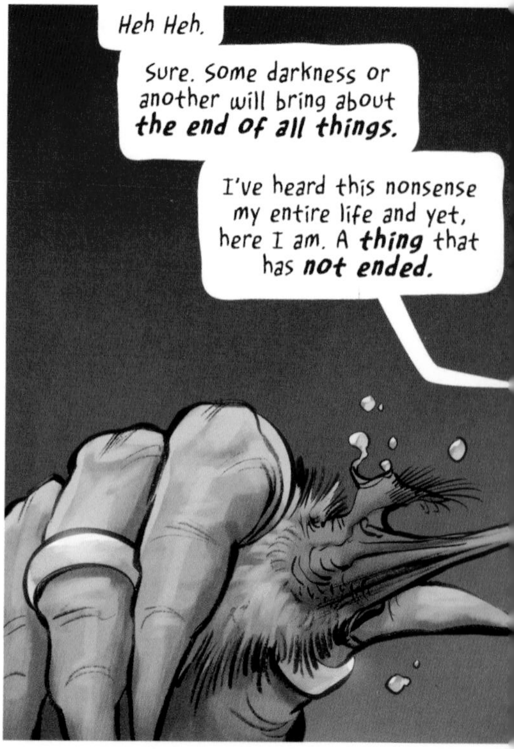
Heh Heh.
Sure. Some darkness or another will bring about **the end of all things.**
I've heard this nonsense my entire life and yet, here I am. A ***thing*** that has ***not ended.***

You're a **Placeling,** which means you're rare and will fetch a mighty high price.

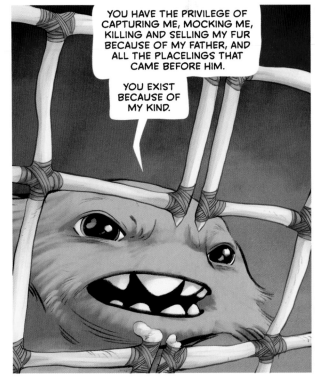

YOU HAVE THE PRIVILEGE OF CAPTURING ME, MOCKING ME, KILLING AND SELLING MY FUR BECAUSE OF MY FATHER, AND ALL THE PLACELINGS THAT CAME BEFORE HIM.

YOU EXIST BECAUSE OF MY KIND.

That may very well be true. You failed your journey by getting yourself caught, so you may prove me wrong, little one. You just won't be around to see it.

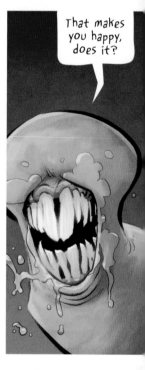

That makes you happy, does it?

YES...UH, I MEAN, NO!

I WAS JUST SMILING AT YOUR, UH, FOOD. I'M JUST SO HUNGRY...

...THERE'S NOTHING QUITE LIKE A WELL DONE QUIPPLE OVER A...

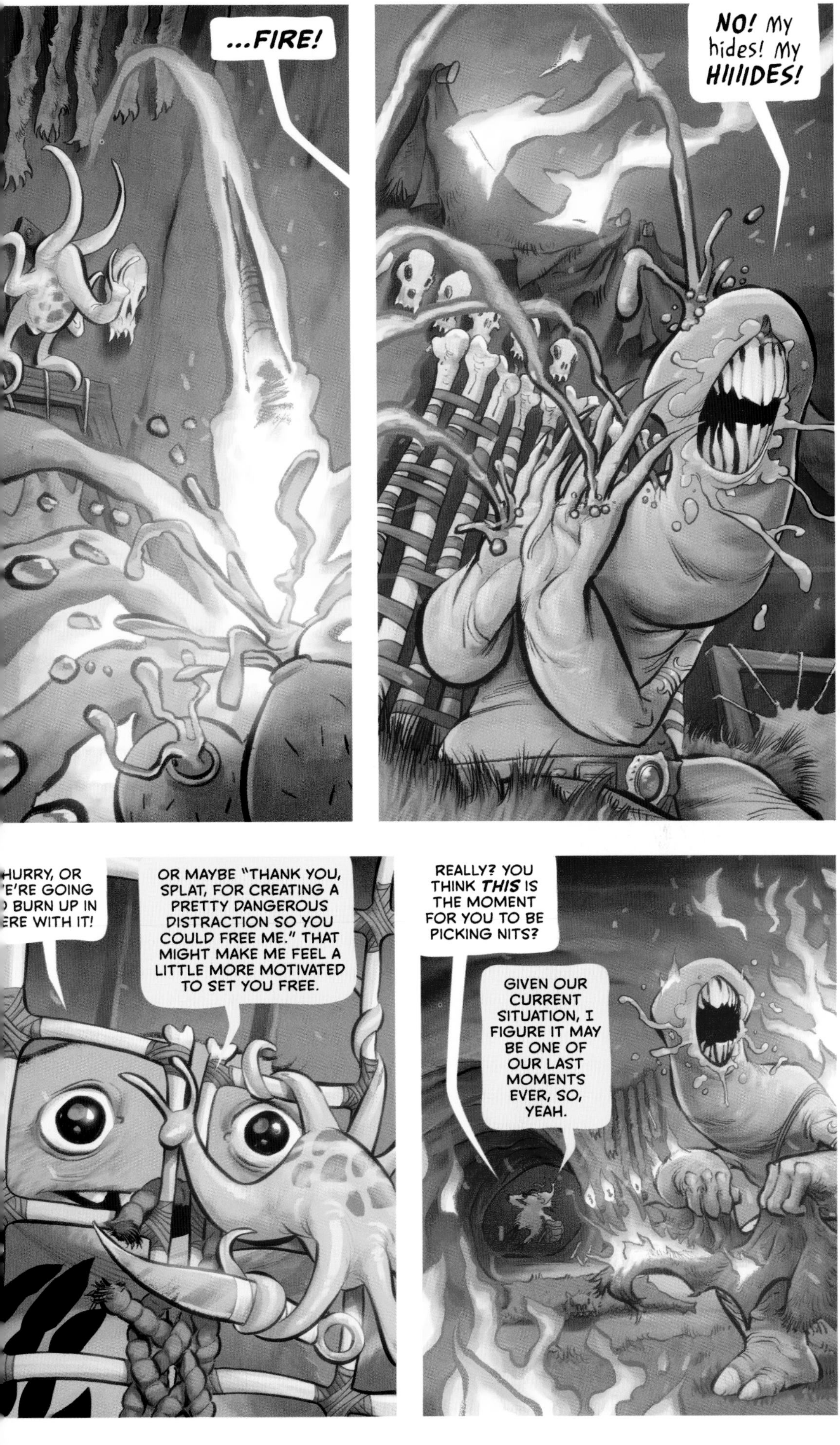
...FIRE!
NO! My hides! My HIIIIDES!
HURRY, OR 'E'RE GOING) BURN UP IN ERE WITH IT!
OR MAYBE "THANK YOU, SPLAT, FOR CREATING A PRETTY DANGEROUS DISTRACTION SO YOU COULD FREE ME." THAT MIGHT MAKE ME FEEL A LITTLE MORE MOTIVATED TO SET YOU FREE.
REALLY? YOU THINK THIS IS THE MOMENT FOR YOU TO BE PICKING NITS?
GIVEN OUR CURRENT SITUATION, I FIGURE IT MAY BE ONE OF OUR LAST MOMENTS EVER, SO, YEAH.

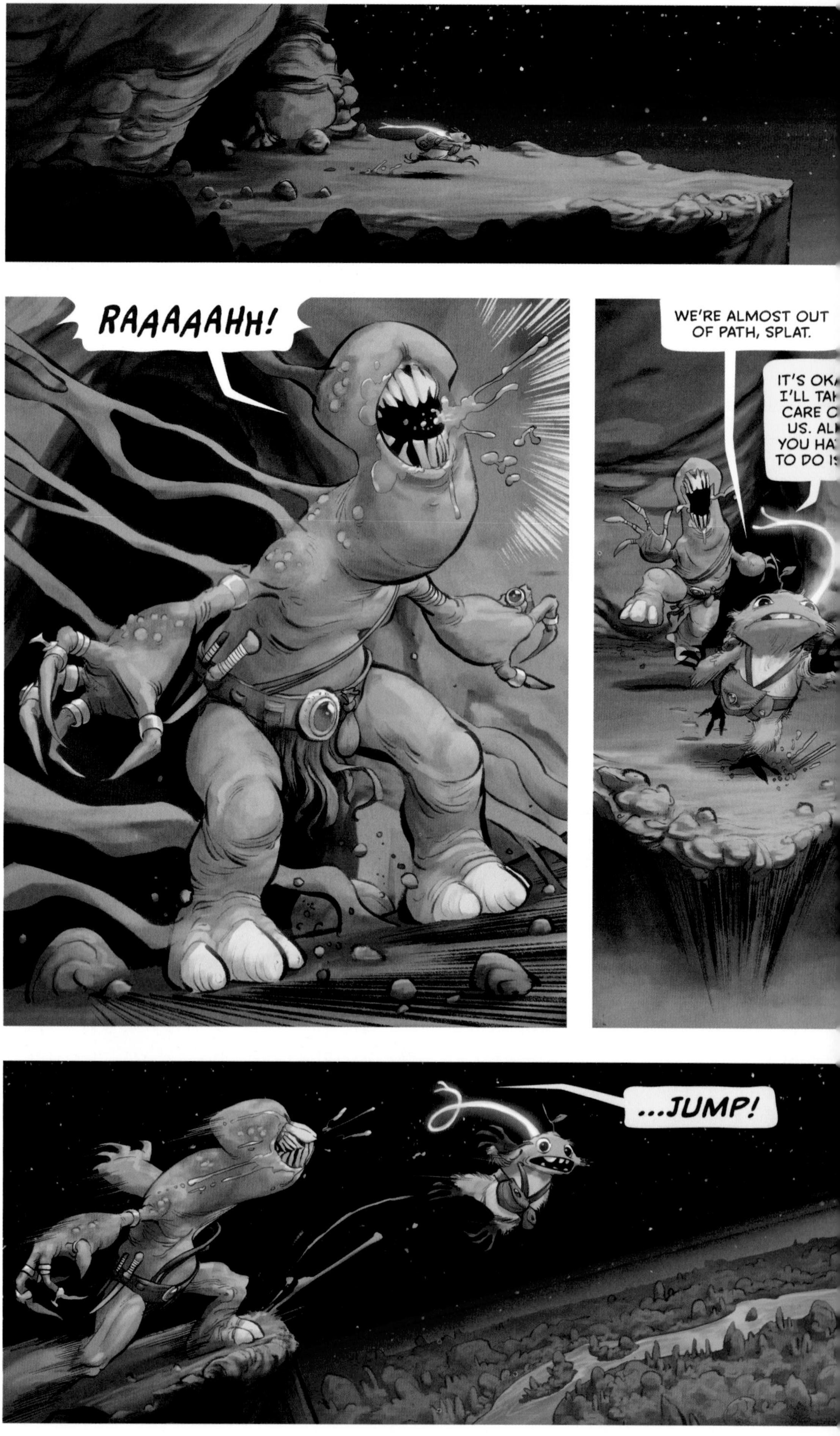

RAAAAAHH!
WE'RE ALMOST OUT OF PATH, SPLAT.
IT'S OK
I'LL TA
CARE O
US. AL
YOU HA
TO DO I
...JUMP!

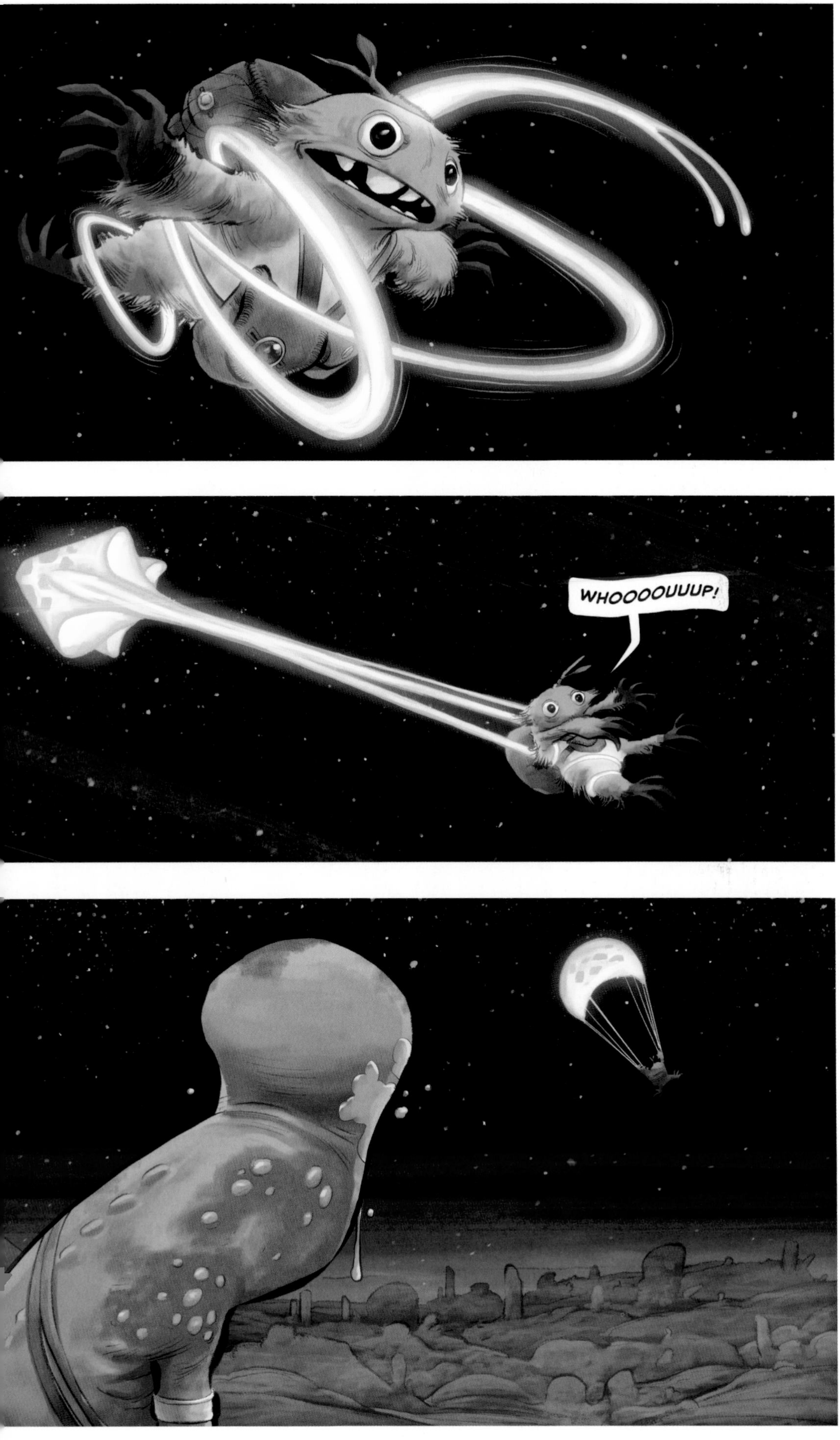
WHOOOOUUUP!

OUR RUN-IN WITH THE TRAPPER THREW US OFF COURSE QUITE A BIT, BUT ACCORDING TO THE NEKTARMANCER'S HANDBOOK, WE'RE ON THE RIGHT TRACK.

EEEEAGG!

EEAAAG!

EEEA

WE SHOULD MAKE IT TO THE WESTERN PLAINS SOON.

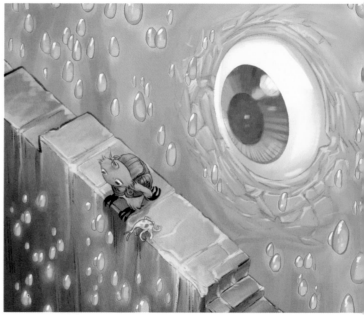

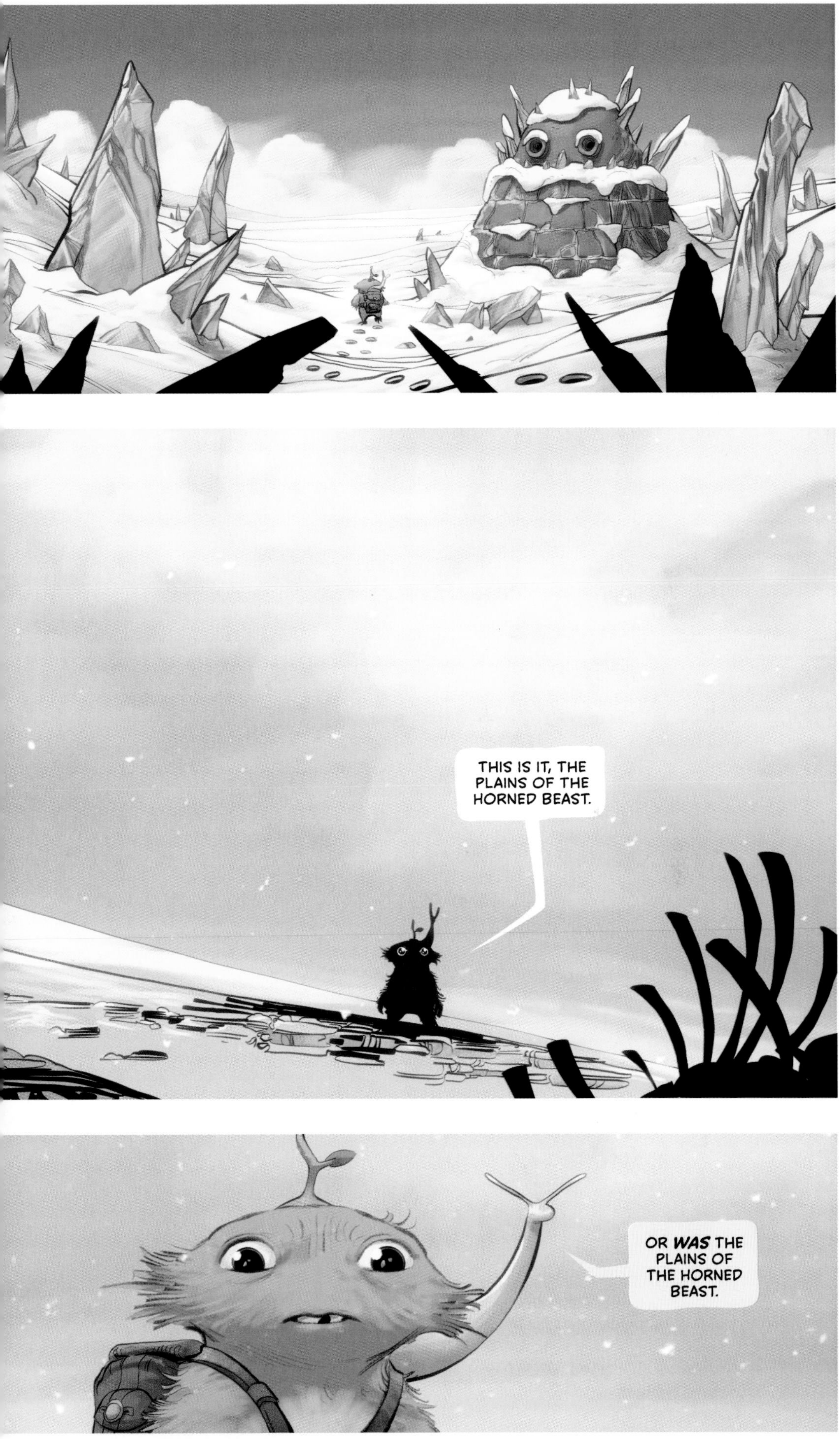
THIS IS IT, THE PLAINS OF THE HORNED BEAST.
OR *WAS* THE PLAINS OF THE HORNED BEAST.

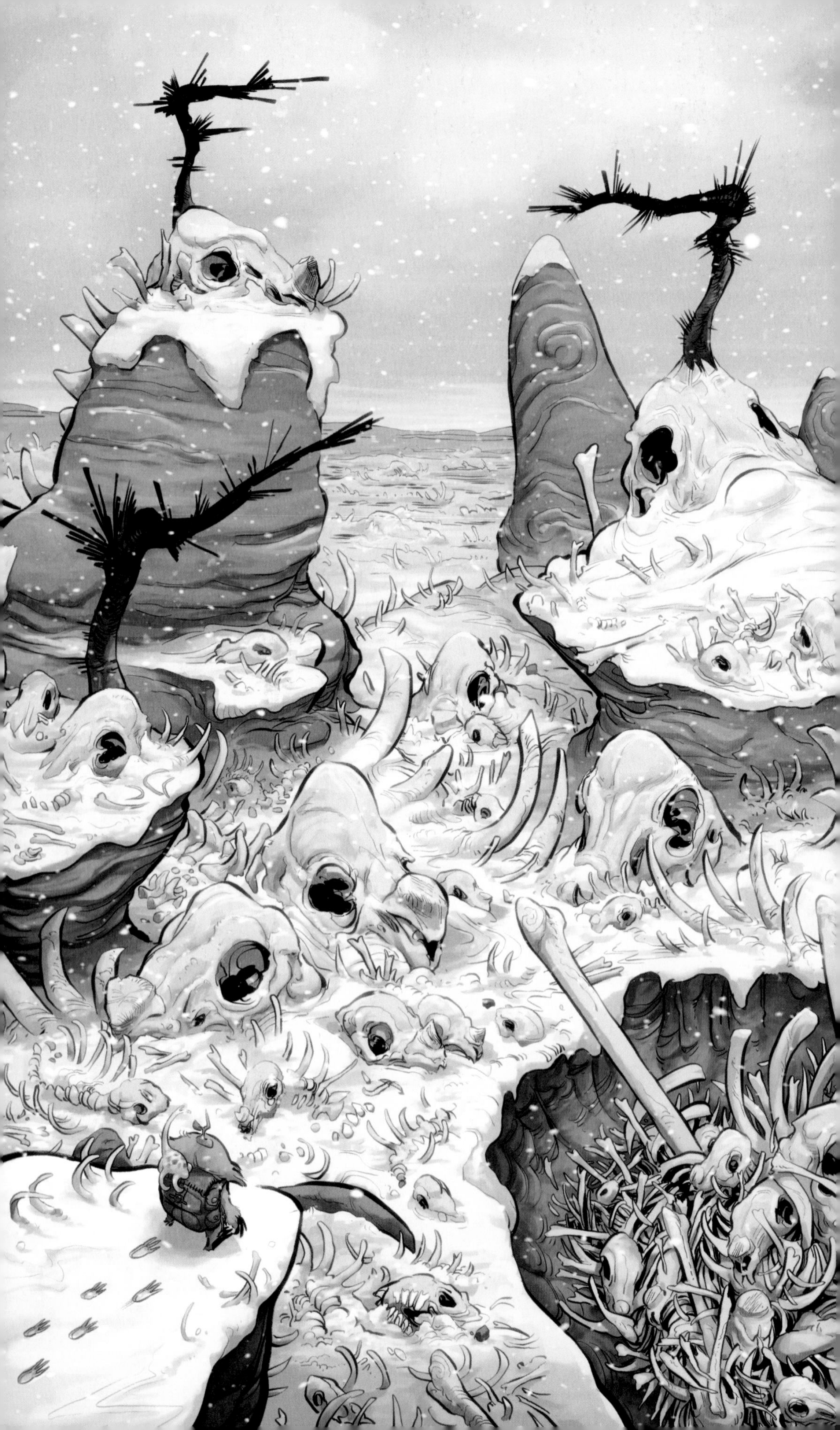

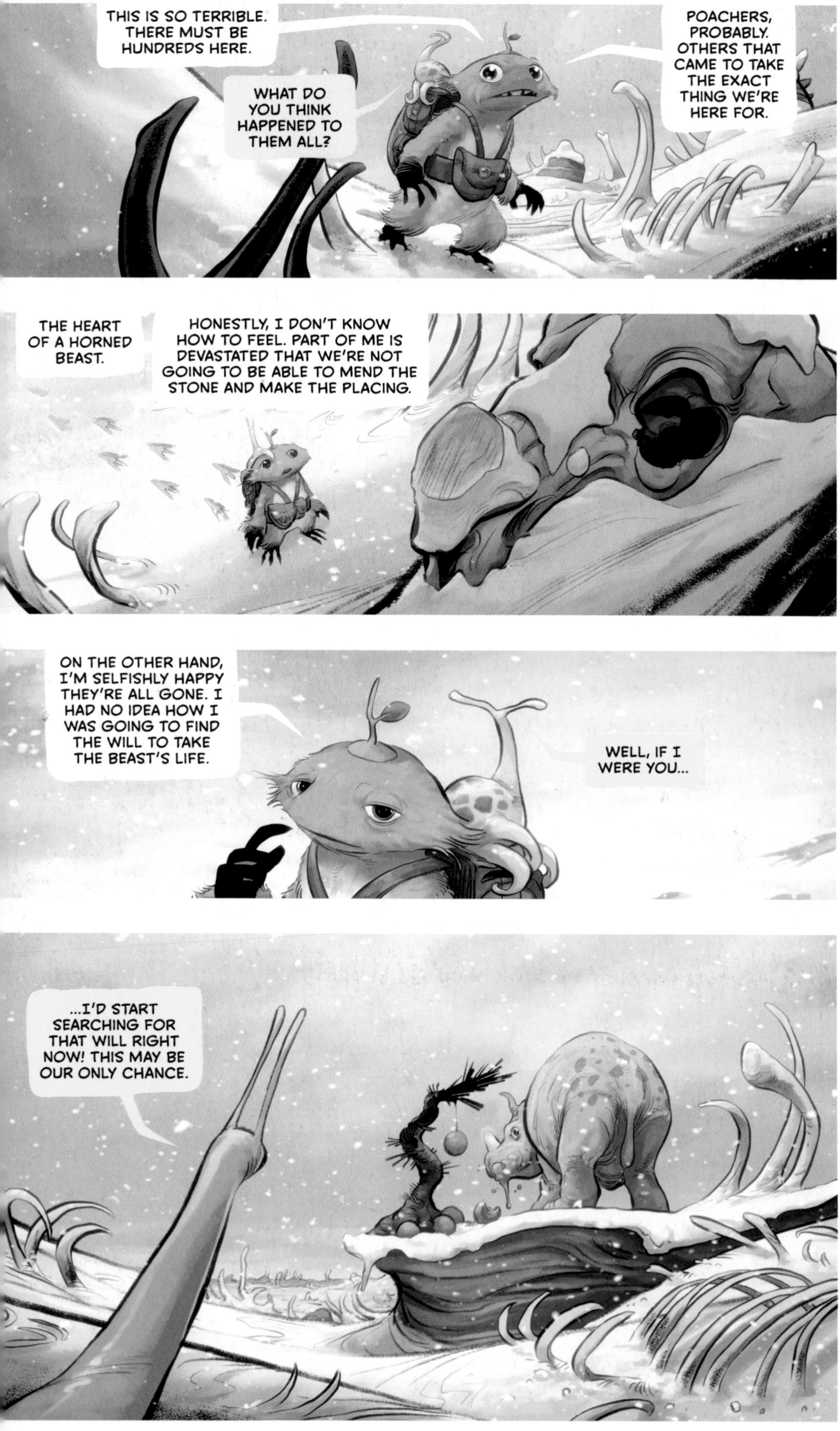
THIS IS SO TERRIBLE. THERE MUST BE HUNDREDS HERE.
WHAT DO YOU THINK HAPPENED TO THEM ALL?
POACHERS, PROBABLY. OTHERS THAT CAME TO TAKE THE EXACT THING WE'RE HERE FOR.
THE HEART OF A HORNED BEAST.
HONESTLY, I DON'T KNOW HOW TO FEEL. PART OF ME IS DEVASTATED THAT WE'RE NOT GOING TO BE ABLE TO MEND THE STONE AND MAKE THE PLACING.
ON THE OTHER HAND, I'M SELFISHLY HAPPY THEY'RE ALL GONE. I HAD NO IDEA HOW I WAS GOING TO FIND THE WILL TO TAKE THE BEAST'S LIFE.
WELL, IF I WERE YOU...
...I'D START SEARCHING FOR THAT WILL RIGHT NOW! THIS MAY BE OUR ONLY CHANCE.

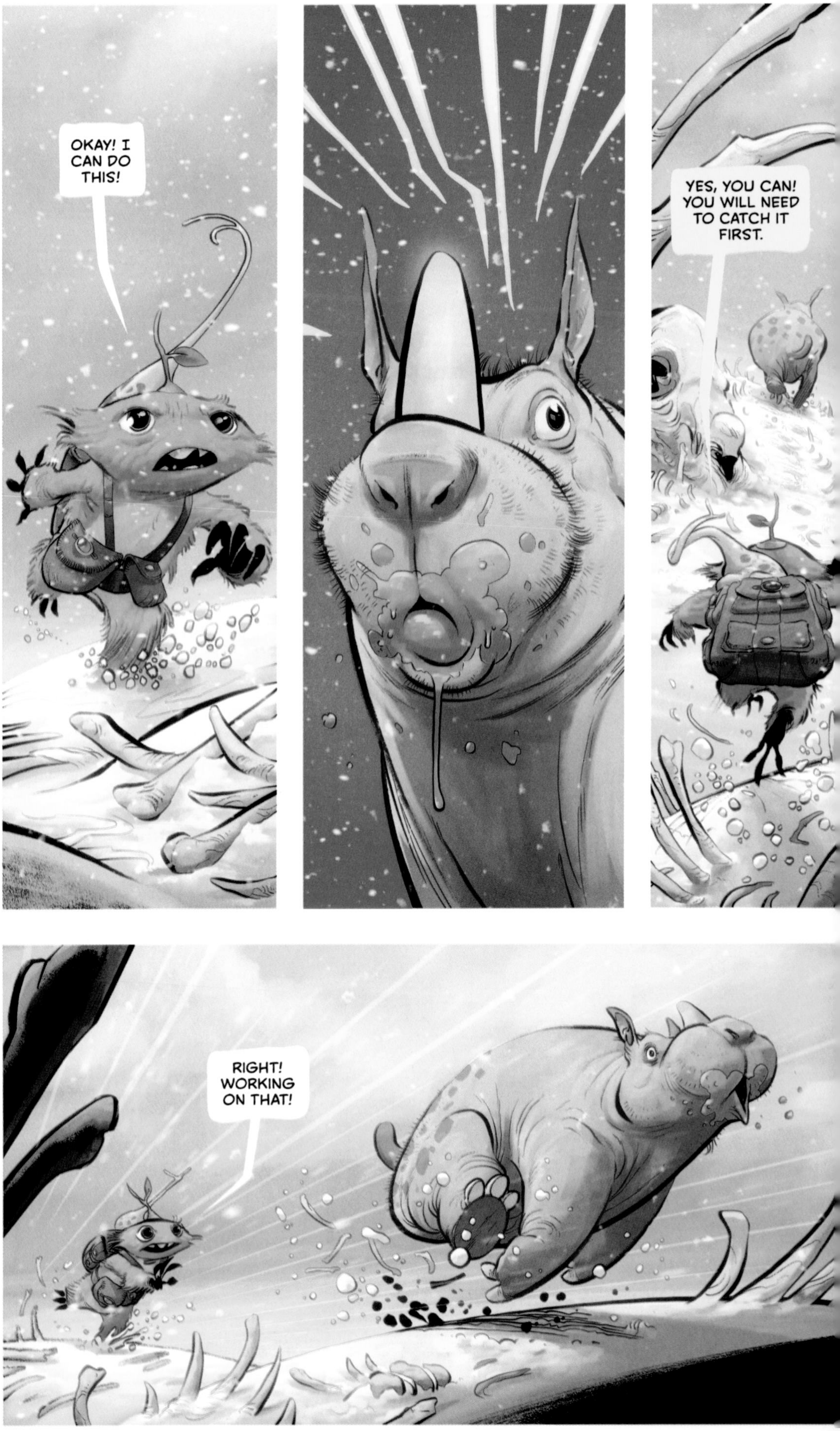

OKAY! I CAN DO THIS!
YES, YOU CAN! YOU WILL NEED TO CATCH IT FIRST.
RIGHT! WORKING ON THAT!

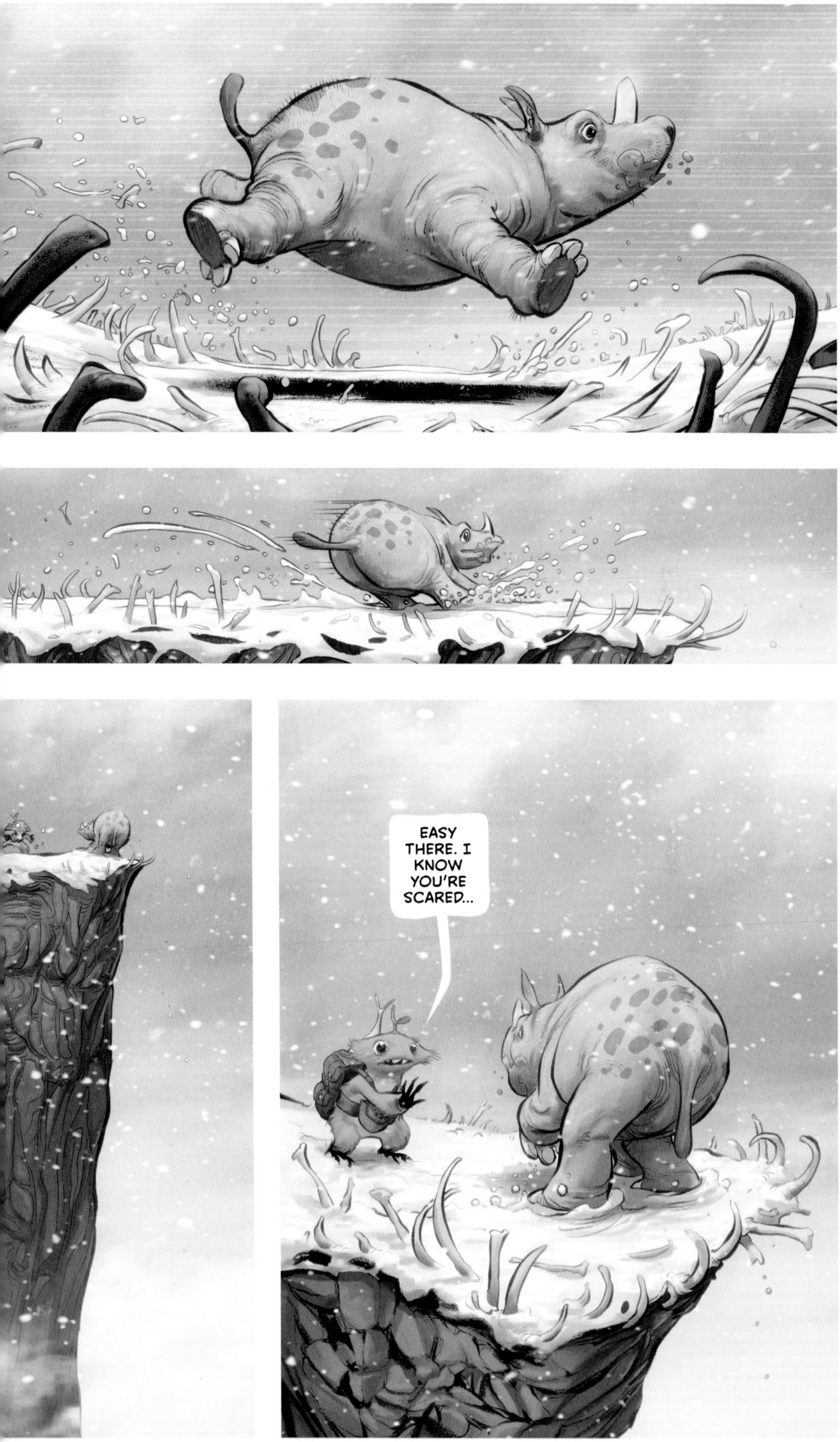
EASY THERE. I KNOW YOU'RE SCARED...

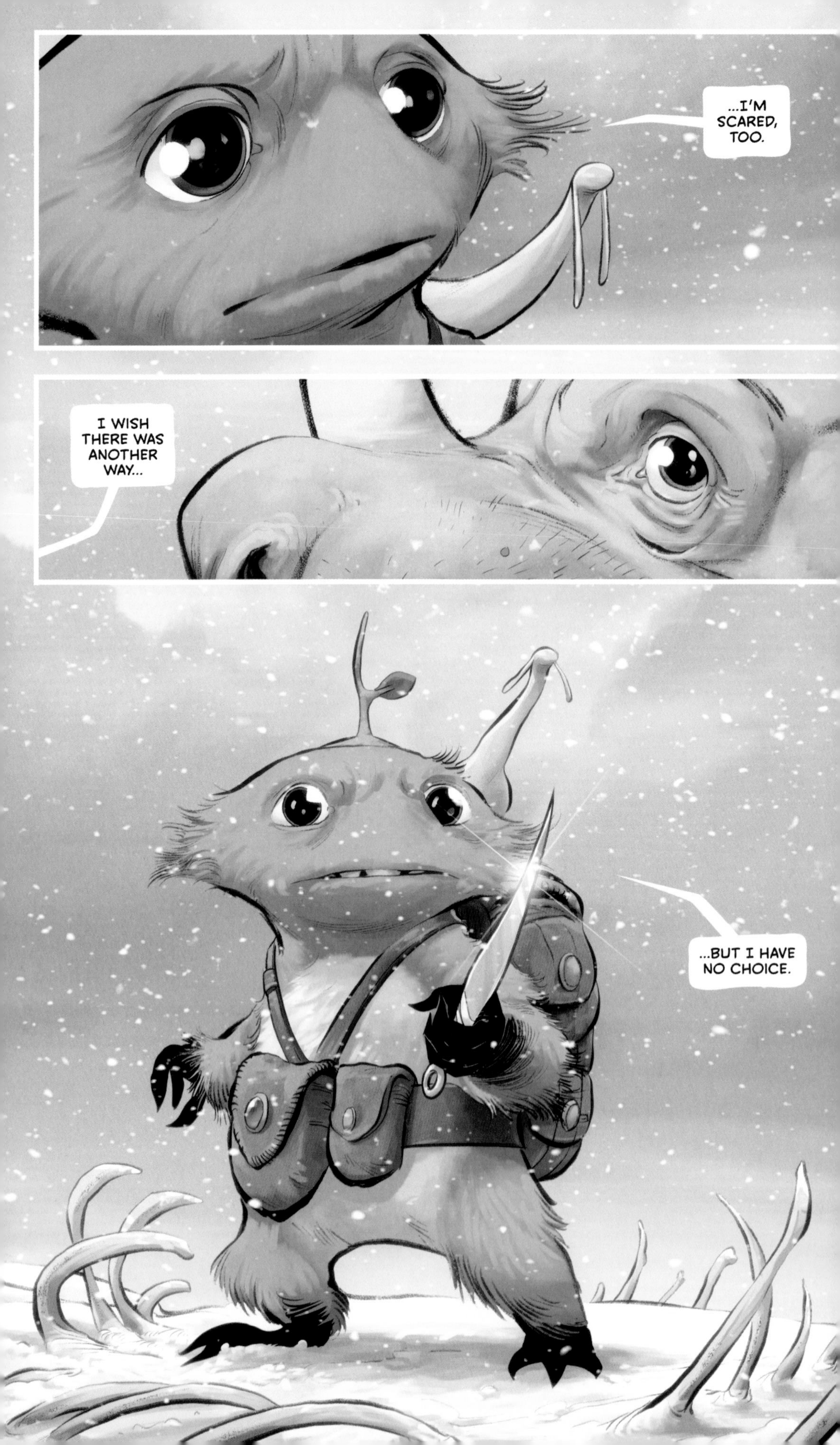
...I'M SCARED, TOO.
I WISH THERE WAS ANOTHER WAY...
...BUT I HAVE NO CHOICE.

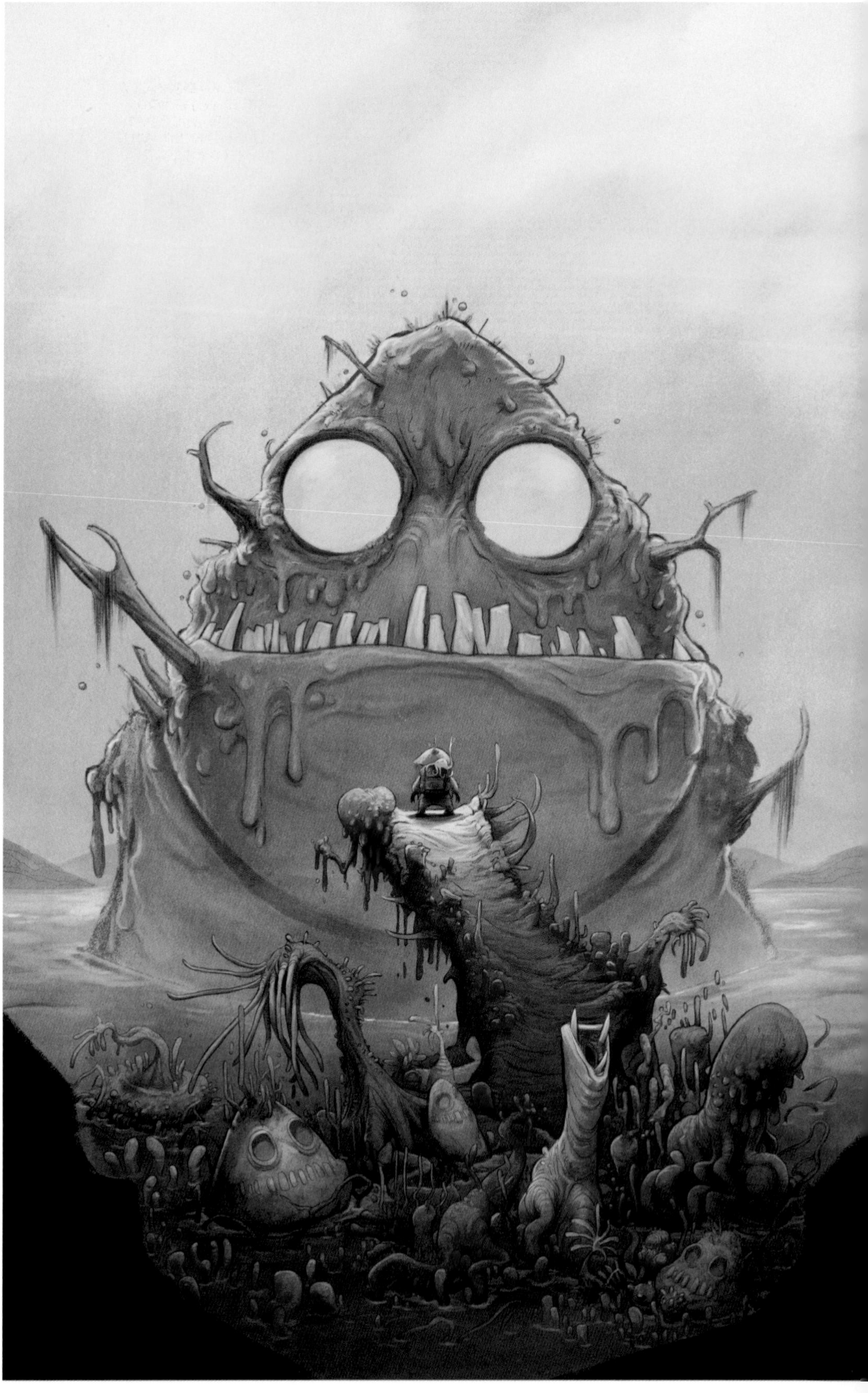

FOUR

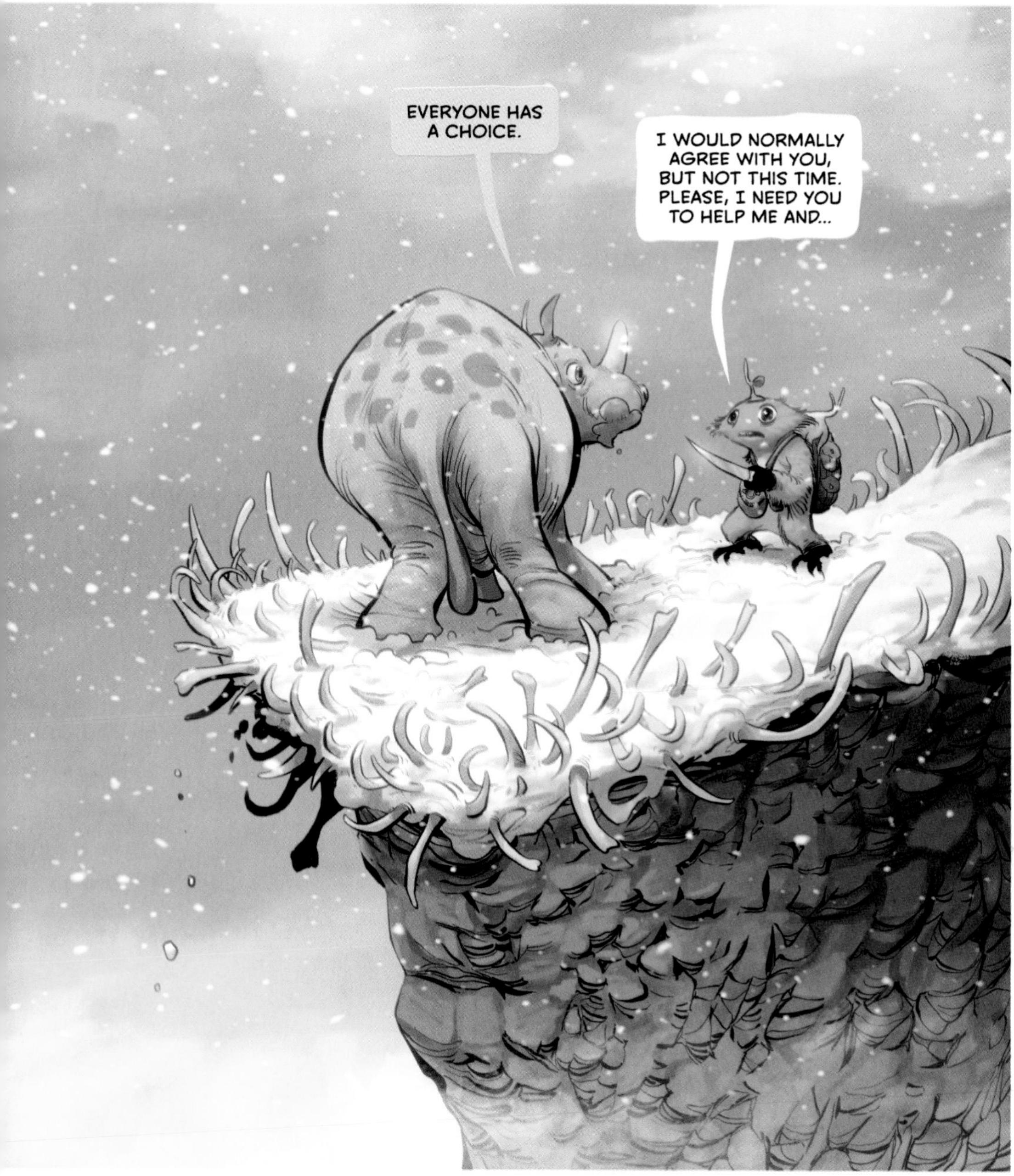
EVERYONE HAS
A CHOICE.
I WOULD NORMALLY
AGREE WITH YOU,
BUT NOT THIS TIME.
PLEASE, I NEED YOU
TO HELP ME AND...

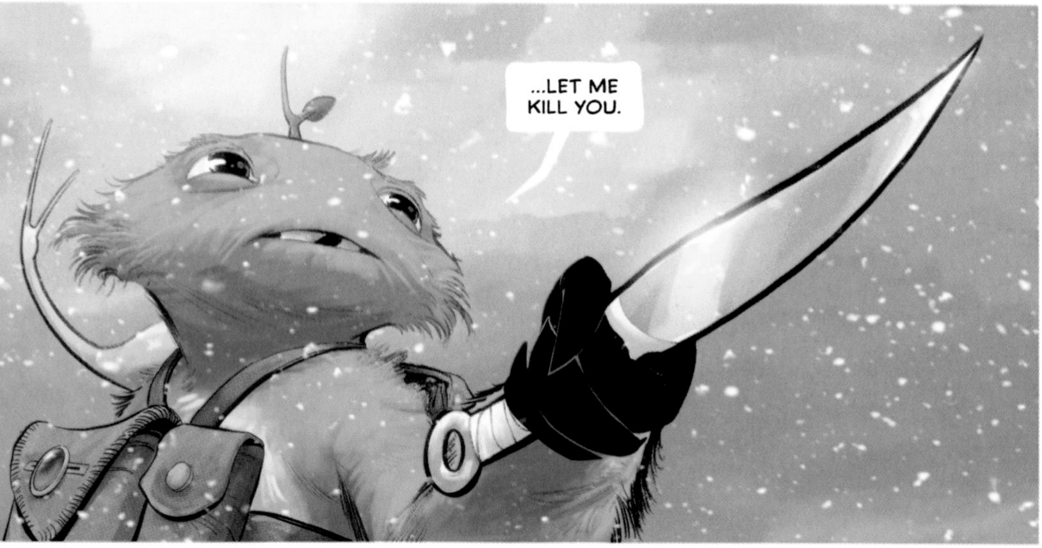
...LET ME
KILL YOU.

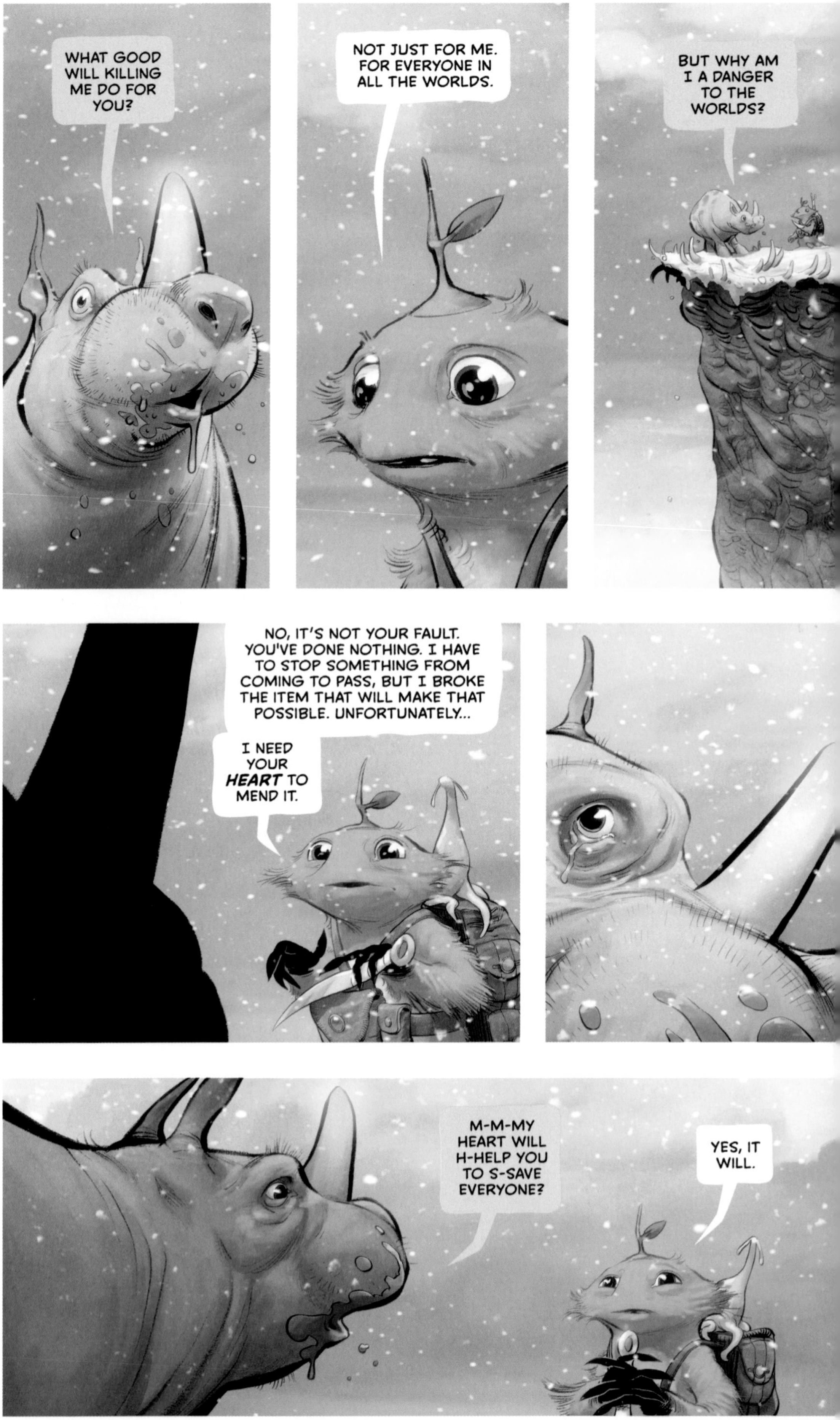
WHAT GOOD WILL KILLING ME DO FOR YOU?
NOT JUST FOR ME. FOR EVERYONE IN ALL THE WORLDS.
BUT WHY AM I A DANGER TO THE WORLDS?
NO, IT'S NOT YOUR FAULT. YOU'VE DONE NOTHING. I HAVE TO STOP SOMETHING FROM COMING TO PASS, BUT I BROKE THE ITEM THAT WILL MAKE THAT POSSIBLE. UNFORTUNATELY...
I NEED YOUR ***HEART*** TO MEND IT.
M-M-MY HEART WILL H-HELP YOU TO S-SAVE EVERYONE?
YES, IT WILL.

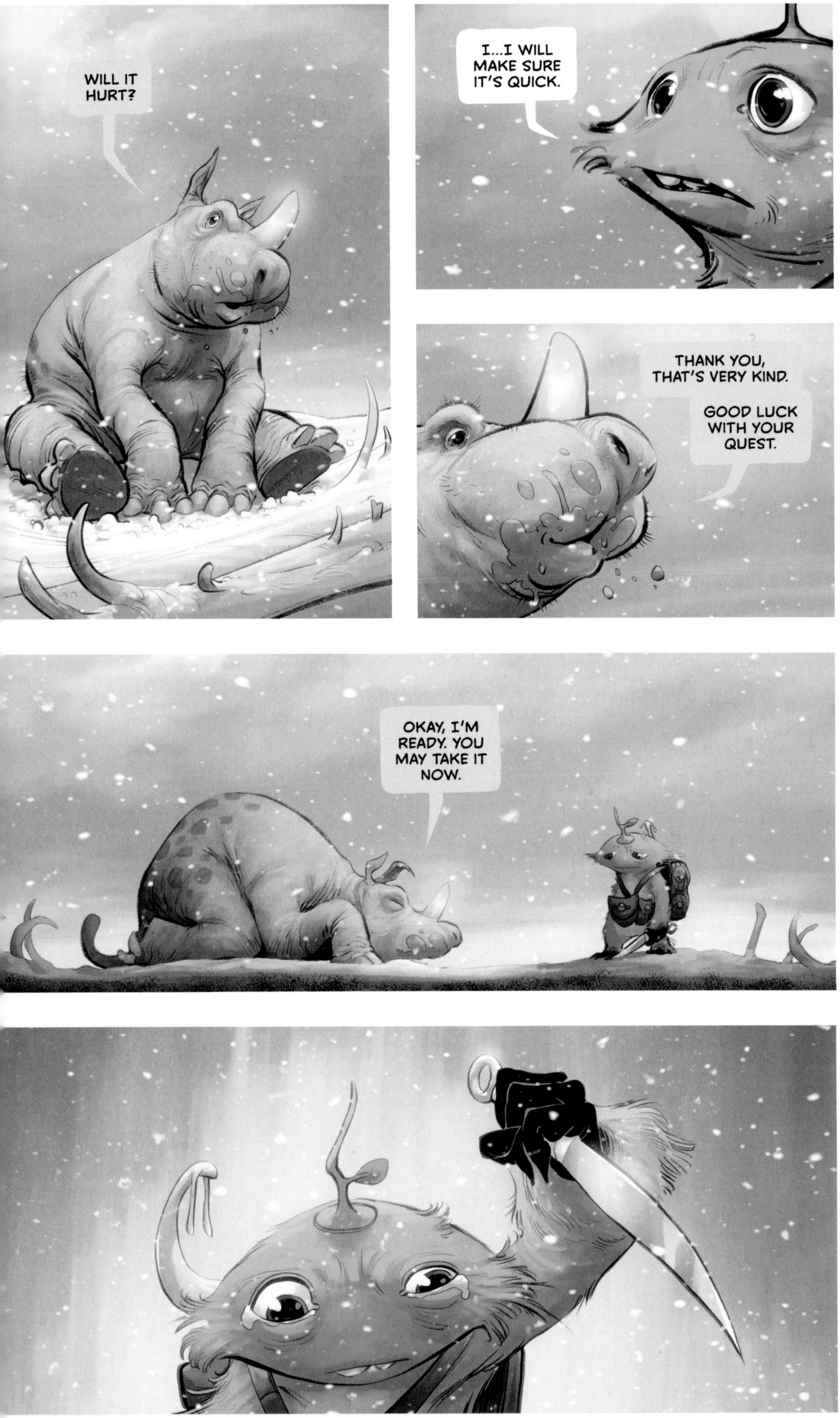
WILL IT HURT?
I...I WILL MAKE SURE IT'S QUICK.
THANK YOU, THAT'S VERY KIND.
GOOD LUCK WITH YOUR QUEST.
OKAY, I'M READY. YOU MAY TAKE IT NOW.

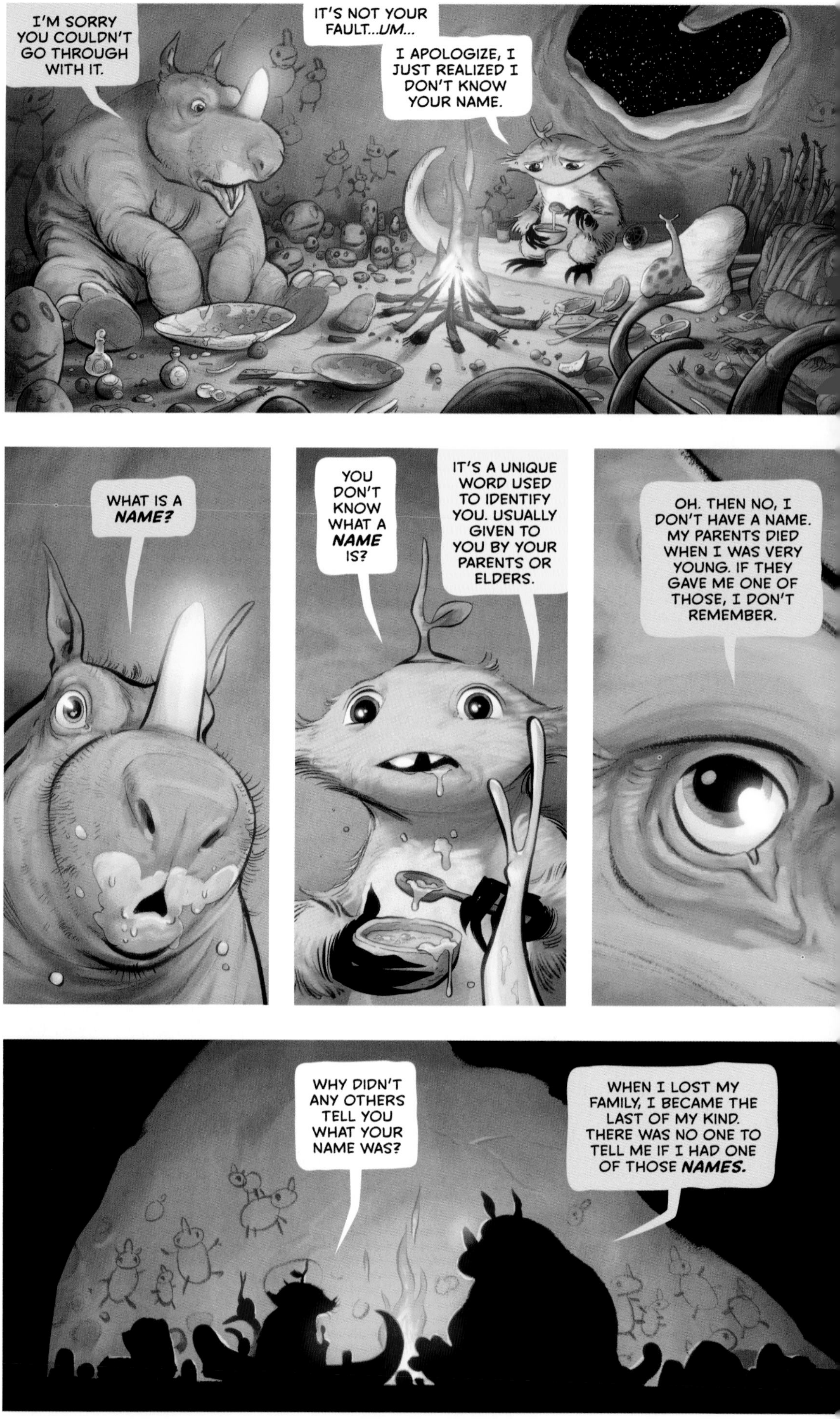
I'M SORRY YOU COULDN'T GO THROUGH WITH IT.
IT'S NOT YOUR FAULT...*UM...*
I APOLOGIZE, I JUST REALIZED I DON'T KNOW YOUR NAME.
WHAT IS A ***NAME?***
YOU DON'T KNOW WHAT A ***NAME*** IS?
IT'S A UNIQUE WORD USED TO IDENTIFY YOU. USUALLY GIVEN TO YOU BY YOUR PARENTS OR ELDERS.
OH. THEN NO, I DON'T HAVE A NAME. MY PARENTS DIED WHEN I WAS VERY YOUNG. IF THEY GAVE ME ONE OF THOSE, I DON'T REMEMBER.
WHY DIDN'T ANY OTHERS TELL YOU WHAT YOUR NAME WAS?
WHEN I LOST MY FAMILY, I BECAME THE LAST OF MY KIND. THERE WAS NO ONE TO TELL ME IF I HAD ONE OF THOSE ***NAMES.***

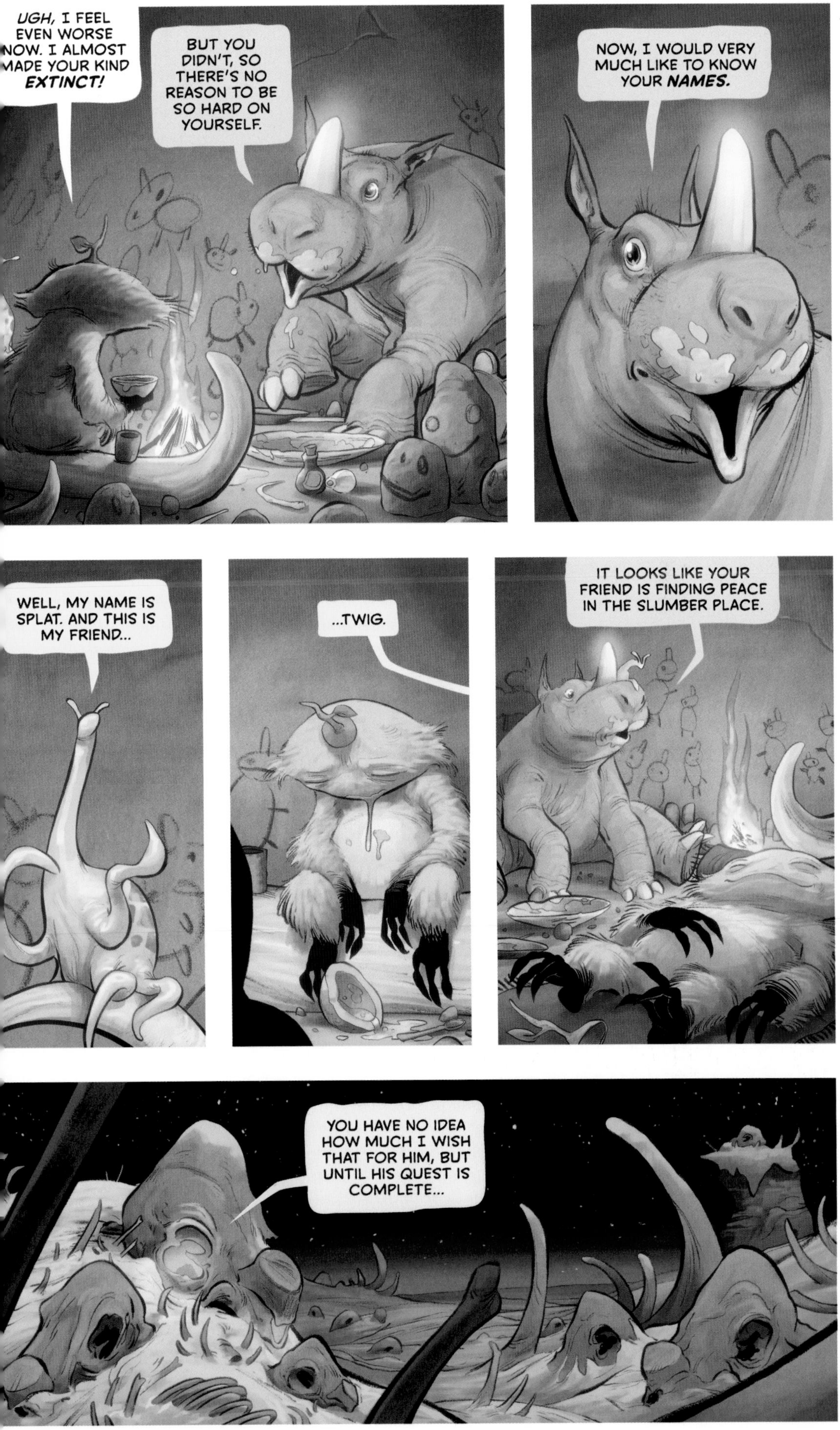
UGH, I FEEL EVEN WORSE NOW. I ALMOST MADE YOUR KIND *EXTINCT!*
BUT YOU DIDN'T, SO THERE'S NO REASON TO BE SO HARD ON YOURSELF.
NOW, I WOULD VERY MUCH LIKE TO KNOW YOUR **NAMES.**
WELL, MY NAME IS SPLAT. AND THIS IS MY FRIEND...
...TWIG.
IT LOOKS LIKE YOUR FRIEND IS FINDING PEACE IN THE SLUMBER PLACE.
YOU HAVE NO IDEA HOW MUCH I WISH THAT FOR HIM, BUT UNTIL HIS QUEST IS COMPLETE...

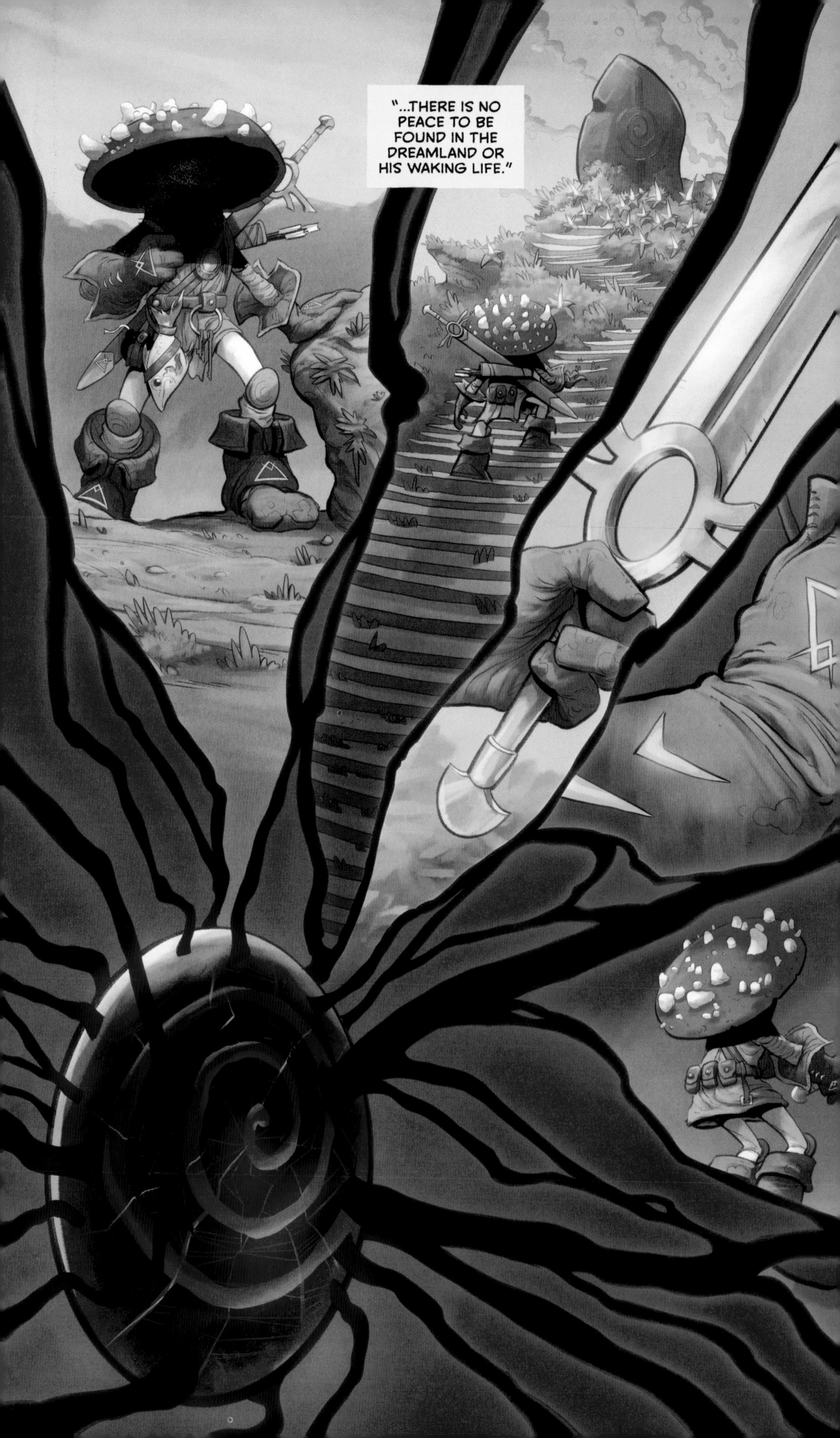
"...THERE IS NO PEACE TO BE FOUND IN THE DREAMLAND OR HIS WAKING LIFE."

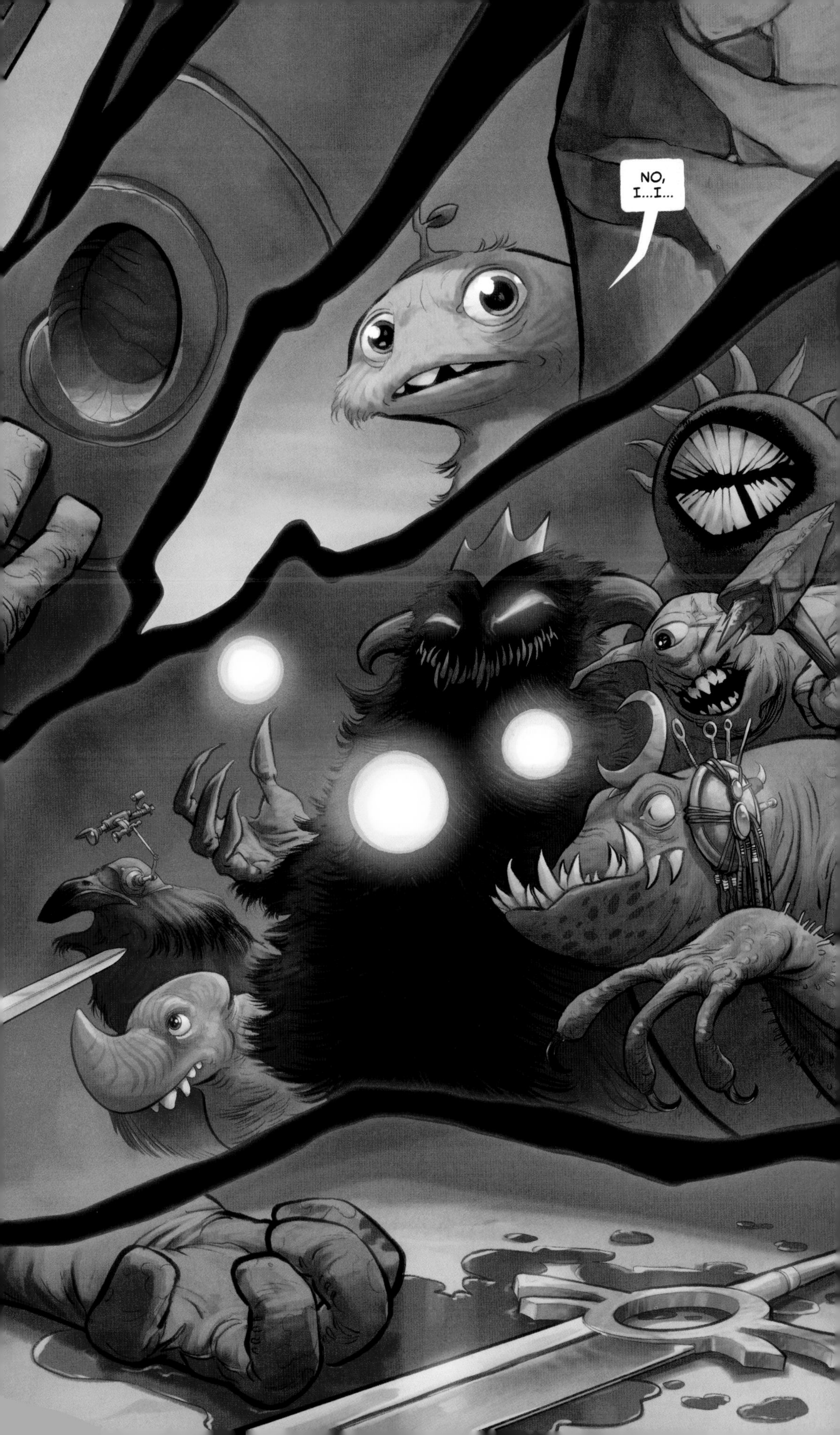
NO, I...I...

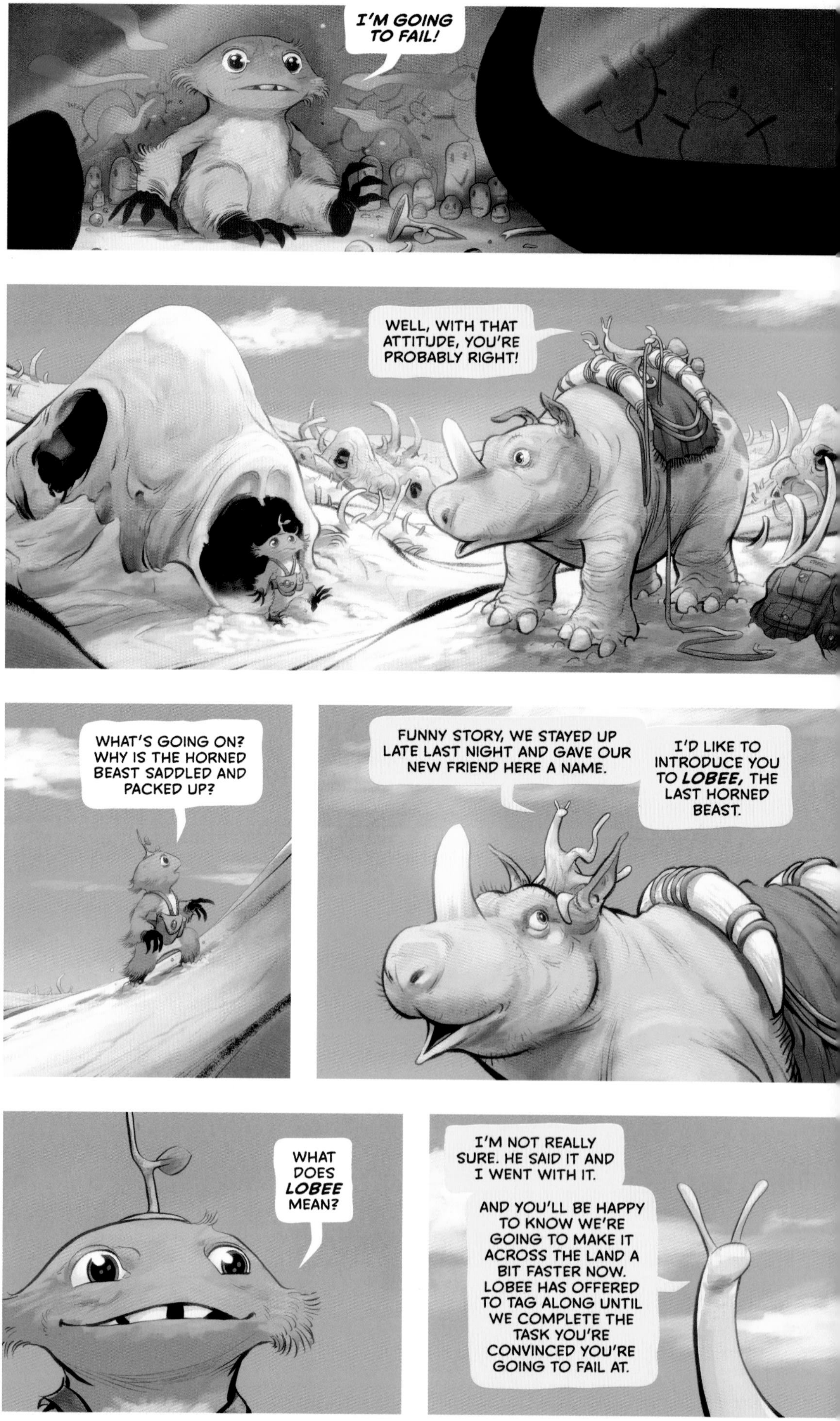
I'M GOING TO FAIL!
WELL, WITH THAT ATTITUDE, YOU'RE PROBABLY RIGHT!
WHAT'S GOING ON? WHY IS THE HORNED BEAST SADDLED AND PACKED UP?
FUNNY STORY, WE STAYED UP LATE LAST NIGHT AND GAVE OUR NEW FRIEND HERE A NAME.
I'D LIKE TO INTRODUCE YOU TO ***LOBEE,*** THE LAST HORNED BEAST.
WHAT DOES ***LOBEE*** MEAN?
I'M NOT REALLY SURE. HE SAID IT AND I WENT WITH IT.
AND YOU'LL BE HAPPY TO KNOW WE'RE GOING TO MAKE IT ACROSS THE LAND A BIT FASTER NOW. LOBEE HAS OFFERED TO TAG ALONG UNTIL WE COMPLETE THE TASK YOU'RE CONVINCED YOU'RE GOING TO FAIL AT.

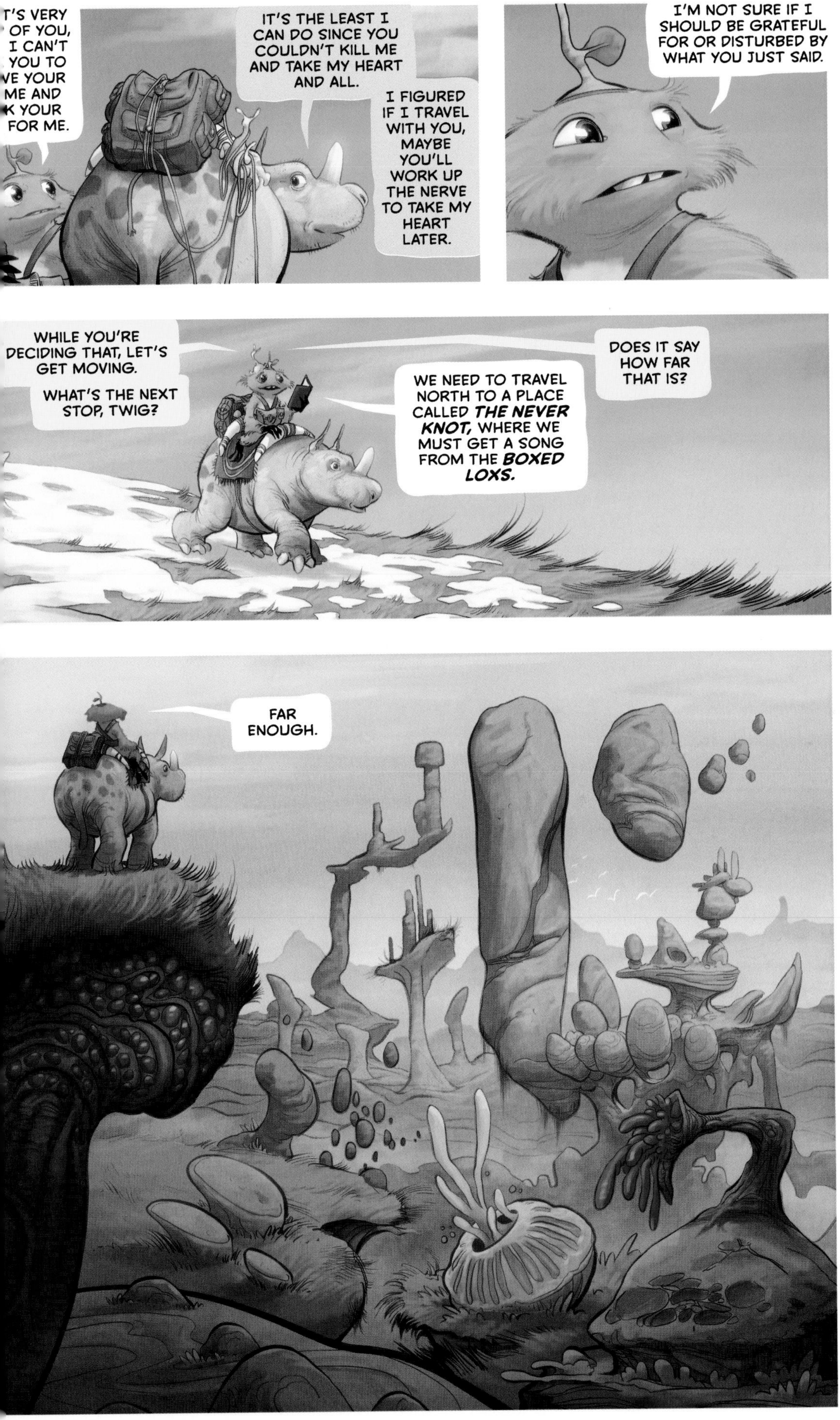
T'S VERY OF YOU, I CAN'T YOU TO VE YOUR ME AND K YOUR FOR ME.
IT'S THE LEAST I CAN DO SINCE YOU COULDN'T KILL ME AND TAKE MY HEART AND ALL.
I FIGURED IF I TRAVEL WITH YOU, MAYBE YOU'LL WORK UP THE NERVE TO TAKE MY HEART LATER.
I'M NOT SURE IF I SHOULD BE GRATEFUL FOR OR DISTURBED BY WHAT YOU JUST SAID.
WHILE YOU'RE DECIDING THAT, LET'S GET MOVING.
WHAT'S THE NEXT STOP, TWIG?
WE NEED TO TRAVEL NORTH TO A PLACE CALLED ***THE NEVER KNOT,*** WHERE WE MUST GET A SONG FROM THE ***BOXED LOXS.***
DOES IT SAY HOW FAR THAT IS?
FAR ENOUGH.

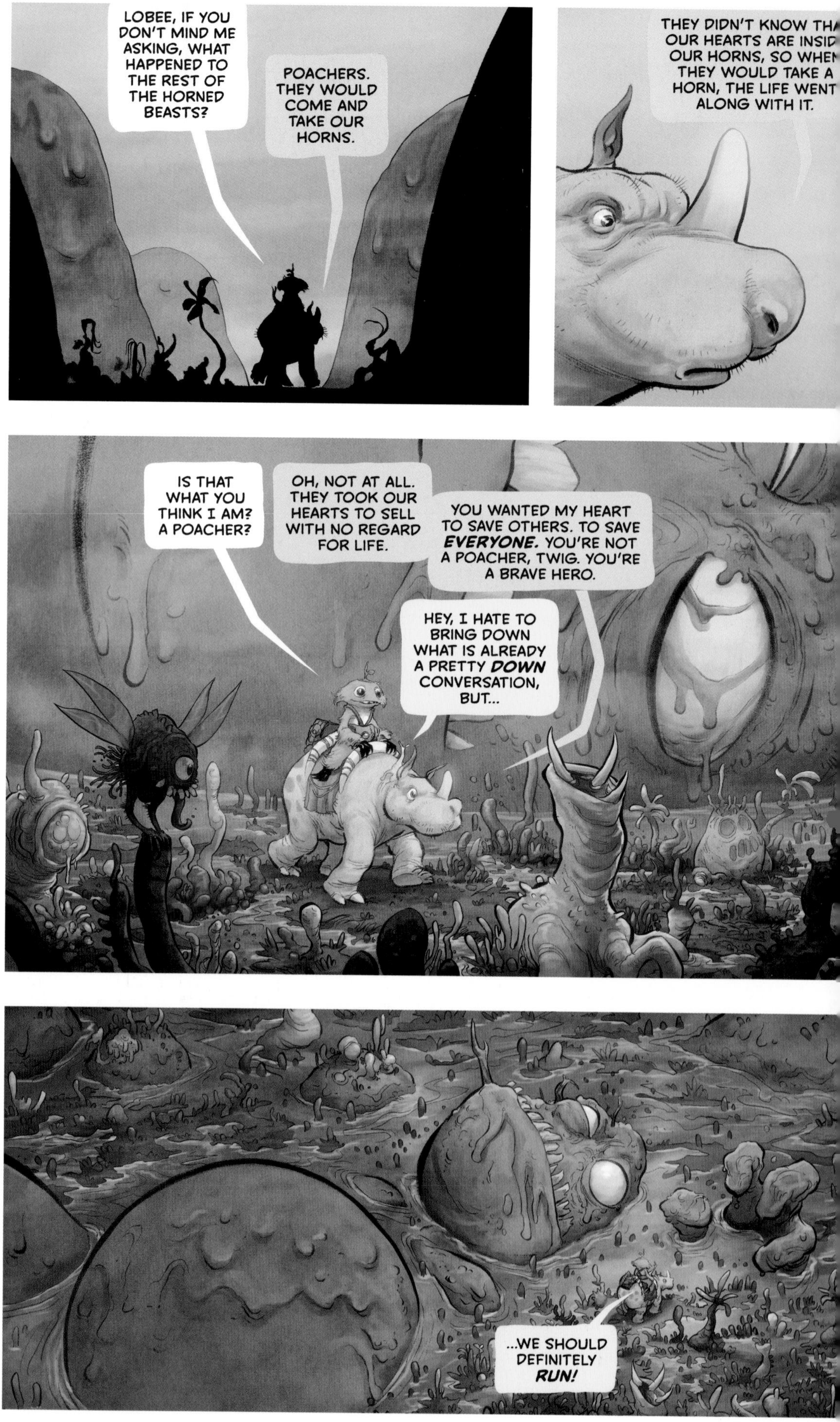

LOBEE, IF YOU DON'T MIND ME ASKING, WHAT HAPPENED TO THE REST OF THE HORNED BEASTS?
POACHERS. THEY WOULD COME AND TAKE OUR HORNS.
THEY DIDN'T KNOW THA OUR HEARTS ARE INSID OUR HORNS, SO WHEN THEY WOULD TAKE A HORN, THE LIFE WENT ALONG WITH IT.
IS THAT WHAT YOU THINK I AM? A POACHER?
OH, NOT AT ALL. THEY TOOK OUR HEARTS TO SELL WITH NO REGARD FOR LIFE.
YOU WANTED MY HEART TO SAVE OTHERS. TO SAVE ***EVERYONE.*** YOU'RE NOT A POACHER, TWIG. YOU'RE A BRAVE HERO.
HEY, I HATE TO BRING DOWN WHAT IS ALREADY A PRETTY ***DOWN*** CONVERSATION, BUT...
...WE SHOULD DEFINITELY ***RUN!***

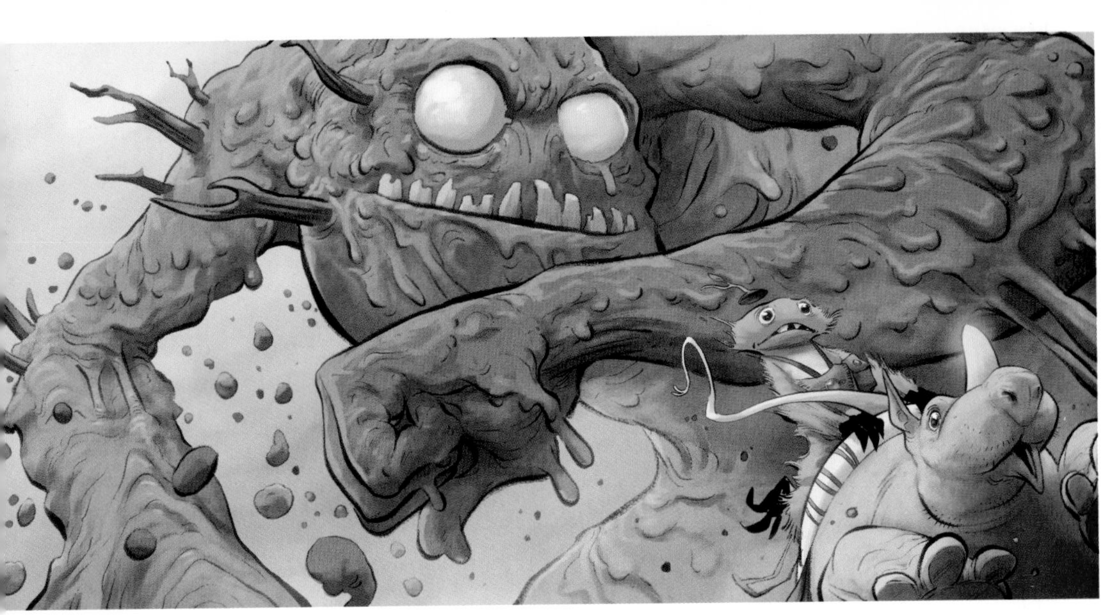

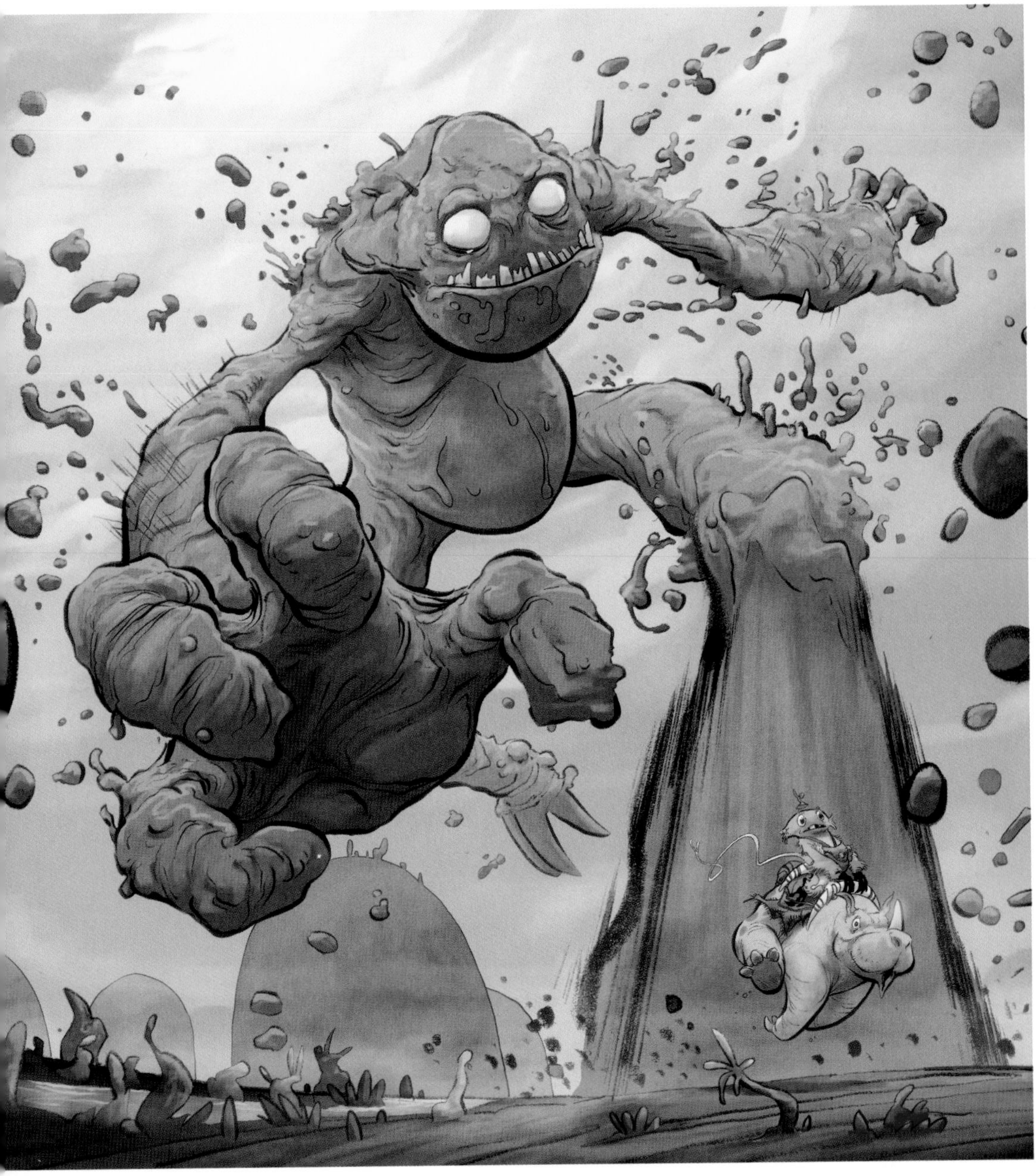

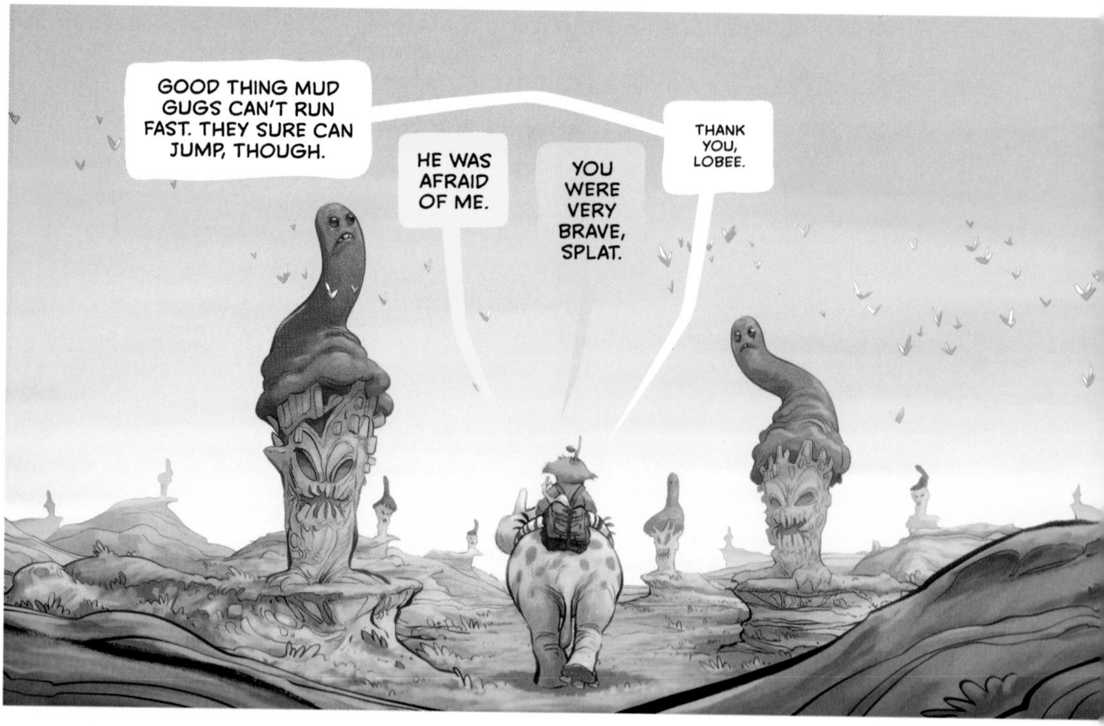
GOOD THING MUD GUGS CAN'T RUN FAST. THEY SURE CAN JUMP, THOUGH.
HE WAS AFRAID OF ME.
YOU WERE VERY BRAVE, SPLAT.
THANK YOU, LOBEE.

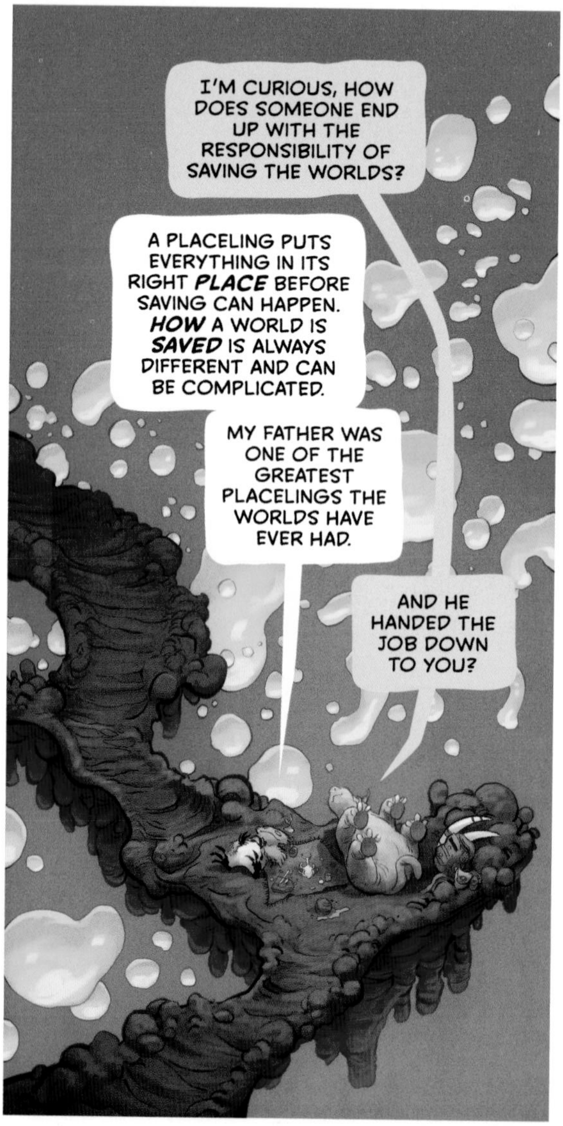
I'M CURIOUS, HOW DOES SOMEONE END UP WITH THE RESPONSIBILITY OF SAVING THE WORLDS?
A PLACELING PUTS EVERYTHING IN ITS RIGHT ***PLACE*** BEFORE SAVING CAN HAPPEN. ***HOW*** A WORLD IS ***SAVED*** IS ALWAYS DIFFERENT AND CAN BE COMPLICATED.
MY FATHER WAS ONE OF THE GREATEST PLACELINGS THE WORLDS HAVE EVER HAD.
AND HE HANDED THE JOB DOWN TO YOU?

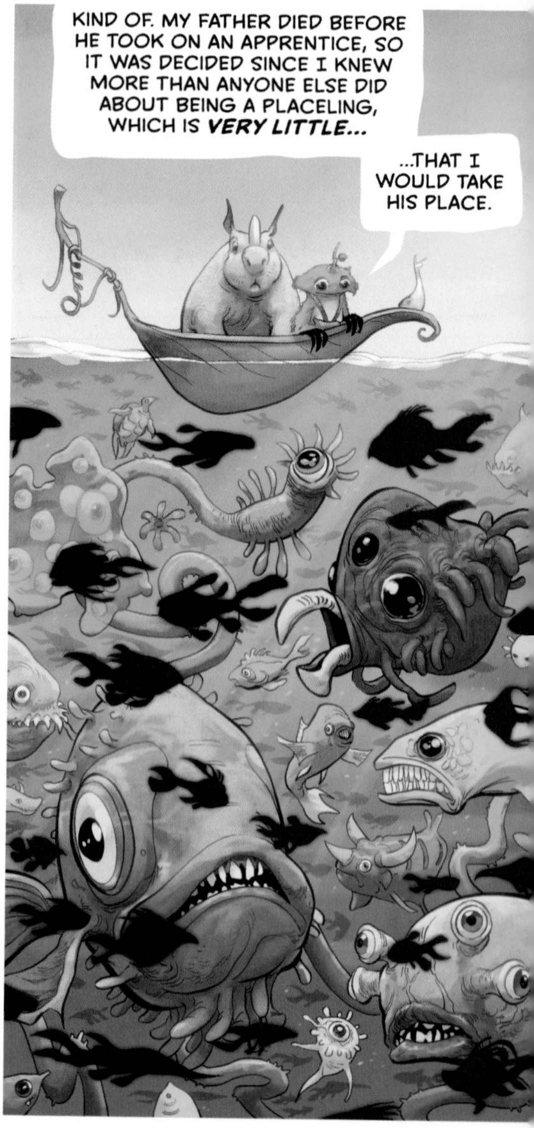
KIND OF. MY FATHER DIED BEFORE HE TOOK ON AN APPRENTICE, SO IT WAS DECIDED SINCE I KNEW MORE THAN ANYONE ELSE DID ABOUT BEING A PLACELING, WHICH IS ***VERY LITTLE...***
...THAT I WOULD TAKE HIS PLACE.

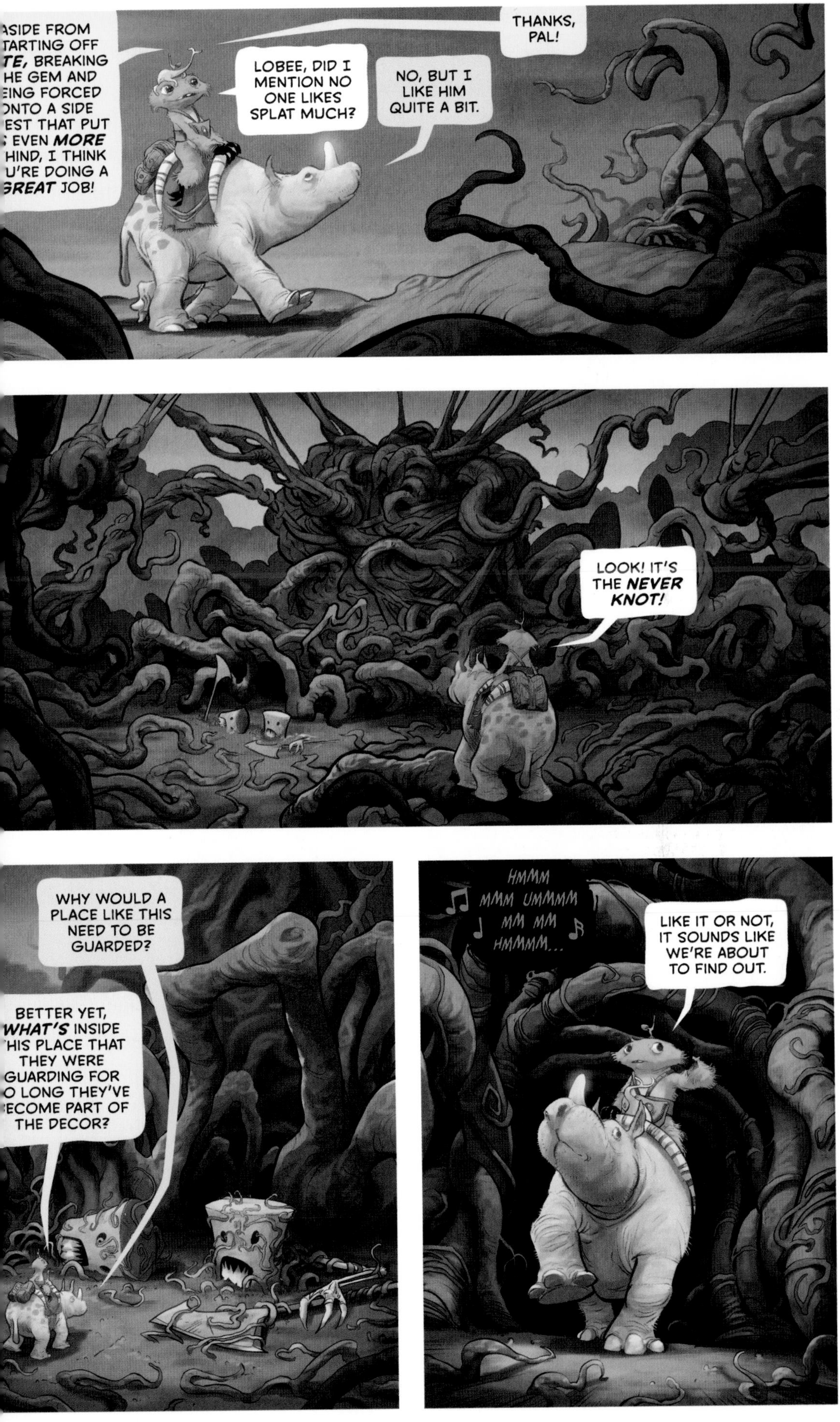
ASIDE FROM TARTING OFF TE, BREAKING HE GEM AND EING FORCED ONTO A SIDE EST THAT PUT EVEN MORE HIND, I THINK U'RE DOING A GREAT JOB!
THANKS, PAL!
LOBEE, DID I MENTION NO ONE LIKES SPLAT MUCH?
NO, BUT I LIKE HIM QUITE A BIT.
LOOK! IT'S THE NEVER KNOT!
WHY WOULD A PLACE LIKE THIS NEED TO BE GUARDED?
BETTER YET, WHAT'S INSIDE HIS PLACE THAT THEY WERE GUARDING FOR O LONG THEY'VE ECOME PART OF THE DECOR?
HMMM MMM UMMMM MM MM HMMMM...
LIKE IT OR NOT, IT SOUNDS LIKE WE'RE ABOUT TO FIND OUT.

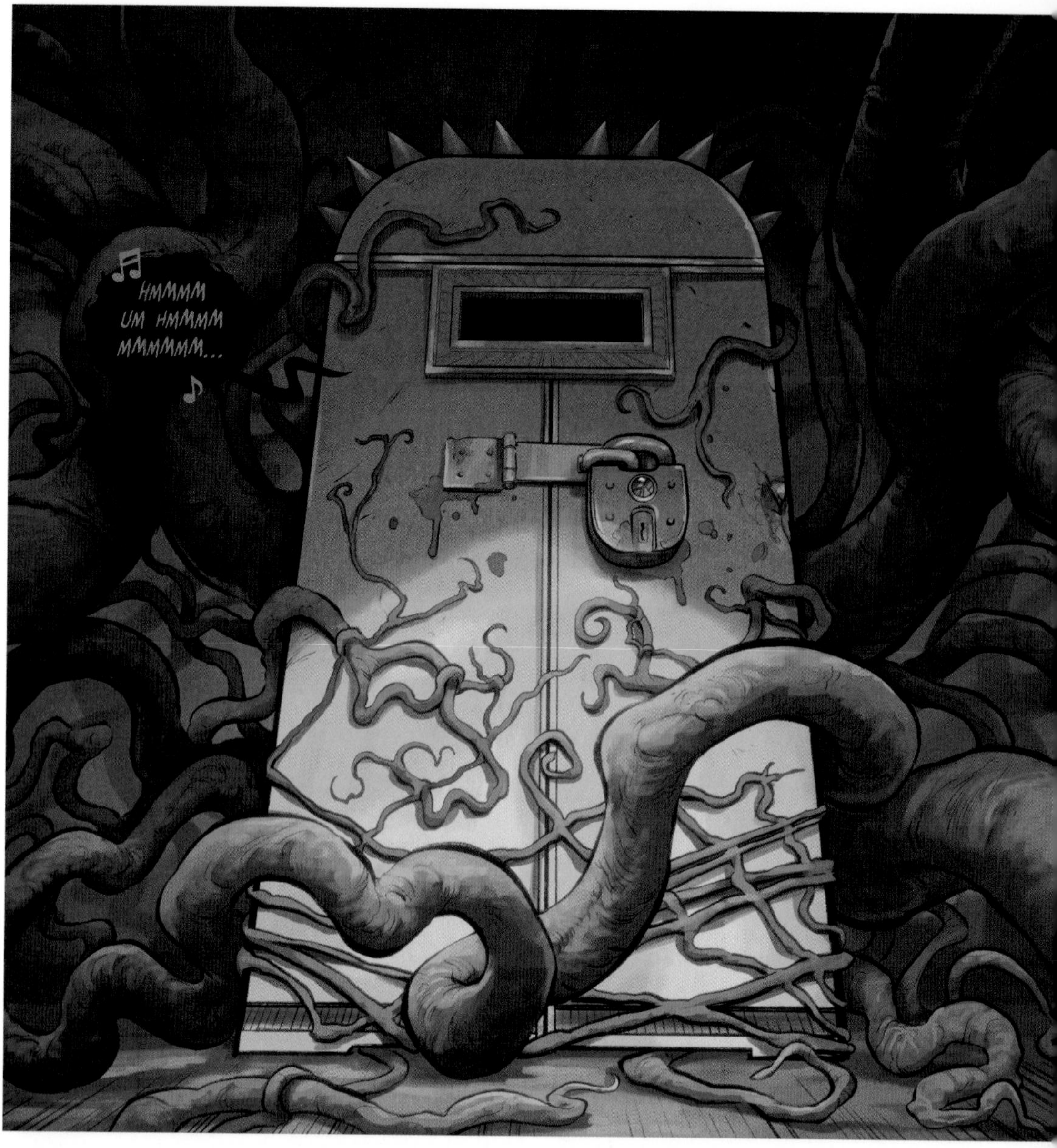
HMMMM UM HMMMM MMMMMM...

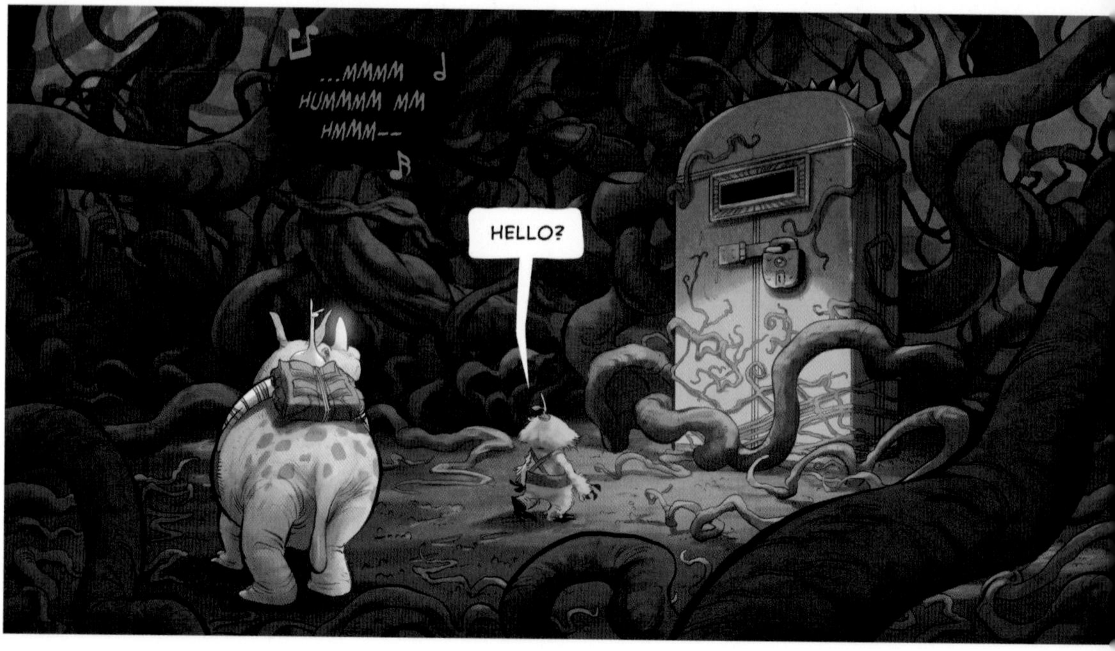
...MMMM HUMMMM MM HMMM--
HELLO?

IS THAT YOU, MIND, TEASING ME AGAIN? WHY DO YOU TORTURE ME SO?
OR...COULD IT BE...
SOMETHING BESIDES YOU IS SPEAKING TO ME?
YOUR MIND IS NOT BETRAYING YOU. I AM REAL, AND I'VE COME TO ASK FOR YOUR HELP.
HOW COULD I POSSIBLY HELP A THING SUCH AS YOU FROM INSIDE THIS MADDENING BOX?
WITH A *SONG.*

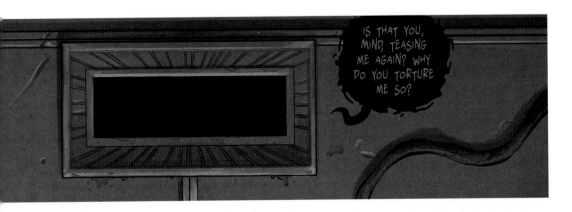

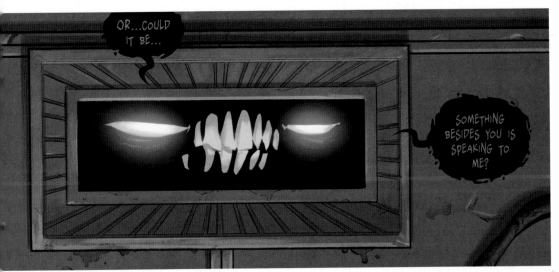

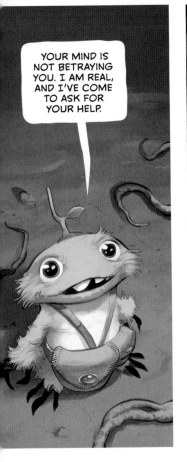

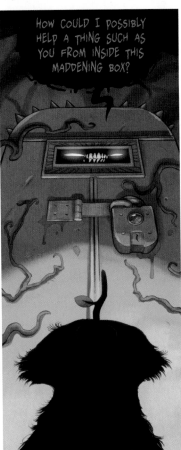

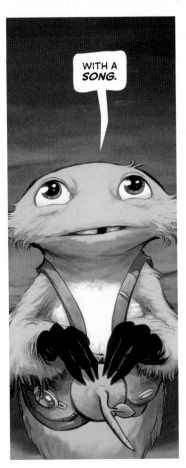

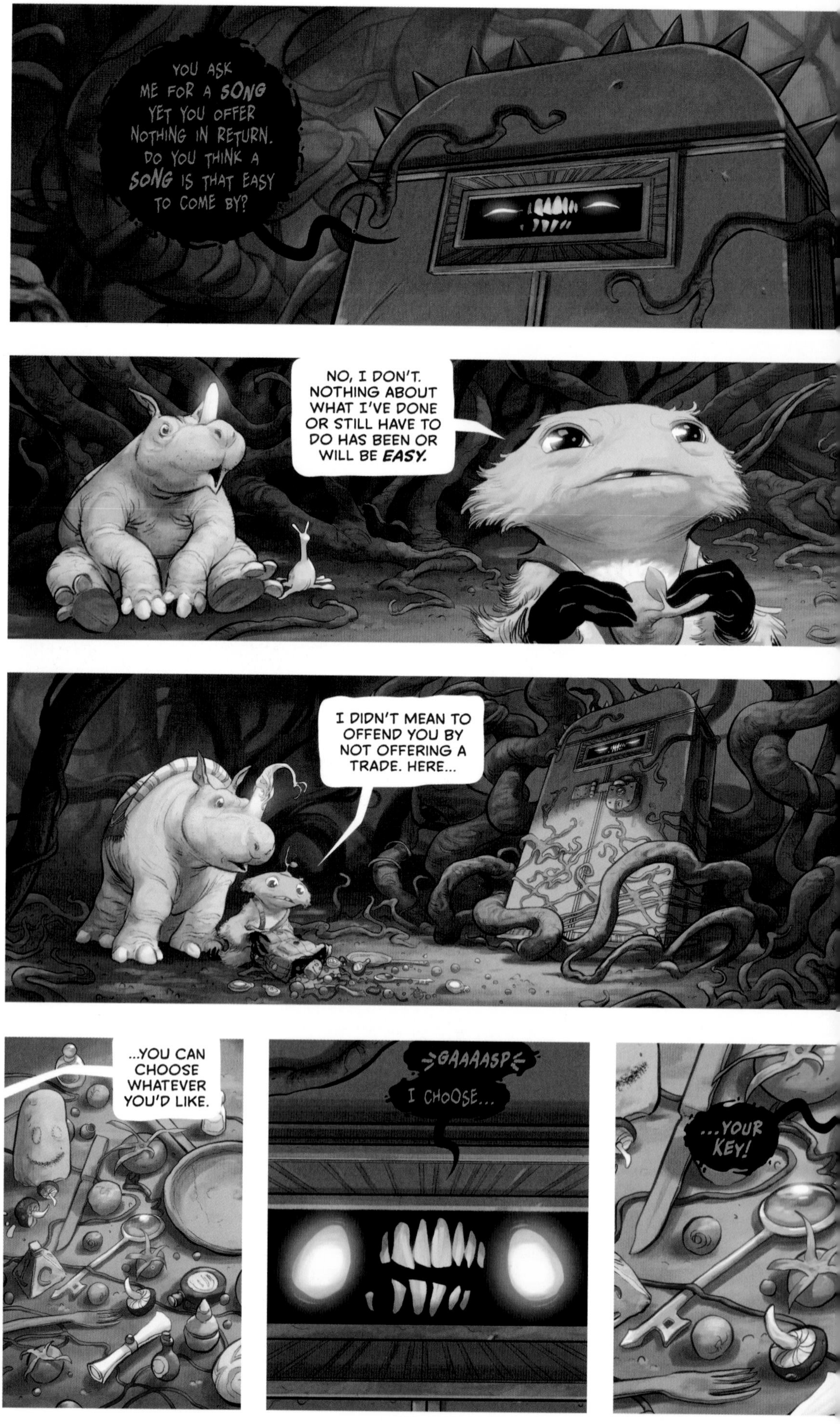
YOU ASK ME FOR A SONG YET YOU OFFER NOTHING IN RETURN. DO YOU THINK A SONG IS THAT EASY TO COME BY?
NO, I DON'T. NOTHING ABOUT WHAT I'VE DONE OR STILL HAVE TO DO HAS BEEN OR WILL BE EASY.
I DIDN'T MEAN TO OFFEND YOU BY NOT OFFERING A TRADE. HERE...
...YOU CAN CHOOSE WHATEVER YOU'D LIKE.
GAAAASP
I CHOOSE...
...YOUR KEY!

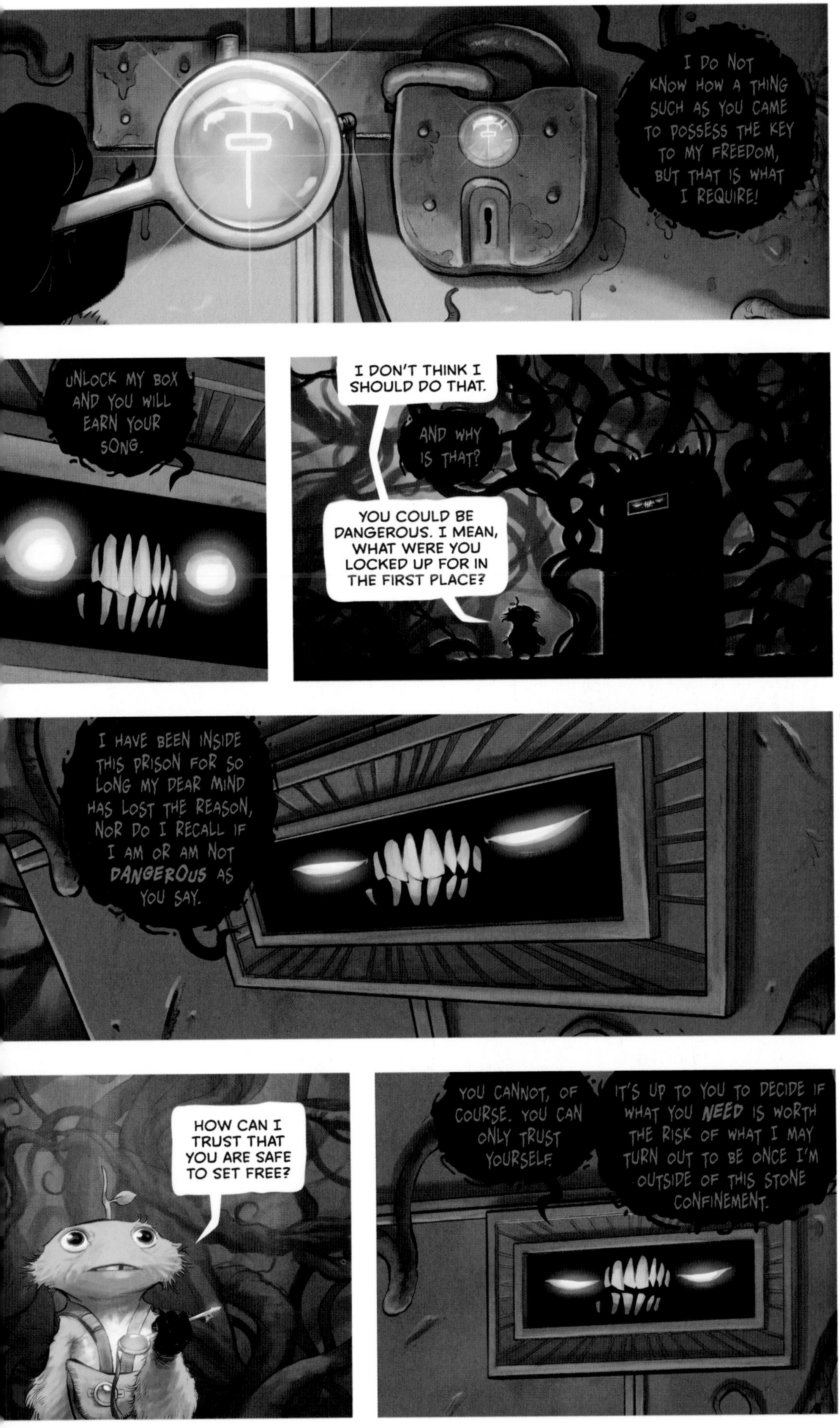
I DO NOT KNOW HOW A THING SUCH AS YOU CAME TO POSSESS THE KEY TO MY FREEDOM, BUT THAT IS WHAT I REQUIRE!
UNLOCK MY BOX AND YOU WILL EARN YOUR SONG.
I DON'T THINK I SHOULD DO THAT.
AND WHY IS THAT?
YOU COULD BE DANGEROUS. I MEAN, WHAT WERE YOU LOCKED UP FOR IN THE FIRST PLACE?
I HAVE BEEN INSIDE THIS PRISON FOR SO LONG MY DEAR MIND HAS LOST THE REASON, NOR DO I RECALL IF I AM OR AM NOT DANGEROUS AS YOU SAY.
HOW CAN I TRUST THAT YOU ARE SAFE TO SET FREE?
YOU CANNOT, OF COURSE. YOU CAN ONLY TRUST YOURSELF.
IT'S UP TO YOU TO DECIDE IF WHAT YOU NEED IS WORTH THE RISK OF WHAT I MAY TURN OUT TO BE ONCE I'M OUTSIDE OF THIS STONE CONFINEMENT.

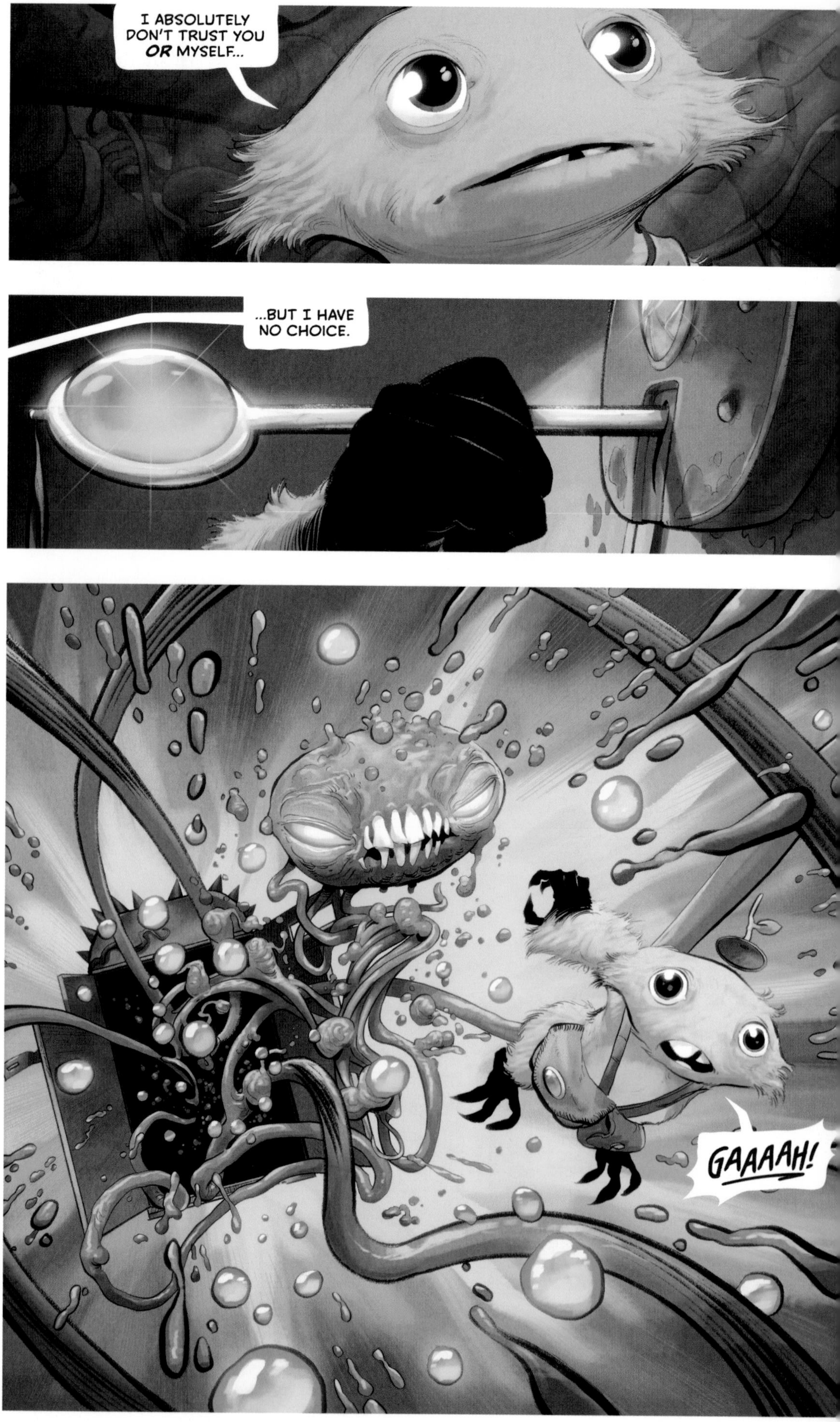
I ABSOLUTELY DON'T TRUST YOU *OR* MYSELF...
...BUT I HAVE NO CHOICE.
GAAAAH!

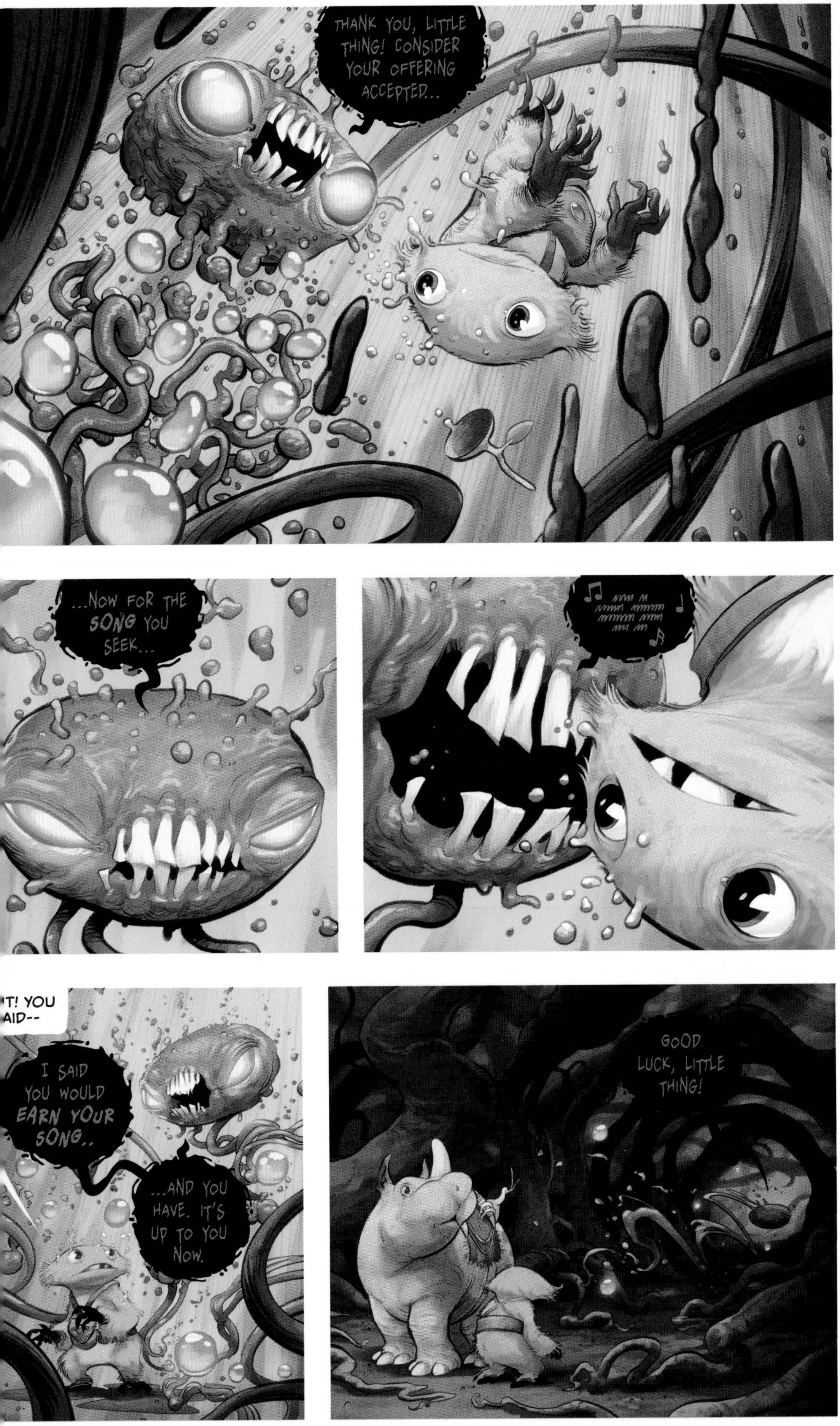

THANK YOU, LITTLE THING! CONSIDER YOUR OFFERING ACCEPTED...
...NOW FOR THE SONG YOU SEEK...
'T! YOU AID--
I SAID YOU WOULD EARN YOUR SONG..
...AND YOU HAVE. IT'S UP TO YOU NOW.
GOOD LUCK, LITTLE THING!

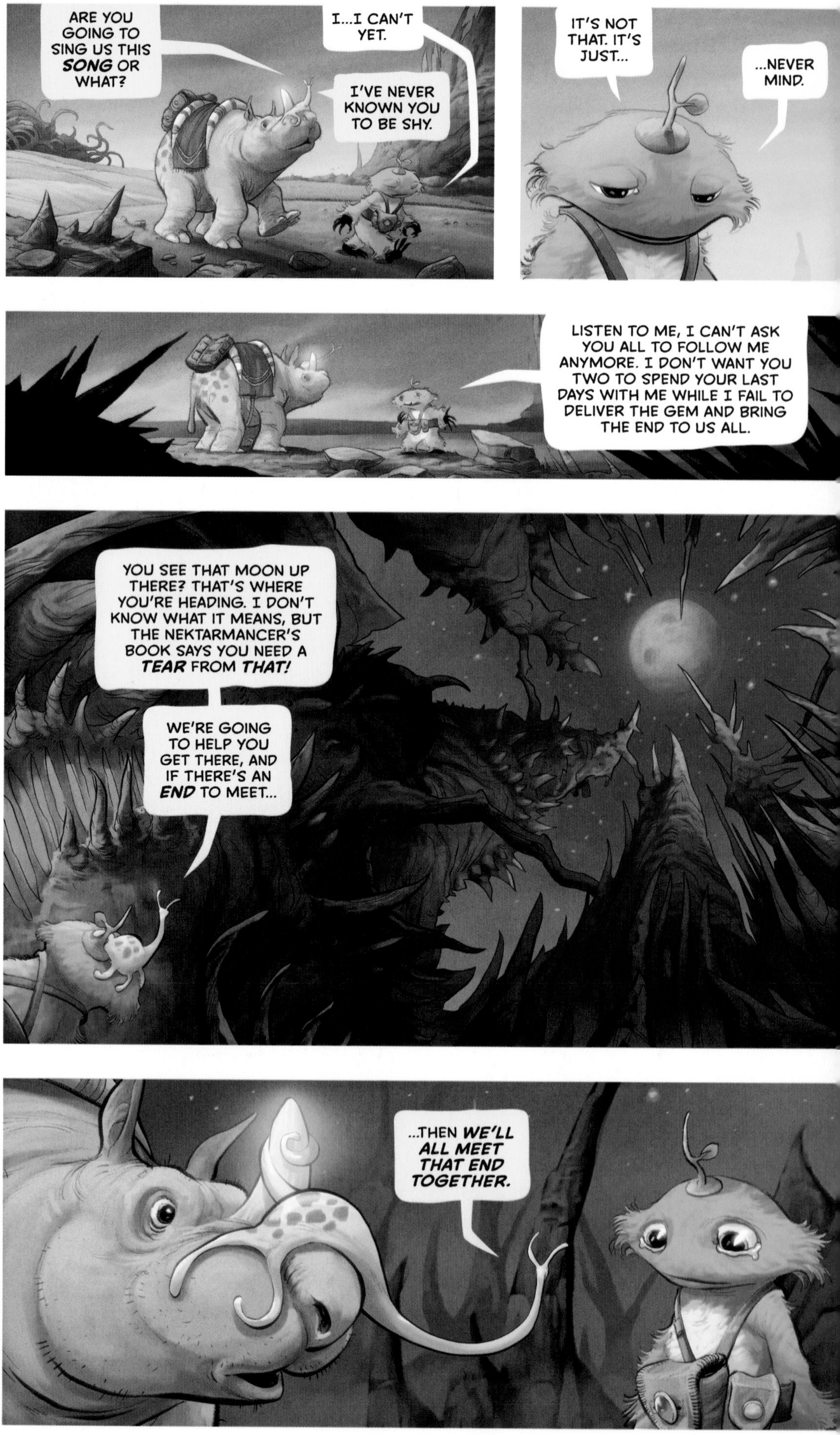

ARE YOU GOING TO SING US THIS ***SONG*** OR WHAT?
I...I CAN'T YET.
I'VE NEVER KNOWN YOU TO BE SHY.
IT'S NOT THAT. IT'S JUST...
...NEVER MIND.
LISTEN TO ME, I CAN'T ASK YOU ALL TO FOLLOW ME ANYMORE. I DON'T WANT YOU TWO TO SPEND YOUR LAST DAYS WITH ME WHILE I FAIL TO DELIVER THE GEM AND BRING THE END TO US ALL.
YOU SEE THAT MOON UP THERE? THAT'S WHERE YOU'RE HEADING. I DON'T KNOW WHAT IT MEANS, BUT THE NEKTARMANCER'S BOOK SAYS YOU NEED A ***TEAR*** FROM ***THAT!***
WE'RE GOING TO HELP YOU GET THERE, AND IF THERE'S AN ***END*** TO MEET...
...THEN ***WE'LL ALL MEET THAT END TOGETHER.***

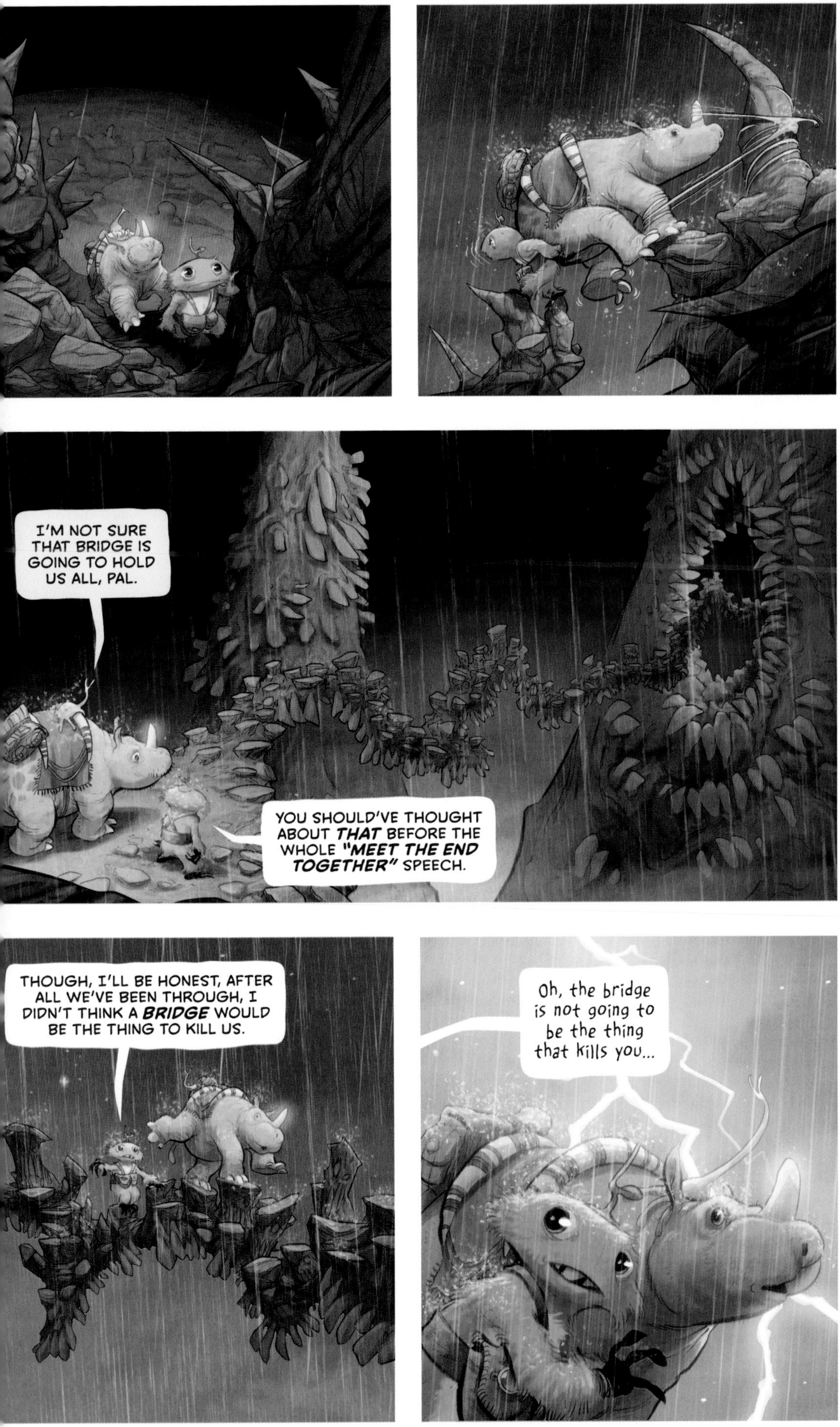
I'M NOT SURE THAT BRIDGE IS GOING TO HOLD US ALL, PAL.
YOU SHOULD'VE THOUGHT ABOUT THAT BEFORE THE WHOLE "MEET THE END TOGETHER" SPEECH.
THOUGH, I'LL BE HONEST, AFTER ALL WE'VE BEEN THROUGH, I DIDN'T THINK A BRIDGE WOULD BE THE THING TO KILL US.
Oh, the bridge is not going to be the thing that kills you...

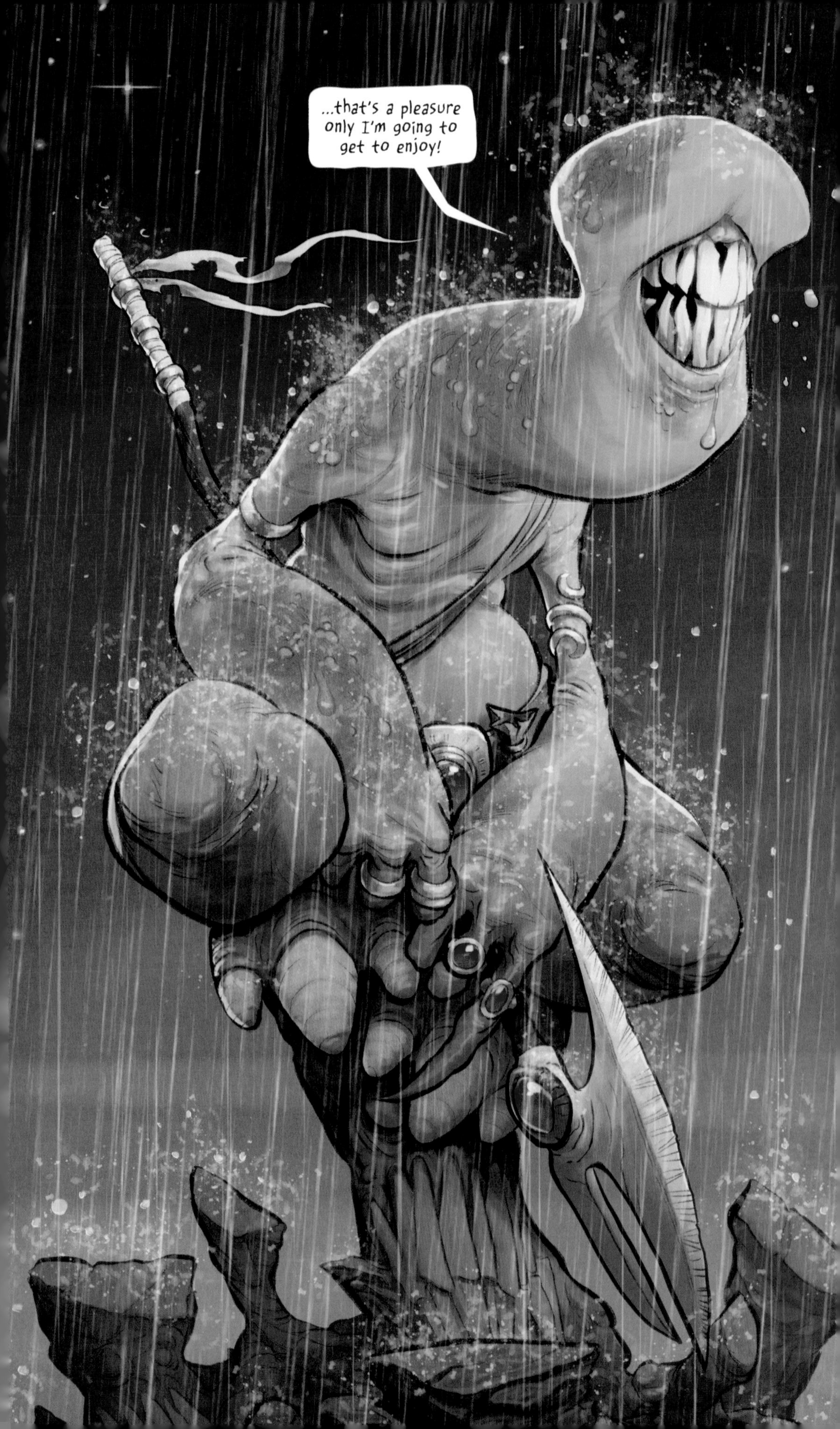
...that's a pleasure only I'm going to get to enjoy!

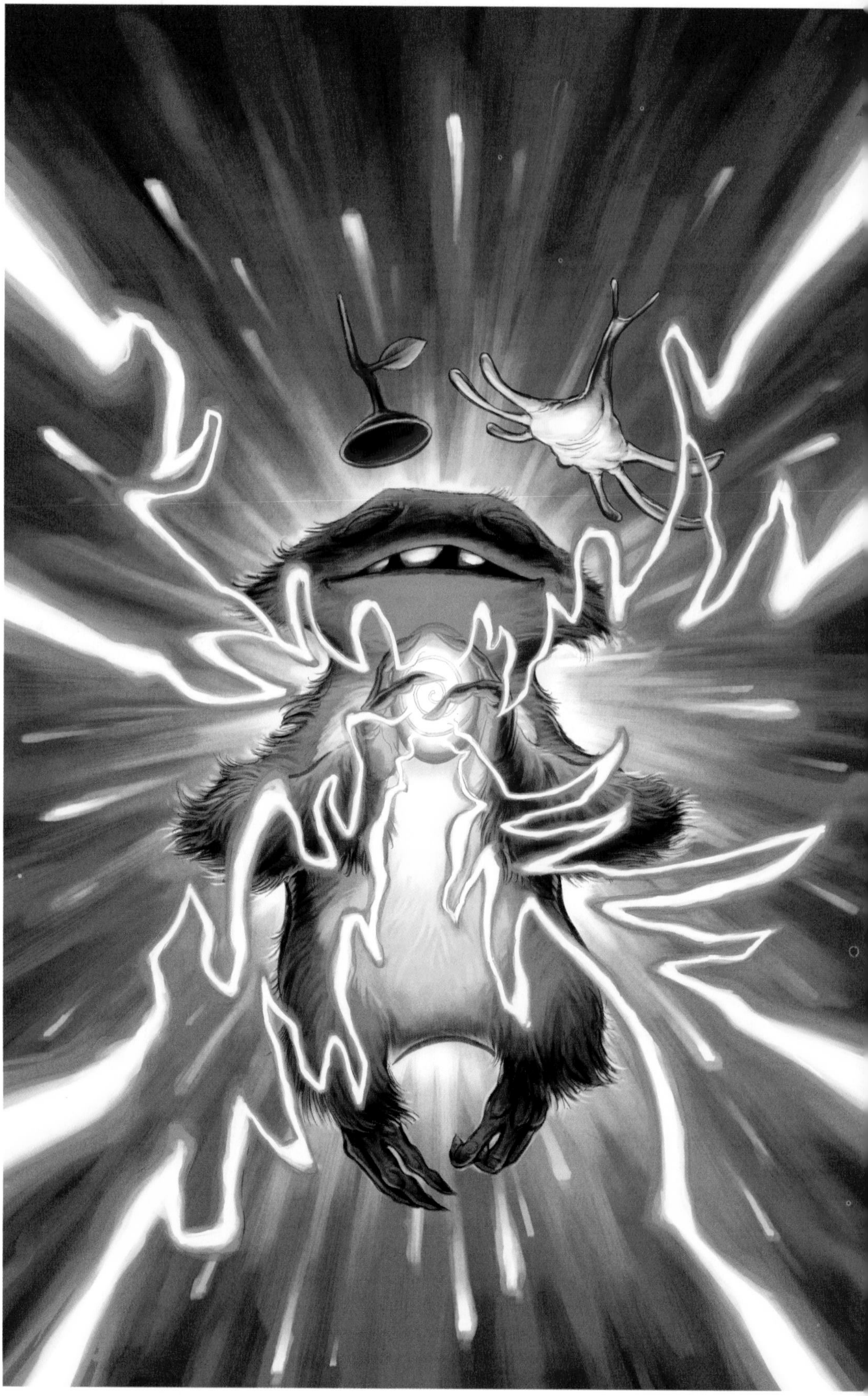

FIVE

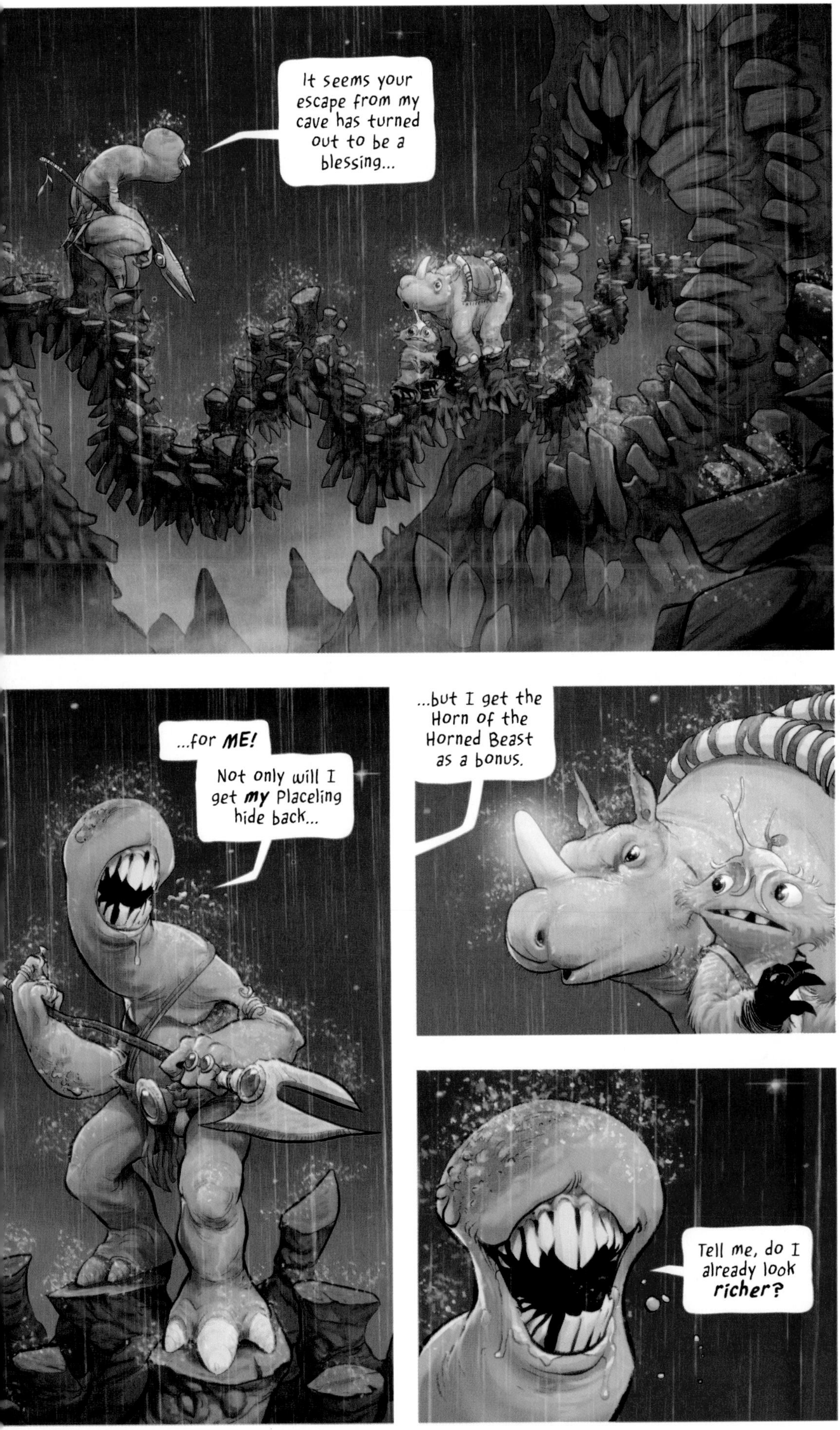
It seems your escape from my cave has turned out to be a blessing...
...for ME!
Not only will I get my Placeling hide back...
...but I get the Horn of the Horned Beast as a bonus.
Tell me, do I already look richer?

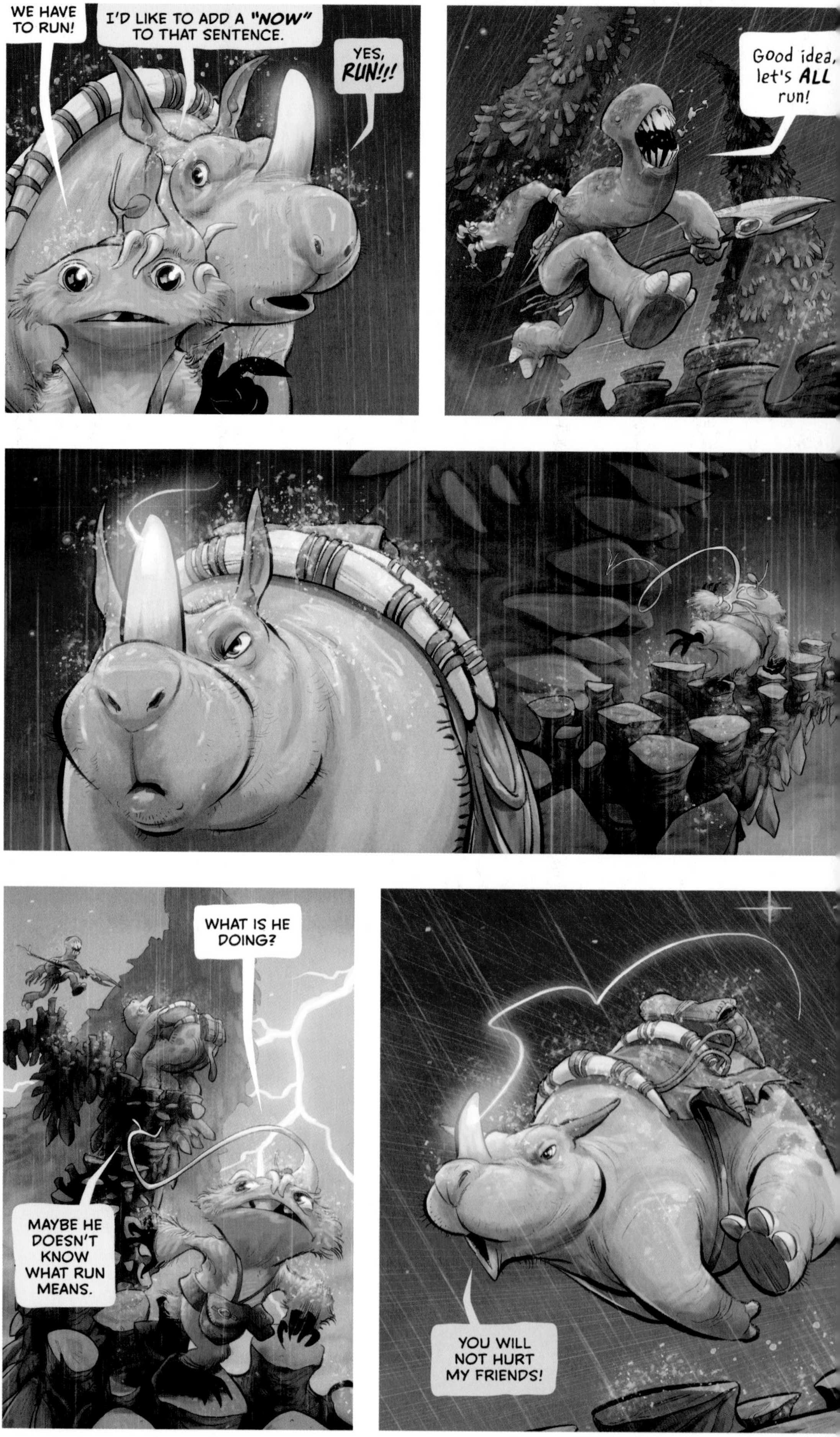
WE HAVE TO RUN!
I'D LIKE TO ADD A "NOW" TO THAT SENTENCE.
YES, RUN!!!
Good idea, let's ALL run!
WHAT IS HE DOING?
MAYBE HE DOESN'T KNOW WHAT RUN MEANS.
YOU WILL NOT HURT MY FRIENDS!

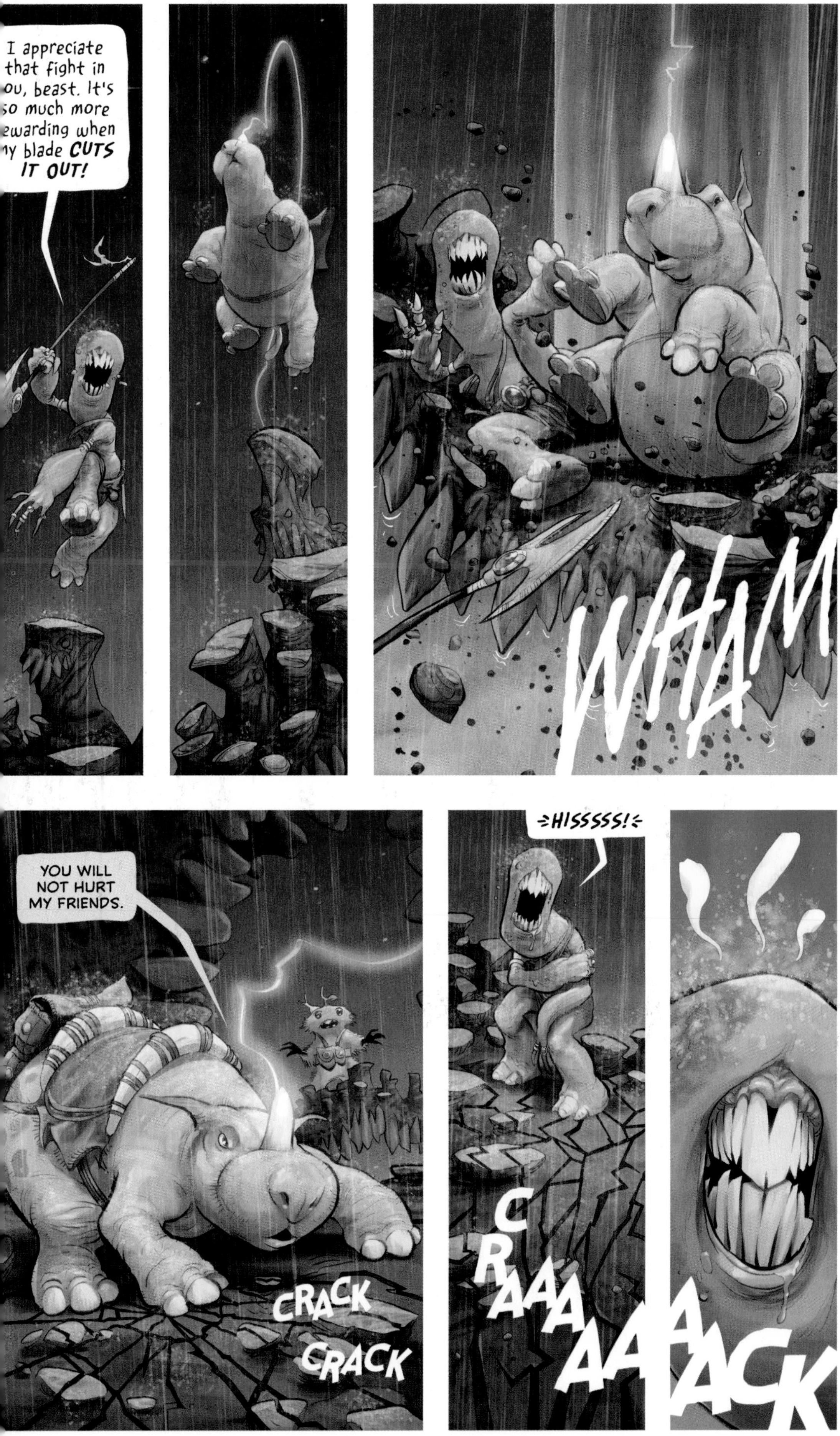

I appreciate that fight in ou, beast. It's so much more ewarding when ny blade CUTS IT OUT!
WHAM
YOU WILL NOT HURT MY FRIENDS.
CRACK
CRACK
HISSSSS!
CRAAAAAAAACK

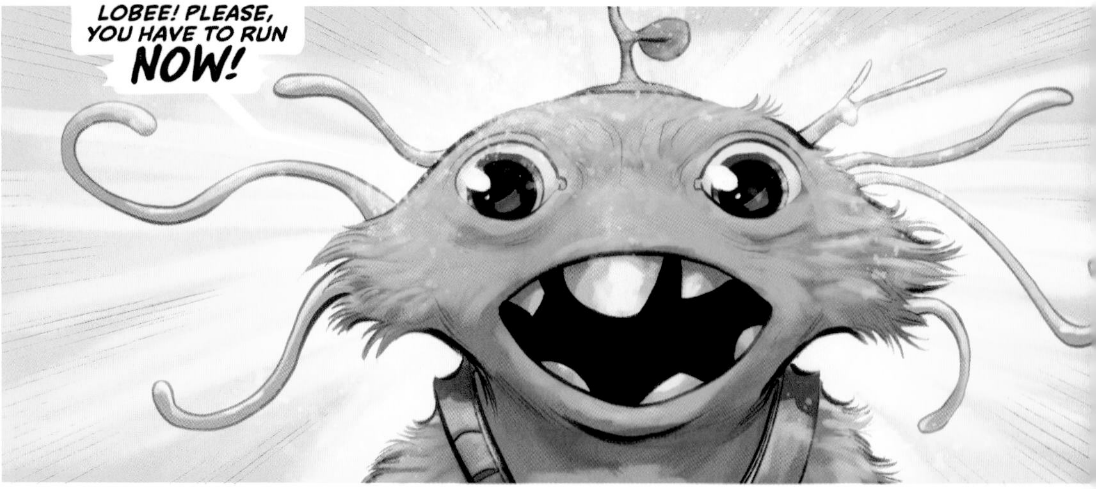
LOBEE! PLEASE, YOU HAVE TO RUN NOW!

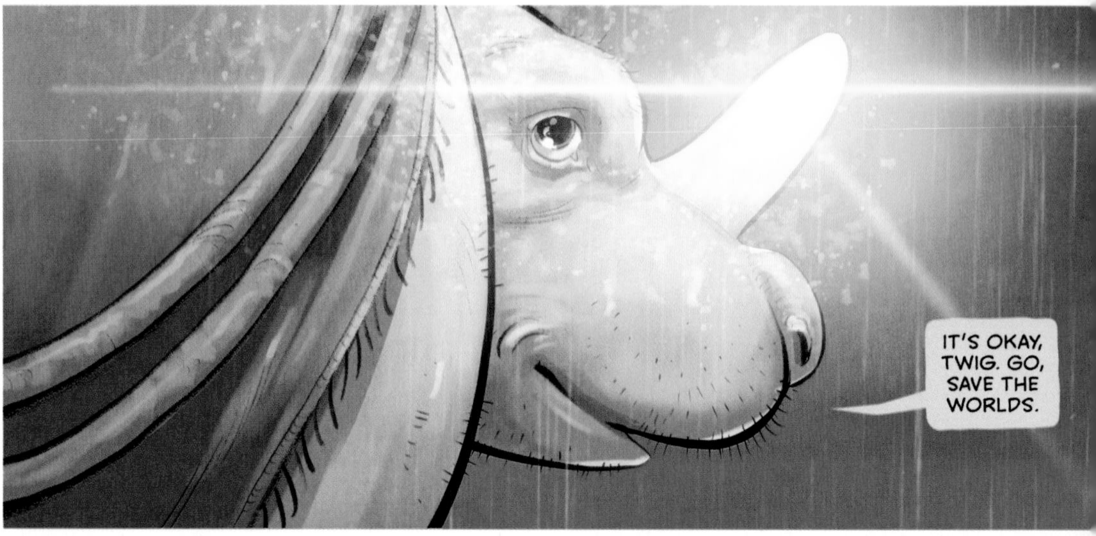
IT'S OKAY, TWIG. GO, SAVE THE WORLDS.

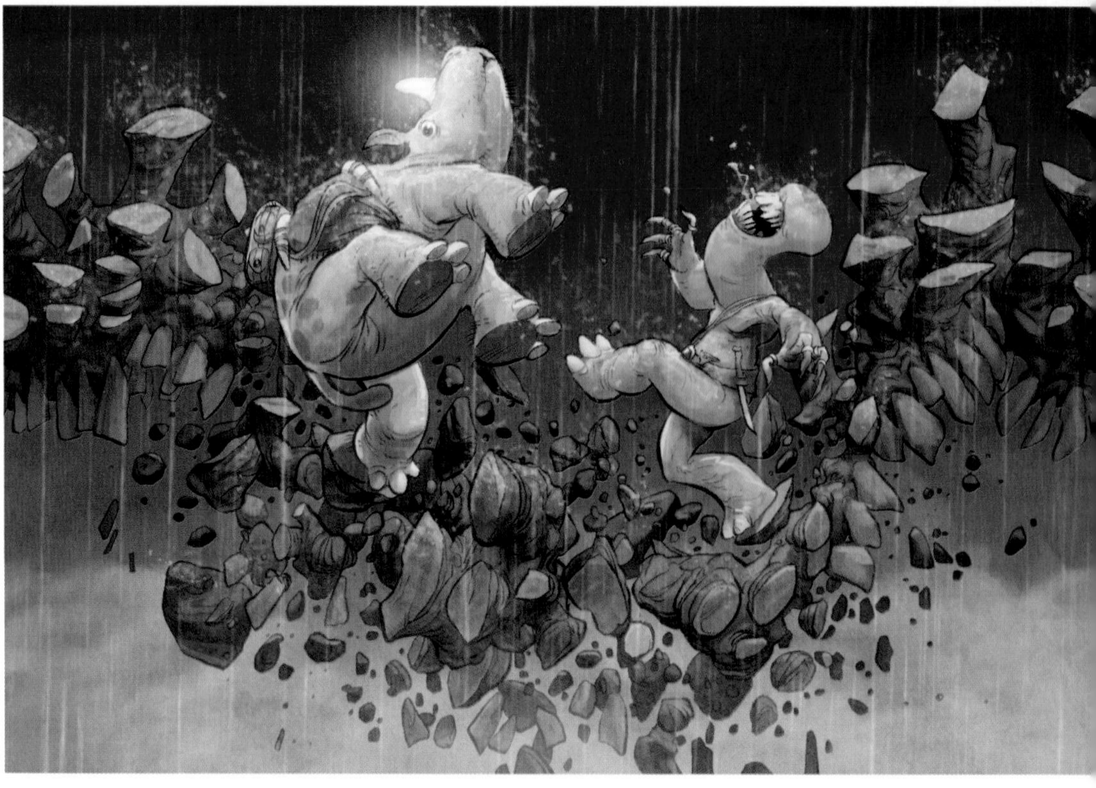

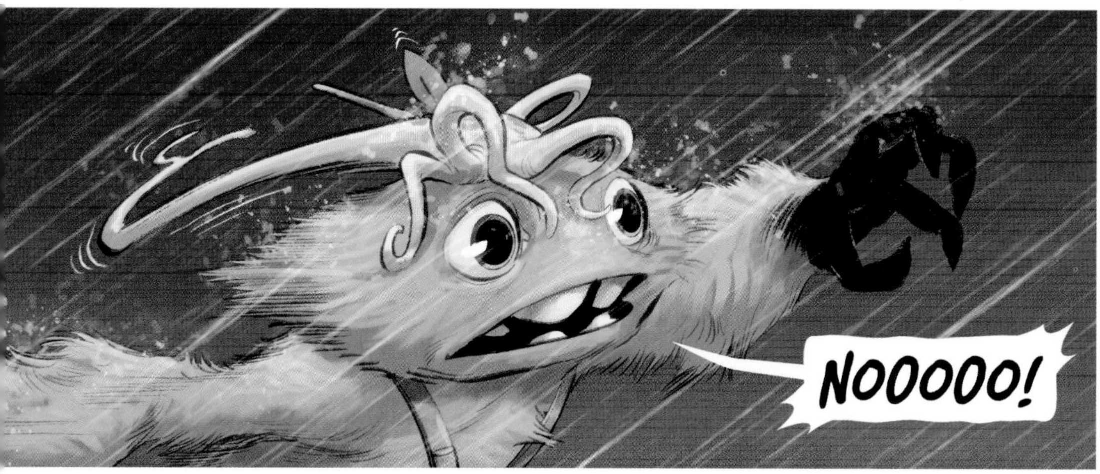
NOOOOO!

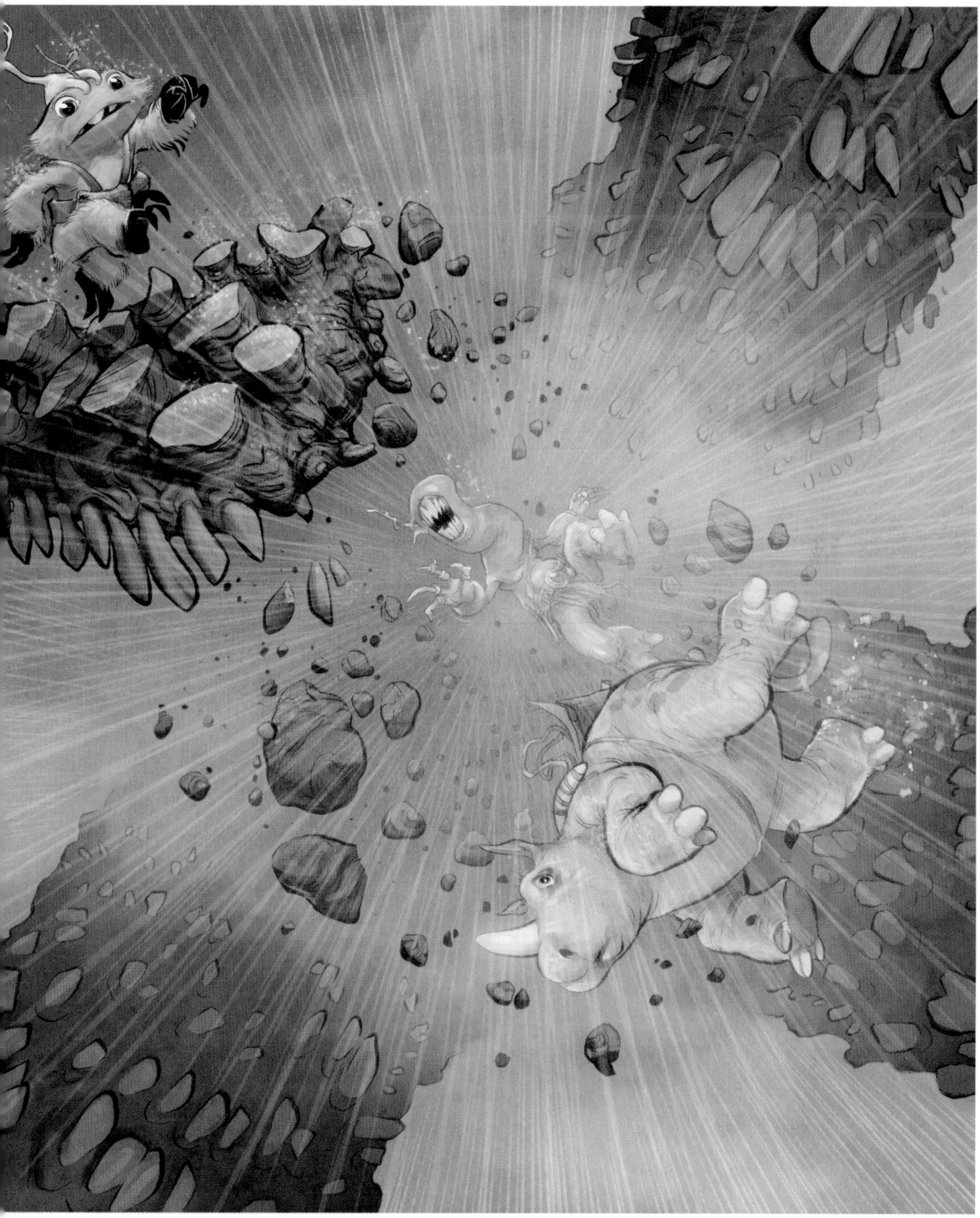

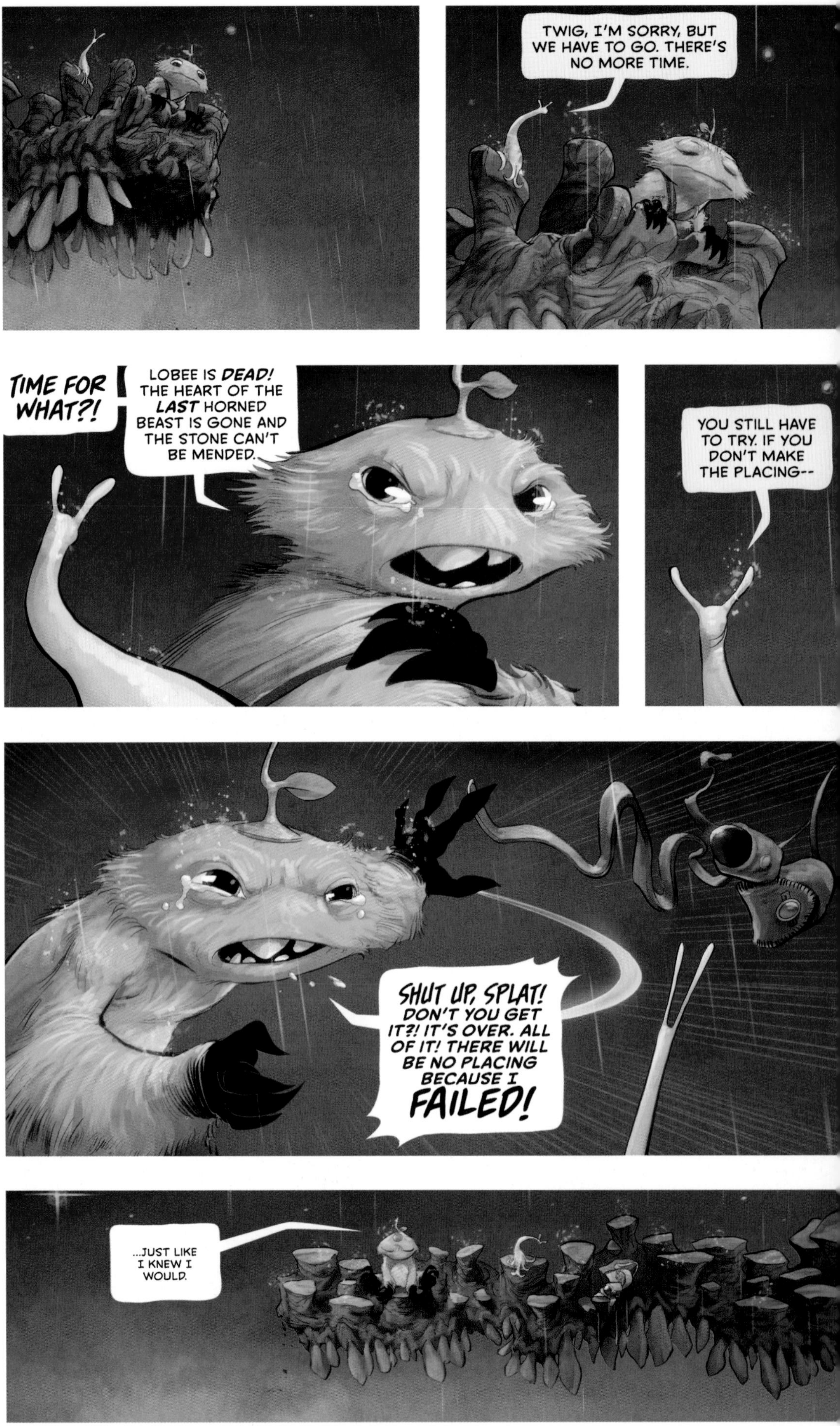

TWIG, I'M SORRY, BUT WE HAVE TO GO. THERE'S NO MORE TIME.
TIME FOR WHAT?!
LOBEE IS DEAD! THE HEART OF THE LAST HORNED BEAST IS GONE AND THE STONE CAN'T BE MENDED.
YOU STILL HAVE TO TRY. IF YOU DON'T MAKE THE PLACING--
SHUT UP, SPLAT! DON'T YOU GET IT?! IT'S OVER. ALL OF IT! THERE WILL BE NO PLACING BECAUSE I FAILED!
...JUST LIKE I KNEW I WOULD.

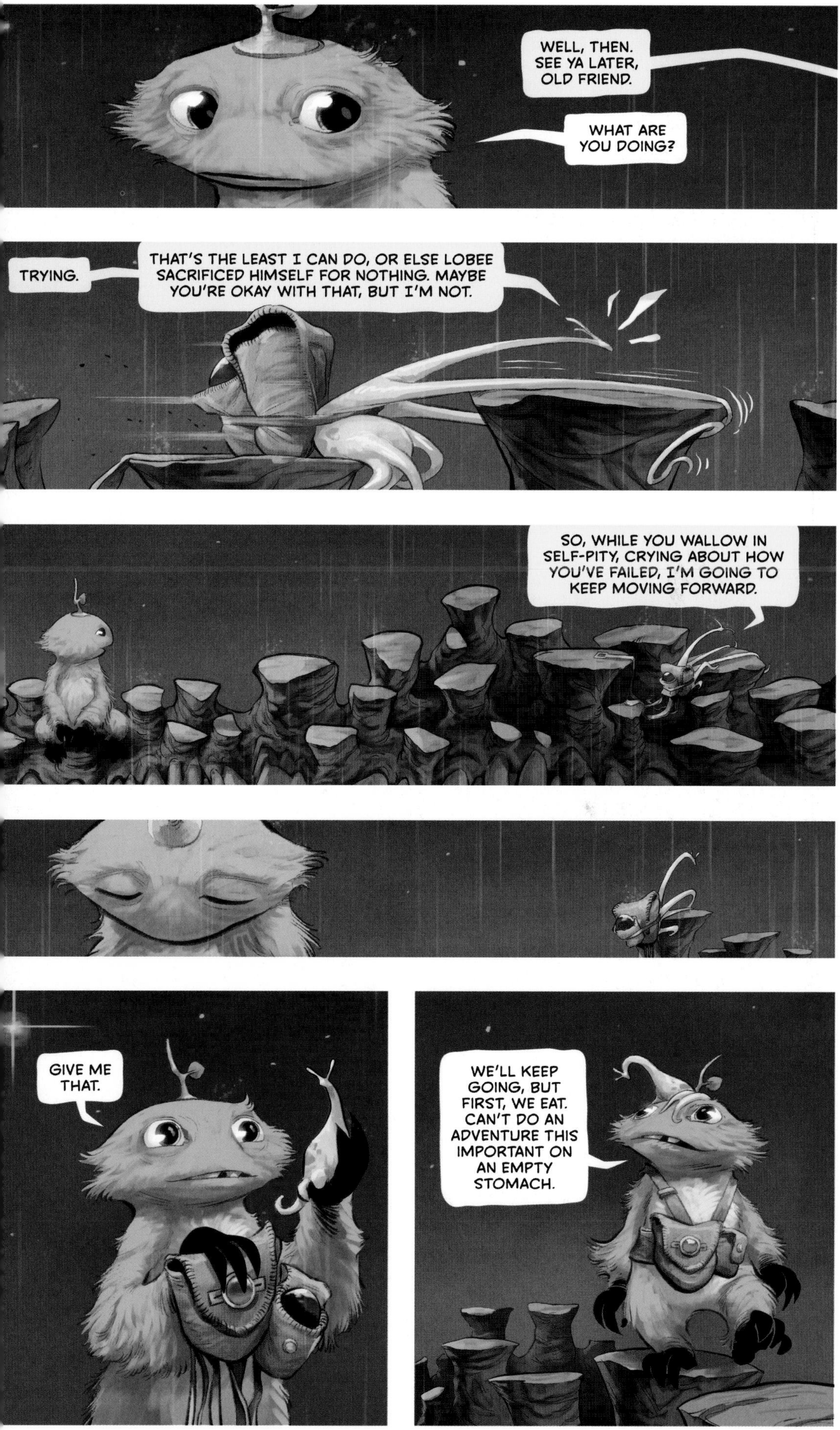
WELL, THEN. SEE YA LATER, OLD FRIEND.
WHAT ARE YOU DOING?
TRYING.
THAT'S THE LEAST I CAN DO, OR ELSE LOBEE SACRIFICED HIMSELF FOR NOTHING. MAYBE YOU'RE OKAY WITH THAT, BUT I'M NOT.
SO, WHILE YOU WALLOW IN SELF-PITY, CRYING ABOUT HOW YOU'VE FAILED, I'M GOING TO KEEP MOVING FORWARD.
GIVE ME THAT.
WE'LL KEEP GOING, BUT FIRST, WE EAT. CAN'T DO AN ADVENTURE THIS IMPORTANT ON AN EMPTY STOMACH.

WHAT'S ON THE MENU THIS EVENING?

I FOUND SOME POWDER OF PEEZER PETAL AND A NEST THAT HAD A BIT OF YOMO YEAST.

DON'T TELL ME YOU'RE MAKING AN IZIPA FLAT!

YES, I AM. EV[E]... TIME MY FAT[HER] RETURNED FR[OM] A PLACING, M[Y] MOTHER WOU[LD] MAKE HIM ON[E].

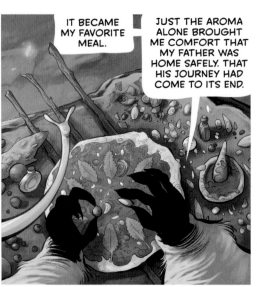

IT BECAME MY FAVORITE MEAL.

JUST THE AROMA ALONE BROUGHT ME COMFORT THAT MY FATHER WAS HOME SAFELY. THAT HIS JOURNEY HAD COME TO ITS END.

SINCE WE DON'T KNOW IF WE'LL EVER BE MAKING IT HOME, SAFELY OR OTHERWISE, I THOUGHT IT WOULD BE FITTING TO PREPARE THE SAME MEAL FOR US...

...SO WE CAN ENJOY IT BEFORE OUR WORLD IS IN DARKNESS.

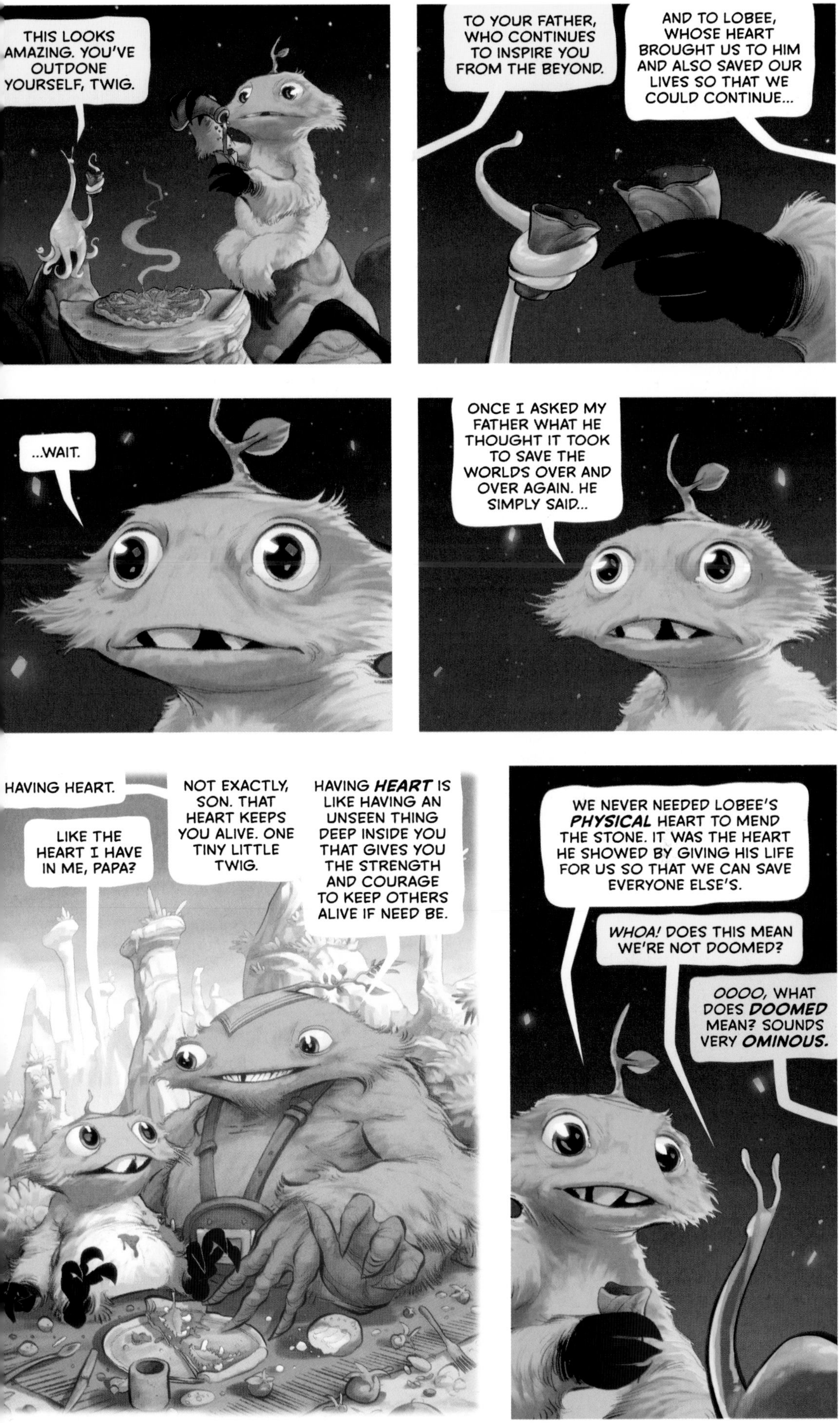
THIS LOOKS AMAZING. YOU'VE OUTDONE YOURSELF, TWIG.
TO YOUR FATHER, WHO CONTINUES TO INSPIRE YOU FROM THE BEYOND.
AND TO LOBEE, WHOSE HEART BROUGHT US TO HIM AND ALSO SAVED OUR LIVES SO THAT WE COULD CONTINUE...
...WAIT.
ONCE I ASKED MY FATHER WHAT HE THOUGHT IT TOOK TO SAVE THE WORLDS OVER AND OVER AGAIN. HE SIMPLY SAID...
HAVING HEART.
LIKE THE HEART I HAVE IN ME, PAPA?
NOT EXACTLY, SON. THAT HEART KEEPS YOU ALIVE. ONE TINY LITTLE TWIG.
HAVING *HEART* IS LIKE HAVING AN UNSEEN THING DEEP INSIDE YOU THAT GIVES YOU THE STRENGTH AND COURAGE TO KEEP OTHERS ALIVE IF NEED BE.
WE NEVER NEEDED LOBEE'S *PHYSICAL* HEART TO MEND THE STONE. IT WAS THE HEART HE SHOWED BY GIVING HIS LIFE FOR US SO THAT WE CAN SAVE EVERYONE ELSE'S.
WHOA! DOES THIS MEAN WE'RE NOT DOOMED?
OOOO, WHAT DOES *DOOMED* MEAN? SOUNDS VERY *OMINOUS*.

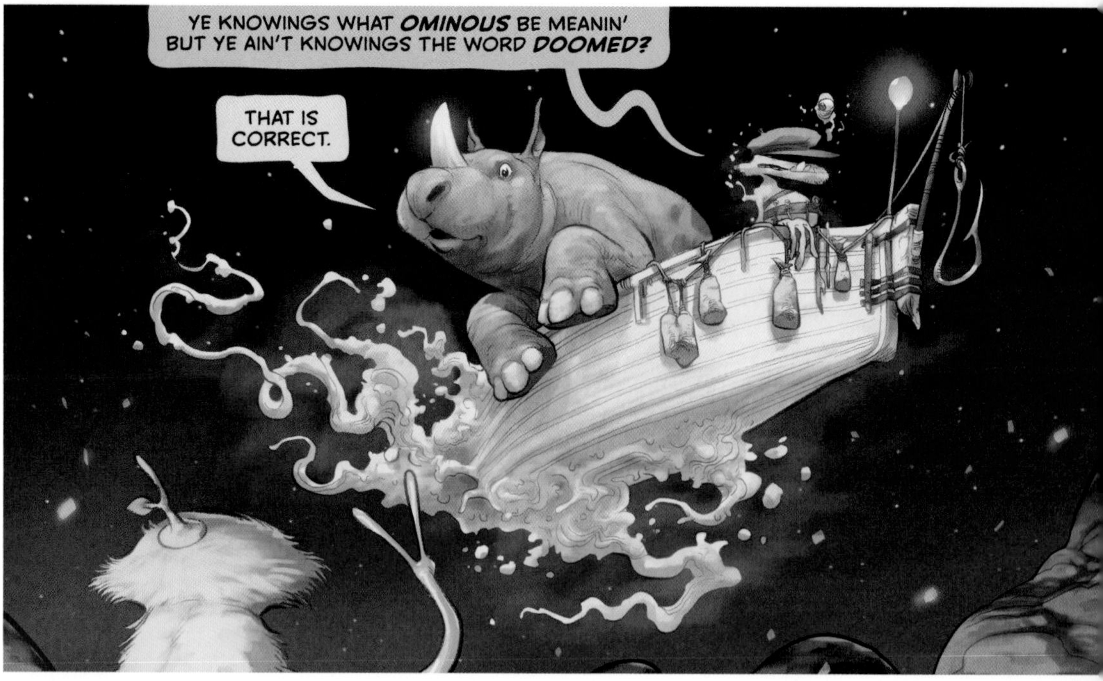
YE KNOWINGS WHAT *OMINOUS* BE MEANIN' BUT YE AIN'T KNOWINGS THE WORD ***DOOMED?***
THAT IS CORRECT.

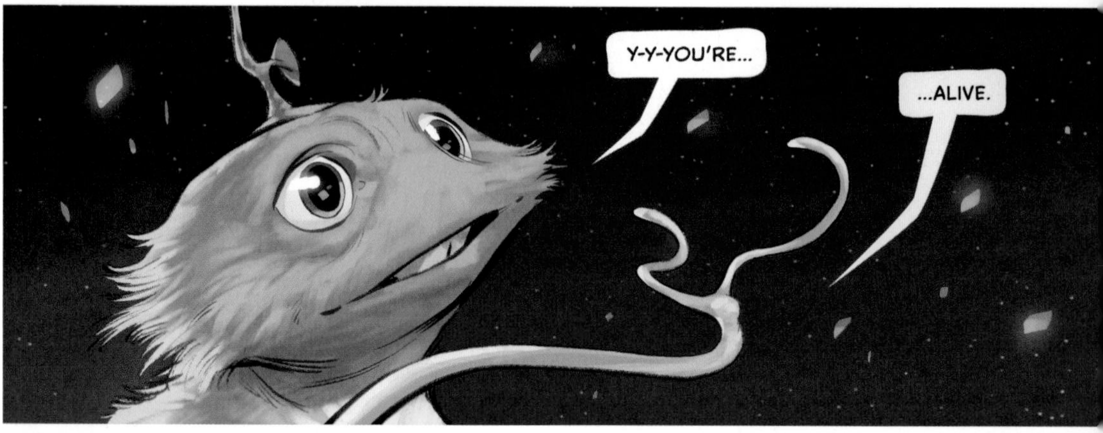
Y-Y-YOU'RE...
...ALIVE.

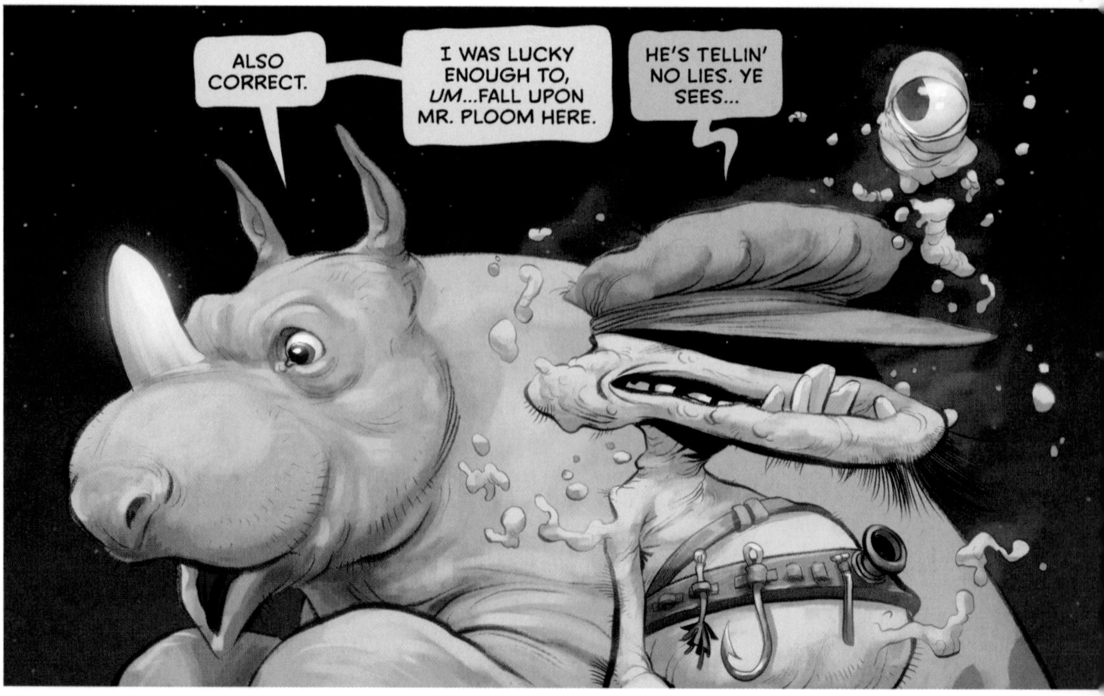
ALSO CORRECT.
I WAS LUCKY ENOUGH TO, *UM*...FALL UPON MR. PLOOM HERE.
HE'S TELLIN' NO LIES. YE SEES...

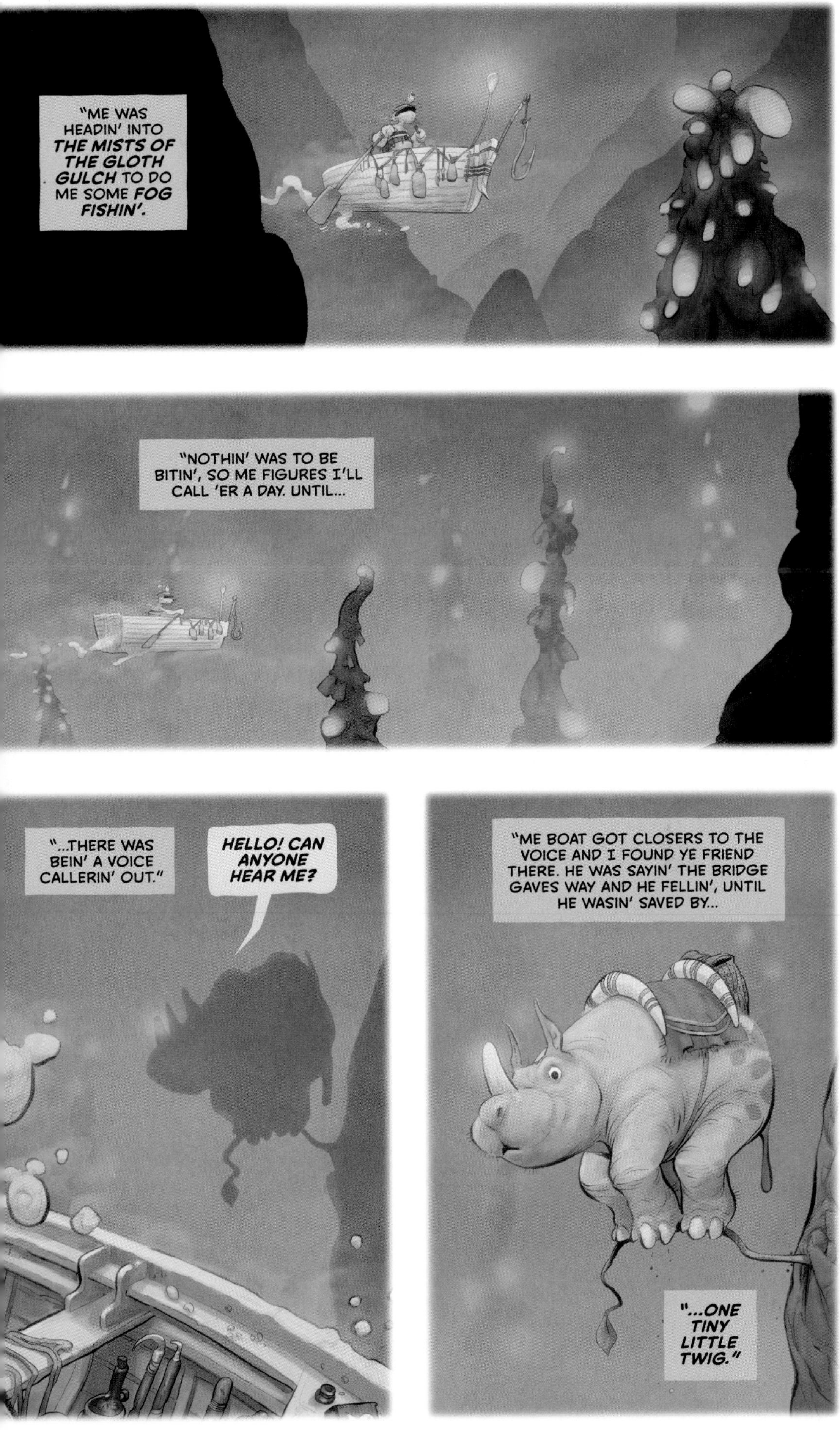
"ME WAS HEADIN' INTO THE MISTS OF THE GLOTH GULCH TO DO ME SOME FOG FISHIN'.
"NOTHIN' WAS TO BE BITIN', SO ME FIGURES I'LL CALL 'ER A DAY. UNTIL...
"...THERE WAS BEIN' A VOICE CALLERIN' OUT."
HELLO! CAN ANYONE HEAR ME?
"ME BOAT GOT CLOSERS TO THE VOICE AND I FOUND YE FRIEND THERE. HE WAS SAYIN' THE BRIDGE GAVES WAY AND HE FELLIN', UNTIL HE WASIN' SAVED BY...
"...ONE TINY LITTLE TWIG."

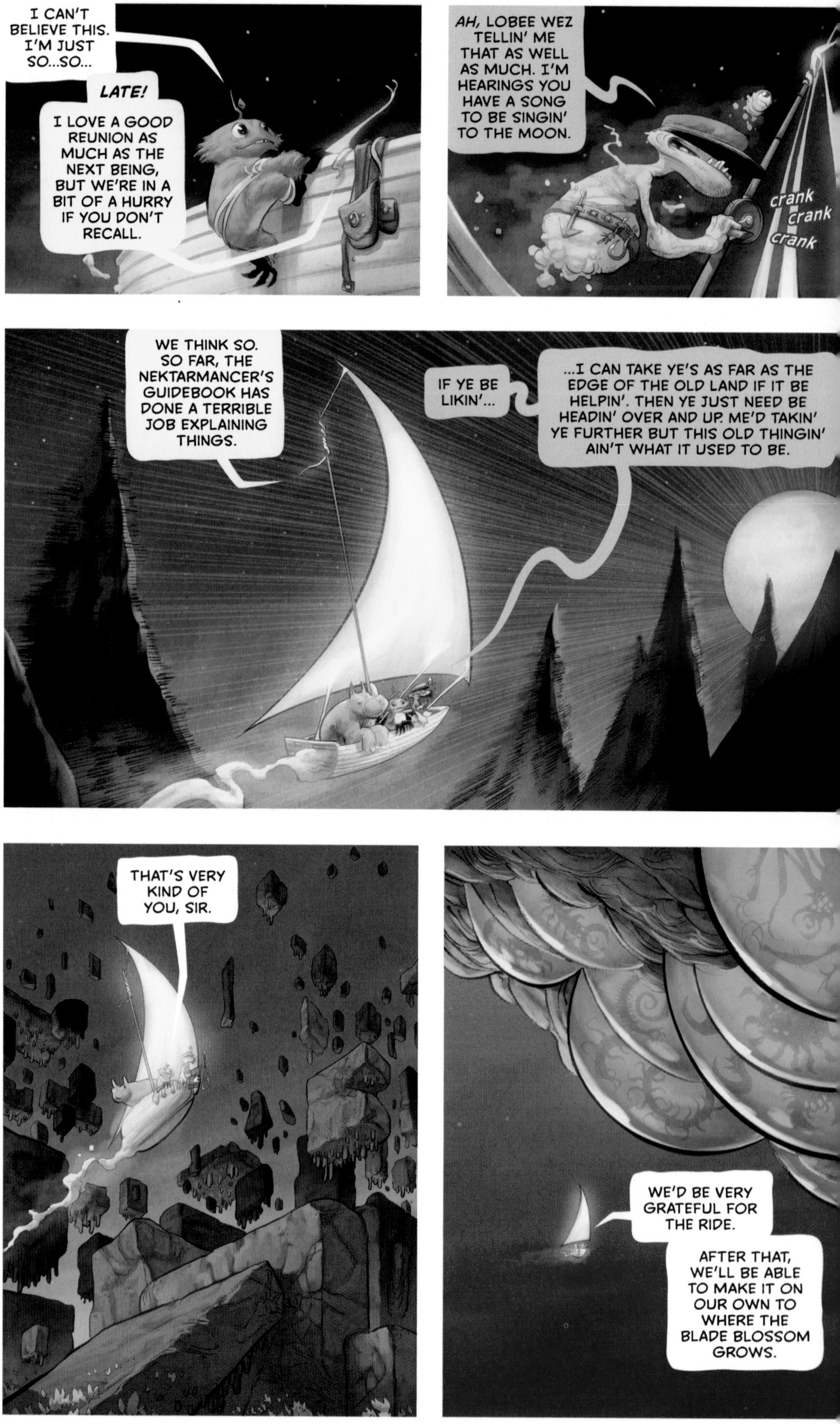

I CAN'T BELIEVE THIS. I'M JUST SO...SO...
LATE!
I LOVE A GOOD REUNION AS MUCH AS THE NEXT BEING, BUT WE'RE IN A BIT OF A HURRY IF YOU DON'T RECALL.
AH, LOBEE WEZ TELLIN' ME THAT AS WELL AS MUCH. I'M HEARINGS YOU HAVE A SONG TO BE SINGIN' TO THE MOON.
crank crank crank
WE THINK SO. SO FAR, THE NEKTARMANCER'S GUIDEBOOK HAS DONE A TERRIBLE JOB EXPLAINING THINGS.
IF YE BE LIKIN'...
...I CAN TAKE YE'S AS FAR AS THE EDGE OF THE OLD LAND IF IT BE HELPIN'. THEN YE JUST NEED BE HEADIN' OVER AND UP. ME'D TAKIN' YE FURTHER BUT THIS OLD THINGIN' AIN'T WHAT IT USED TO BE.
THAT'S VERY KIND OF YOU, SIR.
WE'D BE VERY GRATEFUL FOR THE RIDE.
AFTER THAT, WE'LL BE ABLE TO MAKE IT ON OUR OWN TO WHERE THE BLADE BLOSSOM GROWS.

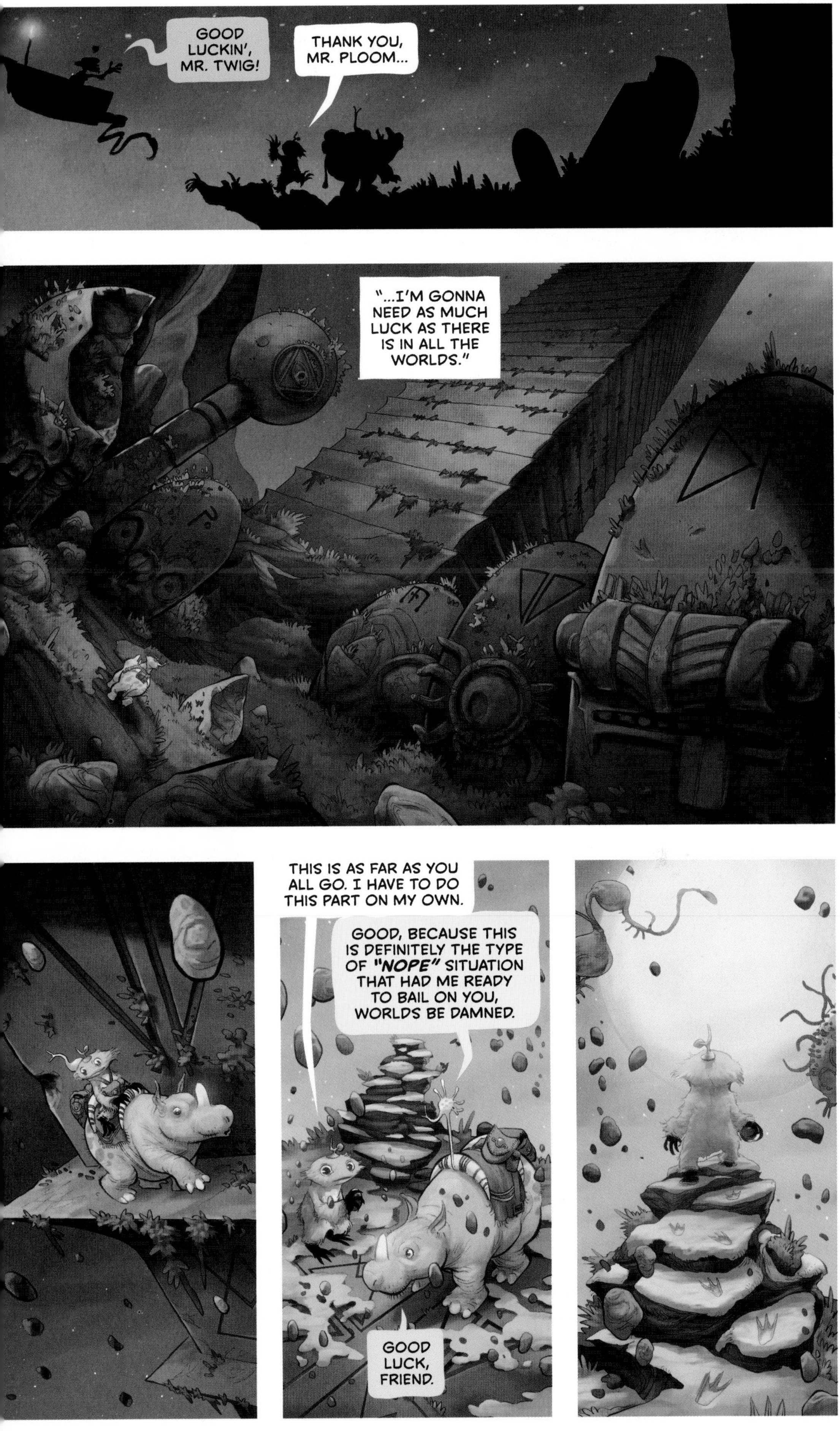
GOOD LUCKIN', MR. TWIG!
THANK YOU, MR. PLOOM...
"...I'M GONNA NEED AS MUCH LUCK AS THERE IS IN ALL THE WORLDS."
THIS IS AS FAR AS YOU ALL GO. I HAVE TO DO THIS PART ON MY OWN.
GOOD, BECAUSE THIS IS DEFINITELY THE TYPE OF "NOPE" SITUATION THAT HAD ME READY TO BAIL ON YOU, WORLDS BE DAMNED.
GOOD LUCK, FRIEND.

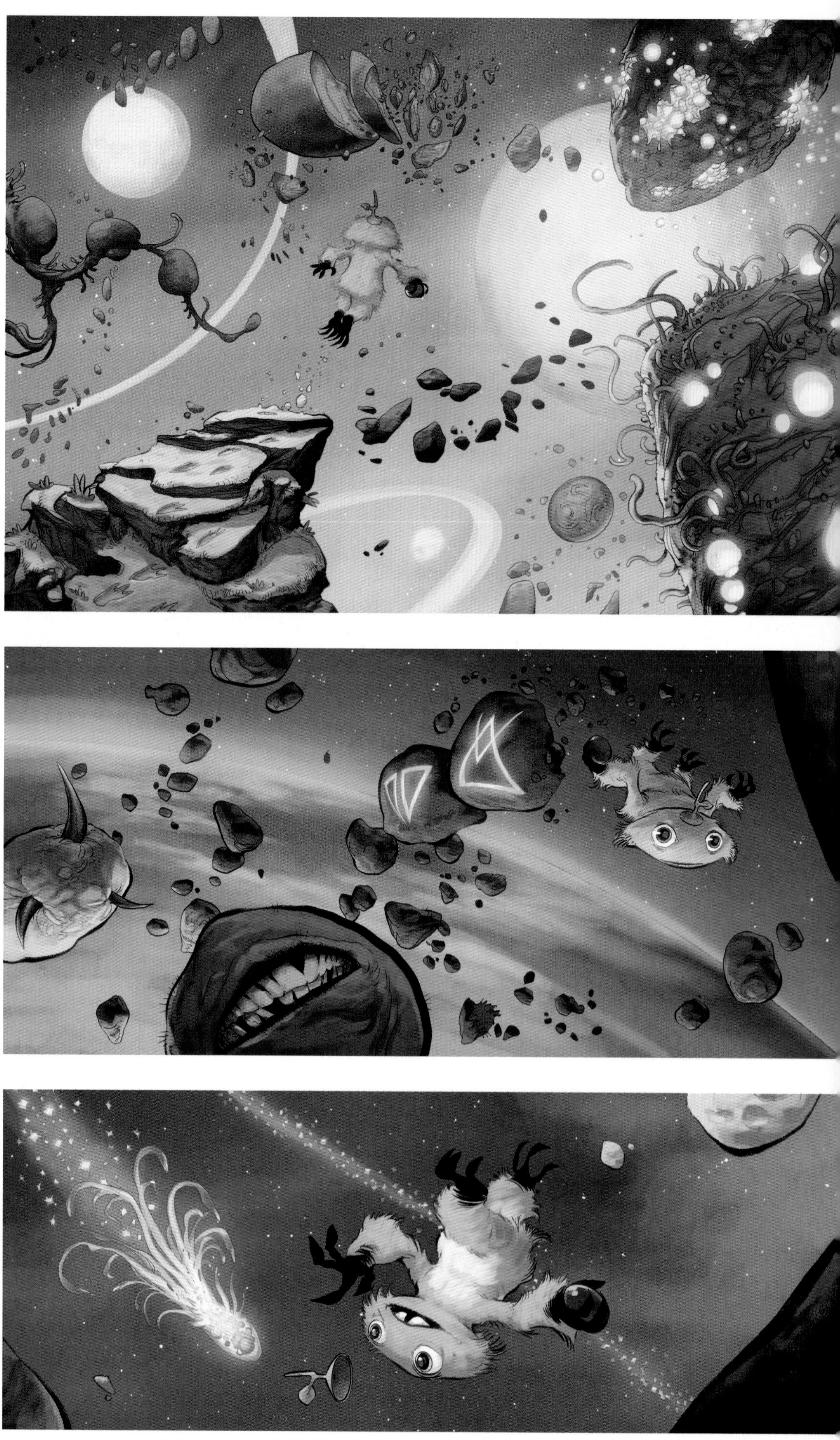

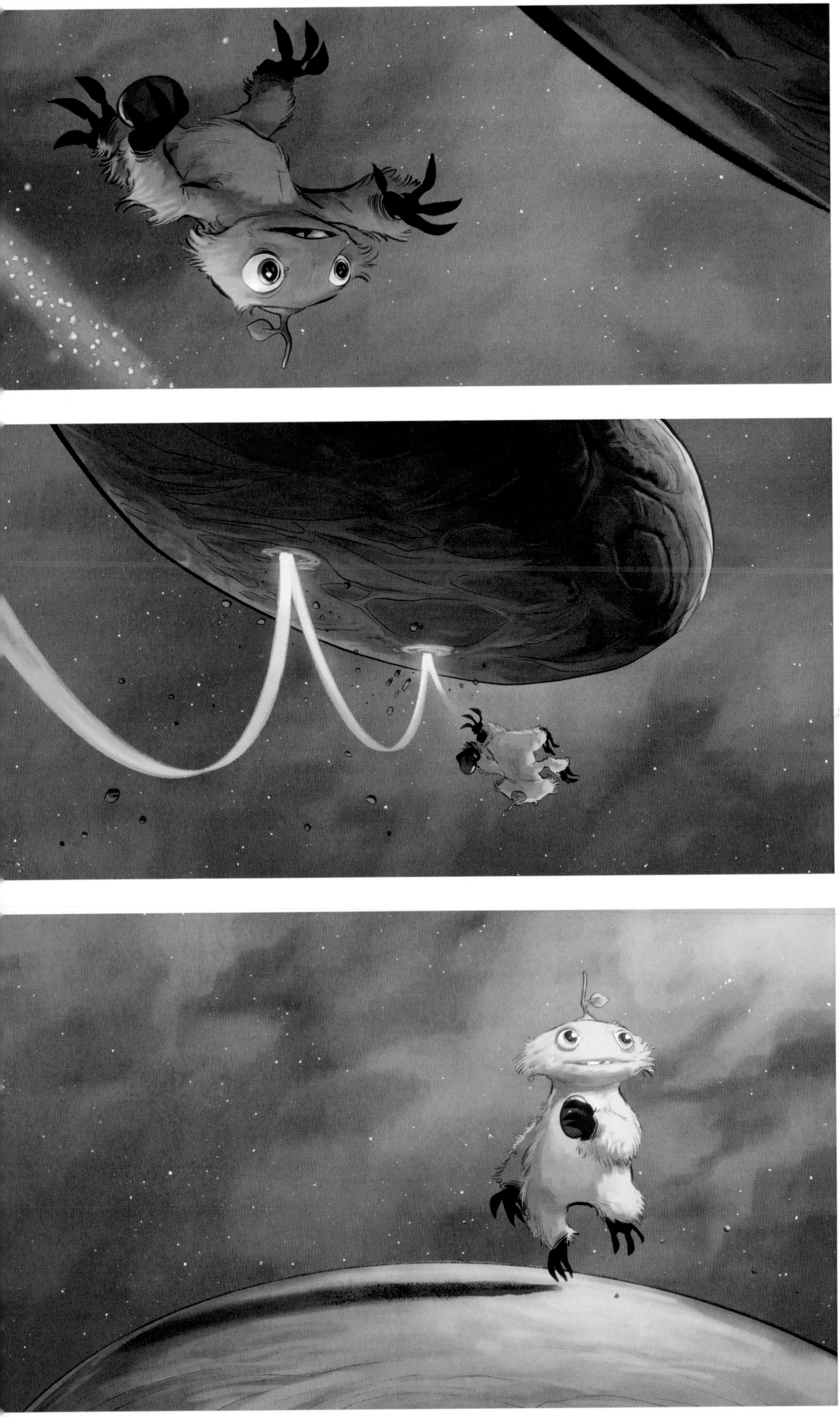

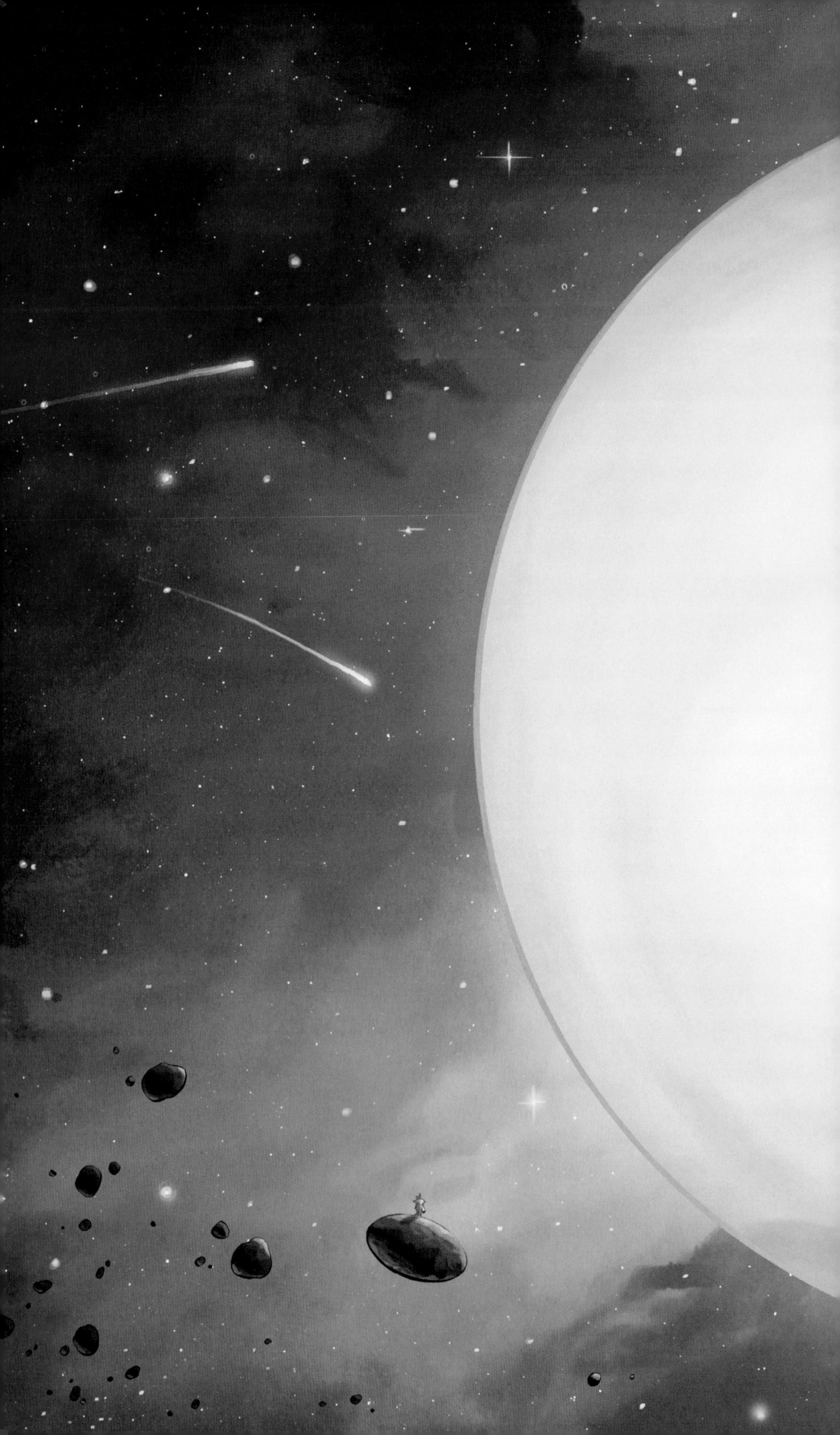

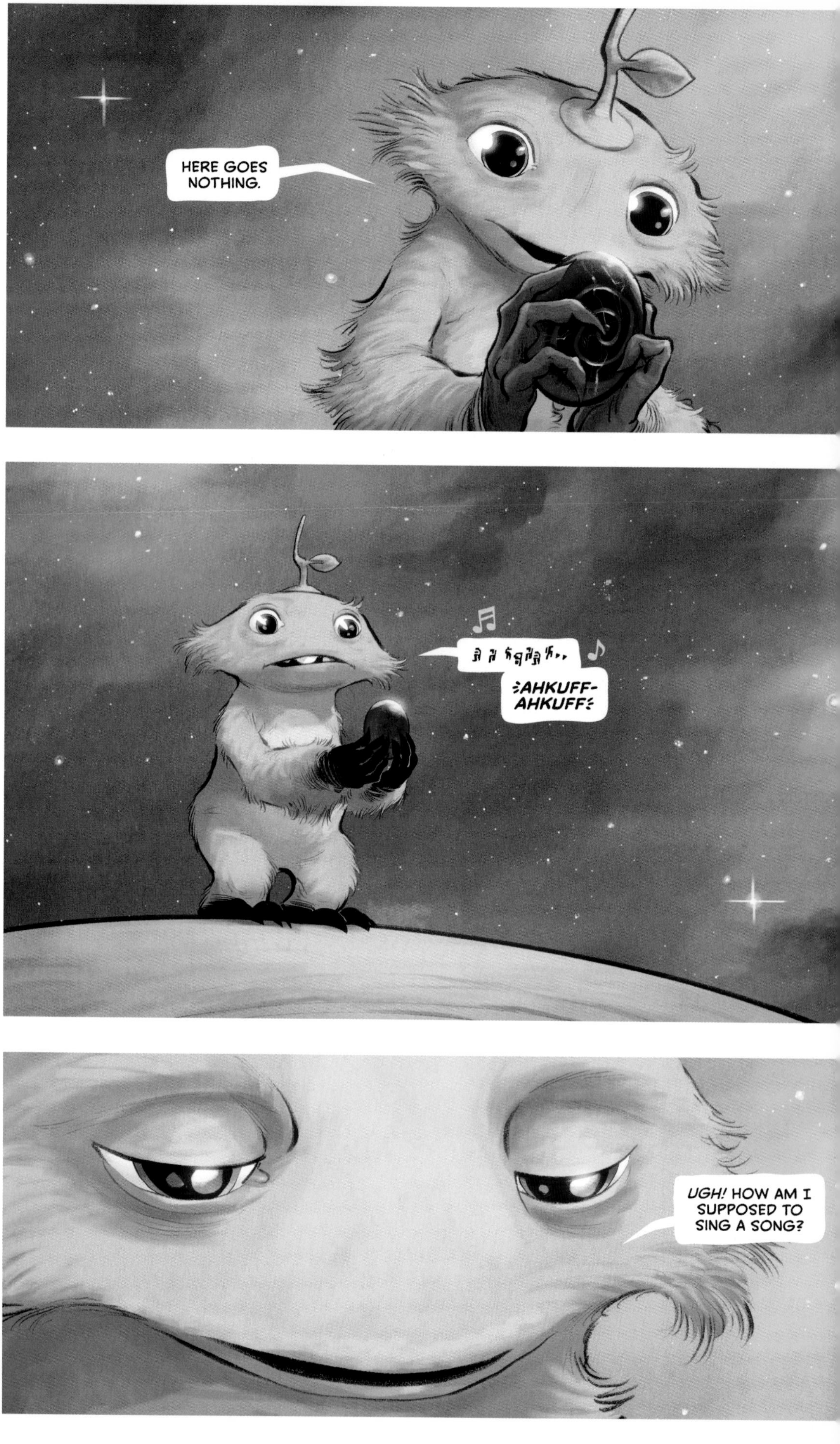
HERE GOES NOTHING.
AHKUFF-AHKUFF
UGH! HOW AM I SUPPOSED TO SING A SONG?

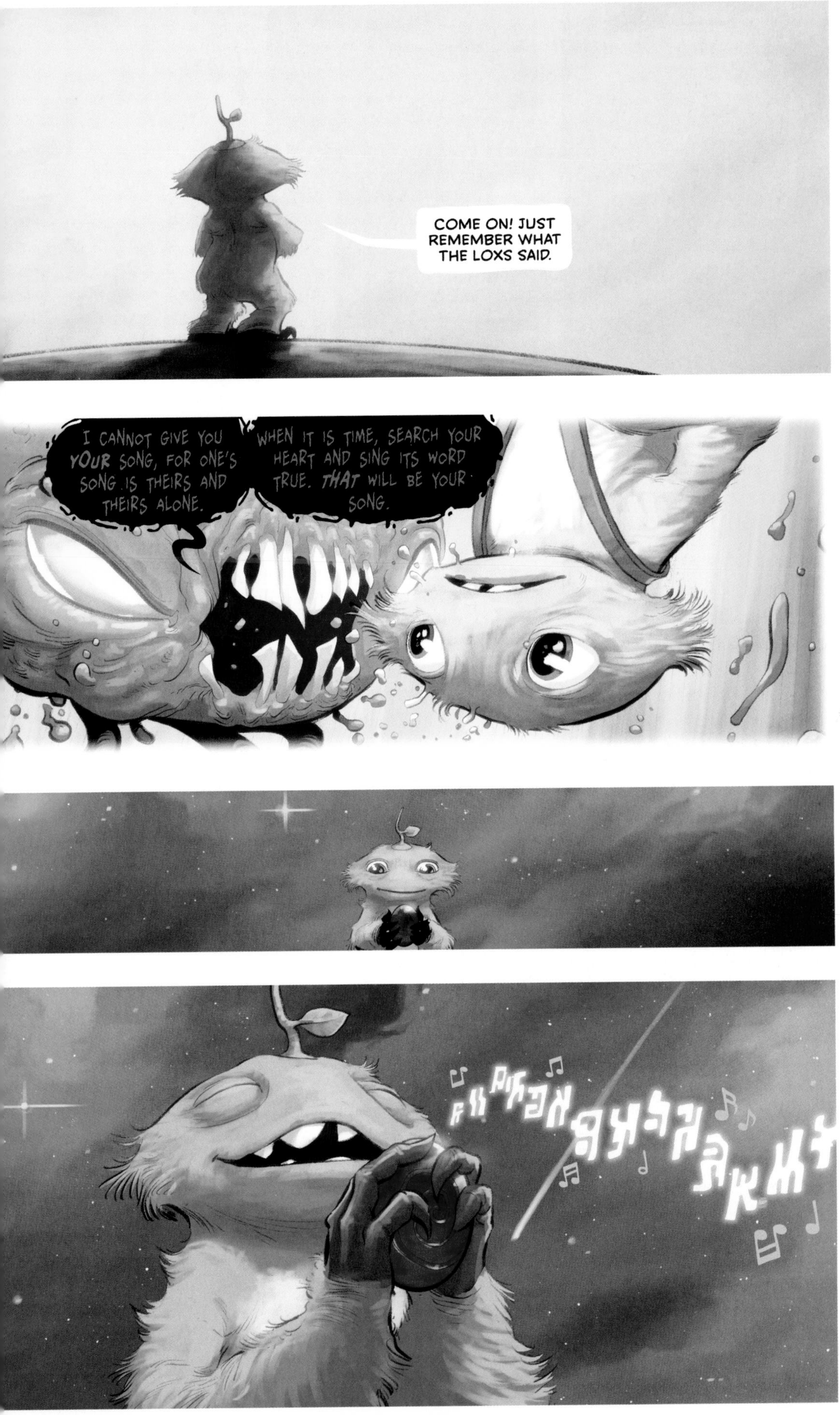
COME ON! JUST REMEMBER WHAT THE LOXS SAID.
I CANNOT GIVE YOU YOUR SONG, FOR ONE'S SONG IS THEIRS AND THEIRS ALONE.
WHEN IT IS TIME, SEARCH YOUR HEART AND SING ITS WORD TRUE. THAT WILL BE YOUR SONG.

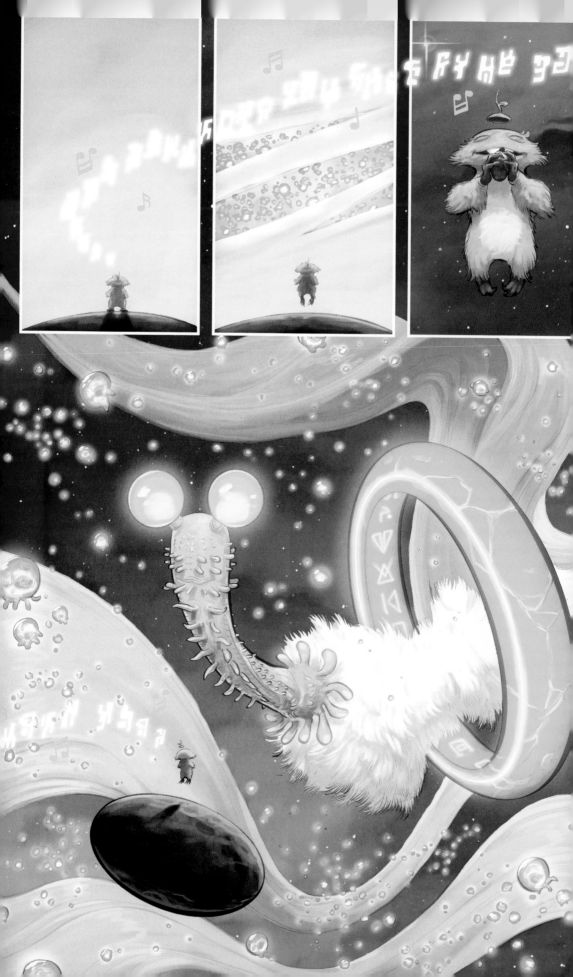

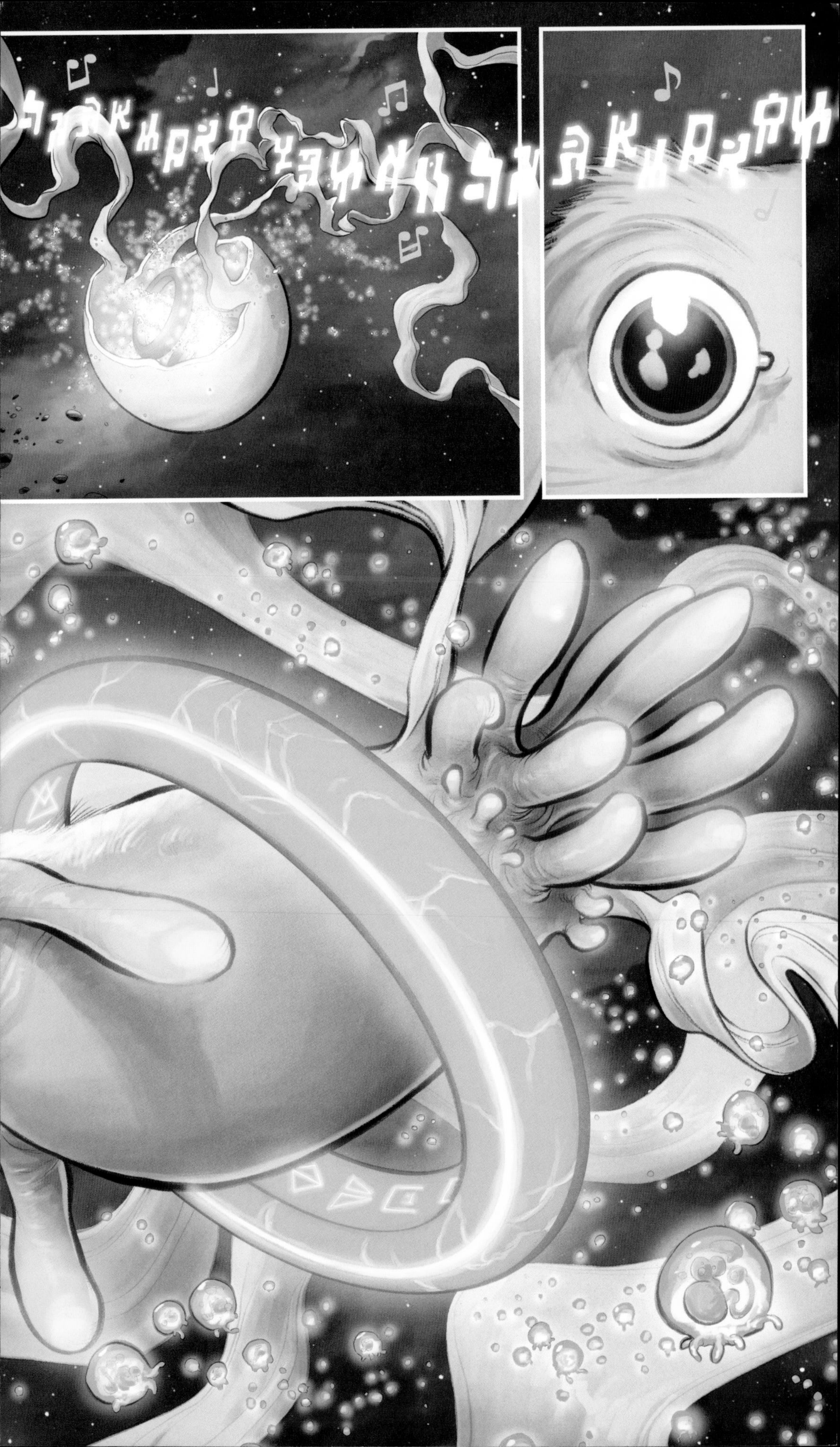

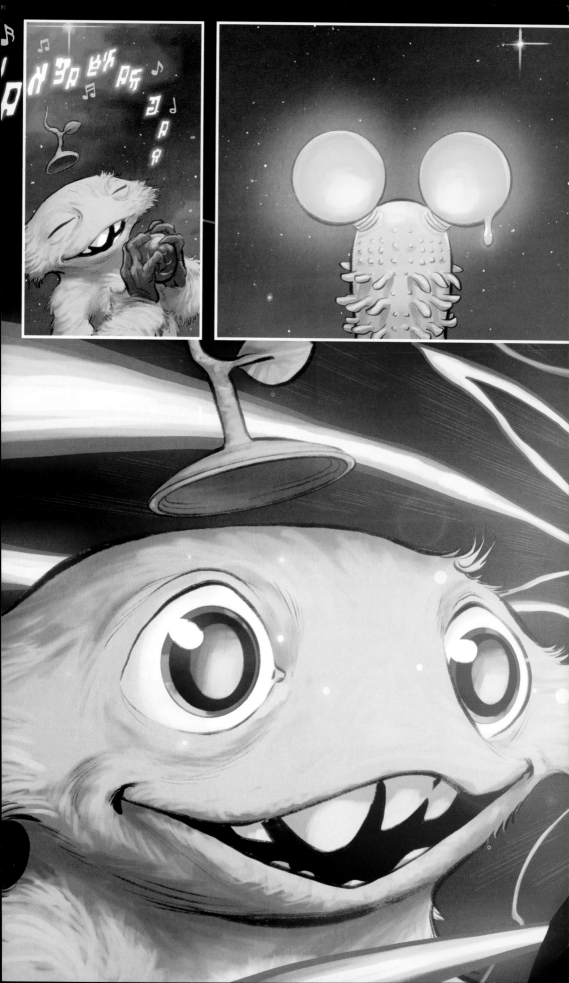

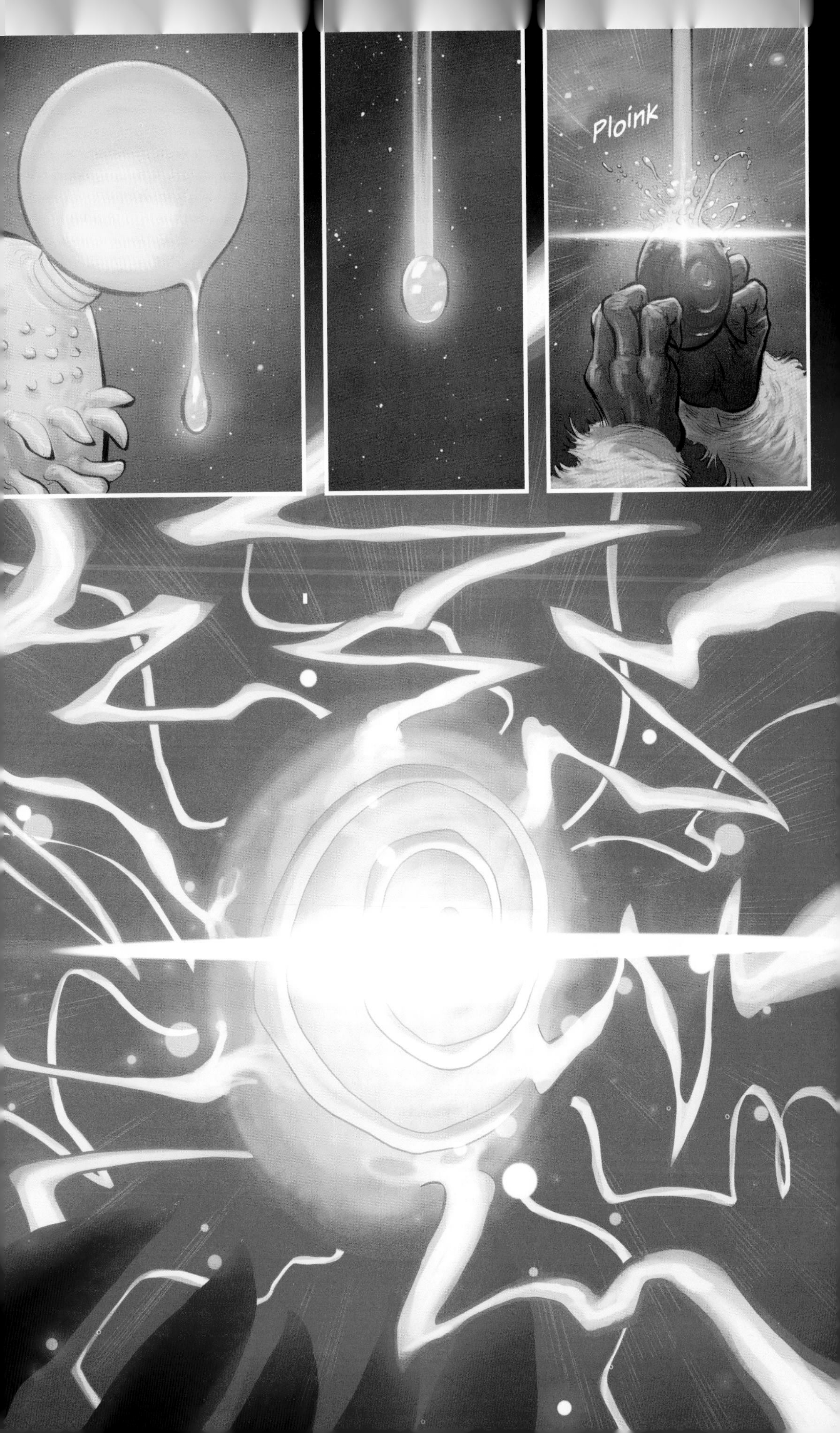
Ploink

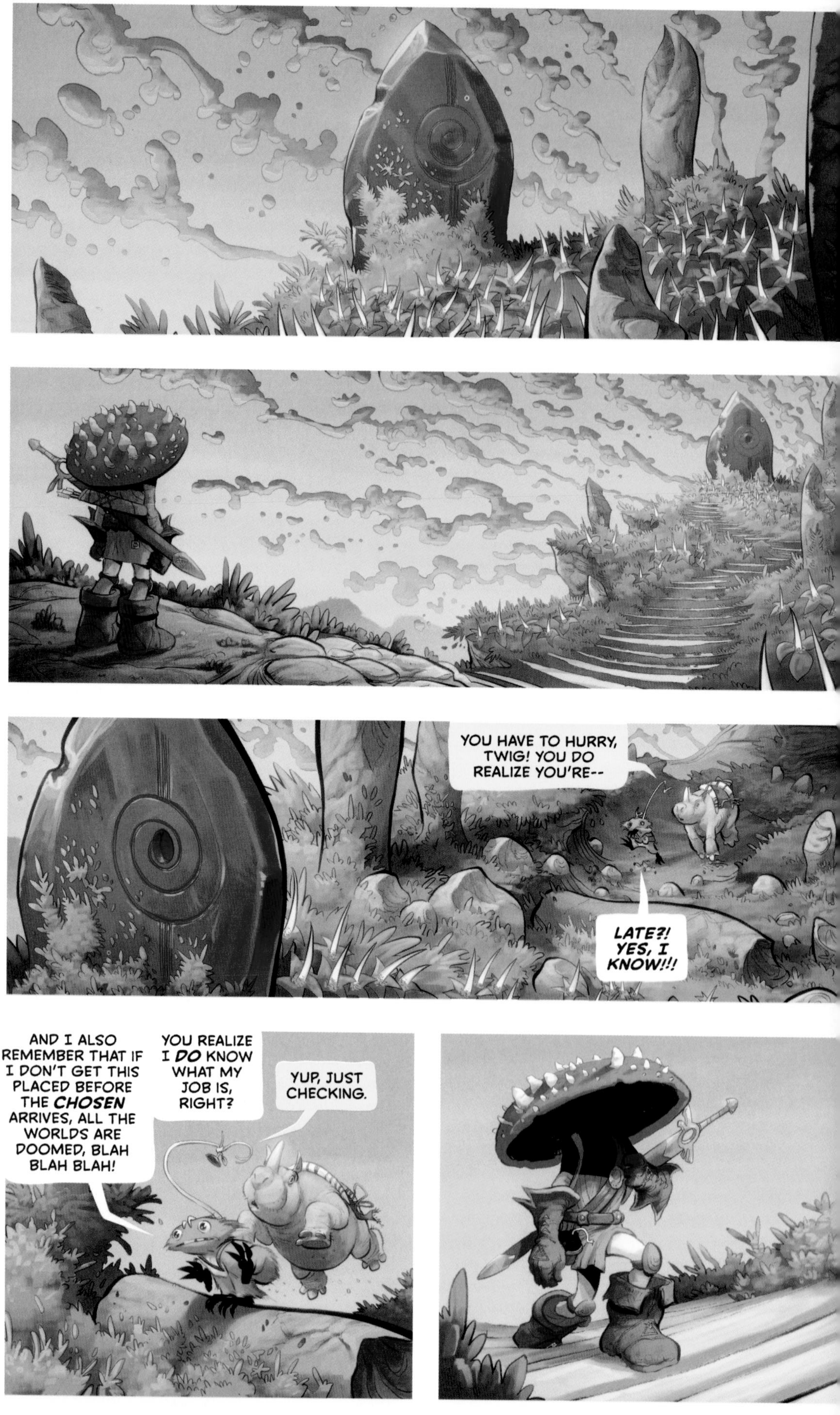
YOU HAVE TO HURRY, TWIG! YOU DO REALIZE YOU'RE--
LATE?! YES, I KNOW!!!
AND I ALSO REMEMBER THAT IF I DON'T GET THIS PLACED BEFORE THE CHOSEN ARRIVES, ALL THE WORLDS ARE DOOMED, BLAH BLAH BLAH!
YOU REALIZE I DO KNOW WHAT MY JOB IS, RIGHT?
YUP, JUST CHECKING.

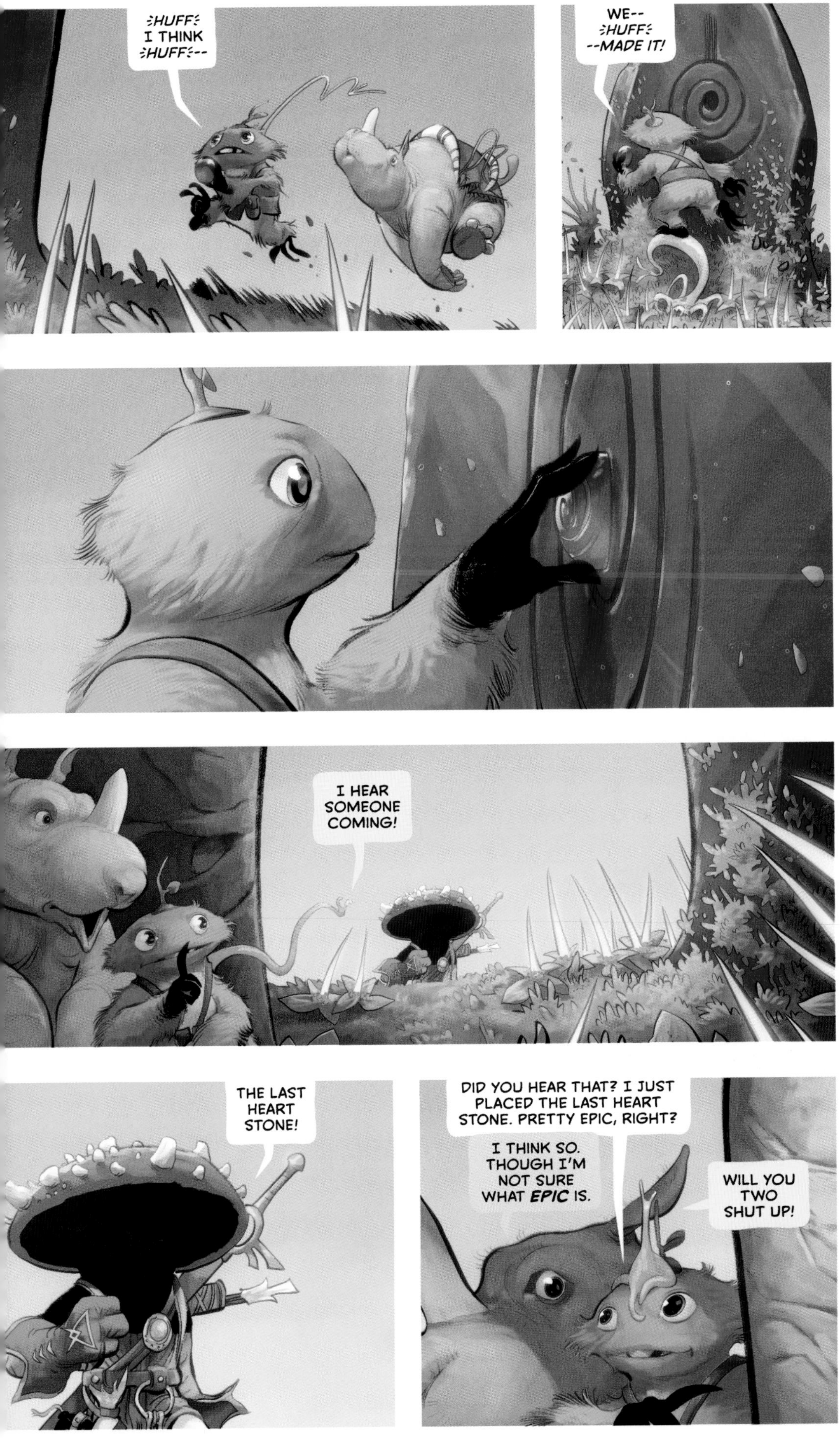

⋮HUFF⋮ I THINK ⋮HUFF⋮--
WE-- ⋮HUFF⋮ --MADE IT!
I HEAR SOMEONE COMING!
THE LAST HEART STONE!
DID YOU HEAR THAT? I JUST PLACED THE LAST HEART STONE. PRETTY EPIC, RIGHT?
I THINK SO. THOUGH I'M NOT SURE WHAT *EPIC* IS.
WILL YOU TWO SHUT UP!

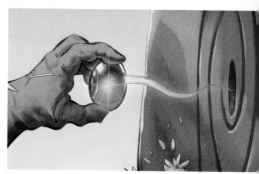

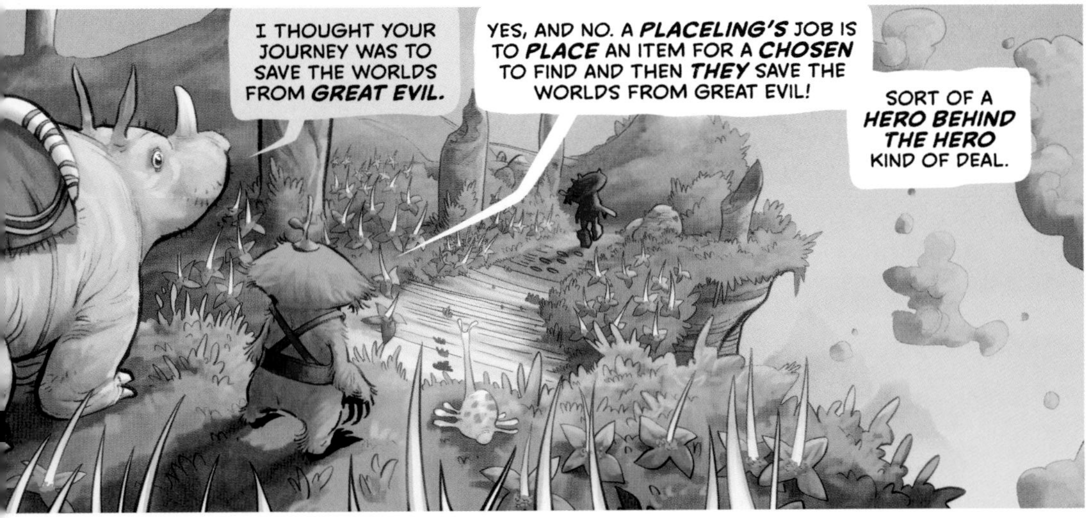
I THOUGHT YOUR JOURNEY WAS TO SAVE THE WORLDS FROM GREAT EVIL.
YES, AND NO. A PLACELING'S JOB IS TO PLACE AN ITEM FOR A CHOSEN TO FIND AND THEN THEY SAVE THE WORLDS FROM GREAT EVIL!
SORT OF A HERO BEHIND THE HERO KIND OF DEAL.

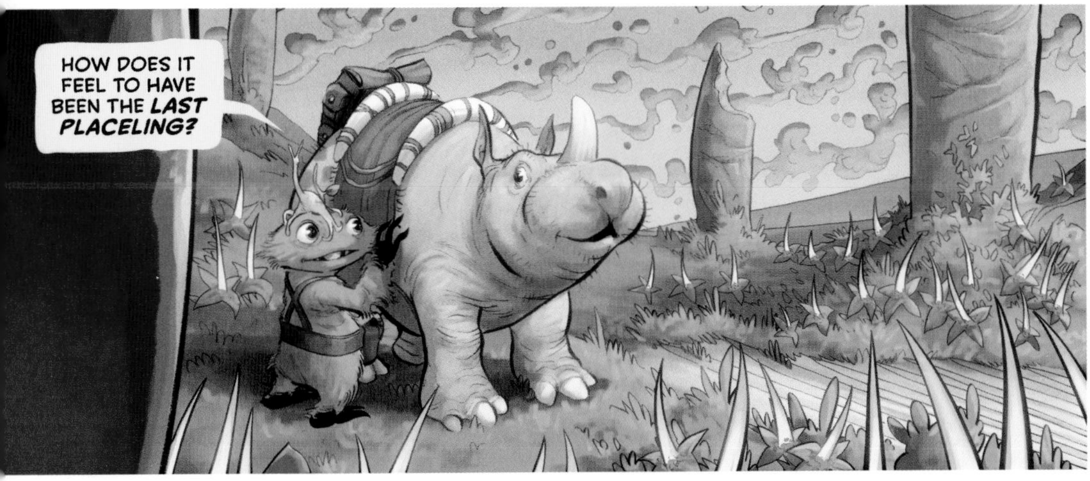
HOW DOES IT FEEL TO HAVE BEEN THE LAST PLACELING?

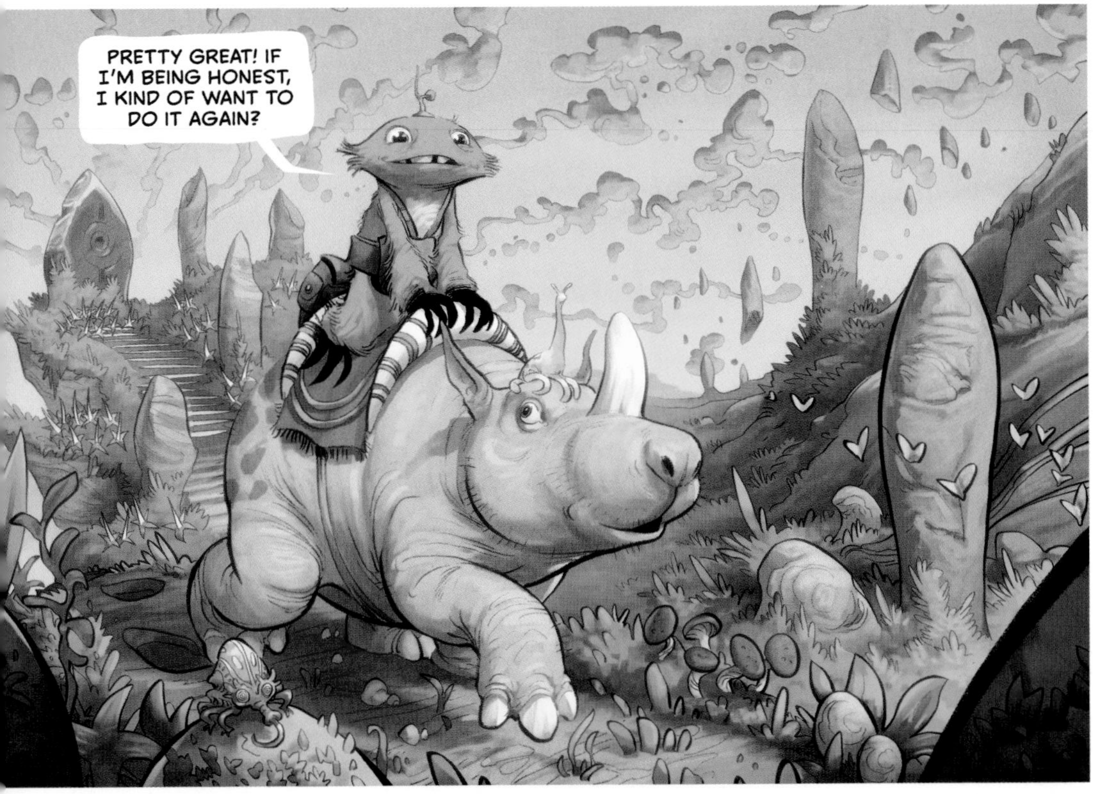
PRETTY GREAT! IF I'M BEING HONEST, I KIND OF WANT TO DO IT AGAIN?

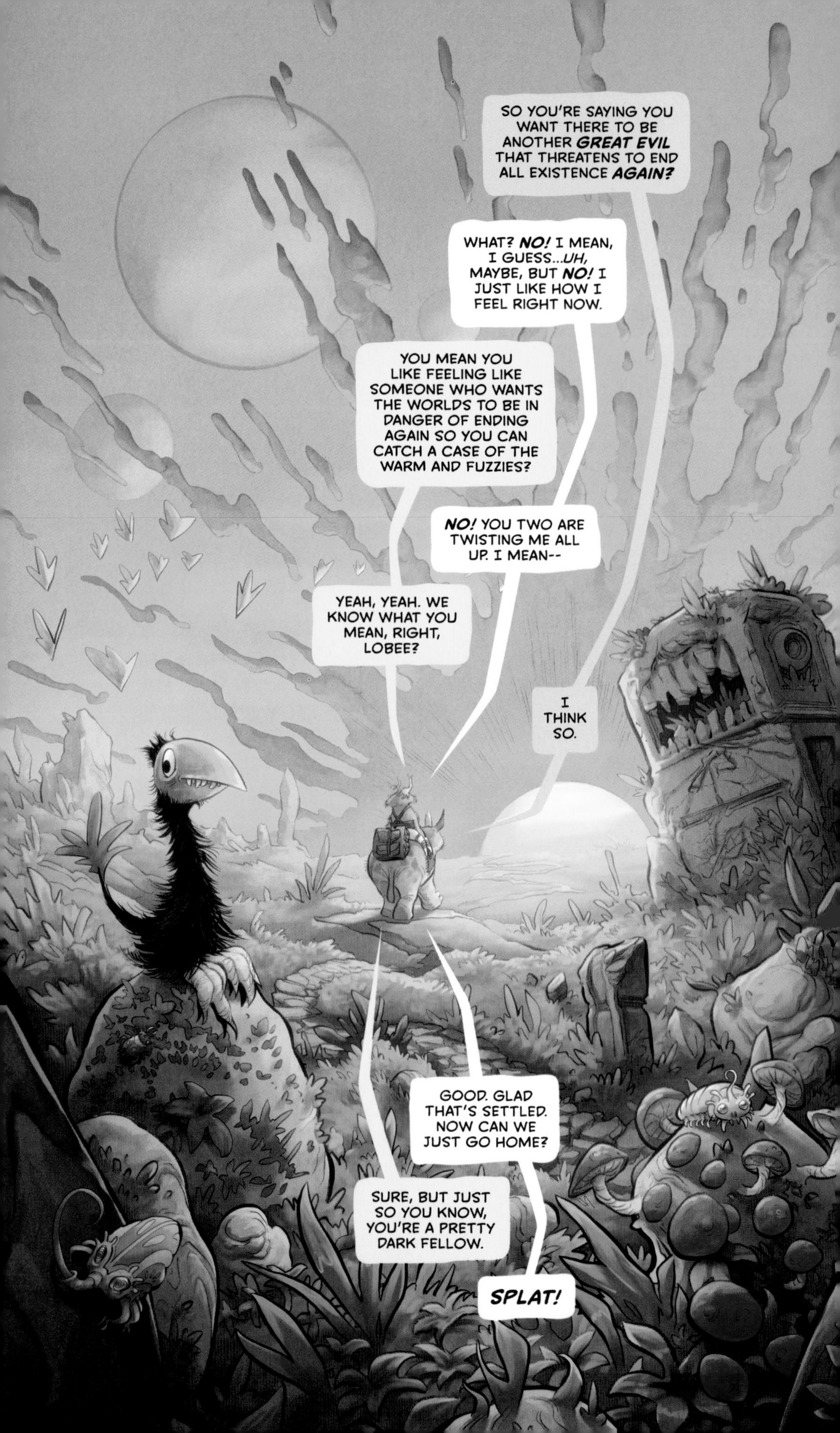
SO YOU'RE SAYING YOU WANT THERE TO BE ANOTHER GREAT EVIL THAT THREATENS TO END ALL EXISTENCE AGAIN?
WHAT? NO! I MEAN, I GUESS...UH, MAYBE, BUT NO! I JUST LIKE HOW I FEEL RIGHT NOW.
YOU MEAN YOU LIKE FEELING LIKE SOMEONE WHO WANTS THE WORLDS TO BE IN DANGER OF ENDING AGAIN SO YOU CAN CATCH A CASE OF THE WARM AND FUZZIES?
NO! YOU TWO ARE TWISTING ME ALL UP. I MEAN--
YEAH, YEAH. WE KNOW WHAT YOU MEAN, RIGHT, LOBEE?
I THINK SO.
GOOD. GLAD THAT'S SETTLED. NOW CAN WE JUST GO HOME?
SURE, BUT JUST SO YOU KNOW, YOU'RE A PRETTY DARK FELLOW.
SPLAT!

TWIG

COVER GALLERY, ISSUES 1-5

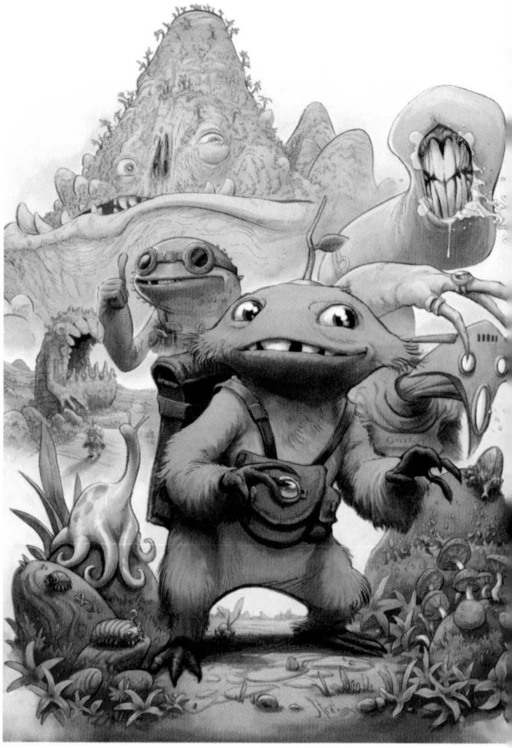

TWIG COVER, ISSUE 1: KYLE STRAHM

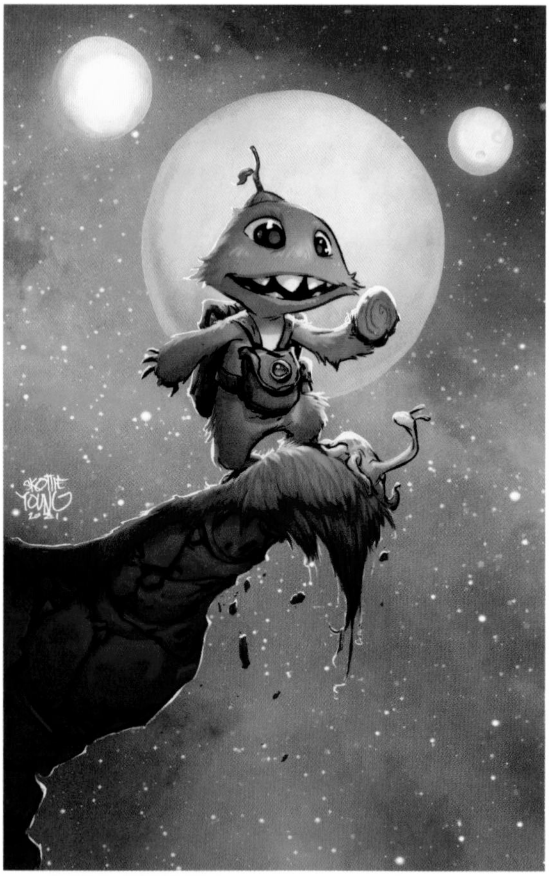

TWIG COVER, ISSUE 1: SKOTTIE YOUNG

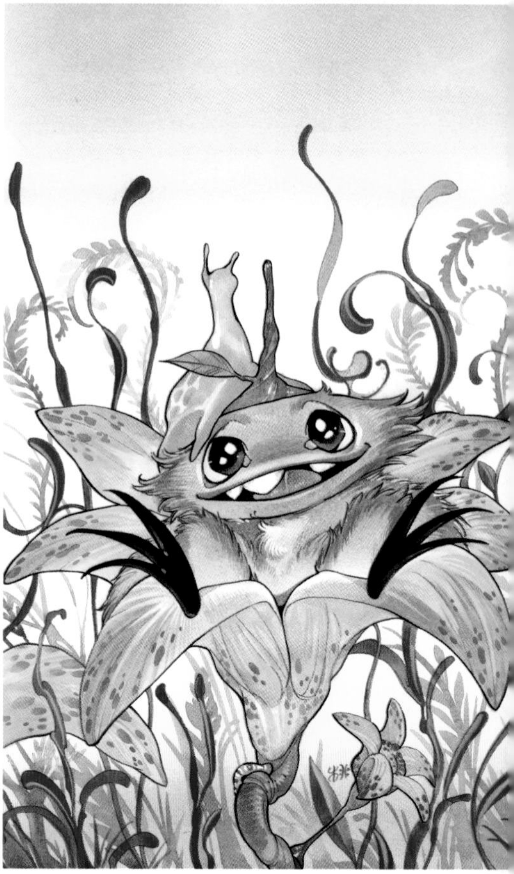

TWIG COVER, ISSUE 1: PEACH MOMOKO

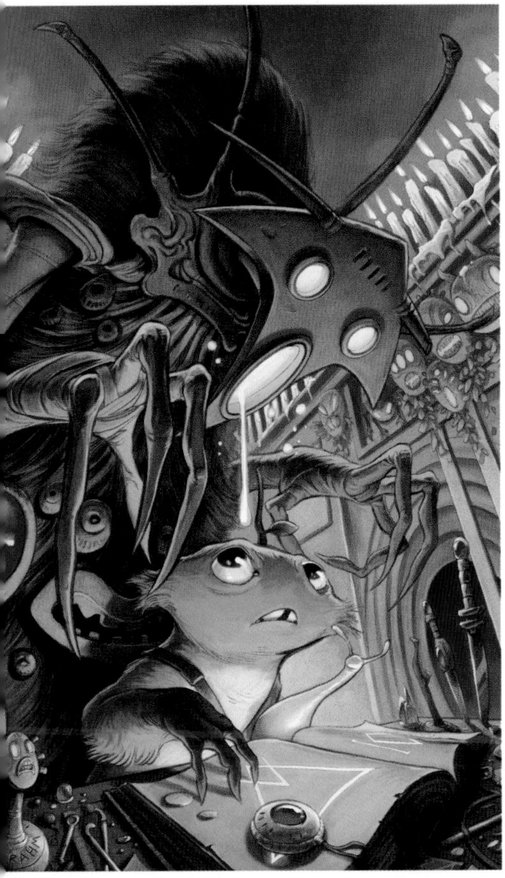
TWIG COVER, ISSUE 2: KYLE STRAHM

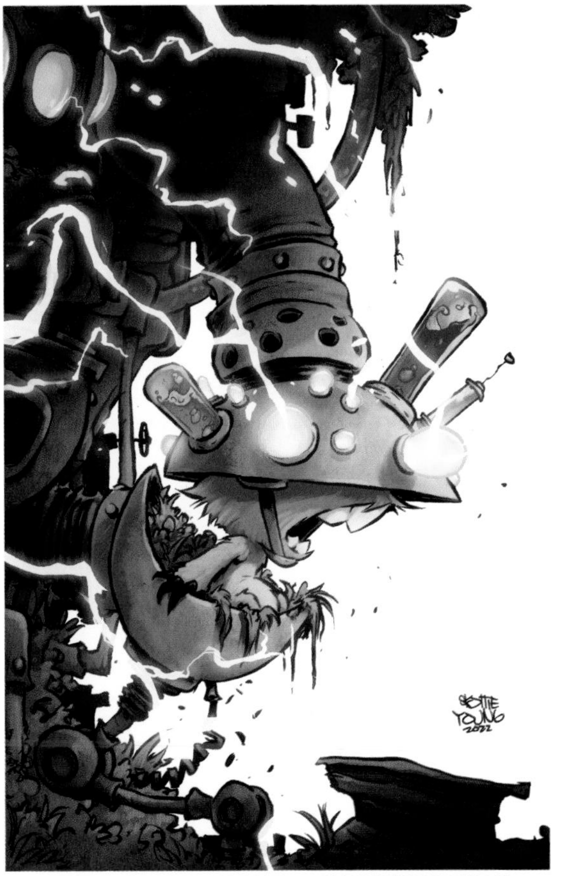
TWIG COVER, ISSUE 2: SKOTTIE YOUNG

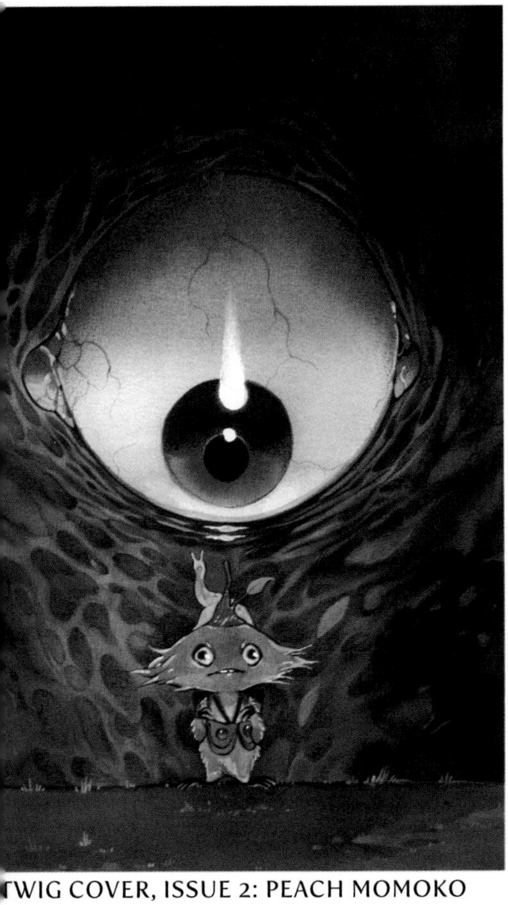
TWIG COVER, ISSUE 2: PEACH MOMOKO

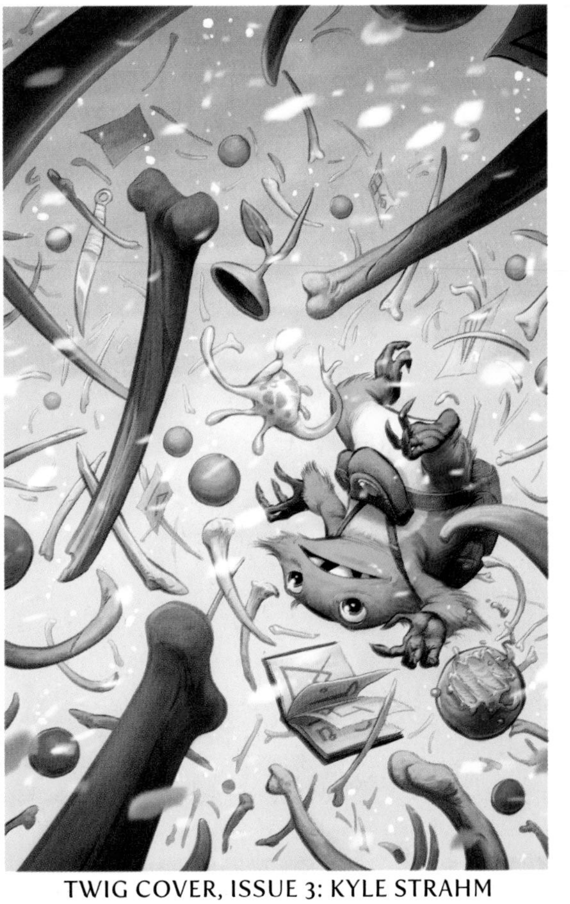
TWIG COVER, ISSUE 3: KYLE STRAHM

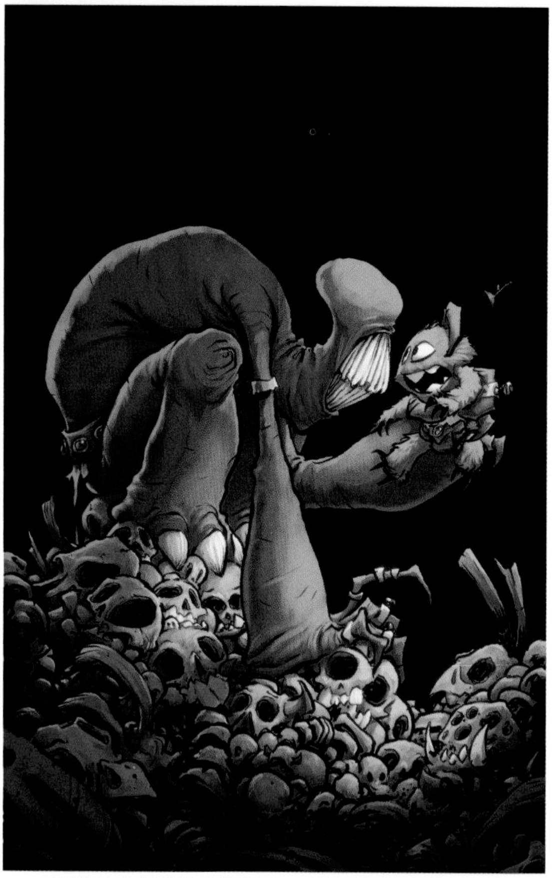

TWIG COVER, ISSUE 3: SKOTTIE YOUNG

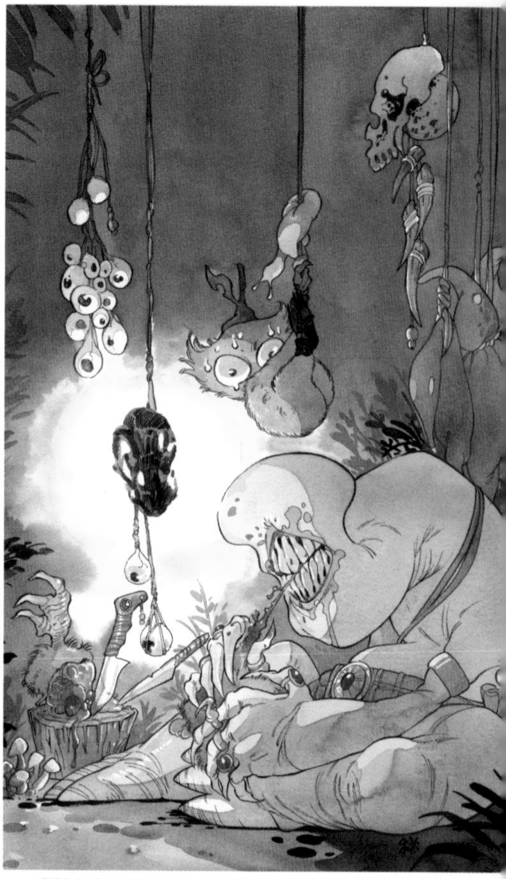

TWIG COVER, ISSUE 3: PEACH MOMOKO

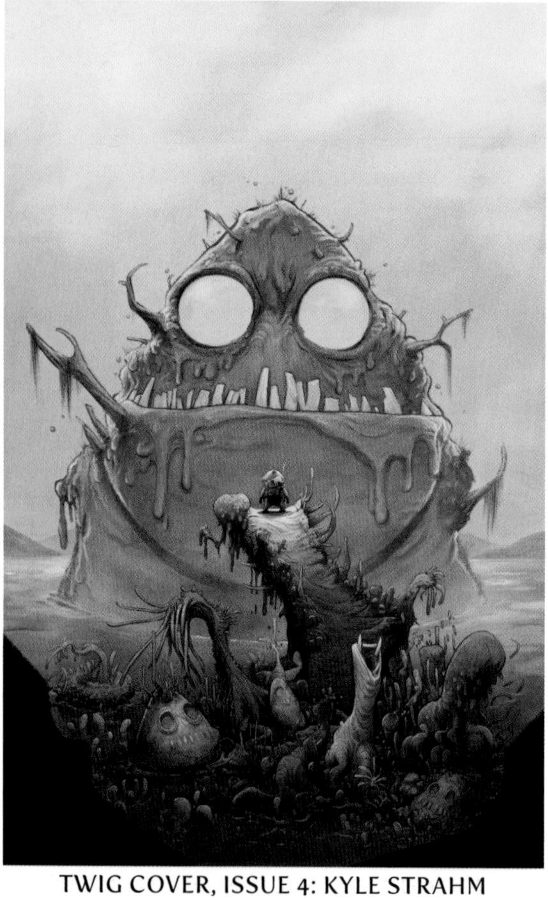

TWIG COVER, ISSUE 4: KYLE STRAHM

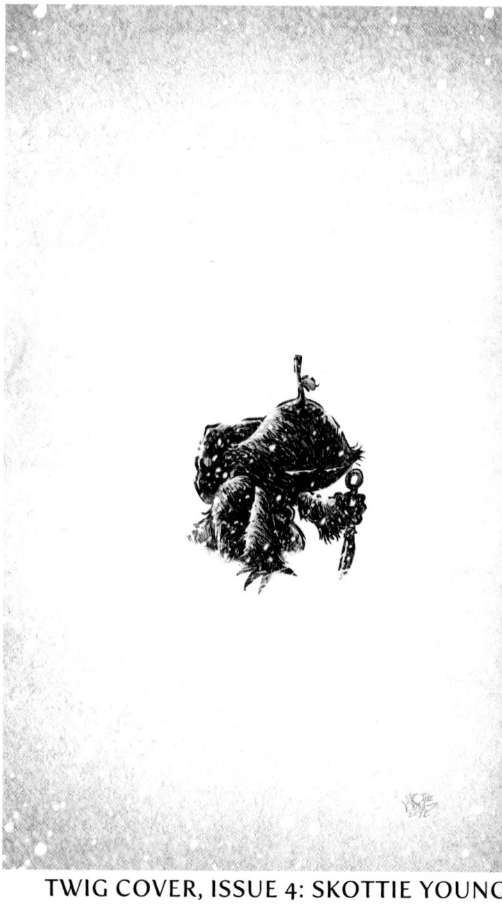

TWIG COVER, ISSUE 4: SKOTTIE YOUNG

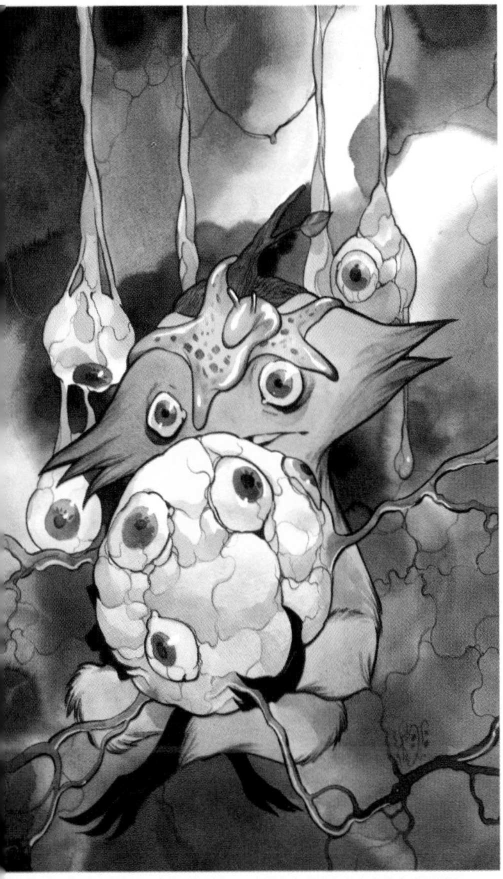

WIG COVER, ISSUE 4: PEACH MOMOKO

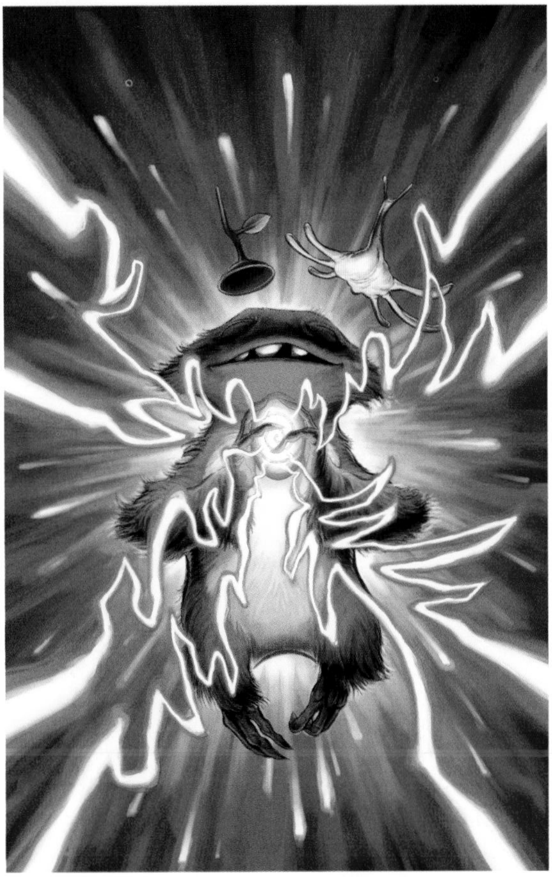

TWIG COVER, ISSUE 5: KYLE STRAHM

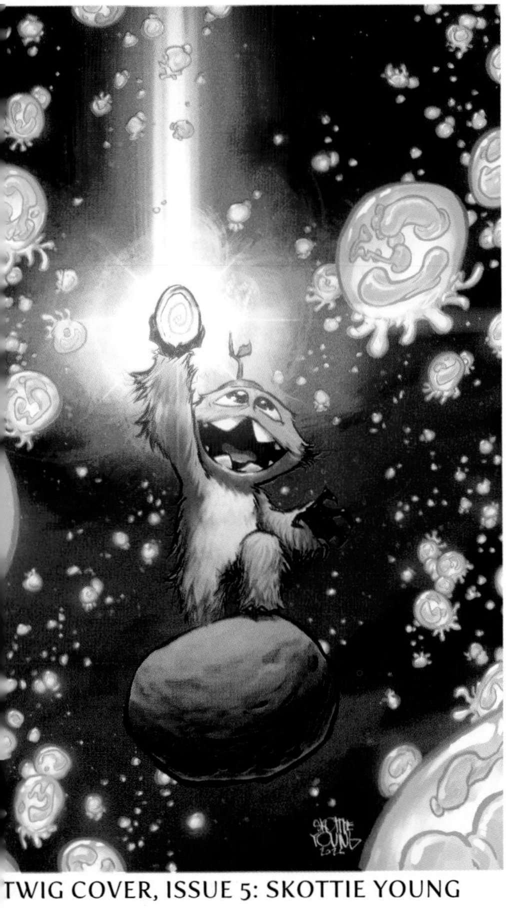

TWIG COVER, ISSUE 5: SKOTTIE YOUNG

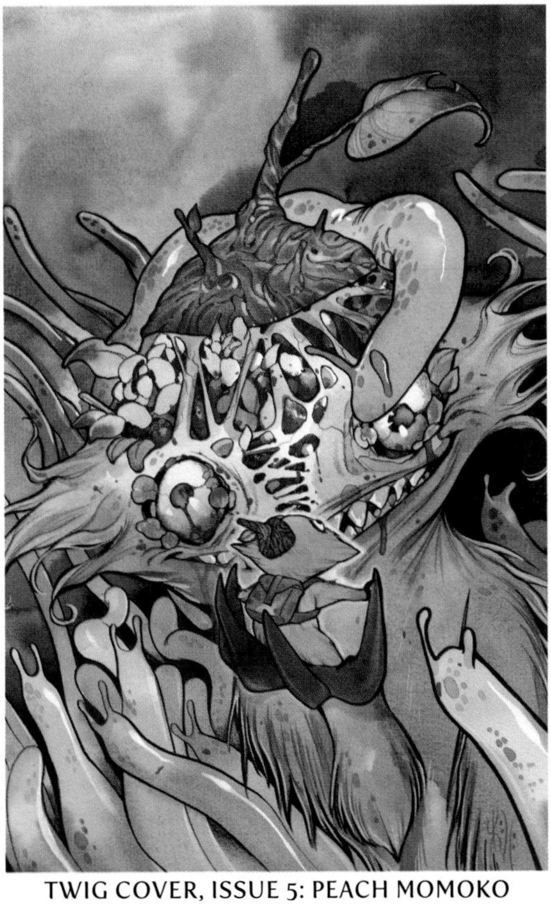

TWIG COVER, ISSUE 5: PEACH MOMOKO

SKOTTIE YOUNG

is the *New York Times*-bestselling, Eisner Award-winning creator best known for his art in Marvel's *Wizard of Oz* graphic novels, his writing and art in *Rocket Racoon*, his illustration work for Neil Gaiman's *Fortunately, The Milk*, and his Young Marvel variant covers. For Image Comics, Skottie created, wrote, and illustrated the widely popular series I HATE FAIRYLAND and recently finished writing MIDDLEWEST and THE ME YOU LOVE IN THE DARK, both collaborations with artist Jorge Corona. Skottie lives in Kansas City, Kansas with his wife, two boys, and a very large dog.

KYLE STRAHM

Kyle Strahm has been a freelance comic book creator since 2006. In that time he has had work published by Image Comics, Marvel Comics, DC Entertainment, Aftershock, Todd McFarlane Productions, IDW Publishing, Dark Horse, Dynamite, Valiant Entertainment, Black Mask, and others. As an adjunct professor, Kyle teaches Illustration to seniors at the Kansas City Art Institute. He lives and works in Kansas City, Missouri.

JEAN-FRANCOIS BEAULIEU

is an acclaimed comics colorist with a bright and exciting palette. He is widely regarded as one of the industry's top colorists and has worked on countless properties for Image, Marvel, DC, Dark Horse, and more. He is also a longtime close collaborator with Skottie.

NATE PIEKOS

is an award-winning comics letterer and the founder of Blambot.com. He has created some of the industry's most popular fonts, and has provided lettering and design for virtually every major comics publisher. His book THE ESSENTIAL GUIDE TO COMIC BOOK LETTERING is available now from Image Comics.